Praise for *Siege*

"Russ Schneider's *Siege* is in the same league as Theodore Plievier's classic *Stalingrad*—haunting, mesmerizing, and spellbinding."
—NELSON DeMILLE

"While this novel only deals with two small cities under siege by the Russians on the Eastern Front during World War II, it manages to give us the face of all war, the horror, blood, exhaustion, hunger, and sacrifice of human conflict wherever it has raged over the face of the world. This darkly painful narrative by a writer himself too early dead will change you forever. Such is art on its highest level."
—HARRY CREWS

D1059331

SIEGE

A Novel of the Eastern Front

1942

Russ Schneider

PRESIDIO PRESS • NEW YORK

A Presidio Press Book
Published by The Random House Publishing Group

www.presidiopress.com

ISBN 0-345-47585-2

This edition is published by arrangement with Bookspan

Manufactured in the United States of America

OPM 9 8 7 6 5 4 3 2 1

First Presidio Press Edition: November 2004

Contents

Prologue

Vorkuta lay just before the Ural Mountains. It lay not in remotest Siberia, but at the gates of Siberia.

But what difference does this make? Men describe the geographic locations of places only because they are in the habit of doing so.

It was all unspeakable. Names of places serve only as certain reference points for treachery.

The Gulag is everywhere, and everywhere in Russia there are rivers of death and long stretches of railroad track laid yard by yard upon the bones of men.

The Kolyma is one such river, where high water in springtime erodes the riverbanks and unearths the bones of thousands who have been buried there. The earth slides into the spated river like the collapsing wall of a glacier, and the bones embedded there slide in as well, thus to be carried away to the Arctic seas, or perhaps merely to settle into the silt a few dozen feet below.

And even upon the ocean there are rivers of death—for how did all those wretches arrive upon the banks of the Kolyma in the first place? This region of our country was so remote—beyond the farthest eastern sunrises—that it could only be reached by ocean travel. Railroad tracks would convey the wretches four thousand miles to the ports of Okhotsk and Vladivostok on the Pacific Ocean, and from there they would embark upon the high seas—the ocean thus to become a river of death—aboard ships that would take them after a voyage of two weeks to Magadan, at the entrance to the Kolyma country. Those who had not already died along the way saw the ends of their lives approaching at last, as the ships carried them between the bleak hills, treeless and bereft of all human encouragement, around Magadan harbor.

The Ob is another such river of death, thousands of miles nearer to European Russia than is the Kolyma. But otherwise it is all the same, all the same. In the springtime the waters of the Ob rise in spate and erode away the banks, clay banks packed with human bones that collapse into the water, thus to be carried away to the Arctic seas, or merely to settle into the silt a few dozen feet below.

I know, for I saw this spectacle each year from our tiny labor camp on the banks of the Ob. It was a vast and marshy country along the Ob, where in summer dense mists would hang over the land, mists composed entirely of insects that would form part of our suffering. Other forms of suffering were in equal measure, each blurring with the other.

Then one year barges arrived, and we were packed on board them. Our little camp by the river was abandoned, and we were conveyed slowly down the river to the site of another labor project, which would become known to us as Vorkuta. Occasionally a few of us would be allowed to emerge from the stinking holds to walk about on deck. Sometimes we would see other barges, no doubt carrying others like ourselves from other little camps abandoned along the Ob, all traveling slowly downstream to the great project of our people at Vorkuta. Sometimes we would pass other places where the bones, packed into the blue clay banks, were sliding quietly into the river.

One day we glimpsed the low insignificant hills of the Ural Mountains some distance to the west. The appearance of these hills indicated that our journey was near its end, though we did not know this at that moment. After only a few minutes in the open air we were forced to descend again into the hot, suffocating, and stinking holds of the barges. This abrupt change from sweet breathable air to thick, dark, almost unbreathable filth was yet another form of the unspeakable, which we wretches had come to know in many forms over these years. Could there not be some way for a man to shoot himself, some way that would not inflict death or permanent injury, but which would merely allow a man to sleep until journey's end, without being forced to endure such awful transitions? Some way for a man to shoot himself while still out in the sweet, breathable air of the open deck, and simply sleep there for a few days?

Questions such as these would be among the finer points of a philosophy of human pain. And no doubt such questions would be perfectly valid, perfectly meaningful—but we had become too much like beasts to really ponder such things except in the most fleeting of ways. Only a short time later we came to our journey's end near the great mouth of the river. Some of us were assigned to remove the dead from the hold and drop them overboard, while the rest of us were taken off the barges and assembled along the shore, next to the railroad tracks that led to Vorkuta.

The train took us there. We were loaded onto open cars. Many of us had already experienced, at one time or another, traveling for days and weeks in boxcars that were locked and sealed, but I myself was not to undergo that particular fate until several years later, near the true and God-given end of my journey.

Here the train pulled us in open cars at low speed away from the banks of the Ob, and we steamed slowly toward the Urals, which were not so far away. We felt the breeze of the summer Arctic. The sun hung low in the sky, and thus was often obscured by horizon clouds although much of the sky was blue above us. After those weeks in the stifling holds of the barges we stood in the open cars and felt the fresh breeze against our cheeks with a kind of dull animal ecstasy, a fleeting sensation in which deep gratitude was mixed as always with foreboding, implacable resentment, and an even, deep resignation that was almost beyond words. Smoke and blowing cinders from the locomotive also blew back in our faces, but this bothered us only a little.

We entered the insignificant Urals, barren mountains a few thousand feet high that seemed scarcely larger than burial mounds set down for no reason among the infinite lowlands of the taiga. Many of us did not recognize these mountains, but a few did. "Behold, comrades, we are leaving Siberia!" a few men said. "We are on our way back to old Mother Russia," a few said. It was true, what they said. In the past we had all been punished for the truth, or at least told we were sadly mistaken about it, but at this moment few were listening, and we traveled slowly onward along a flat valley between the hills. The sun disappeared behind the mountains in the evening but did not set, though we grew cold in the shadows standing on the moving train.

A day passed and we left the mountains behind us and were upon the yellow and grey tundra, the green and brown tundra, the brown and grey tundra. We began to pass other encampments of wretches along the tracks, camps and cemeteries both generally of equal size. For a few moments they looked up from their labors at us, and we looked down at them. The camps grew more frequent, spread further into the distance, and then the tracks came to an end.

We were ordered to descend from the flat open cars, and we did so. We were not in Vorkuta precisely but in the neighborhood of Vorkuta. Beyond the end of the rails we saw only the empty land and the sky and the prospect of the toil that awaited us. We saw also the gravel bed stretching to the horizon where the rails had yet to be laid, and all of those condemned working out there.

We were hungry and thirsty and knew from long habit that we might be fed a little bit now, perhaps, in all likelihood, and as we moved away from the train we were, after a patient wait of five or seven hours, all ladled a bit of nourishment from several large drums that arrived from somewhere on the beds of wagons pulled by horses. After this we were immediately hungry again, and could not so easily reckon when next we might be fed.

We were fed small amounts at regular intervals, the same as it had been at the small camp along the Ob, but as the work here was much harder, far more died and were buried along the tracks as they progressed, rail by rail, across the tundra. Survivors anywhere in the Gulag had to be cunning and resourceful, gregarious also to the extent that we might gradually meet with different people who could provide us with the little extras that would help us to survive. Yet along the tracks to Vorkuta we were worked so hard that we had almost no time or strength left to devote to such necessary resourcefulness. In small and less important camps across the nation the authorities sometimes considered it in their interest to keep us wretches alive, in body if not in soul, because we could not be easily replaced. But the Vorkuta railroad was deemed an important project by our country's fathers, and so more and more wretches arrived to work here all the time, and apparently it was more efficient to work us and work us to the point of death in light of the fact that there would always be more workers available to continue our labors. Oh God, as you did not hear our pleas last year or the year before, or four or five years ago, we understand that you will not hear them now. It is understood. And so quiet reigns in the souls of beasts, quiet anguish, quiet despair, quiet starvation and weakness and disease, quiet words spoken in the dead wilderness, comforting a comrade who is dying, or encouraging a comrade to find some way to go on. Though at times we had neither the spirit nor the strength to offer even that much fellowship. And so they died, or fell into despair and then died.

In summer whole sections of the track bed would disappear into the boggy ground, requiring rebuilding. It was like forever rebuilding a sand castle that was being forever overrun by the tide. We lived for the most part not in stockades but in tents that were often flooded and led to much disease, various fevers, among us. If a man was so sick that he must go to the infirmary he would find his rations greatly reduced, and so he would often starve quietly to death or die more quickly from his illness. If a sick man was determined to keep on working so that his small allotment of nourishment would not be reduced, he might simply drop dead somewhere along the tracks, simply fall over and be dead.

One thing that we did was to form small pools of six or seven comrades who would try and look after one another; more than anything this was done so a truly desperate man could find a reprieve in the infirmary for a time, knowing that his comrades would bring a small amount of extra food, enough perhaps that he could recover somewhat rather than sink into a completely hopeless state. But there was not always the self-discipline or group discipline to maintain such pools, or at least not for very long. More than by betrayal and

selfishness, the bonds of human fellowship which might encourage survival in the long run were weakened by apathy
and exhaustion. Selfishness was present too, of course; this
went without saying, as it was the deepest of all human
traits, the very last thing to endure before the level of utter
bestiality.

Our guards could have made our long, long sentences
much worse; killed us sooner, in other words. But by and
large they were not cruel and showed little interest in us. The
few cruel ones stood out in our memories and sometimes we
devised plans of vengeance, which we never carried out except on one occasion. Malik disappeared inside a crowd of
us one summer day, and we beat him to death, and then his
body subsequently disappeared within the ever-shifting bog-
beds beneath the tracks. This was done as we had planned it,
and it was the only time we had the will or the hate to carry
out any such thing we had planned, which otherwise was
only idle and useless talk. His body had to disappear, for if it
were found then suspicion and severe punishment would inevitably fall upon a certain group of wretches, and the dull
nature of our anguish was such that no form of vengeance on
even the most brutal oaf—as he was—would be worth such
a price. But his body was never found and neither the commandant nor other guards or informers were able to piece together enough evidence to single out his murderers, the
result being that the camp (a word I use only loosely for our
desolate and oft-moved village of tents and stockades along
the eternally progressing tracks) was merely punished as a
whole. And this was not overly severe, when compared with
the normal day-to-day pace of our ordeals. The deputy commandant, Baryushin, a vicious young idealist of the Party,
announced that the commandant, Barzhevsky (who may almost have been a decent kind of man, from what little we
saw of him—may his soul be cursed forever), had decided
to punish us by reducing our rations for a week. Clearly
Baryushin thought this too mild a reprisal for Malik's death,
but even he expressed his contempt for us with a certain lofty
and pig-eyed detachment, as if such matters were as much
beneath him to worry about as they were for Barzhevsky. For
after all the very nature of our existence was killing us, and

brutes like Malik were unusual. And so probably only a few more men died from this week of reduced food than would have died otherwise.

One must understand how the whole incident, within the toil and drudgery and despair of months and years, was almost indescribably trivial. We remembered it because it was unusual, that was all. There were many who deserved to die but the pig Malik had to die; and then it was over with and we continued to endure our sentences across the tundra toward Vorkuta, a place we never reached and never saw.

For most of the guards were not like him and would not exert themselves to make our lives miserable. The throngs along the railroad tracks, ever-toiling, ever-arriving, ever-dying, were vast and rather impersonal. In the winter during the worst weather the guards would often remain indifferently inside their quarters, after taking the morning roll and turning us out into the unbelievable cold to either fulfill our day's quota or freeze to death. We were allowed to divert some of our labor to build snow-fences along the tracks, to shield us somewhat from the gales, though the snow frequently drifted right over them, onto the completed tracks or still-empty bed, covering those frozen to death also. How ordinary it all was, the lonely terror, the gales, the looks of men who could no longer even speak, above all the endless hours of a day, any day, even the cannibalism that happened sometimes. The cannibals were not punished but only ostracized, and generally they were recognizable because there grew to be something about the looks in their eyes. Enforced ostracism from all the other living souls would often amount to a kind of death sentence in itself. For as I have said, the very possibility of long-term survival hinged on a certain necessary degree of gregariousness. But perhaps the cannibals had stumbled upon another and better method, secrets which they kept to themselves and which no one except others of their ilk sought to pry out of them.

In smaller camps like my old labor camp along the Ob men who lost the will to live would try to escape through the barbed wire, entangling themselves, and the guards would then machine-gun them without rancor. In fact if a man was cunning and had a good plan it was not all that difficult to escape, though they were almost always caught and brought back from wherever the dogs tracked them down out in the marshy or snowbound wilderness. In fact the authorities showed very little concern about these escape attempts, and when caught these stubborn and determined souls were usually given only slight punishments. Often they would attempt to escape again six months or a year later, and would only be caught again. The fathers of our country seemed to understand in a very deep sense that the great majority of us wretches would always be too weak or hungry or confused or resigned or already near death to ever attempt to escape.

But along the tracks leading to the polar seas in the neighborhood of Vorkuta there was never, or almost never, any barbed wire. Without much difficulty a man could simply walk away, but this would not be really to escape but only to die out there. Men also frequently died along the snow-fences, lying down to rest in the unbearable cold, doing this at Vorkuta just as they might have entangled themselves in the barbed wire at other places.

At last, when it was time to go, I was ill. This was always dangerous, for it made everything impossible, or nearly so. I had no choice but to go to the infirmary, for I could barely stand. I was too sick to want to eat, so I did not suffer hunger from the reduced rations there. I lay there in my lice and filth and thought how good it was, to lie there and do nothing. I was inured to the stench of the place even though it was worse than the overall stench of the camp, because it had been years since I had really smelt anything, it seemed. There was only the nagging worry that I might waste away and die here; it was tiresome to have to worry about this, for otherwise it might have been peaceful. It seemed that most of us wretches had some kind of inner mechanism, which felt rather like the sands running away in an hourglass, to tell us that we had crossed a certain point and were thus near to the legitimate realm of death. How tiresome to have to be aware of this, to have to exert one's will, for the thousandth or ten thousandth time, to have to struggle with the temptation to sink into sweet and hopeless apathy. If only one could get a little rest. But such thoughts were dangerous; that is the point, everything became dangerous when you fell ill. Every day the dead were dragged out of the infirmary. The soup tasted like food that had already been vomited once, just as it did out in the camp; only there was less of it here. At this time I had no comrades who might sacrifice a little of their nourishment to bring to me. Too many were dead, or had retreated into themselves, nearly insane, and for some time I had fallen out of the habit of allying myself with other small groups.

If you did not recover after a certain number of days you would be placed in another part of the infirmary, where your rations would be reduced even further. At that point it was intended that you should die; that was how it worked.

So I knew I must raise myself to my feet somehow, and go back to work. I had been sick before, been through it all before, but it was always so hellish. To face the endless hours of toil when your head roared with a kind of nausea that spread throughout your body, that made the whole prospect of staying upright a horror, a sheer horror. The will to live was an unending, terrible ordeal, so much like everything else.

It was at this moment, during one of these days, that I discovered it was time to go. I had managed to pull myself erect, leaning against the log wall of the place, seeing God swimming like a tadpole at the bottom of some filthy vision of something that seemed to reside along the rims of my eyeballs. I had not quite gathered the stamina to report myself to one of the guard-attendants in the outer rooms next to the sickrooms.

Then, unexpectedly, one of these men entered and stood in front of me, motioning me out the door. I struggled toward the door and heard him announce to the other wretches lying in there that a special opportunity awaited all those who were fit enough to rise. Those not fit enough would be allowed to remain, as they were not desired in any case.

A few other men rose and walked out of there with me. Their faces more or less resembled hardened puddles that had human eyes set into them.

We could not expect much from whatever this opportunity might be. There was always a hope, seemingly impossible to

kill, that it might mean some alternative to going back to
work along those railroad tracks. Though it might simply
mean some other kind of work just as bad.

We were led outside, and kept waiting for some hours in
the mud. Graciously none of the guards forced us to remain
standing for all this time, and so we could settle down to wait
upon our knees or our elbows, gathering a little stamina. Inevitably some fool among us began muttering that it would
not do to be lying about like this, as no good would come of
it. One could not just be seen lying about, if any good at all
were to come out of whatever awaited us. "Get up, comrades. Get up. Try to stand for a little while." Perhaps he was
right. But I was simply too sick to make myself stand and
wait and wait. The guards nearby showed no interest in any
of this.

Finally, perhaps with a strange benevolence, they did
make us stand, and a few moments later Deputy Commandant Baryushin arrived to speak to us.

The motherland needed us. For what purpose we were not
told until later, I forget when exactly. In the intervening days
rumors began to circulate that our country was at war. Perhaps this was so, though it seemed that during all the years of
our servitude we must have been at war at other times as
well.

We were set off marching across the boggy tundra in high
summer. Not just we few from the infirmary, but hundreds of
others as well, perhaps thousands, who had been told to
cease their labors along the rails and march away. All were
needed. We marched alongside the bed where no rails had
yet been laid, and then one day the bed also came to an end
and we marched on across the brown unstable land through
the insect fog. I told myself that marching was easier than returning to the normal toil. Still, I was always on the point of
collapse and do not know for sure how I did not join all those
others who collapsed and died along the way. It was a nightmare beyond words. Then somehow I began to recover
somewhat from my illness, and this horror as well receded
into the past, gone forever.

I walked on in a stunned or dazed state that was maybe almost cheerful, like a new day rising as it always did. Though

the sun never rose and never set along the march, as it was high summer there. We came to a place where again there was a long lonely somehow profound-appearing empty bed waiting for rails to be laid down on it. We marched along beside it and at length came to the actual terminus of the tracks, where a number of trains were waiting for us.

We were loaded onto boxcars, packed in so tightly that there was room only to stand, and then the doors were sealed shut behind us and we moved slowly away.

There was barely enough room to breathe through cracks or apertures in the walls of the boxcars. It was like the journey down the Ob in the holds of the barges, but then it grew to be worse than that. In the barges there had been room to lie down. In the boxcars we could not lie down or move in any way, except perhaps to sink slowly to our knees, but then it became apparent that those who succumbed in this manner were dying of suffocation. They died and somehow over the course of hours and days they were slowly trampled down into the layer of human excrement that had come to cover the floor of the car. Others died and remained upright, corpses squeezed against their fellows. We had all been fed out upon the tundra before boarding the trains. After that we were given nothing. No water. No food.

Men began to lose their minds and days on end were filled with babbling and louder noises of delirium. Men—somehow we were no longer wretches but actual men, though I could not imagine how this had come to pass, and perhaps I myself began to suffer from hallucinations. In all these years I had never traveled aboard these closed boxcars. But there were others who had done so, and before thirst robbed them of their power of speech they began to cry out in rebellion, especially during long hours when the train was halted somewhere along the way. They cried out to guards or other people that they could see standing outside, through little cracks in the wall. Water. Food. Anything, comrade, for the love of God. At least unload the dead. At least give us water. How can we be made to work again if we are left to die here? How, comrade, how?

Never, never in all these years had I heard resigned and beaten wretches speak so beseechingly. To plead was an act from another world, but still they pled and pled, speaking, at first, with a pleading outrage, as even the most abased prisoners will do when their sense of privilege has been violated. Men who in years past had been carried in these hellish cars for thousands of miles back and forth across our country, who now insisted that at least they had been fed once every two or three days, that at least they had been allowed to descend and drink water during such halts along the tracks.

"Open the doors, comrades. We will do anything you ask, just open the doors for a few minutes. For the love of God. Water. Water."

This was whenever we stopped during the first several days, when men were still able to speak. I found myself hoping only that death would come quickly, more quickly. I thought of other opportunities I had had to die during all these years, along the Ob, or at Vorkuta, regretting that I had not availed myself of them then, to spare myself this. There was a kind of sleep that came when standing upright, a rattling, suffocating sleep, squeezed upright among other men, drifting in and out of sleep yet never entirely collapsing. I dreamed that I had died years ago, along the Ob, before I ever came to Vorkuta, and that this was death, and that there was after all a hell for the dead, for some of them, for all, I did not know. I dreamed other things, awoke, drifted off again, wondered if I might somehow make myself die a little more quickly.

For a day or two, perhaps longer, there was a voice beneath me. Unbearable heat had come. I licked the sweat off the shoulders of the man crushed against me. But we were already too parched and there was only a little to lick. My tongue could barely move, it was too stiff. We had left the Arctic. I was incapable of knowing anything anymore, but still some stubborn horror of awareness remained. And then this voice, this voice coming from down below.

"It's the angels, my love. Dear God, Elisabet, I can really see them. Oh my God, it's all right now, sweetheart. At last, everything will be all right. Don't fear for me now. At last, at last, oh God, thank God, at last. I can see the angels. I'll be going soon, my dear. The pain is going away. Oh dear God, thank God, thank God."

He was somewhere near my feet, a small pile of flesh down in the darkness. Somehow he had not yet suffocated or been trampled. But still he must be on the verge, near the end, to be talking thus. My whole being was palsied with agony and hallucinatory sensations, yet persistently I felt a dull jealousy that I had not yet reached the glorious peace felt by this creature below me. So it was true then, just as men have always been told—that at the point of death, all of it, all of it, all of it, the pain, will lift away, there at the very end. But if the fortunate bastard was so near the end then why did he not die? And where, oh where, dear God, did he find the strength to speak in this car full of death-thirsty tongues? For it seemed he went on like this for days, for hours at least, a day, I don't know, a long, long time.

"Don't worry about me, Elisabet. It is much better now. I should tell you about the angels so you'll know too. They're here, they really are here, my dear."

It was never entirely dark in there, and when not clouded with dreams or hallucinations my eyes could see well enough the ordinary unspeakable place where we were. Once I looked down and saw him down there, crushed down in a corner of the boxcar into such a small space that I could not believe a human being could be contained in it. There was no space to lie down, he had collapsed down into himself in a space that seemed less than a foot high. I could actually see him talking, telling his Elisabet about the angels; it seemed there was nothing but a head down there, about the size of a large frog or hedgehog. There came a time when he repeated over and over something about rising away, rising away. I do not know when he died. I forgot all about him, fogged by my own madness.

At some point the train stopped and the doors opened and we were allowed to get out and drink, as if this were an ordinary stage in the course of things. I was too weak to get down and had to let myself fall out of the car onto the cinder bed. But my fall was cushioned by the bodies of dead men, who must have fallen onto the siding the moment the doors were opened. Out of the corner of my eye—for I seemed incapable of seeing anything in any kind of direct fashion, or perhaps it was the sun that was simply so blinding—I saw the doors of the next boxcar behind us being slid open, and I saw the dead spilling out the door like logs bursting out of a collapsed timber rick, all tumbling down onto the cinder bed, and the guards as if anticipating this dodging nimbly out of the way, all except for one, who was buried momentarily beneath the log-pile of the dead.

Then those still alive inside slowly followed the dead out into the sunlight.

At first most of us were too weak to move, except for a few who began to stagger toward the drums of water set up beside the tracks. There were too many of us still alive to all drink at once, but we were too weak, almost beyond thirst itself, to rush up and crowd around the water barrels. A few of the guards looked almost puzzled, as if they might wish to help us or would this be unseemly? A chief guard or an officer began walking among us, brandishing a pistol in an odd sort of way.

"Come now, prisoners! Drink and you'll feel better! Get up now, prisoners! The train won't wait here all day! Drink and you'll feel better! Get up, you sorry bastards! There is soup as well! Your country has need of you! Your journey will be over soon! Come now, prisoners!"

The stronger ones were allowed to throw out the dead still in the car and then rake out a good deal of the excrement and other filth, assisted by some of the guards, as there were only a few of us strong enough. Even after drinking and eating a little bit most could barely climb back into the cars unassisted. The guards then hoisted a water barrel into our car, so that we should be thirsty no more. It tasted of motor oil, almost undrinkable, but we were thirsty no more. With all the dead removed the cars were crowded no more, and we could lie down or sit down among the remains of the filth. The doors were slid shut again. The train remained at this siding for some hours. Then our journey continued.

We were let out again, a few days later, at an actual station, called Cholm from its hanging signboard, and told that our journey was over. It was very hot. I myself was beginning to feel like an angel, or so I thought once or twice, though in truth this idea did not seem to have any meaning to me. We

were fed again, watered, watered like horses. During our
march out of this small town I began to feel better. So much
horror was now in the past, gone forever. It was impossible
to understand.

Now there were men dressed like soldiers, they were soldiers. I had forgotten about the war. During the long hot
march away from this small town we passed through fields
and all kinds of staggering greenery. In the deep blue sky
clouds such as I had not seen in over ten years billowed up
overhead, miles high, like God manifesting himself near to
his earth. All was strange, all was familiar. Ahead of us there
grew a deep rumble which without being told I understood
must be the sound of the war. I had first been condemned in
1930. I no longer knew what year it was.

The soldiers dispersed us into smaller groups along a line
of low cement structures covered with earth. Myself and
three other men were made to enter one of these, which was
sunk partway into the earth. It was like a kind of jail but I understood it was a fortification of some kind. It was dark, dark
like the boxcar, except for a slit in the cement that looked out
blindly across the countryside. Two soldiers who had come
in with us quickly chained us to several sets of manacles that
were bolted into the wall beneath the slit. Then they left and
left us in there. Within reach of the three of us, mounted in
the slit, was a machine gun with belts of ammunition. It was
curious, all this, ominous also, though I was pretty much beyond reacting to anything in any particular way. Given more
time to react or gather our strength or our wits, we might
have given some thought to our situation, discussed it among
ourselves. But for the first few hours we sat dumbly, no more
than dogs at rest, beyond satisfaction or discontent.

The sound of gunfire, cannon fire, rumbled through the slit
and made the cement walls tremble.

At length another man was brought in and left with us,
wearing a soldier's uniform. His comrades did not chain him
to the wall but his ankles were chained together, so that he
could hobble about the interior of the place a bit. At first he
said nothing, but crawled furtively to the rear entrance a few
minutes after his comrades had departed.

"Very well, they've locked us in. Very well then."

He looked back among the three of us and announced himself as Sergeant Jefremov of the Red Army, and immediately took to ordering us about like children, instructing us in the use of our weapon. He was a very strange and feverish little man, like some kind of man I had not seen for a lifetime, though perhaps all this had to do with our coming under attack from the enemy very soon, as he declared.

"Fuck your busyness. Fuck your enemy. You're no better than one of us now," said my fellow convict Anton Fyodorovitch, with whom I had conversed a bit during our march from Cholm. How quickly the normalcy of speech returns to a man under almost any circumstances, once his lips have been wet enough that he can speak. Even chained to a bunker wall set beneath the earth, we seemed almost to float upon a small cushion of air, now, after what we had endured in the boxcars.

Jefremov, who if possible seemed more deranged than the three of us, or maybe only different somehow, took only slight offense at the impertinence of Anton Fyodorovitch.

"It's all very well to talk that way, but you are prisoners and know-nothings and you would do well to listen to me! The enemy will be here soon! You need only look out there and watch for yourselves."

"Fuck your enemy," Anton Fyodorovitch repeated stubbornly.

The sergeant shouted at him, "When the Germans are driven off we will be sent for and taken out of here. But you, you will stay! We'll leave you locked in here."

"Fuck your mother," declared Anton Fyodorovitch calmly, as if he sensed, though perhaps mistakenly, that he had gotten the upper hand. "I'd rather stay here anyway. Ha. Ha, ha!"

Slowly we all, except for the sergeant, began to laugh, quietly, on and off, for a minute or so. Jefremov simply looked at us dubiously, busying himself with a bit of newspaper and some bits of majorka taken from his pocket.

"You'll give us some of that," said Fyodorovitch. I had sized him up as a difficult type by nature, perhaps a criminal, one of those who tended to fare better in the camps. Or per-

haps he simply had courage. I had only had a short time to
talk to him, even to notice him.

"Yes, yes, all right," said Jefremov. "Fuck the enemy. I'll
show you how to operate the gun and then we'll see how it
goes. If we are to have any chance you had better pay attention. The Germans are difficult little bastards, you'll see."

Fyodorovitch only glared at him. Jefremov lit the smoke
and passed it first to me. I smoked, then passed it. I did not
know the name of the third man with us.

"So. The Germans," said Fyodorovitch. "I told you so,
didn't I?"

It was to me he said this. We had heard different rumors
bandied about.

"I've forgotten your name," he said.

I couldn't remember if I had told it to him. Maybe I had.

"Vasily Osipov."

He shrugged and grunted. Suddenly I began to feel ill
again, hungry and terrible. Sitting down against the wall beneath the slit, I hoped it would pass. Yet all the same, all the
same, even chained like this to a wall, it seemed that some
curious feeling of freedom had come over us. Another hallucination. But all the same it was there.

Fyodorovitch began to badger the sergeant again, who
again uttered his earlier threats, though not as loudly now. I
saw him staring carefully out the slit; then he began explaining to Fyodorovitch how to load the belts into the machine
gun, ignoring me and the other man. He fired a few rounds
and announced that the weapon worked satisfactorily.

"What was your crime?" demanded Fyodorovitch. "Cowardice? Rape? Stealing?"

"Worse," said the sergeant. "My unit was destroyed. I survived along with a few others."

"Cowardice in the face of the enemy." Fyodorovitch
laughed unpleasantly.

"Shut up now and do as I tell you. There they are. Look for
yourself."

I looked up to see the faces of Fyodorovitch and Jefremov
lit up in the bar of sunlight let in by the slit, both staring out
there. I realized that the continuous deep noise and vibrating
from earlier had diminished considerably. I could hear indi-

vidual shots though, machine guns and rifles, what seemed like shouting in the distance.

The sergeant began firing. The noise thundered in the dark bunker. I moaned and shut my eyes. I heard a peculiar whooshing noise and smelt something foul. Suddenly Fyodorovitch went off in a terrible rage.

"So that's it, you whores? I survived that stinking train so I could be chained to a wall like this? You bastard of a fuck!"

I looked up to see him attempting to strangle Jefremov with his chain, but it was not long enough and he threw it down and made to throttle him with his hands instead.

"Pick up the belt, you idiot! Feed the gun!" shouted the sergeant. He started to back out of Fyodorovitch's reach, fending him off with one hand while still firing the gun, and then the length of chain hobbling his own ankles caused him to lose balance and he fell. Fyodorovitch could no longer reach him and the sergeant began to crawl back into the darkness, back toward the locked door at the rear. Fyodorovitch looked out the slit again, in the beam of light.

A violent whoosh and stench.

I may report, in conclusion, that the screams of men burning, those screams, do issue in the first instants from the shock and horror of seeing that one is consumed entirely by fire, and not instantly from the unbearable pain which follows momentarily; and as with human affairs in general, there may be different cases to enumerate, as with a man who is completely burned over in an instant, but not deeply into his vitals, and whose outer layer of sensation has been so entirely burned away that he in fact feels nothing, screaming from shock only and also horror, or perhaps too shocked to utter even a single sound; whereas in another case a man is so entirely consumed by jellied corrosive flame that it eats immediately or else very very quickly into the inner vitals where such nervous sensation remains as to evoke an unimaginable agony that is also, in part, the utter horror of this, unleashing such screaming as is sometimes heard from burning people, this pain and the ineradicable horror of being witness to one's skin draining away and the flame reaching into the brain cavity and also simultaneously into every other inner place, with myself, for example, feeling the flame burning entirely through my chest to allow my beating heart to beat against the open outside air before being itself consumed in the very last moments; thus in these different cases the horrible screams may have a different nature, which may at times be combined or uncombined in still other different cases.

PART ONE

Cholm

Chapter One

Private Kordts cackled in spite of himself. A nervous outburst, it was over before he could hold it back. He didn't know if anyone else had heard him. Freitag picked himself up off the ground and glanced over at him, his face black with greasy smoke. Kordts was too tired to care anyway. He wanted to sit down, but he didn't see anyone else sitting down, so he didn't.

The Russian had emerged almost nonchalantly, it seemed, from some opening in the bunker, with his arms raised and his face bearing what seemed like a preposterous kind of smile. Hard to say really, startling though it was, as he had collapsed facedown at Freitag's feet only an instant later. Freitag had leaped aside and nearly fallen over backward.

The Russian's uniform was smoldering faintly, maybe his skin too, though he hadn't looked that bad when he first came into view. Kordts nudged the body with his boot. He thought of turning the head up so he could see the man's face again, to see if he had really looked that way.

Then he changed his mind and stepped back. Another impulse to laugh came over him and he simply let it out, a quiet groan. He looked over toward the next bunker in the system, about a hundred feet away.

Some of the others ran up past him now. The flame section was already over by the next bunker, which was throwing up smoke like a burning oil derrick. The screaming over there was horrible and it sobered Kordts immediately.

It affected the others also, who simply stood around listlessly, staring over there while the flame team finished the place off. Goertz slowly moved the nozzle back and forth, which bucked slightly whenever he exerted a slight extra pressure on the release valve. The thing did not have a proper trigger. It was easy enough to operate once you got used to it. But Kordts had heard of an incident in training, a man from some other unit, who had not taken a firm grip on the nozzle and the first jet of flame had bucked it up into his face. He didn't know if this had really happened or if it was just a story, though he found no reason to doubt it. In general people did not want to have anything to do with the flame guns. The job often seemed to go to some naive, cheerful, practical-minded, unafraid sort of fellow, who also frequently seemed to be among the very youngest of a given group of men. Though such personal attributes might begin to change some-what over the course of prolonged stretches, and they had been at it among these bunker complexes for a week now, this so-called Stalin Line.

Kordts blinked, dazed, for he had fallen back into some kind of inner silence where he did not seem to hear anything. As if the whole area had fallen silent. Then suddenly the hor-rible screaming burst into his ears again. And then it ceased, this time for good it seemed. The flames continued to lick out hypnotically from Goertz's nozzle. The final jet of flame seemed to follow itself strangely into the bunker, as if the bunker were sucking it in. Goertz lowered the gun and sat down wearily on a stump. The area all around the bunkers was dotted with stumps. Now Kordts sat down on the ground, looking away from the whole business.

Beyond the low stumps was a depression covered with green meadow grass and the summer flowers of northern re-gions, about two hundred yards across, and then the ground sloped up again to the edge of a pine forest. The forest was of thick old pines, spaced widely enough that sunlight fell between them and a sparse cover of grass was able to grow among the trees up to the brown needle-littered circumfer-ence of each bole.

They had emerged from the forest and been taken under fire from the bunkers hidden among the stumps on this side of the depression. So they had retreated back into the trees and called for artillery support, after spying out the well-camouflaged line of bunkers, which they had gotten more

adept at recognizing during these recent bad days. A few
minutes later the artillery fire had come in, well-spotted,
well-directed. During these first weeks of the invasion the
infantrymen had been gratified to see that their artillery support worked well with them and generally with a good deal
of precision. The fire had been laid down for fifteen minutes
and from the cover of the old pine forest they had watched
the bunkers get pretty well smashed up. But those were
sturdy places, built low in the ground with reinforced concrete under all the foliated camouflage, and the shells had not
finished them off completely.

They had emerged from the forest again and been taken
under fire again and advanced in groups of twos and threes in
scattered lines across the depression and up toward the
stump-field, taking casualties. For many of them it was all
still too new to have any kind of grasp of it all, of the dead,
of the wounded, of themselves still going. The dead and the
wounded were separate, the way rear-echelon troops or civilians or other kinds of people were also separate. Advancing
quickly in scattered echelons as they had been trained to do
they had taken only one man killed and several wounded;
they had taken cover among the stumps. Some of them, a
few officers or some of the quicker studies who were beginning to piece together some of the bewildering elements of
combat, cannily thought that the Russians had not been wise
to leave so many of these obstacles scattered about and
blocking their field of fire. The rest were just grateful for the
shelter afforded by the stumps. A year later, maybe, after the
Russians had begun to work through their long initial phase
of chaos and idiocy, they might have sited several small infantry mortars onto the stump-field and brought a great deal
of harm down on the Germans who had instinctively paused
to regroup their surge in that area.

But on this particular date in late July there were no mortars or other supporting weapons, no other men in fact, positioned behind the bunker line. Though still under fire from
the machine guns the Germans were able to regroup and send
the flame teams in.

About a half hour later Kordts was sitting on the ground,

looking back across the terrain they had covered, or else simply not looking in the direction of the one stinking bunker in particular. Freitag wandered into his field of view, still looking jumpy, then walked off somewhere.

Kordts was hungry. His mind flitted from one thing to another, and suddenly he was hungry. He fished out a piece of hard sausage he'd taken from a civilian some days earlier. It was partly eaten and he chewed some more off, not bothering with his pocketknife. A thick smell of frying chicken fat, which he had noticed a moment ago and now noticed again, began to coat his lips and nostrils and he chewed tepidly, persisting in keeping his back to things for a few more minutes.

"How can you eat?" said Brammler.

"I don't know," said Kordts.

He glanced over to see Brammler seated on the ground beside him. Then there were Moll and Erickson seated on two stumps, their faces dirty, their throat-hollows shining with sweat, their helmets off and their hair tousled and dirty, passing a canteen back and forth. Brammler drank from his own canteen and Kordts, feeling the same urge as to light a cigarette when three or four other men have done so, drew out his own nearly empty canteen and took a few swallows, still chewing a few grains of taste out of the sausage before gulping it down.

He saw Lautermann, the platoon sergeant, coming over their way. But then there seemed to be some kind of commotion over by the stinking bunker and Lautermann looked back and then went over that way.

The rest of them looked to see what it was.

Goertz was still seated on a stump next to the place and several men from the next platoon were gathered around the blackened bunker embrasure. The smoke had pretty much lifted away now, and the flames were gone.

"Will you look at that," said Brammler, standing up. He began to walk over there, catching up with Lautermann.

"I can see," said Kordts. Or he thought he could; yes, when one of them over there stepped aside for a moment he could see, and now someone was gingerly pulling what was left of the defender partway out of the embrasure. The man's black arms were manacled together by a length of chain, which was in turn bolted through its middle to a longer length of chain that hung down against the bunker wall, its other end disappearing somewhere back into the darkness of the embrasure.

After a moment or two Kordts could make out each of these peculiar features pretty clearly. Moll and Erickson, too, remained imperturbably where they were on the stumps, quietly studying this latest curiosity of the country they had entered some weeks ago.

Kordts took another swallow to clean out some aftertaste, spitting, spitting again, then probing around the inside of his mouth with his finger, feeling for some film or deposit though there didn't seem to be anything.

Down in the meadowy depression the corpsman, the *sanitäter*, was kneeling over a man who looked to be dead. Three wounded men had gathered in the thick grass nearby. Another wounded man with his shirt off and blood and dirt crusted on one arm and shoulder was walking slowly out of the stump-field down that way. Private Freitag was standing by himself down there a ways, dark and still in the burning sun with the hot green grass and pine forest in the distance beyond him, standing still like a sentinel, thought Kordts, or a Red Indian or something.

Chapter Two

From this point they were about ten miles from Cholm.

To this point they had done a great deal of marching, more of it than fighting. For hours and days they were aware of little other than their own fatigue. The fighting had come to seem like grisly, unaccountable way-stops along an endless highway. Only there were no highways. There were dirt roads, sometimes broad and fairly well-maintained, at least before the weight of thousands of German boots and vehicles had abused them and broken them up. More than anything else there were only meandering dirt tracks through the unending countryside of their enemy. The countryside was not wilderness exactly, insofar as the deep forests were frequently broken up by rolling grasslands and fields—long vistas from atop any small hill—and there were human settlements scattered frequently enough across the land. But the settlements were primitive, and not constructed from the shabby dregs and litter of industrial civilizations, as remote settlements in remote parts of the world in the latter part of the century would tend to be, but constructed almost entirely of wood. Unpainted wood, bereft of signposts or numbers. Just collections of small wooden buildings, isbas or somewhat larger houses, barns, storage sheds, sometimes put together with a strangely appealing craftsmanship, but more often poor and slipshod and untidy-looking, creaky, tilted, old, so that each settlement as a whole would have this kind of appearance.

As if they had rested there in thus and such a way for many hundreds of years, without change, without the normal meddlesome human tendency toward progress and change at any kind of pace at all, either gradual or swift.

So if the land was not entirely wilderness it was still a vast strange place, rendered almost stupefied or quiet by the forces of nature, for good or ill.

Many of the invaders were impressed in a bad way by the general shabbiness of things; others were somewhat more mystified by it all. If not entirely a wilderness, the land still did not seem to belong to the human domain, which was what they were used to in their own country.

In any case they were frequently so exhausted from marching twenty or thirty miles a day to really make much sense of this, what with the dust raised by their marching clouding the landscape and caking moistly to the sweat rimming all their eye sockets. They would collapse in exhaustion at the end of a day's march, seeming to fall down in their tracks like dead men along the sides of the dirt roads. One not used to the sick squalor of combat might even believe they were dead at first glance, so still did they lie in exhausted sleep, if one was not used to the unmistakable attitudes that dead, terminated human beings almost always had in death, as opposed to those merely sleeping.

They had almost no vehicles; a few cars for the generals and staff officers, that was about it. The other vehicles they did have were only rubber-tired carts pulled by horses, carrying supplies, ammunition, or the paraphernalia of the artillery trains. The horses too raised a lot of dust, plodding relentlessly and patiently forward, eastward.

The modern army, the tanks and armored cars of the mechanized units, the half-tracks and trucks, would sometimes pass them by, choking them with dust that was more billowing and obnoxious than their own tramping boot-stirred dust, unless perhaps a traffic jam ensued on one of these miserable roads, slowing the motor vehicles down with everything else.

The first days at the end of June had been very hot and hazy, the hot sunny land seeming to lie in a murky sweat of such weather, hard to even look at, the country seeming to lie underwater in the waterless heat. They all suffered greatly from thirst. The roads also, in the border territories, had all been very sandy, difficult to struggle through.

At some point in July though, deeper into Russia, the hot air had begun to feel clearer. Individual clouds took shape above and the sky was bluer. The still very primitive roads were not as sandy.

It was about this time that they first approached Cholm, after that bad stretch, the first really bad fighting they had encountered really, among the bunker complexes of the Stalin Line. These fortifications erected about a decade earlier under the direction of Stalin had in fact done almost nothing to prevent the Germans from penetrating still deeper into the country. The invaders themselves would remember the bunkers and the hot July days only fleetingly, after the other ordeals in the months and years to come.

Cholm itself was a more established place. It was not large, but many of the buildings were of stone which stood up in powerful white shapes against the deep blue sky and against the brilliant green of the marsh grasses that lay all around Cholm. The white buildings. Instead of hot they appeared cool to the eye, because of the intense blue above and green below among which they were situated. Even so the sun shone blindingly off them from a distance.

Many of the most ancient towns in northern Russia— Pskov, Novgorod, Staraya Russa, Velikiye Luki, Nevel, to name a few—would have this stone appearance.

Most of these same towns were surrounded by a watery kind of country. There were a few lakes here and there, though not that many compared with other watery places in the world. There were mostly shallow seeps and bogs and marshes scattered about, puddled between gradual rises that were drier though still covered with green grass and stands of birch, all of this moisture seeping one way or another into the rivers along which these towns had been built seven or eight hundred years before.

Rarely were any large bodies of water visible to the advancing invaders, but often there would appear to be glints of it here and there, flashing irregularly beneath tall marsh grass. They were all still very tired, but it began to be more pleasant and easier to look at than the sand and dust and scraggy trees of the border areas. More and more vast clouds began to take shape overhead, though the blue sky was also still vast.

The first time they passed through Cholm they did not linger there. The place was not defended and they kept on going, toward Staraya Russa and Ostashkov and the upper reaches of the Volga River. Almost all of them would never return to Cholm and never remember it.

In the winter everything was changed. The great agony, which had already begun before then, achieved its worst dimensions.

By the winter the division's manpower had nearly petered out, not just from casualties and sickness but from being strung out across such large areas of the enemy country. In December they were stationed still further to the east, around Lake Seliger—not a lake but a reservoir dozens of miles long near the upper end of the Volga. Their defensive lines were thin, their outposts scattered, and in the first days of the Red Army's great counteroffensive the division was nearly destroyed.

The survivors were pushed back scattered in many directions, mixing with shattered units from other divisions likewise sent reeling back through the terrible winter, driven back toward Rzhev, toward Toropets, back and back for scores of miles through the blizzards and the gales. A few company- and battalion-sized units of the division fell back in disorder upon Cholm in the first weeks of January.

They—the few hundred still alive—would have barely remembered passing through this place back in July. In any case it was unrecognizable, even to those who did remember it, buried under snow, heavy blizzard clouds like fish bellies blowing over the stone buildings from the east, the stone buildings seeming desolate and pointlessly scattered about in the unbearable cold.

Scherer was in charge here. The generals and colonels of the frontline divisions had been killed or wounded or simply separated from the widely dispersed groups of their men. None of the ranking officers reached Cholm. Only a few battalion and company commanders led their men in here, men looking like starving wolves or like frightened fleeing herds that had been set upon by wolves, stumbling into the town with almost their last strength. They were all placed under

Scherer's command. He was the leader of some kind of rear-area garrison unit. None of the exhausted stragglers had heard of him before.

Before the crisis Scherer's greatest worry had been dealing with the partisans. Cholm was the only town of any size in one of the most isolated and undermanned of the German rear areas. Partisan activity had picked up in the autumn and then grown steadily worse. Cholm itself had not been threatened, but outlying villages along the lonely supply roads to the front had been garrisoned by only handfuls of men from Scherer's so-called security division, older, poorly trained soldiers mostly, living much of the time in a state of fear in their outposts. It was a climate of stress and fear brought about by being isolated in what they called "Indian country," a phrase that tended to be spoken with little irony. As the snows grew worse they became still more isolated, with German supply columns pushing through only once or twice a week, greeted by these men with almost embarrassing cries of relief; but then after the half-frozen drivers or small batches of replacement soldiers had warmed themselves for a night in the tiny isbas they would move on, and the lonely garrison of perhaps half a dozen or ten of Scherer's men would watch them depart anxiously into the empty distance.

For then only the partisans would remain, invisible out there in the snows and the forests, coming out every so often without pattern or warning to murder an isolated man here or some poor unwary bastard there. And one could be as wary as one liked; it didn't help much when you were so alone. . . .

Scherer was not exactly a humorless and ruthless, by the book kind of general. He had done fairly well in his career, in postings both as leader of an infantry regiment and as a staff officer attached to higher command levels. In fact he was a rather cheerful sort of fellow; perhaps it was perceived that he did not have quite the stuff to command a combat division, and so instead he was assigned to head this security unit behind the lines. It was a dismal enough job for whatever kinds of men, good or evil men, for asses, ignoramuses, unimaginative careerists, or perhaps for somewhat better men than these. Conditions such as these could turn any commander into a sick, flinty-eyed sort of man, retreating because he did not know what else to do into that stern, vindictive, and narrow-minded German longing for order, which all too often led to hangings and shootings of the uncooperative natives. And the commanders of these security divisions were not, after all, among the army's best men. (Nor were the commanders of the frontline divisions always among the army's best men. The army, like any large organization, rewarded mediocrity as a rule and talent as a vaguely defined exception to the rule. Sometimes, in the ongoing crisis that was to unfold over the next few years, even mediocre men felt some kind of call that allowed them to rise above themselves; this only made matters more complicated.)

Scherer, in any case, as the commander of one of these security divisions, had to do something. His men had already burned down a number of partisan camps and killed a few partisans in confused gun battles. But he had not yet crossed that peculiarly infamous line of simply rounding up hostages and executing them in reprisal for the murders, sometimes very grisly murders, of his lonely soldiers, though he might wake up before dawn in his quarters in Cholm and be beset by the urge to do just that. He hadn't though. Still, he had begun to have people shot.

These had not been hapless bystanders caught up in one of the remorseless German roundups. No, they had been guilty of something, of violating the curfews or of wandering into prohibited areas, of traveling without proper papers outside their designated villages, guilty of bearing arms or of consorting with others caught bearing arms, guilty of some capital offense according to the long list of regulations and bans the Germans had posted in every miserable town and miserable village.

Scherer was troubled by all this, though it hadn't prevented him from seeing that his soldiers carried out these duties. But it put him into a lonely uncertain mood and he did not have the proper, small-minded, orderly and vindictive streak in him that would allow him to think that all this was very unfortunate of course but it was not his fault if the natives would not obey.

He never really articulated all this to himself, and he never looked in the mirror early in the morning to see if he was blameworthy or not. But this lonely uncertainty troubled him and it troubled him that he had not somehow risen above this filthy mess and found some way of dealing with it. Except, that is, by continuing to enforce the regulations and shooting the violators. He might think—and of course he did think this—that very few others anywhere in Russia, and perhaps no one at all, knew any better how to deal with this than he did. And many of them were far more insipidly remorseless and self-satisfied bastards than he was. He might think, and he did, of the mutilated bodies of his own men found hanging in a tree or dumped upside down in the snow.

Still, he could not hide from himself, as many others did, that all of this was simply no good, no good. He tried though. He tried not to think about it too much.

A career military man, even a great leader, must always have a certain innate streak of unimagination, which he had either been born with or else acquired over the long course of the years.

By definition, almost, the commander of any of these rear-area security divisions had not previously evinced any great leadership traits or other outstanding qualities. But perhaps Scherer was an anomaly in this respect. It was hard to say—hard to say what he was by his own nature, and what he was by the force of events that were soon to be thrust upon him. Long before the siege of Cholm was over he had begun to walk among his frozen and desperate men almost like a pirate captain, or perhaps, more humbly, like the captain of some doomed merchant vessel struggling along with his small crew in terrible seas. During the siege he grew a full beard—a seemingly insignificant characteristic, especially in the midst of such desperate fighting—but as far as is known he was the only German general ever to grow a beard and wear the same haggard facial growth as his men.

And this included a lot of generals fighting elsewhere in situations that were no less desperate. Von Paulus at Stalingrad had no beard, only a ragged and defeated-looking stubble when he finally gave up at the end of that shambles. Cocky Model, pulling the front of 9th Army around Rzhev together with little more than his manic busyness and contempt for danger, let a dirty stubble grow when he was too preoccupied with everything, but it was never more than a few days before he was clean-shaven again. The same with Seydlitz and Eicke around Demyansk, or Guderian around Tula before he was sacked for his disobedience; in the Crimea von Manstein would never think of sporting any kind of unkempt appearance. Halfway around the globe, though still fighting the Russians in the high Arctic, Dietl, a wiry, knobby little outdoorsman and faithful Nazi, always kept a clean ruddy hardness on his face.

Insignificant perhaps. In the end it is only a fact that by its singularity becomes noticeable, whatever it might mean. German seamen and U-boat men had always worn beards, remote on the high seas from any authority but their own, though there was also the lack of fresh water for shaving. Whatever this might have to do with Scherer hopelessly besieged for one hundred and five days at Cholm is anybody's guess.

Almost certainly he was not panic-stricken to see the entire front collapsing and shrinking back to his very doorstep. Apprehensive maybe, but not alarmed. For at least if the Red Army came he would be fighting soldiers instead of partisans. Anything to divert his duties from this filthy war against civilians. He must have realized this and felt better one morning, even while bedraggled and frightened men were marching grimly past his headquarters at Cholm from seemingly all points of the compass.

The soldiers on security duty in their snowbound outposts in partisan country were no doubt also relieved to have to fall back on the safer environs of Cholm. These men mixed with strange relief among the scarecrows retreating from the disintegrated front. They all collected in the town, ultimately about four thousand souls from a dozen different units. The temperature continued to drop, the wind continued to blow even icier on clear days than during the blizzards. The blizzards would blow for a few days and then the clear razor-light of the sun would emerge and be every bit as cold. The first packs of T-34s and Soviet ski troops kept right on going past Cholm and by January 18 of '42 the place was entirely cut off.

Chapter Three

Kordts and Freitag came in with the few hundred other survivors of their division, having marched a hundred miles back from Lake Seliger. They had been followed at every step by the Russian spearheads and by the ever-worsening cold. Among the men they knew, the immediate circle of their platoon, company, and battalion, Goertz had been wounded and then frozen to death because he could not keep up, Brammler had disappeared, Sergeant Lautermann had been killed leading a counterattack, and Erickson had also been killed somewhere. Kordts and Freitag had frostbitten feet and Moll, who was also with them, was even worse, both his hands and feet so badly frostbitten that they looked mangled. But he was lucky, at least in a way, because he was flown out in one of the first planes to come in after the siege had begun.

Meanwhile Kordts and Freitag stayed there as part of the bedraggled force that was now under the command of General Scherer, known as Kampfgruppe Scherer.

They were still there in April, almost three months into the siege. Freitag was out on the defensive perimeter somewhere, which in places ran right through the middle of the town. Kordts was in the field hospital, housed inside the old GPU building, burning with fever that carried him in and out of delirium like a tide ebbing and surging.

It was unfortunate that the GPU building was within spitting distance of the perimeter, and at times the Russian storm parties had been beaten back with spades and machine-pistols and grenades right at the front door of the place. But there was really no other place to keep the wounded and the sick. Cholm had been blasted to rubble by the Russian artillery or by the German artillery called in out of desperation to drive back the Russian attacks. The ancient stone town had not been burned to the ground like so many outlying wooden villages; rather, it had been pulverized. The GPU building, site of unknown infamies from the days when Stalin's policemen had operated out of there, was not imposing-looking but had the fortresslike construction common to grim jails in Russia and elsewhere. It was chipped, gouged, cracked, pockmarked, blackened with flame, but otherwise still standing solidly in the middle of the debris-field that Cholm had become.

Scherer's headquarters was also inside this edifice, and frequently the moans of the wounded men were audible to him, and he flinched at foul smells until he became inured and could no longer smell them.

Or he may at times have heard Kordts talking in loud delirium to some invisible visitor hovering by the straw pallet where he lay. During lucid moments Kordts lay in pain and miserable boredom, alternately very hot or very cold, the tedium of the hours barely dispelled by the nearby sounds of fighting which he and everyone else could hear. The windows had all been blown out since the beginning, and only the boards that had been nailed up prevented Russian infiltrators from tossing grenades into the sickrooms, though many of the boards were also smashed in or sagging brokenly in the window frames.

In April the cold was still freezing but not unbearable, as it had been two months earlier, sometime in late January or early February, when he had been wounded the first time and made his first visit to this place. A splinter, either a piece of shrapnel or a shard of ice from one of the snow walls they had built, had laid open his left cheek from the corner of his mouth almost to the cheekbone. Grotesque as it was, he might have been patched up by one of the medics and stayed in the line. They'd tried it that way at first, and Kordts himself had little desire to be stuck defenseless in the GPU building with the Ivans crawling up to that place almost every night. Having to stay out on the perimeter depressed him as well, with his pain and the anger his pain made him feel; a wounded man deserved a breather, but there seemed no safe place to get one and so he just stayed where he was.

The terrible cold had done much to numb the initial pain of the wound, and with this additional crooked grin slashed into the left side of his face Freitag had dubbed him Smiley, ha, ha. Filling his mouth with cigarette smoke had also eased the pain and of course it had been amusing to all to see the thin wisps of smoke seeping out through the gash. But he could not keep consuming his and everyone else's meager ration of tobacco and after a few days the cold and bitter gales seemed constantly to be working into the deepest recesses of the wound and causing him agony, exciting jagged nerves even into his teeth. Then someone had removed the bandages to have a look and told him gangrene was going to come if it hadn't already. Kordts still didn't want to go to the field hospital—he feared he would be murdered lying there—and he wasn't so sure you could get gangrene on your face. But maybe you could. It was an evil malodorous pollution, which he had seen on other people's legs and feet, not only here but also during the agonizing retreat from Lake Seliger. It was something to be afraid of, and anyway the pain was driving him into momentary bouts of hysteria—whenever his teeth began chattering from the cold the gash in his cheek would flex and he had to bite into his hand to make it stop.

So he went, unescorted, to the wretched sick dens of the GPU building, taking his rifle and a few grenades with him so he would at least have something if the Russians broke in.

The doctors saw he was still capable of moving about and assigned him to help defend the building while he was there, and he was glad he was not hurt worse and forced to lie unattended and defenseless for hours and days. Now he started worrying about the gangrene, fearing one of the scalpel-wielders might come up on him while he was sleeping and decide to carve half his face away. The exhausted doctor tried to reassure him; it hadn't set in yet and he should try and stay as warm as he could and not move about too much.

Stay warm though . . . it was a joke. It was as cold indoors as out; every building and every house was so thoroughly wrecked that it was impossible to heat them, though fires in clay ovens or wood fires on open floors were kept going day and night. The massive GPU building was as cold as death and the wounded moaned from their wounds and from the cold. At night some of them if they could crawl at all tried to huddle together for the extra body warmth, though moaning still to have their hurts nudged and elbowed by their equally suffering neighbors, all staring into the iron stove glowing in the middle of the room, a dozen pairs of eyes staring from a small cramped corner of the darkness.

Others unable to move still lay scattered about in the straw. More than a few gradually froze to death; or else a combination of the cold and their injuries, and shock and whatever else, did them in.

Kordts tried to stay warm to keep his teeth from chattering, and so sometimes he too huddled down in the midst of a heap of men, though it was distressing to be squeezed so tightly among foul-smelling terribly hurt strangers. If he could stand it he tried to stay warm by walking around and swinging his arms near the stove, chewing on a rag so his teeth wouldn't rattle so. Orange light glowed through cracks in the stove and out there in the night tracers from every caliber of gun crisscrossed spectacularly above the roofs of Cholm. It never stopped and this intensely vivid multicolored web of fire grew to be like some celestial phenomenon, Saint Elmo's fire clinging to the broken roofs or lopped-off cornices, to a few brutally decapitated steeples . . . or maybe like some unknown manifestation of the Aurora Borealis, which Kordts had seen too, hanging out there above the icewastes on a few unearthly nights.

The risk of gangrene lessened, though the wound, being so deep and in a hard place to keep bandaged, was not healing all that well. Stitches helped, though such binding seemed to aggravate the pain when his teeth chattered. During the week or so that he was there the Russians did not try one of their rampages into the center of town and he did not see any hand-to-hand fighting around the front steps. Bodies from other such occasions still lay there though, sprawled and petrified in the air, unburied—the ground was too hard to bury anyone—nor even dragged out of the way. Finally he asked if he could return to his unit—his group, you could hardly call it a unit. The exhausted doctor nodded after barely examining him, and he made his way back out through the rubble to the perimeter, the same two stick grenades stuck in his belt that he had brought with him the week before.

"Nice patch job," said Freitag upon his return. They huddled behind one of the head-high snow walls that girdled the outskirts. The ground was too frozen to dig into and these snow walls had been piled up everywhere, both around the town and inside it, anyplace where the Russians had a clear field of fire. The maze of snow walls began to look like the foundation for some other town that would be built upon the ruins of the present one.

"Give me a smoke," said Kordts.

"Didn't you bring any with you?"

"God no, they hardly have anything for anyone over there."

Freitag looked at him doubtfully, extracting a cigarette from somewhere under the white bedsheet he was wrapped in, then muttering with a kind of lighthearted annoyance, "Well, just don't take advantage of us, Smiley. Looks like they sewed you up pretty well. And you've had a week to rest now."

"Rest, my ass," said Kordts. Still in constant pain he was in a foul mood, though he was glad to be away from the field hospital. He knew he would change his mind about that too, as soon as he had been back on the perimeter for a few days.

"And don't call me that either."

"What's that? Ah," said Freitag. "Why not?"

"It sounds stupid, that's why."

Freitag shrugged agreeably and the nickname disappeared just like that into the crystal air of midday. They smoked together, sharing the one cigarette. The sky was razorously blue and peculiar, as it often was for days on end. The cold seemed to suck the atmosphere out. The sky was so bright and seemed so damnably close overhead that it was unnerving sometimes. Men often shut their eyes just to retreat into the black more familiar shadows of their own heads for a few moments; they both did this as they sat there talking to each other, or else peered out through slitted eyelids.

Other men from their squad, their platoon, their group, were manning weapons or sitting idly behind the snow wall nearby, though the force of the light seemed to put a peculiar almost palpable distance between yourself and every other man either nearby or far away, even while you could make out their features with strange clarity. The smoke from the one shared cigarette curled up.

"Thanks," said Kordts. "I didn't mean to take your last."

"It's all right," said Freitag. "They'll drop some more in sooner or later."

The smoke that came from men's breath also issued out everywhere, though this seemed to evanesce more quickly.

A shot was fired somewhere. It was nothing unusual. A man sitting by the snow wall a few feet away yelped in surprise.

"To the devil with all this!" cried someone, reacting more quickly than the others. Kordts didn't recognize this man, who was now shouting at them all to get away from the wall. The one who had been struck now lay groaning on his side in the snow; Freitag and the stranger ran over to him while the others started to scatter.

But there wasn't much other shelter nearby; the snow wall was their shelter. They moved with a strange laboring slowness, some at hardly more than a walk. The nearest building was several hundred feet away and several took cover over there, running bowleggedly the last little stretch over ice and squeaking hard-packed snow when another shot rang out. Others simply flopped down behind small mounds of debris or out in the open snow in places where it was a little deeper, burrowing in, lowering their heads.

Kordts was already worn out after walking all the way from the GPU. His lungs ached from the icy air, just from the extra bit of breathing that walking half a mile had required. And he could not properly take in air without stretching the stitching on the left side of his mouth. The thicker place where the corner of his lip had been slashed always hurt the worst. He scuttled off a little way along the snow wall and dropped down into a bit of shadow.

All of them . . . all of them were in great physical misery, and even though they tried to take cover and avoid being killed, they would not really have thought it an unwelcome thing.

Some of them were raising their heads and shouting across

the snow at each other, though it was clear that none knew where the firing had come from. Freitag was dragging the wounded man by himself; the other one, the stranger, seemed to have vanished. The wounded man was moaning and crawling and staggering with Freitag's assistance. Blood was on his white sheet, his snow-cape. In the intense invisible air the color red stood out like a beacon. They made it over to where Kordts was and both collapsed, the wounded man no longer groaning but ashy-looking and Freitag gasping for breath.

"This is my place," said Kordts.

"Swine," gasped Freitag.

Kordts didn't really mean it; it was only some dry obstinate humor that even he didn't seem to find very funny. Freitag, dully aware of this as he had known Kordts for nearly a year, shook his head but said nothing more.

Baer, the wounded man, stared up into the sky, seeming to collect himself a little, breathing hard but not looking quite as frightened. He cursed, he muttered. It looked as if he had been shot through the shoulder. Red blood was now black in the patch of shadow, or rather grey like something colorless; it always took thirty seconds or so for their eyes to adjust from brightness to something not in brightness.

"He's dead?" said Kordts.

Freitag looked back along the short path he and Baer had plowed up.

"Looks like it."

"Who was it?"

"I forget. Fritsche, something. He came over with a few jaegers yesterday."

The stranger, who Kordts thought had vanished, lay back there in the churned-up snow. They could only make out part of his bedsheet there, rippling a little in a gust of breeze. It looked like no more than some random bit of trash that could be seen lying about in the ruins or in the blazing-white, unnaturally wide-looking streets.

"If he moves I'll go back for him."

"Let his own friends help him out," said Kordts. "Don't be an ass."

Freitag, who was impulsive and energetic rather than a

hero, was used to this also and offered no reaction other than to glance at Kordts. They both looked out there and the jaeger sergeant made no movement. For quite some time now Kordts had come to despise the war and everyone in it, including himself sometimes, but especially including all officers, whom he believed with maybe only one or two exceptions suffered from some kind of genetic illness, including most NCOs and even his own comrades, though in a spontaneous moment when he had no time to think how much he hated everything he might still risk his neck to help someone. But not a stranger.

Freitag seemed uncertain what to do and finally looked down at Baer.

"How are you doing?"

"Are the planes still flying in?"

"You know they haven't been," said Freitag.

Baer looked angry, as if he had been caught up in a lie. But then the expression vanished, replaced by a look of pain and resignation. "I can't tell. Maybe it's not that bad."

"Your shoulder," said Freitag, peeling back the bedsheet from the center of the bloodstain and examining the threadbare tunic underneath. "Are you cold?"

"Yes, yes, I'm cold. What kind of question is that?" Baer became angry again, addled, almost drunk, from the throbbing of the pain.

"All right. I suppose you'll be fine then," said Freitag.

He didn't seem to be suffering from shock. His irritation and suffering and disgust were too strongly focused for that. The cold would often bring it on quickly when a man was struck by even a minor wound. Well, the wind was not howling today and the sun, useless sun, was shining brightly at midday. One of the JU-52s, before the planes had ceased flying in, had brought in several crates of adrenalin ampules. Scherer had ordered some to be stored at the GPU but had decided to distribute most of them to the men out on the perimeter, ready for instant use, though there hadn't been enough to go around for everyone. Still, the decision had saved some lives.

Baer had had something different in mind though, about the planes, thinking that a wounded man might still have a chance to be flown out of here. Even though he knew better than that, as Freitag had quickly reminded him. Daydreaming it, then.

"*Heimatschuss,*" he muttered forlornly or in resignation. Or else refusing to let go of the daydream for a moment longer.

"Forget it," said Freitag. "A shoulder wound wouldn't have gotten you out of here anyway."

"Maybe it would have. How about a cigarette at least?"

"Kordts stole my last one."

"No. Look in my pocket. I can't reach."

Freitag searched Baer's pockets but couldn't find anything. Baer cursed. Kordts, seemingly lost in thought for a few minutes, blurted, "*Heimatschuss* only gets you a ticket to the GPU. It's a disgusting place. You'll like it there."

Kordts often said things like this and Baer ignored him. "How am I going to get out of here?" he said to Freitag.

It was a good question. After the initial confusion they realized what had happened. There were snipers inside the town. To their backs, in other words. This had been going on for some time. About ten days before five civilians had been located in the upper rooms of a house with radio equipment and rifles equipped with telescopes. Scherer had had them hung in the town square. Things had quieted down, at least inside the perimeter. But now it seemed the bastards were at it again.

They were crafty of course and it might be hours before they let off another shot. Or perhaps they were waiting for the Germans to move, to haul a wounded man across open terrain.

Kordts looked back into the town, not really looking for snipers because he felt it was useless, but just looking. He could see down one of the streets a long way away where a few people, he couldn't tell whether soldiers or civilians, were walking about unconcernedly. Distance and perspective were given illusory qualities and for a moment they appeared as creatures a few inches high walking about in front of his nose. In the background to this odd tranquility was the noise of gunfire and shelling from some other part of town.

A desultory racket—the Ivans were not attacking, it was just people shooting and shells bursting here and there as they did at all hours.

Baer still craved tobacco and he was falling into depression. And he was cold. Color had returned to his face for a few minutes but now it was leaching out again. Their faces were mostly dark from the sun and snow-glare and so the ebbing paleness of an injured man became more noticeable. His shoulder was throbbing and sending deep iron pulses into his body and he was thinking too that with a difference of a few inches he could have gotten his head blown off. He was frightened.

Freitag thought Baer ought to be able to walk but now he wasn't so sure. He didn't look good. He wanted to get him standing, try it at least, but he was afraid of drawing more fire and an uncertain lethargy was settling on all three of them.

"Goddamn it, look again," said Baer, almost whining, looking like a boy, his jaw beginning to tremble. "I know I had some."

Freitag was about to go through his pockets again when they saw someone running across the exposed white glare of the middle distance. As he came nearer Freitag could see it was another one of the jaegers. The man floundered up to the dead sergeant and reached down into the snow, rolling him over. Then he dodged more quickly along the path Freitag and Baer had churned through the snow and knelt down beside the three of them.

"Somebody should get word back to Scherer," he said. "If this business starts up again there'll be hell to pay."

He looked at the dead man, someone he must have known for some time, cursing to himself then falling silent, staring intently here and there. "I hate those bastards. Do you want to come with me, Baer? We'll talk to Scherer."

Baer didn't answer. The cold was beginning to paralyze them all. They would often speak in this direct kind of fashion, as if Scherer were their company or battalion commander, their immediate superior, in other words. He did make himself available, and he was out touring the perimeter every day, talking to the men with the ragged, hard-bitten,

disgruntled look that the lower ranks seemed to recognize as
their own kind of everyday look. It was Scherer who went
around talking to people and maintaining that they would
hold here, uttering this not with confidence but with simple
determination. Yet he could be disarmingly cheerful at
times. Meanwhile his second-in-command Colonel Mabrius,
more experienced in matters of basic infantry tactics, did much
of the actual planning of things, constantly shifting the defenders around from one point to another, wherever the Russians
were gathering for the next blow out there. So if Scherer was
not at the GPU right now they would wind up talking to
Mabrius or some other officer; when they said Scherer's name
they were referring to him and to these other people too.

They had tried to get Baer to walk, both Freitag and the
other jaeger helping him a way, but he kept leaning on them
and laboring so slowly through the drifts that they got one of
the metal saucer sleds and laid him in that and began pulling
him into town. Kordts could still see them crossing the open,
outlying snow; it was then that the alarm bell rang.

It rang in a steady metronomic panic through the blank air,
the urgency too familiar.

The men who had scattered began surging back toward the
snow wall.

Perhaps the Russians still had contact with observers inside the town, who had reported the momentary confusion of
the defenders during the sniping. It didn't matter. German
observers watching from their own lookout posts had seen
them coming from a distance, out there in the snow-covered
swamps and meadows, still laboring far away while the
clanging sound carried everywhere.

Shells came in and mortar fire and a few of the defenders
were hit in the open before they could get back to the snow
wall, but not that many; for a long time they had learned
never to collect in groups of more than a few people and so
only a few people were hit now, and maybe some of them
only stunned as the deep snows tended to absorb a great deal
of deadly force.

Back to the wall and still they did not fire right away, peering out to see just how far off the enemy was, then hunkering
down again to make themselves small amidst the bursting

shells, knowing instinctively as well that the snipers in the town would take advantage of the confusion to start picking them off again and in the confusion few would know whether they were being shot down from the front or from the rear. There was nothing they could do about it. The beginning of another attack drew all their attention, anxiety, adrenaline. The heavy machine gunners began firing first and then at closer range the riflemen began firing. Between shots they began priming more grenades to set within easy reach beside the other grenades that they always kept primed and waiting, the wooden handles of the things lining the snow wall like kitchen utensils.

The Russians kept coming, floundering on through the cold glaring quicksand, dying, still coming.

"Oooooooouray!" they shouted en masse once or twice. Their Red Indian yell, their Russian yell. It must be hard to yell laboring through the snow for hundreds of yards, gasping, being shot down in large numbers, and so the yelling diminished raggedly and pathetically and they just kept on.

The defenders, impressed for weeks now by the seeming hopelessness of their own situation, were also much impressed by the stubborn hopelessness of the Russians, who struggled forward to be killed out there almost every day in scenes little different from this one, an ongoing repetitive blur beneath the sky-arc of frozen light; or in the gloomy intimacy of the blizzards when they sometimes managed to sneak much closer and kill the defenders hand-to-hand before being driven back.

If they were driven back. For every few days it was the defenders who were overwhelmed, saved only by Mabrius's cunning shuttling around of his scant few alarm troops who waited round the clock for such emergencies; even so the perimeter was shrinking, from one week to the next.

The Russians attacked according to fixed, unchanging schedules that must be graven in stone—in a tombstone maybe. A child would have displayed more cunning than they did, attacking like clockwork in those clustered waves regardless of whether conditions were favorable for them or whether—as it was right now—the conditions were the worst possible.

The snow was deep, the light was bright, and the Germans although outnumbered ten to one were able to see everything spread before them and amass every bit of deadly metal in their small arsenal at the critical point at the critical moment. Heavy machine guns would often jam or freeze up but the alarm troops would quickly bring up more machine guns from out of the ruins, the scant few that could be kept in reserve; but each such weapon was a murderous metal-spewer. The standard MG 34 had been a good weapon, the best of its kind in fact; but during the first days the JUs had flown in a few of the newer model gun, the MG 42, whose rate of fire was faster still; the defenders christened it the bonesaw.

The Russians, familiar enough with seeing their ranks cut up by the older 34, would still keep coming on with a brutal calculated perversity, knowing that during some point of continuous firing the German gun would almost always jam or seize up from the cold—that being the time when the surviving attackers might surge on through the forward-most dead-heaps and overrun the crew with bayonets or hand grenades, knives, anything, in a last rage.

But the newer 42 was of simpler construction and rarely jammed, nor was it so sensitive to cold. Sometimes the Russians, when they could pinpoint one of these infernal devices, would call in whole batteries of artillery just to silence the thing. But their communications were never very good and as often as not their artillery might as well be firing at some other town altogether.

Kordts watched them come. And there were tanks too.

The infantry could not close, could not keep up. Exhausted, demoralized, dead, wounded, screaming, enraged, or in dull despair at the stubbornness of the officers who drove them on. Finally their officers could drive them on no longer, no matter what threats or demented patriotic shouting.

The tanks, though, pulled away and kept coming and the men along the snow wall knew that nothing would stop them.

Such thoughts as a man could have at this time occurred only in small claustrophobic corners of the brain. Kordts only reckoned that if one came at him, him personally, then he would find someplace to get out of the way.

The defenders, small in number and scattered thinly

around their little strongpoints, would each often get the notion that a tank was heading for him and him alone. There were no antitank guns in Cholm, not even the smallest caliber weapon; there was only such a weapon as an individual man himself constituted out of his own flesh and blood, with a Teller mine or grenade-bundle clenched in his fist.

So the defenders could only wait until the tanks were right on top of them, and soon they were.

The first crashed the snow wall, rising up like the hull of a speedboat bucking up on a high swell. It stayed there, almost stuck for a few moments, tracks churning, grinding down the thick wall like a belt-sander, gears shrieking and downshifting. It was vulnerable then but men rarely could keep enough of their wits about them during the moment of initial shock to react; to react other than to get out of the way or crouch down in terror. There were a few men near the tank. From some distance further away along the snow wall another man came running up with a Teller mine. But then the tank was through before he could get close enough, dropping down over the wall like a huge iron lid and then driving straight on into town along one of the main streets.

The machine gunners were trained—if the word "trained" made sense in this case—to ignore the tanks and keep their fire laid on the following infantry to make sure they did not regather their impetus and storm the wall in the wild confusion the tanks always brought about.

Then it was up to the rest of them to deal with the tanks; or up to those with enough courage by nature or by desperation to do it. Because you could not train a man to take on a tank all by himself, though all had seen some men do it by now.

Kordts was not such a man, though he remained calm and collected enough. That is to say he was not panicking, though the sight of one of those things lurching about close by often induced a kind of mental paralysis where it was impossible to think clearly, even if you were not exactly crippled by terror. After some months of this kind of thing you could teach yourself to react instinctively, if such a way of saying something is not too paradoxical or inane; to actually be able to think clearly and cogently during a tank attack might take several years of experience, pending your own survival for that long.

As always though, some men were quicker studies or else braver. The second tank burst through the breach made by the first one and likewise kept on going into the town. Kordts sidled back along the wall to keep clear of the thing, glancing over the snow wall to make sure their infantry had not come up, his fingers kept gripped tightly around the first of his grenades just in case. The man with the Teller mine had been run over by the second tank, a horrible sight though unnoticed by many; but someone now picked up the mine from the mangled remains and leaped onto the third tank, which was slowed down by a part of the wall that had been doused with water and become a solid rampart of ice. He wedged the cumbersome disc-shaped explosive under the turret and pulled the ring and jumped, landing on the piled ice and losing his balance and sliding sideways into the snow below.

The explosion lifted the turret partway from the hull. It was a very quick and highly concussive bang felt by everyone around, a stunning and satisfying sensation when you knew the work it had done, satisfying and awesome as well to see the engine deck blown off and soaring fifty feet into the air, thudding down into the snow over there.

There were four in all. But the fourth T-34 now kept its distance out there, shelling and machine-gunning the snow wall out of anyone's reach.

Kordts saw all this and then felt a prickling in his scalp. There was an engine racing and gears shifting somewhere close behind him. He turned to see the second T-34 wheel about, no longer following the first toward the town center to blast away at Scherer's headquarters in the GPU. Kordts was afraid it was going to come back and run down everyone from the rear. Perhaps the Soviet crew had this in mind. There were some men though back there in the middle distance behind the snow wall and the T-34 first approached them and they approached the T-34, two of them.

Kordts now saw a third man roll out of the aluminum sled he had been lying in and realized it must be Baer. Baer got to his feet and staggered off and the tank crushed the saucer sled and sent part of it spinning off across the snow, flashing twice upon specific angles from the sun's rays. One of the other two men had climbed up on the engine deck now; it had to be either Freitag or the jaeger though Kordts could not make out which, though he could make out that the man seemed to be carrying no weapon except a rifle. He was shot in the face by a crewman who pushed back the wide ungainly hatch firing with a pistol. The crewman ducked back inside as gunfire from somewhere raked the turret. The hatch remained open and the tank again slewed about and resumed its advance up the main street, where in all likelihood it and the first tank would spend half an hour or so shooting up everything in sight around the GPU building before someone finally knocked them out; either that or they would head on straight through the town and make their escape out the other side.

Meanwhile Kordts caught sight of Baer again, staggering over to the other man, the one who hadn't climbed on board and gotten shot. Kordts looked to see if it was Freitag.

Scherer had just returned from one of his daily or sometimes twice daily tours of the perimeter and he was unable to get back inside the GPU before the first T-34 took it under fire. He and his aide took shelter behind a collapsed wall on the other side of the street. From here they were able to watch the second T-34 come up less than a minute later.

"The lid's not closed," said his aide, Gadermann. He was armed with a captured Russian submachine gun, a goat's leg; they all coveted these guns and took them from the dead whenever they could. Scherer carried one too. The number of enemy dead in and around the town had been enough to supply much of the garrison with arms.

He and Scherer kept up a steady fire along the top part of the turret. An arm reached up, a hand scrabbling about for the hatch handle, but then the hand disappeared and the heavy awkward lid remained open.

"I'll do it, Herr General," said Gadermann.

Scherer looked at him, said nothing, not wanting to lose such a valuable man. He would have done it himself; though in an instant's sublimation of thought he knew he should not risk himself. He knew his duty, suffered no doubts as to his courage, and kept calm. He placed his hand on Gadermann's back and Gadermann loped out from behind the wall. Nei-

ther had any grenades though. Scherer cursed, on the verge
of yelling at Gadermann to come back.

The act of clambering on board a moving tank was nearly
suicidal in itself; to justify such a risk a man ought at least be
carrying something he could kill a tank with. Scherer yelled
at Gadermann to just get out of the way, or began to cry these
words before he clenched his teeth and just watched, letting
off another burst at the turret and then holding fire for fear of
hitting the other man.

The T-34 slowed as it came up near the first tank and Gadermann, with the quick marionette lope common to people
trying to dash about on unfirm footing, was able to get up
alongside it and grasp hold of one of the equipment racks
along the fender. Unexpectedly the tank picked up speed
again and Gadermann was jerked off his feet though he managed to roll out of the way.

The crew sitting under the wide-open hatch must have
sensed something or else panicked. Scherer watched the vehicle roar away, past the first tank, past the GPU building,
down the rubble-clogged street heading at full speed for the
other side of town, from where they would try to make it
back to their own lines. Maybe. There was no telling what
the Soviet tankers would do. He had seen the clockwork pigheadedness of their attacks from day to day, yet once inside
the town they seemed to burst free of such restraints and
wander about like rabid dogs, their movements unnerving
and unpredictable though at some point almost always coalescing around the shattered pile of the GPU as if drawn to
the largest offal heap.

Gadermann remained in the street, crawling over to pick
up the goat's leg which he had lost hold of. He stared at the
first T-34 still idling in the main square a hundred feet ahead.
Scherer stood up. "Come back over here, *junge*!" Then he
too looked at the first tank, which had fixed its cannon upon
the GPU entrance; the shell went out and struck the building
at point-blank range, sending debris and stone-dust billowing up like billowing snow.

All this mess now settled slowly and stunningly back toward the earth. The Soviets drove off, gradually disappearing, and then quickly at a high rate of speed.

As if the whole enterprise had been nothing more than the carrying out of some crazed dare. Storm into town . . . get off a good shot or two . . . get out again. . . .

Scherer walked out and helped Gadermann to his feet. They continued slowly toward the GPU, stepping through quiet fits of their own trembling, though this had mostly passed by the time they stepped inside. Mabrius and a few others were standing in the entrance now among fallen blocks and dust still settling.

It had taken scarcely an hour for the midday brightness to pass to the dimness of dusk.

Someone was shrieking in pain from inside the building. Mabrius started to speak but Scherer shook his head and led him into a smaller room, closing the door. Gadermann lit an oil lamp sitting atop an old chest of drawers covered with maps and scribbled notations.

"The Russians are still going at it in the Paupers' Field sector," said Mabrius.

"I know. I started back when I heard the alarm," said Scherer.

"The forward observers say there's still one T-34 out there shelling the perimeter. The enemy infantry was dispersed initially but the latest report says they're regrouping and closing on the first strongpoints. It seems that tank is making it difficult for our men to man their positions."

"Who's in command at Paupers'?"

"The jaeger lieutenant. Ohlsson."

"All right. What's the enemy strength at this moment?"

"The last report was five minutes ago. A company, perhaps two hundred men. The attack was initially reported as regimental size, but Ohlsson says we hit them pretty hard before they could get close."

"As usual, as usual," muttered Scherer tersely.

Still, two hundred of them, if they had not been cut up into a demoralized leaderless mob, could present quite a threat. Especially with the tank still out there. Always these damned T-34s, he thought. It seemed inconceivable to Scherer that the JUs had been unable to fly in a single antitank gun; he had spent a good deal of the first few weeks on the radio to the outside, calling Pskov and Riga and demanding that heavy weapons be brought in. He did not believe that none were available and yet still none were brought in. Lately he had given up trying, devoting himself to more pressing concerns inside the perimeter. And so the damned T-34s. The GPU seemed to draw them like flies to shit, which was fortunate in its nerve-wracking way; sooner or later they would learn to stay more patiently out on the perimeter until their infantry had followed them through into the breach. And then what? Another crisis. Perhaps even today. . . .

Even one tank still roaming around out there could cause havoc if it remained beyond the reach of individual tank killers.

"All right. Let's get to the radio," Scherer said.

In the radio room they made contact with Ohlsson again. Scherer got on the speaker.

"All right, Ohlsson, listen carefully. If things don't clear up out there I will call in artillery support. Which you may find landing on your own heads. Do you understand?"

The lieutenant reported that he understood. They were taking casualties but he believed they could hold, T-34 or not. Scherer said, "What do the observers say? Are the Russians assembling a second wave? Or is this it for today?"

The question came out with a dry sardonicism, which Scherer had not intended. The implacably curious manner with which the enemy conducted their operations would elicit such remarks.

They waited for Ohlsson to get in touch with one of the observers. The observers were also in direct contact with the radio room in the GPU, but he had confidence in Ohlsson and didn't want to muddle things by hearing from too many different people right now.

Ohlsson spoke again. He reported no sign of any further enemy assembly positions out there. No follow-up attack. He wanted to keep talking about the Russians still fighting at the perimeter; Scherer listened for a moment more, gave Ohlsson some encouragement, then nodded at Mabrius to stay in contact while he stepped into the doorway to think for a moment.

The hallway outside still reeked of cordite and dislodged filth and dust and plaster from the tank shell delivered through the front entrance ten minutes earlier. He had already decided not to call in artillery fire unless of course the Russians did assemble a second assault wave outside the town. If he called in fire support directly on Paupers' he would have to tell Ohlsson to withdraw; in spite of what he had told the lieutenant a minute before, he had no intention of bringing shellfire down on his own positions, on his own men. They could no longer afford casualties like that, even if the Russians were on the verge of breaching the perimeter.

Yet he knew somehow that today was not that day. Ohlsson would hold. He scowled, wondering why Mabrius had not called for artillery support from the very start, before the enemy had a chance to get right into the middle of the defenses.

What else, what else? He was constantly worried that one day they would deceive him, that their pigheadedness was no more than some long, drawn-out, incomprehensible ruse of some Asiatic mind. Actually he no longer thought even that. He worried that the clearly incompetent commanders out there would sooner or later be replaced by others who knew how to mount an effective siege. Perhaps such fears were groundless, perhaps every high-ranking officer in the Russian army was completely mad, but he could never quite bring himself to believe it. Nor could Scherer quite believe, like every other man in the ever-shrinking garrison, that they were still holding on in Cholm after all these weeks. Yet so they had done.

For days the Russians had been going at the Paupers' Field sector and he had thought, correctly, that today would not be any different, yet some nagging thought had driven him to tour the perimeter on the other side of town, where the strongpoints had been left weakly manned due to the ongoing business at Paupers'. A concerted attack at both Paupers' Field and against these more vulnerable sectors might mean disaster. Yet he had walked out there with Gadermann and seen nothing at all, no signs of activity out in the bright wastelands, nor any reports of such from the observers in that sector.

And even all the way across town, the perimeter of about one square mile that they still held, he had heard the alarm bell ringing clearly and knew that it came from Paupers' and that this day would only be another like all those preceding.

Night was falling. The rank-smelling corridor was dark
and carried drafts of knifing cold and Scherer stepped back
into the radio room. Mabrius had already sent up the alarm
troops some time before and now the reports coming in from
Ohlsson were more encouraging. The remaining T-34 out
there had finally withdrawn.

"All right, that should do it for now," muttered Scherer to
no one in particular. The tense postures of men in the room
relaxed noticeably for a few minutes—Scherer, Mabrius,
Gadermann, the radio operator, the signals officer, the two
runners kept on duty in there. He would not have to pull back
the perimeter any further. Another day had passed. There
would only be more casualties, more casualties.

He did not like having his headquarters in the same building with the wounded. He pitied them moaning and crying,
or lying in oppressive, hanging silence on the floor above,
and such a distraction made it hard for him to concentrate.
Yet at this point, even if it were feasible, he doubted he could
bring himself to move his headquarters somewhere else.
They were all in this together. Interwoven in suffering, hope,
and lack of hope. Anyway it was not feasible to move and
every day and night the ceiling overhead moaned and cried at
ragged intervals, or else was silent and ominous hour after
hour, the days passing. He visited them often, and when he
was out on the perimeter he often personally assisted
wounded men trying to limp or crawl back to the GPU, putting his arm around a man's shoulder, helping him to walk.

To Mabrius he said, "Why didn't you call for artillery
from the start?"

"They're out of shells."

Scherer looked hard at him and knew he would pass another sleepless night.

"Why didn't you say so right away?"

"I should have mentioned it. I'm sorry. I was coming out to
look for you when the damn T-34 came up to the door."

Mabrius like Scherer seemed oddly indestructible, inde-
fatigable at least, and it had not occurred to the general to ask
if he had been injured by the shell blast.

"Are you all right?"

"Yes. But it slipped my mind. Then with Ohlsson."

"Yes, yes, I know. But how can they be out of shells? For how long then?"

Mabrius explained. Scherer thought the man must be addled with exhaustion but simply hiding it; something so critical could not just slip Mabrius's mind. But then, of course, it could; it had. Mabrius was a rough and solid leader who automatically commanded the respect of his men, a heavily built combat officer who might have intimidated a more studious type like Scherer. But Scherer was at ease with himself—with his ego, as it were—and thus was also at ease with all other kinds of people. Not having to devote energy to sorting out personality conflicts, he was able to devote himself entirely to the predicament they were in. Mabrius had not belonged to Scherer's security outfit; he had come to Cholm from the outside, leading in the remains of a shattered infantry regiment, which nonetheless remained the largest coherent fighting force inside the town. At least for a while the men of this group had continued to look more to Mabrius than to Scherer as their leader, as their hope for somehow finding a way through this ordeal. He was more familiar with frontline fighting tactics in any case, and Scherer had no qualms about listening to his advice. As for Mabrius, he had seen from the start that Scherer was a calm and unshakable sort of fellow; as the days went on he began to appreciate that Scherer also displayed a good deal more competence and energy than he might have expected from a rear-echelon general. Theirs was not a natural partnership, but it had worked well enough thus far.

Even so, Scherer might have felt some brief satisfaction to see the rugged Mabrius not in full command of the situation for a few moments, whether addled from exhaustion or perhaps more stunned from the blast of the tank shell than he had let on. But if he thought this at all it was only in passing. It was only natural to take some satisfaction when another man, a competing force of personality, faltered momentarily, but Scherer evinced rather little of this all-too-typical human trait. It did him well, and the people around him worked better for it.

Mabrius went on, "Understand it's only for today. They hope. They reassure us anyway." Mabrius's lips tightened in a thin wry line, though he was not much given to irony. "The supply train was ambushed by partisans. They were beaten off but it took most of the day. The shell stocks should be replenished by tonight. They're doing everything they can. I do believe that."

This was not quite so bad but Scherer still wondered how well he would sleep. It was bad enough inside the town, and this weighed on him still more whenever he was reminded of his powerlessness to deal with conditions on the outside.

For that was where the artillery was, massed in an exposed feeble salient of the German front line about ten miles to the west of the besieged town. Often without antitank guns the men defending the perimeter felt almost naked in the face of the enemy assaults, but strictly speaking they did have some support from heavy weapons. It just happened that these weapons were all located outside of Cholm, and if the Russians succeeded in pushing back or cutting off the dangerous salient where the artillery was massed then the town would surely fall.

That, at least, seemed fairly simple. Self-evident, in fact.

The general of the German division nearest to Cholm had responded to Scherer's predicament by bringing every available heavy gun as far forward as he could, in effect placing the artillerymen in the front lines, which were scarcely better manned than those of Scherer's own perimeter ten miles away. For weeks now this critical weight of shellfire had smashed down on the enemy assembly positions around Cholm.

"Partisans. Partisans," said Scherer. He too was very tired and out of nowhere a blackness suddenly took hold of him.

"Yes, that's right," said Mabrius. "It never ends. They've started it up inside the town again as well. There was a report of sniper fire inside the perimeter, just before the attack started. You know I've got no more patience with these bastards."

Nor did Scherer, though he didn't say as much. He didn't like to talk about partisans, didn't like to think about them. He'd had enough of that back in the autumn and earlier in the winter. He listened to Mabrius and blackness possessed him. The last time this had happened he had scoured the entire town. He wondered if he had enough men left to do this again. There were few enough buildings still standing for snipers to hide in, though he supposed the bastards could hide themselves just about anywhere in all the rubble about. He began to feel again some of the sickness inside him that he had felt the previous fall, and which he had largely put out of his mind since the siege had begun.

He told Gadermann to fetch him some tea. He felt a feeling like a block of stone resting against his forehead and decided he would not have that, one way or another. He said, "Never mind, Mabrius. We'll hang some more. That's all there is to it. Get hold of Ohlsson again and tell him he's done well. I'd come up and decorate him in person but the last box of Iron Crosses got left behind at Riga. I'm going to lie down for a few hours. You too, Mabrius. Get some rest."

Gadermann came back with the tea. But Scherer walked past him without a word into the dark corridor.

Chapter Four

The small sun bulged like an aneurysm in the thin line of red stretched across the horizon. Evening twilight. The sky was ice-clear, palpably invisible; one of nature's paradoxes, the palpable void. The earth—the stomped ruins of Cholm and all the rest of the earth—was nudged tight against the vacuum of space, the normal gradations of the atmosphere sucked away, gone.

The small aneurysm dissolved. There remained only the blood-vessel-thin line across the horizon, now perfectly smooth, even, healed of its agony for these few lingering moments. Such a perfect narrow line across the ice-waste must be pumped through with the blood of Christ himself. Easy, easy. Already the stars were rolled out overhead, like the vast inner constellation of synaptic firings, calm with such an utterness up there.

At many places in the town the ruins were so stomped that it was easy to get a good view of the horizon, of the end of the day. The Russians were massed out there. And then beyond the horizon, scarcely ten miles away, were the German guns, the guns that had been brought up into that exposed and perilous salient of the main line to offer all possible fire-support to the encircled defenders of Cholm.

The guns had not fired today. Scherer and Mabrius and a few others knew the reason for this. All the rest of the garrison knew only that the enemy had nearly broken through in the Paupers' Field sector, that their artillery support had not delivered them from this danger as it had so often done on preceding days, and that they had managed to throw the Russians back anyway.

The Russians, or at least their leaders—commanders and

commissars—may have been particularly enraged that they had failed to take advantage of this excellent opportunity. By now, more than six months into the war, they were used to their failure to take advantage of almost any opportunity; their leaders no less enraged for all that, possessed by an intolerant rage that yet coexisted somewhat dementedly with a kind of tolerant stoic fatalism.

The reality of such a conflicting and unstable mind-set would be a moody vacillation, commanders and commissars perhaps deciding to forego the usual expedient of executing a number of the survivors of today's debacle, men who by late afternoon had broken and fallen back across the snow-fields, back to the dismal Russian encampments in the snow-marshes around Cholm.

Instead they decided to try again, as night fell.

Kordts, as the last man to have seen Baer and Freitag alive, was sent back to look for them. Baer had been wounded in any case, and if he hadn't been killed during the tank attack then he was probably at the field hospital by now. Or perhaps he was simply holed-up in some other ruin, tended to for the time being by some other group of men. He could be anywhere and in fact it was only Freitag whom Kordts had been sent back to look for. Freitag was a reliable fellow and should have reappeared at the perimeter by now. The perimeter was so thinly held that the absence of even one man could plague the thoughts of group or section leaders. Kordts had been told to look back in the town and then return within an hour, with or without Freitag. For Kordts too was one man, one more hand.

There was a good deal of open space between the few buildings around the edge of town. They seemed set up randomly, without corresponding to any street plan. Thus men moving back and forth between the perimeter and the center of town were more exposed to sniper fire, or any kind of fire. There were stretches that men always tried to cross at a dead run, clearly visible to enemy observers on the outside or to civilian snipers still hiding inside the town, if Scherer hadn't hung them all by now. Kordts doubted the general had had any chance to find much less hang whoever had been sniping at noon before the attack began. Even so, he did not make a quick dash, as most men did, across the open stretches. He was too tired. When men were tired they were not necessarily careless, insofar as they knew the risk they were running; they were simply tired, and walked when at another time they might have run.

Night was falling and he might have waited for night to conceal his movements. True, he had been given only an hour to look for Freitag, but Kordts was not the type to observe instructions to the letter. He just thought he might as well get it over with. Survival instincts, experience, and cunning warred dully at all hours of the day, any day, with fatalism, with the stupid hand of God, like altering casts of sunlight that fell upon the snowfields throughout all the hours of the day. The last of the day lay in a thin red line behind him. The night would be as cold as it had been before. His boots squeaked grudgingly across one of these open stretches in the twilight. Even so he began to stagger a little more hurriedly because the cold impelled him to do so. He was not fired upon and came to the relative safety of a street lined with buildings. The buildings, or ruins of them, were more tightly clustered together toward the center of town. There were streets and side streets, some of them quite narrow. He had walked only a short distance from the strange, scattered-about nakedness of the perimeter, of the snow walls and randomly scattered structures out there. He looked over his shoulder. The long red horizon line was now abbreviated, a short red bar at the far end of the street, bracketed by the black cracked shapes of buildings that stood shoulder to shoulder on either side of him now.

Fires glowed within many of these ruins nearby, the fires of men trying to stay warm.

The idea of walking all the way back to the field hospital in the GPU—the most obvious place to look—depressed him, so he looked in a few other places first.

He stopped at an oil drum with a fire going in it at the entrance to one crowded ruin, with long thin planks leaning up from the top of the drum like the framework of a teepee. Flames licked up. A few men standing watch there acknowledged him by staring back at him through the flames. It was too cold to speak except when necessary, or when boredom or physical distress compelled a man to mumble something. Kordts stamped his feet, feeling something like a brick attached to either of his ankles, a dull worrisome bricklike pain resonating up his shinbones.

It was too cold to think. The question, Have you seen Baer or Freitag? formulated in his head. The garrison was small enough that one of these men might easily have seen Freitag or Baer during the day; but they wouldn't know them by name. He couldn't think how to express what he wanted.

"A smoke?" he said finally.

The three other men standing there trembled with sardonic depression.

"Maybe we could offer you some schnapps," one of them said. They laughed faintly, a scarcely audible rumble that seemed to issue from their navels, hhnh-hhnh.

It was difficult for Kordts to talk normally anyway, from the deep hideous gash in his cheek. The other three glanced once or twice at this dramatic disfigurement, a bit more remarkable than the normal run of things.

"Hm," said Kordts, clenching his teeth to keep them from rattling. He took hold of one of the planks sticking up from the drum, feeling the warmth in the wood, the warmth also from flame and spark shooting up around his pathetic gloves. Healed by hypnosis . . . this idea came from nowhere, as if from a voice whispering against the inside of his ear, as he stared into the hypnotic white structure of the fire.

The flames leaped up in front of the faces of the other men, then subsided; each time they subsided it seemed their eyes were closer to his own. Smoke, sparks, and then the clouds of their own breathing issuing up feebly.

"A pale skinny fellow, almost an albino sort of *Kerl*," he said finally. "Short, curly red hair?"

He was describing Freitag, who—as was obvious—was easier to describe than most men. Though characteristic features tended to diminish, beneath the haphazard swaddling of all their garments, ransacked from anywhere, beneath the red patina of snow-glare and sun-glare and frost-burn, beneath the grey patina of smoke and grime and fatigue that tended to make brothers of them all. Still he felt a small tremor of accomplishment in describing Freitag pretty unmistakably. My God, this cold, he thought.

"*Ja, ja,* I think I did see him," one of them said. "What is his name?"

"Freitag," said Kordts.

"*Ja,* was," said the man. "I've seen him about. Has he gone missing?"

"He was bringing back a wounded man today. A tank came up on them."

"We saw the tank," another said. "It drove right by here, toward the GPU."

"There were two tanks," the first man said.

"*Ja, ja,*" the other nodded. As if they were inhabitants of a village mulling over some unusual incident.

"Yes, yes, I saw him today. He came by here too, a little later it might have been."

"All right," said Kordts, vaguely surprised that he was getting somewhere. Yet he was still too cold to pursue his inquiry in any logical fashion. Tears started to form in his eyes, partly from the smoke. He said, "Which way was he going?"

"Ah, for the love of God," one said. "Here, I'll take you inside. In fact he might have stepped inside here."

"Swine," another man said to this one, who laughed a little more loudly, waving Kordts toward the entrance of the ruin, leaving the other two at their assigned post.

There was a kind of lurid cheer to the inside of this ruin, fires going in several more drums planted on the floor and inside the cracked tiles of a shattered clay oven. About thirty men were crowded in here, in various states of undress, body-heat and drafts of flame-heat circulating and then seeping out through the cracks in the walls. There were holes in the ceiling through which could be seen further holes in the roof, sparks rising up past the stars overhead.

An officer told Kordts's escort to return to his post.

"Your relief will be out in a few minutes. Tell the other two."

"*Ja,* all right. Thank you, Herr Hauptman."

"Anyone of you named Freitag?" the officer said to the room at large. Most of them gave the captain their attention but none answered. "These are all my men anyway," the captain said. "A few other people took cover here during the day, but they might have gone back to their own groups by now."

He walked over to an NCO sitting cross-legged beside the shattered oven, a hundred cracks seamed with fire, warmth.

"Any strangers still in here?"

The NCO replied that he did not believe so; then with some effort he stood up in a heavy and deliberate articulation and bellowed the question to the thirty or so others crowded about or in nooks and corners.

Whereas none had responded directly to the captain, perhaps half a dozen quickly answered the NCO.

The captain turned to Kordts.

"You're shorthanded, I expect."

"*Ja,*" said Kordts. "He'll probably show up. Probably he'll be there already when I get back."

"We only came in two days ago," said the captain.

This seemed a kind of preamble.

"*Jawohl,* Herr Hauptman," said Kordts quietly. He was not eager to go back out into the black cold and waited to see if the man had more to say to him. Thick warmth and thin terrible cold eddied back and forth in this drafty house; many of those in here had at least partially unwrapped the swaddling of bedsheets, greatcoats, stolen civilian garments and scraps of material, even scraps of newspaper, which they all used to insulate their persons, so that Kordts had a better look at the standard uniforms they wore underneath. They were from the police unit that had been flown in on the last JUs to land at the airstrip on the outskirts, that operation being terminated since then; the Russians now held the landing zone.

Rumor had spread quickly through the garrison, perhaps because some of these newly arrived policemen had spoken openly enough about certain hair-raising operations they had conducted before being so abruptly flown in to reinforce the Cholm defenders.

Some of them—a minority probably—may well have been ashamed or disturbed, though not ashamed enough to keep from relating with dully awed matter-of-factness what they had been up to. Others were simply matter-of-fact and that was that; still others—there were always a fair share of fanatics among them—might have recounted their experiences with a certain gusto, though somehow this would come out matter-of-factly as well.

Kordts knew only the rumors though, not having seen any of these policemen before now. He did not place much credence in rumors. They were useful, almost like food in a way, something for people to gnaw over and over during the frozen hours; or perhaps more like tobacco than food, really. During an idle hour he, Freitag, and Moll, before Moll had begun to suffer so terribly on the march back from Lake Seliger, had calculated that it was impossible to go for more than three or four minutes without thinking about a smoke— except during a long firefight, which changed everything.

On the other hand, Kordts believed, there were certain kinds of rumors that could only arise because they were true, or had a grain of truth in them. So he tended to believe the stories that had so quickly gone around, after the arrival of the policemen.

The captain went on, "So you've had it pretty rough here. I understand that. But I don't expect you would envy us either. We received orders that we were to be flown in to Cholm and less than twenty-four hours later we found ourselves here. This is the first time any of us have faced the Red Army. We'll do all right though. In fact we've done pretty well already, since we got here."

"The Russians are easy to kill," said Kordts. "But there are quite a lot of them, you know."

The captain drew his head back sharply upon hearing this remark. Kordts had only uttered the kind of obvious thing one brings up in idle conversation. For he thought the captain had been speaking to him that way; officers would do that from time to time, without even condescension often enough. Kordts blinked, not certain if the captain's face had paled suddenly; he really hadn't been paying close attention. Nor did he scrutinize all the other men gathered in this ruin too closely. He did find himself looking at them, it was true, once he recognized their uniforms, looking to see if he could detect anything different about their expressions, their manner of carrying themselves, their eyes, their bones; yet doing this somewhat offhandedly. Perceiving subtle differences, like warps or bends in the very constancy of reality, yet at the same time not certain if he was perhaps just imagining these things.

"Ah," he muttered to himself, yet blinking with dull surprise to hear himself speak.

The rumors had been quite horrible; though how horrible could anything be, really, anymore? But because they were horrible they were also interesting. And because the rumors were interesting they were also, in the deep inversion of force laid upon all their lives during these months, profoundly uninteresting. It would take a lengthy course through a twisted maze of reasoning to arrive at such a conclusion as this—and Kordts for one was not inclined to follow such paths around inside his head—but somehow this conclusion would present itself entirely alone like a newborn babe, and needed no reasoning to be found. Entirely uninteresting, entirely uninteresting. . . .

"All right, I suppose I should be going," he said. "If I don't find him soon, I'll just have to head back."

"This is a very small place," said the captain.

"*Ja,* Herr Hauptman. Next time maybe they'll send us people overland, instead of by air. Then maybe we can all get out of here."

"How long have you been here?"

"I've lost track of time. I think it's been over a month now."

"You were here when it started?"

"*Ja.*"

"All right. Get on with your business then."

"*Jawohl*, Herr Hauptman."

Kordts saluted, lost in a kind of abstractedness in which he did not feel any of his normal antagonism.

The policemen—thirty of them in this room that were part of a larger unit of about one hundred that had stepped down from the last JU-52s to fly into Cholm—also understood that the logic of their destinies was somehow uninteresting. They understood there was a certain justice, or doom rather, in being flown in at the last moment to this doomed place, this frozen little ass-crack in Russia isolated behind Russian

lines. Up until a week previously they had been engaged for
months in an enormous and arduous operation, assisting the
SS groups in the German-held hinterland, in fact performing
exactly the same tasks as the mobile SS groups. The SS had
not had enough manpower to take care of the operation by
themselves. Kordts had said the Russians were easy to kill,
which was certainly true; but the policemen already knew
this, even though they had not served at the front before, had
never faced a Red Army man in combat before, even though
their own experience was limited to a very specific group of
Russians. The blood they had spilled, for months on end, was
too much for them to understand. Some felt guilty, but most
did not. Some who had felt guilty for a little while felt guilty
no longer, had left all that behind them months ago already.
They understood that a tidal wave of blood had somehow,
according to some unfathomable but perfectly logical doom,
unexpectedly swept them up and cast them ashore at the very
end upon this frozen, besieged, tiny island. But because it
made so much sense, and was obvious to every last one of
them, it really was not interesting at all. The ordinary chaos
of all things—and not just of the last several months, but of
all things—was simply too great a distraction. Though only
policemen, they had earlier been put through a good deal of
regular military training, and for the moment were intent
only on putting that training to good use here at Cholm, intent on not embarrassing themselves, shoulder to shoulder
with all the other ad hoc formations fighting here, for survival. Scherer welcomed any kind of reinforcements whatsoever and when it was all over he would consider that the
police battalion had acquitted itself well, as had the men of
his own security division, and the men from the broken and
retreating infantry units that had found themselves under his
command, and the small group of naval personnel that had
inexplicably been stationed at Cholm, and the two platoons
of Latvian soldiers, and the jaegers and handful of para-
troopers and the rear-echelon misfits and supply units.

Kordts found himself outside again, without even having
braced himself to go back out into the black cold. He had
simply walked out through the blanket draped over the ruined door frame.

"You again," said the man who had led him inside a few minutes before. The three of them around the fire-drum in the street were clearly anxious to be relieved.

"Cold, isn't it?" said Kordts, mustering a certain cheerful contempt, if only because they were newcomers. But that was all he could manage; within seconds he was too cold himself. He had not braced himself and his body heat was sucked out instantly into space. It stunned him but it was too familiar. He hunched up his muscles the same as he would do when a barrage was coming down. A stab of pain in his slashed cheek blinded him momentarily. He recovered, and stood next to the glowing drum almost directly in the flames. The other three stood almost as close.

Again he felt the temptation to study them, but he could not even concentrate. He stood nearly in the fire, having to remind himself of what he was supposed to be doing. He should just get back, he thought, empty-handed or not. Still, he felt a dull urge to be able to tell Ohlsson something definite.

"You see that church?" he said to the other three, their eyes hidden then revealed by the flames.

Two looked around. The third simply looked at Kordts, said, "What about it?"

"Come with me. Your captain will need to know about it, if he doesn't already."

"We'll be relieved in a minute."

"It's right there," said Kordts. "Bring a torch. We like to keep things nice and tidy."

This odd comment elicited dull stares, unchanged stares.

Kordts pulled a thin flaming piece from the drum. He withdrew another and handed it to the man who had spoken. Removed from the fire, the flames shrank at the ends of the makeshift torches, tipped now with embers, only a few tiny white flames licking up.

"Hold it down," said Kordts.

He lowered his piece so the flames could crawl up the wood again, feed. The other man did likewise.

"Come. It will just be a minute. I'll need your light."

Diversion, curiosity, might bring another small force to bear upon the clear and terrible cold. A kind of knavery was working, very slowly, through Kordts's mind.

"All right, I don't give a damn. Stay where you are then."

He walked off, thinking perhaps they would just ignore him. The cold made a precise mask, death mask, of his face, the hideous gash in particular replicated exactly. When the nerves were not too sore or excited he could just feel it there, a precise tracing, somewhat painful, somewhat numb, very exact. He looked back and saw the one with the other brand following him.

He recognized it silhouetted against the starlight. Large holes gaped in the onion-dome, so it looked somewhat like a torn paper lantern. Next to the church was a collapsed shack or shed, outbuilding maybe, with an alley threading back between the collapsed beams and the ruin where the policemen were housed.

The medieval stone of the church was pockmarked from flying metal. The wooden door hung massively askew on twisted hinges. He thrust his flame through the doorway, staring into the interior for a moment until the other man came up; then they went in.

"This is storage until spring," said Kordts. "We don't bury anyone. You'll bring your fellows here."

"*Ja*. Spring," said the other one. They were too cold to consider the implications. It was just a way of saying something. Kordts would think they must all be killed, or marched off to Siberia, or rescued if one dared hope for it, long before spring ever came. The policeman would be too new to all this to think that far ahead. He merely stared at the dead piled on the floor of the church.

They were partially clothed, unwrapped as it were, as the policemen had been in the drafty warmth and cold of their house next door. To leave the dead in whatever warm clothing they had possessed would be an unbearable waste to those still surviving in the cold. Yet none were completely stripped. Some feeling of terminal sacrilege might account for that. Mufflers, scarves, blankets, bedsheets, lengths of cloth, civilian parkas, Russian felt boots or fur hats, had been taken from the dead. They still wore their uniforms, and most still wore their standard issue greatcoats like simple shrouds, as those still living had their own greatcoats anyway; and anyway, as winter garments those were not much valued. Neither were the standard issue jackboots, which most of the dead still wore.

"It's only the Russians we leave lying in the streets," said Kordts.

The other man had no comment.

Kordts walked along next to the pile, which was about thigh-high and spread more or less evenly across the church floor. They were all the same, most of them quite whole, others mutilated or fire-blackened, but all of them the same; except for one group stacked in a peculiar tangle over by the wall.

"They were wounded," said Kordts, gesturing at this one glistening lump with his flame. "There was another hospital for a while but the Russians took it. We drove them off again, but they dumped ice water over everyone in there before they left."

The other nodded in the torchlight. "I've heard of that," he said.

The separate group of ice-dead were welded to each other. Their faces and limbs were contorted in the bending shapes one sees in nightmares, nightmares in which the shape of what is is bent, elongated, stretched out, and then snapped. The welded, sickeningly angular-looking heap bore as a whole its own larger contorted shape.

Kordts offered this in the illumination of his brand as if it were some noteworthy display left for ages in a church, museum.

"You are having fun with me," the policeman said.

His tone did not indicate much offense, if any. Perhaps he wasn't sure if Kordts might have some useful reason for showing him this. Or perhaps he thought it was a worthwhile curiosity. The morgue-cold of the place was different somehow from the void-cold outside. Or it seemed different.

"No," said Kordts. "I said we'd just be a minute. He's probably not here."

He walked back beside the larger pile of dead, who lay but were not welded. He removed the small flashlight from within the bulk of everything that he wore, shining it on the faces of the most recent dead, those lying on top or at the edge of the pile, within the larger guttering illumination thrown by the two torches.

"Ah, the albino," said the other. "You are a *Kerl* then. They're all that way here."

"*Ja,*" said Kordts.

In the sharper beam he came across Haik, Birsa, a few others whose names he could not remember. Some kind of knavery was still working through him, but so slowly he hardly knew it any longer.

The policeman remembered piles upon piles of the dead, not soldiers. Nor piled in a frozen church either, but in ditches and pits, in obscure stretches of countryside, back there, back then, where he had been; and all of them coated in fresh, sticky blood, and himself coated in the same blood, from firing into the backs of skulls at such close range. All of it, all of that, had been so absolute that to be reminded of it stirred him very little. He thought he was offended and was about to speak sharply to Kordts, but then realized he was not.

He looked up at the huge tears ripped in the paper lantern, onion-dome, overhead, the cold stars hanging brilliantly there as medieval painters would have wanted them to hang, beautiful and still, from the high vaulted ceiling of any church in any land. The strange flat-painted Russian saints were up there too, their bodies fractured and shattered like the dome itself. But they were covered with centuries of smoke and other grime, and the two torches underneath did little to dispel the night-blackness and make them visible, some thirty or forty feet overhead. A few glimpses of abstract painted designs, icons, if that's what they were, or maybe that was something different. His breath rose up, living clouds that were as constant a feature of this place— Cholm or Russia—as anything else they knew here. His feet felt merged with the stone of the floor, as cold as that. He looked toward the door, could not see where it was, held the flame out a little to see better.

Kordts, standing close beside him, said, "How was it then, with those Jews?"

The other man considered, still looking toward the door. His breath rose up.

"It was quite something," he said.

Kordts laughed a little, then gulped back a wild guffaw before it could shake loose from his gut. He should have just let it out. His body felt twisted into terrible exposed angles that would be chipped at by the cold, chipped right off him. He had had a recurring fancy for months now, ever since this thing had begun (by which he meant not so much the siege or even any of this war in the East, but just the winter, the winter), a fancy of blacking out for weeks on end, months even, and then just waking up somewhere else, he dared not even imagine where. He saw his home, Erika; but it was not even that.

"All right, he isn't here," said Kordts. "But now you'll know where our little closet is, eh?"

"Of course," said the other. "I saw a few men being carried in here today. Yesterday too. We're set up just next door, for God's sake."

"Why didn't you say so then?"

"What of it? I thought you wanted me to help look for your friend."

Kordts shut his eyes. Maybe the other man was dense, or maybe it was the cold. People would often speak in a terse, overly abbreviated fashion, so their words came out not making any sense.

He wondered if he had indeed blacked out somehow, and the place where he was awakening was here, this place. This fancy vanished from his mind as quickly as it had appeared, as had ten thousand other idle thoughts and notions, at their own times. He thought of doing himself in somehow, to escape the cold, a notion that had often passed through his mind and then left it with all the rest.

"That's an ugly wound," the other man said. "You should have it seen to."

"I just came from the damned field hospital today," muttered Kordts.

He stared up at the stars through the shattered dome overhead. They walked out together, into the night-ruin of Cholm. The Russians by this time had already infiltrated well into the town, on the other side of the perimeter from the Paupers' Field sector. A few patrols at Paupers' Field had al-

ready been fired on by German outposts, the enemy then
beating a hasty and rather obvious retreat. This kind of activity was not so unusual. It had served to disguise or cover the
simultaneous movement of many other patrols through the
known gaps in the weakly manned line on the other side of
town. The first of these patrols was already in the alley between the church and police-ruin, while others were working
up to the main streets through other alleys. Still other small
groups that had breached the perimeter remained near the
outskirts, setting up firing positions just behind known German strongpoints.

It was a daring and simple operation, accomplished with
relative ease. Scherer had often lain awake at night in his
room in the GPU and seen it happening in just this way.

Kordts and the policeman walked past the collapsed beams
of the outbuilding—the Russians were lurking in there too, at
this moment—and then passed in front of the alley, where
eyes watched them and weapons were trained on them. Kordts
was looking with dim resignation at the end of the street up
ahead, at the open space where the red line of sunset had been
abbreviated, bracketed, by the last black buildings of the town
center. Now the star-void hung down in that space, shouldered
by the black buildings. His facial nerves trembled with excitement again, or dread, and he felt something like a knife working deep into his cheek. The entire right half of his face pulled
down in pain and his eye on that side went momentarily blind.
He simply had to go inside again before walking back, try and
warm himself with the rest of these swine for a few minutes.

The pain caused him to alter his course for a few steps; he
almost wandered into the alley, but some pile of junk partially blocking the entrance brought him up short. He wasn't
really looking at anything, scarcely capable of it, but the
Russians hidden only a few feet away weren't so sure of this,
and the man was waving his damned torch around in an erratic fashion. A few faces, eyes, even muzzle glints, were actually revealed in the guttering circle of light, but Kordts
though looking right at them saw them not at all. Meanwhile
there was light through cracks and holes and windows, and
sounds of people talking, from the ruin on the other side of
the alley.

They were well-equipped with knives and would have killed him that way, a single man, him plus the other fool standing a few feet behind him. When they began firing their weapons, betraying their presence in the middle of the town, they wanted to take out many more than just one or two men. They were canny though, even when the torchlight fluttered near them, fingering their knives but not yet striking, remaining as still and utterly bereft of sentience as the junk they were hiding behind, as still as the wall of the ruin on one side and the collapsed beams on the other side of the alley, as still as all the pulverized stillness of the town, sucked up very close to the stars. Just to get this far they had, after all, passed equally as close to other sentries or other Germans wandering about randomly in the cold. They had done this tonight and also on earlier nights, learning the best infiltration routes, wandering through Cholm to murder people and harass the garrison and make a nuisance of themselves; tonight though, their wanderings formed part of a larger plan with larger intentions.

Kordts felt better suddenly, as if a switch had been thrown on that side of his face. God in heaven, he thought, tears bulging around his eyes. The pain in his cheek was shut off, leaving only the normal force of the cold. He would just head back then. It would probably flare up again but he didn't care. His fingers and toes dealt him much more prolonged agony than his face did; it was just that the face would paralyze him sometimes. To the devil with it.

He looked ahead and saw the other two still standing around their damned oil drum fire by the entrance to the place. The third man still stood beside him in front of the alley, perhaps having stared curiously at his momentary dance of agony.

"All right, Jew boy," said Kordts. "Enjoy your stay."

"To the devil with you," said the policeman. "I never killed a single one. Not that it's any of your business."

"*Ja,* don't get upset," said Kordts. "Every man here relies on every other man here. There are people in my own outfit I can't abide the sight of anymore. But that's the way it is."

"*Ja, gut.* We hope so too. To the devil with you anyway."

"*Ja,* whatever it is then," said Kordts. If he carried the

torch back across the open spaces on the outskirts he would be killed before reaching his own people. So he thrust it back into the oil drum where he'd gotten it.

The other two there were also looking at him with certain fixed looks, obscured then revealed by the flames. The one who had accompanied him said, "You seem a strange sort of fellow. Not that you know anything about anything. Come see us, maybe, if you wish. This is a small place."

"Sure," said Kordts. The ebbing of the pain in his face had left an odd kind of vacuum in his head and almost throughout his body. He felt that a small gust of wind would lift him from the ground, float him easily beneath the stars. Better than walking, he thought.

"Do you see that, Emil?" said one of the other two by the oil drum. "Over there, where you were just standing."

"Was."

There were in fact faint wisps of steam rising, breathing, back in the alley, invisible in the dark but just visible in a few fractured bands of light cast through the wall of the ruin. Maybe it was only the breath of men gathered inside, issuing through the walls, or smoke from the fires going inside. At first they thought that, the three policemen, and it was too cold to think more than one thing at a time. It didn't look right though.

Kordts could not even make it out at all but he had been here longer and felt his scalp prickle.

Gunfire erupted on the outskirts now, on the weakly manned side that Scherer had toured earlier in the day, before it had begun again at Paupers' on the side where Kordts and the majority of the defenders had been set up. White flashes rippled dazzlingly through the utterness of night, stuttering and abrupt like the lurid streaks that accompany the onset of a migraine. This would have been about a half mile away from where they stood, by the burning oil drum outside the ruin and the alley and the church. Other Russians who had infiltrated yet remained behind, closer to the outskirts, were now firing into the backs of the outposts there. This was the signal for the main force of about a regiment, with six T-34s in support, to launch an all-out assault.

Meanwhile the group lurking in the alley scarcely twenty feet away continued to wait for these last few seconds longer.

Right next to them, within the walls of the ruin, an adjutant was handing the field telephone receiver to the captain in command of these thirty-odd policemen. Colonel Mabrius was on the line from the GPU. The policemen had only been here a few days but had already been thoroughly instructed as to what was expected of them; expected of them and of every other small unit standing by in reserve, that was not already out on the perimeter. The conversation with Mabrius was very brief. The men inside were already rewrapping their filthy garments about themselves and gathering their weapons. Even above the roar of gunfire the alarm bell could be heard tolling through the entire town, tolling too late on this occasion but it tolled anyway, the sound penetrating every cellar and collapsed heap and even out into the black country all around.

The one named Emil and the other two were distracted by the outbreak of the firefight in the distance. But all that was still in the distance and some policeman's instinct—or experienced infantryman's if he had been such—prompted him, Kordts's companion over these last few minutes, to dart over to the alley where . . . whatever it was they'd just seen . . . was. It was probably nothing and it would only take an instant. In one half of his mind he was already preparing himself to follow the captain and the rest of his comrades to the scene of the firefight. Even as he did this the captain and the other occupants of the ruin were spilling out into the street. At other points along the street the tenants of other ruins were emerging. This was what the Russians hidden in the alley, and in several other alleys nearby, had been waiting for.

There was no longer any need to resort to knives, and the one named Emil was shot in the chest by an officer wielding a Nagan pistol, standing up calmly to do this behind the scattering of junk at the entrance to the alley. The men with him there opened fire with submachine guns at the policemen now gathered in the street and running down the street past the alley. So much gunfire concentrated in such a small space was like an explosion and the work done was similar to that

wrought by a shell blast. The Russians also tossed grenades
into the house, ruin, as they figured there might still be a few
German bastards left alive inside there. The captain standing
in the entranceway, urging the last laggards in there to get
going, was hurled out into the street by these blasts, landing
a few feet from Kordts.

Kordts ignored the man. In the split-second before Emil
had been shot he had seen them, all of them, raising their
weapons there in the alley, because he too had smelled a rat
and perhaps because he was the only one on the scene not
looking around for orders from his unit commander. The
Russians had already opened fire and obliterated many of
those still clustered tightly in the street, blown into tightly
clustered heaps or a few staggering by themselves, screaming, collapsing. The pain of being ripped by brute material,
metal, in such terrible cold would drive men insane, those
that were still alive; and after the initial shock wore off those
still alive flopped about or even stood up again howling in-
sanely, not screaming but howling or even barking madly
like dogs. Kordts had thrown himself flat against the iron-
snow of the street the instant he saw what it was, what all of
it was, the instant before they opened fire. He would have
just stayed there, played dead, anything, but he saw they
were coming out of the alley now and firing bursts, coups de
grace, into anyone, dead, living. He unhitched one of the
grenades he kept on his person and slid behind the fallen captain, whose breathing still issued up and who stared wide-
eyed up into space, and hurled it at the pile of junk in front of
the alley. A few were already out in the street but most were
just emerging from the alley, many still firing their goat's legs
from there. He knew he could not look from that distance and
buried his forehead in the captain's armpit. The succinct blast
shaved low through the darkness; he felt it like a dull blade
pressing on his head and shoulders, then echoing with a clatter between the dark buildings faced along the street. The
captain groaned. Kordts looked. He did not see anything at
first; or he saw the whole scene but saw no movement.

For a long, long time he had accepted that he was a bit slower
on the uptake than many of his comrades, as far as his

playing-soldier skills were concerned, though playing at one's very survival, it was true. He had stoically accepted this and refused to be embarrassed by it, doing the best he could though refusing to really even acknowledge his frequent clumsiness, because he knew it was true regardless and anyone else who knew it was true could think what they liked about it. He never apologized, in other words, preferring occasionally bitter arguments to apologizing. As far as he knew he had never been directly responsible for getting one of his comrades killed; though in the back of his mind he assumed this would happen sooner or later, unless he was killed first. He tended not to lay blame on others—he could despise certain people but not blame them—and he refused to accept blame on himself even when he deserved it. Perhaps it was a kind of survival mechanism; but if he had articulated as much to himself a few times—and he had—it still did not interest him much, dissolving into inarticulate shape within a kind of stubbornness he had. He had never asked for any of this. Though clumsy he was also somewhat cunning, understanding the fundamental rule of maintaining a low profile among the ranks of officers, NCOs, and his fellow frontswine; and at least in this regard he was by no means alone. He was used to any number of people looking dubiously at him, though he also understood that at least a few of his fellows held him in some regard. He wasn't sure why that was, but he accepted it as a fact of nature just as he accepted his own clumsiness, thus shielding himself somewhat, in fact pretty well, from whatever feelings of uselessness he might have. He had a certain curious wit and a certain plastic stubbornness that was deeper than he knew or that anyone else knew. He figured that if he was a slow learner he would perhaps still learn eventually; or if he was killed before then, then that was that. He had survived seven months in Russia and a month in Cholm; he wasn't sure how long it had been anymore. He never complained much; he was one of those people who, even on the few occasions when he did complain furiously, was never labeled as a complainer.

He had known these things about himself, or some of them anyway, for a long time, and thus did not need to know them for even a fraction of a second, lying behind the dead or near-dead captain in the iron-snow of the street, the grenade concussion echoing away like some idiot reeling against different objects. He was merely surprised that he seemed to have accomplished something significant. In the sudden silence he was aware of that much. *Ja, gut, gut*, what of it then. . . . But he could not help a little crooked smile, curling back even into the gash. Tears came to his eyes again, and he wiped them with his sleeve.

In fact there had been no silence at all; it was only an instant of deafness and concussed abstraction. Sound returned, the firefight in the distance, also horrible piteous sounds from quite nearby, though on the whole it was quieter now, and various other survivors were staggering around or leaning against walls wondering what to do next.

The surviving Russians in the alley—there had not been that many to begin with—had fled. Their officer had been killed and whoever was still alive could take some satisfaction in having cut up one of the infernal Fritz alarm-units very badly, just as they had been instructed to do hours earlier in the final command sessions in their own positions beyond the perimeter. They would roam the city through the night, perhaps leaving the city entirely or else joining up with the main assault, which had broken completely through the perimeter by now. The tanks were with them, clanking, rattling in the distance down the street, road-wheels creaking.

Kordts heard this. So did the other German survivors. There were men from other alarm units and sundry other personnel in the street now, near and far, mixing with the shattered police unit. A few Russians were still wandering in the street in front of the alley. The police survivors, when they began to recover their senses enough to distinguish this handful of Russians from their own comrades, shot them down one by one, with wounded men still crying out under the feet of everyone. A badly wounded Russian strode up, still emptying his weapon into clusters of men cut down by the first gunfire, until a policeman began shouting at him to stop. Why would he shout that? But he did, several times, before shooting the Russian in the belly.

Meanwhile the main assault had advanced well into town, and those around the church and the police-ruin could hear that it was coming closer. Other reserves, alarm units of ten or a dozen men responding automatically to Mabrius's calls, had also been hit hard by Russian ambushers, and many of these small groups of ambushers were still at work in the town center. So that there was the noise of the most violent firefight coming closer and closer, and the tanks beginning to be silhouetted in flashes down the street there; and then there was the intermittent noise of other gunfire coming from everywhere, from smaller parties roaming around or squirreled away God only knew where.

Get off the street, Kordts told himself. Lethargy possessed him. He was standing, though not aware of having gotten to his feet. He wanted to sink down again where he was. He did not feel the cold, and the iron-snow of the street seemed as appealing as a new white bed. Get off the street, he told himself. He looked down at the police captain at his feet, whose eyes were still open, conscious. The man's eyes were hidden then revealed by flames rising and falling; not flames; it was dizzy blackness rising and falling in Kordts's own head, and a few dull hazy sparks in his brain. It was nothing; he blinked it back, knocked on his temple with the flat of his palm, felt the icy air vented through his nostrils, down into his chest. He ran over to the entrance of the police-ruin.

The place was as cold as death, the fires in there blown-out by the grenade blasts. A few flames licked from scattered pieces of wood but it was mostly too dark to see much. In a strange giddy fit of usefulness, useful activity, he reached inside himself and unclipped his flashlight and began looking around. The place was a mess and even when the beam shone on the face or twisted hand of a dead man these things seemed only part of the overall mess, no different from the bits and pieces of everything else lying everywhere. The miscellaneous units that had been flown into Cholm, before the landing strip was lost, had generally been outfitted with more than their share of heavy infantry weapons, to make up for the dearth of every such thing in the damned town. The reputation of the new 42 gun especially had quickly become known to everyone. He found a box with belts of ammunition, the belts snaked out of the mangled lid all over the floor. He could not get them to fit all back in the box so he picked up the box with the remaining belts draped over his shoulders.

Then he panicked, an alien sensation; he didn't panic much. What am I going to do with all this, he thought.

He heard voices and saw shapes coming up to the entranceway.

"Don't shoot! Don't shoot!" he cried sharply, hoarsely, yet somewhat mechanically for all that.

A beam struck him in the face.

"What are you doing in here?"

"MG," said Kordts.

"Ah, good, good," said the voice. "I thought they'd have some. Did you find any?"

"Ammunition," said Kordts.

"Take it outside. There's one gun already set up in the street. They should have more though."

The voice made this last comment either to itself or to other shapes now entering the ruin, accompanied by a confused latticework of flashlight beams hastily probing around. Something burning up by the roof now burst into a larger flame, lighting up the men in there, throwing their shadows in large shapes against the walls.

"Kordts," said the voice, simply recognizing him, a familiar face.

"Herr Leutnant," said Kordts.

"Go ahead, go ahead."

Kordts hesitated by the entrance, looking at the scene in the street. It didn't look good. He looked over his shoulder at the eerie stage lighting cast down by the roof fire, in which living shapes, some of whom he recognized, were kicking around among the dead inside, picking up another ammunition box, one man dragging another machine gun out of the dead claws of a policeman in a corner.

"That will help," said the lieutenant.

"No," said another shape. "Barrel's bent."

Cursing, frustration, men kicking around more frenetically now, looking for spares, swatting and cursing at burning pieces that were starting to float down on them from the roof. The lieutenant looked up, and saw Kordts still standing there; Kordts left.

Wounded men still cried out in the street. Kordts passed a policeman gibbering, his face wet with tears as if bathed in a fever, pointing a pistol at the head of another man with an unspeakable smile burned into the center of his face, teeth glistening and the smile twisted up where the nose had been, living breath still exhaling from where the nose had been, eyes staring into the gun muzzle of his weeping comrade. He saw two other survivors mounting a machine gun on a dead body; probably whoever had carried it out there. Kordts heard a sharp crack just behind him; ignored it.

"That will never do," said Kordts, setting down the ammunition box.

"It will have to do," said one of them by the gun, a steely-faced man, having calmed himself through the initial waves of terror, regathering years of experience in exercising calm terse authority, on a street corner in the homeland, behind an interrogation desk in the homeland, behind a blood-bog murder-ditch of Jews somewhere in the East, or at last in combat somewhere in the East; it made not the slightest bit of difference. The police unit had been cut to pieces by the ambush but the survivors showed no sign of panic, scarcely even dismay. Kordts was struck by this. So, that's fine then, he thought.

The gun was mounted on the shoulder of the dead man because the tripod was nowhere to be found. Probably still back in the ruin. One of them fired and the recoil threw the gun onto the street. Kordts left them the ammunition and ran for cover again. The ruin was burning vigorously now, too much light there; Kordts hunkered down by the pile of junk in front of the alley. The two operating the machine gun retrieved the piece and one of them lifted the arm of the corpse and the gunner wedged the barrel into the armpit and then the other man, loader, laid his weight down on the dead arm. The gunner fired a short burst. The loader fetched up the box Kordts had left and dragged it around to where he could get at it better, then braced himself against the dead man's arm as before. The gunner fired a longer burst; Kordts looked down the street to see their target. He could see only shapes moving back and forth down there, could not make out whether they were German or Russian, knew the two at the

gun could not make them out either. For all their show of
nerve they were too absorbed in what they were doing to
know what they were doing.

Kordts didn't want to shout, didn't want to say anything.
He did shout though. They couldn't hear him. He ran back
out there, thumping the gunner on the back.

"Our own people are down there."

"*Ja,* all right," said the gunner, startled, yet still masked
with hard calm. He dropped his hand from the trigger, rolled
on his side.

Suddenly the lieutenant was there as well.

"Hold fire! Hold fire!"

"*Ja,*" said the gunner again. Kordts could not help but admire the only slightly embarrassed weariness of the gunner's tone.

"You'll wait for my signal," the lieutenant said. "If anything happens to me then just use better sense. You'll see that
very close range is the best range for fucking them up completely. Wait till you're sure of your target, then keep on
waiting till they're within a hundred meters. It will fuck them
up royally, by God; we've gotten quite used to it here. Is that
clear?"

"Yes, thank you, Herr Leutnant," said the gunner.

The lieutenant led another machine-gun crew over to the
pile of junk where Kordts had been, fence pickets and
chicken wire it mostly seemed to be, junked still more thoroughly by the grenade Kordts had thrown there. He watched
a man with a spare barrel screw it into the piece they'd
hauled out of the ruin and he saw the lieutenant glance back
at the flames throwing more and more illumination from the
ruin and wave the crew off a little way further, out of the
dancing spread of the light, setting up again in the dark
around the collapsed beams, outbuilding, next to the church.
The flames illuminated some movement by the junk pile and
Kordts felt sick to think maybe the Russians had come up
into the alley again. He looked at a few dead Russians
sprawled amidst the blasted junk; he hadn't even noticed
them when he'd been crouched there a moment ago. None
moved. They were dead; he was sure of it. Now he saw the
movement was from a man moving a few feet away, trying to

pull himself away from the flames; the one named Emil, Kordts had forgotten him too, who'd taken it in the chest right at the start.

"Stay with us."

"What?" said Kordts.

It was the gunner, the policeman in the middle of the street. "Stay with us. We might need a spare hand to hold this thing steady."

"Find another one of your people," said Kordts. "I've got to stay with my own bunch."

The gunner gave him a look, raised himself to one knee, seeming somewhat more focused after the lieutenant had talked to him. There were indeed a few of his people still alive nearby, singly or in twos and threes, in the lee of buildings or out in the street. The gunner called out to someone named Paule. That man came over and so did another man. Kordts went over to the lieutenant and the other gun crew over there, none of whom were really from his own bunch, group, back at the perimeter; but at least he knew who they were. Kordts and the lieutenant and those men over there had all marched back from Lake Seliger a month ago now, to this place, Cholm.

He had lost his opportunity to just keep on going, to walk back to his group out at the perimeter, lost his chance to do that hours ago. In truth it had been hardly more than ten minutes ago; but he thought hours ago even though he knew better. It had been inertia, fatigue, the cold, his goddamned face; just wanting to step back into the ruin for a moment, when there had still been cheerful fires going in there, those men lounging in there.

He knew the standard drill with all the alarm units, knew that any spare man who happened to be in the area, himself, could be snapped up in an emergency by any officer leading such a unit. A fate that no one desired, to be snapped up among a group of strangers on what could easily turn into a suicide mission, but a fate they were all trained to accept unthinkingly. He had felt a deep, dull, queasy, yet somehow dully fascinated apprehension the instant the firefight had started off in the distance, in fact during just that one prolonged instant before he'd been shocked to see the Russian infiltrators right there in the alley; dimly revulsed that he might be snapped up by the police captain and led off to his death in the company of these Jew killers. No, a man would have to shy away from something like that, if he could. Perhaps deeper down he really wouldn't give a damn, but he'd had no chance to think that deeply down into himself before all hell had broken loose. Nor had he had a chance to think even more deeply still, to think, no, no, my God no.

The police captain was dead anyway, or dying. Still he could not help but feel he might get swept up among them. So he walked, not running or trotting but walking with black calm, over to the lieutenant whom he knew—Brandeis, his name was.

"Where's the rest of your people, Kordts?" asked Brandeis, under the collapsed beams by the church.

"At Paupers'. We're with Lieutenant Ohlsson."

"You're here by yourself?"

"Sad to say. Ohlsson sent me to look for a missing man."

Brandeis was irked but only for a moment, having hoped that the rest of Kordts's group would be nearby.

"All right. You stay with me now."

"*Ja,*" said Kordts.

"Who are these other men?"

Kordts smiled a little, pressed his lips together. He said, "They're part of the police bunch that came in a few days ago."

"Ah. Really?" The lieutenant seemed to shrug, though his body was quite still. A man could also set his face in a shrug, though Kordts could see nothing of Brandeis's face other than a black outline.

"All right. They seem to have no one in command. So they're with us too."

He declared this quietly to Kordts, to himself, to the machine-gun crew and the few others who had shown up with him. Activity was picking up down the street now, and coming closer. Noise, noise, noise. They could see the first tank down there too, actually the first of several; they'd been able to make them out for a little while now. Brandeis now walked back out into the street, to organize the rest of these men under his command, about ten of them who were left among the dead and mortally wounded.

Scherer said, "Well, we've been waiting for this, haven't we? All right, let's take care of it."

He was speaking to the several operators in the signals room, among the snake-nest of field telephone wires that issued from the building to everywhere. He thought it quite likely that the Russians would make it right up to the GPU before the night was over. Everything depended on the men in here, as much as on the fighting men outside, and he didn't want them panicking if grenades started thumping against the boarded-up windows. He didn't think they would; they hadn't on other nights before this. But already it was clear that more than just the normal wandering parties of murderers had broken into the town tonight.

The weakly manned sector, called the Policeman's Ravine—a nickname of obscure origin that had nothing to do with the police unit that had recently flown in—had already been overrun. Scherer knew nothing of the infiltrators that had opened fire into the backs of the outposts there. The violence of the main assault with the tanks would probably have overrun those outposts regardless. They should have heard the tanks assembling out there; he did not understand why no advance word of this had come over the telephone.

He did not know that the infiltrators at the outskirts had opened fire, taking the outpost line from the rear, before the tanks had even started their engines. The phone lines to the Policeman's Ravine had also been cut at that point. The snow was very deep in the area of the Policeman's Ravine, as deep as the rising waters of a river, and even tanks would have had some difficulty struggling through it, so that the outposts should have had plenty of warning of their approach. In fact in the bell-clarity of the night anyone in the town should have heard them coming. But the tanks had waited silently in their assembly positions in the ice-wastes, the crews nearly petrified within the still deeper cold of their metal hulks, until the infiltrators initiated the firefight. They then started their engines and moved off at full speed toward the German perimeter, a swift advance that normally would have been impossible through the groundless drifts around the ravine. The Russians, however, had labored with great cunning to dig a snow road through the worst of the drifts, more a ship channel or canal than a road. They had done this over the preceding several nights. Tonight the tanks had advanced in column at full speed toward the ravine sector, the tops of their turrets barely visible above the steep sides of the canal-road. The shape of each tank commander standing behind his ungainly raised hatch lid was also just barely visible, himself surging forward above the canal-road as if without visible means of propulsion, his foot resting on the shoulder of the driver below, praying they did not skid or veer in the darkness and block the entire passageway.

They surged through the Russian rear areas and forward areas and through no-man's-land in no time at all. Of necessity the road had had to come to an end just short of the Policeman's Ravine sector. The Soviet intelligence officer who had come up with this inspired idea had nonetheless fretted for several days and nights that it would be yet another exercise in futility, with his own neck laid out on the block, some kind of block—he feared not being shot but some other form of inevitable reprisal—fretting that German patrols or aerial reconnaissance would uncover the whole enterprise, especially the critical terminus near the ravine.

But this had not happened.

The tanks roared up to the end of the snow-channel, where log fascines had been laid to help them negotiate the more difficult drifts in front of the German perimeter. They trundled up, slowing only a little bit here, and blasted through the perimeter. These outposts were weakly manned and already under fire from the rear, so that the tank crews in the dark could scarcely distinguish the German line from their own, except for a few peculiar features of the landscape wellnoted for days.

They now restrained their normal manic impulses to just keep on going right into the center of town. They faced a sentence of death, this time, if they pulled too quickly away from their supporting infantry. Their supporting infantry, a regiment just newly transferred to Cholm, had lain camouflaged in a bone-chilling wait on either side of the terminus of the road. They moved forward like ghosts, clad in white, always like ghosts in daytime or nighttime. They overran the outposts without leaving their usual heaps of machine-gunned bodies in front of the German firing positions. Only a few were killed by German fire, and the infiltrators ceased fire when they saw the attack had broken through, killing only a few of their own men. The assault regiment had rushed in—or labored in, in the deep snow, but rushing it seemed to them, faced with such scant opposition—in dead silence. Only when they came to the first of the outlying streets behind the Policeman's Ravine did they begin to let out their familiar massed cries.

"Oooouuuuuuurayyyy!!!"

The tanks advanced with them, rumbling.

Scherer knew nothing of the mechanics of all this. It made no difference. That part of the Russian operation was already concluded, with great success.

He knew that other parties of infiltrators were already at work seemingly everywhere in the town center. Everyone knew this; the firing of those ambushers was much closer at hand, just out the front door in fact. Gunfire raked the GPU even as Scherer spoke to the telephone operators. Impulsively he had rushed to the entrance, pushed to one side there by his shadow Gadermann, who then began firing with a goat's leg out into the street. Gadermann was shot down and Scherer dragged him back into the building, still alive. Bikers, in command of the headquarters alarm unit at the GPU, led these men out through another narrow entranceway partially underground, built up with sandbags. They were not taken completely by surprise and laid waste like the policemen a few streets away. But they took casualties, the ambushers hidden in their alleys and firing en masse, fulfilling their assigned task of killing any fisheyes that swam out into the streets.

Scherer sent a runner out to find Bikers. The panic let loose in the town center was not the main threat. He sent the runner with orders for Bikers to leave only a dozen men to secure the streets and the main square around the GPU; to take the remainder of his crew and other alarm units nearby and head in the direction of the ravine. Scherer went back to the signals room. Bikers would not make it to the Policeman's Ravine; Scherer grasped that the enemy must have already gotten through there by now, but Bikers would know this too and would set up some kind of firing line as close to the breach as he could.

In the signals room, Scherer asked first if there was any contact with the outposts along the ravine. There was none. The signals officer had already sent out linemen to look for breaks in the lines. This was a deadly exercise, and perhaps useless if everyone along the ravine had already been wiped out. But chances were that many of those men would still be alive; firing pits, wretched sheds, snow forts, bunkers, and fortified rubble heaps still housing survivors attempting to defend themselves in the middle of the enemy onslaught, or already bypassed. Any force they could bring to bear would help; even the smallest elements left in the Russian rear could inflict a lot of harm, but they would need to be told where to do that, if the wire link could be restored.

If not, then surviving officers out there would lead them however they could.

Mabrius meanwhile was already in the signals room, talking to all the units at Paupers' Field. Most of these people, apart from the jaeger company, were from Mabrius's original command that had come in from Lake Seliger a month ago.

The units reported quiet on that side of the perimeter, meaning they could hear the noise like thunder everywhere else but it was quiet along those snow walls. Even before Mabrius's calls Ohlsson and the other group leaders out there had begun divvying up their men, standing by.

"They're ready," Mabrius said to Scherer.

Mabrius was reluctant to use them though. So was Scherer. Scherer was on other lines talking to the commanders of other alarm units inside the town, or waiting tensely for calls to be put through. He was misled for a while—for many leaders of these emergency troops responded initially, and Scherer was unaware how many of them were ambushed and cut up only moments later, after leading their men out into the streets. The police were hit the worst; others kept some kind of coherence and exchanged heavy fire with the infiltrators in the alleys and side streets, but the impetus of any kind of counterattack toward the ravine was seriously disrupted. He understood this by-and-by, as later calls began coming in from the leaders of these units, if they were still alive, or from their subordinates, if they were still alive, describing what the situation was. Scherer told them to place themselves under Bikers's command, if Bikers's people linked up with some or any of them. If not then he or Mabrius would have to go out there personally.

Scherer said, "It's chaos. We'll have to take people from Paupers' Field."

"They're standing by," replied Mabrius.

Scherer said, "If they come in there the way they did this afternoon. Never mind. Send the word."

"We must keep faith, Herr General. Faith that they will continue to fuck their best chances."

"Faith is not your way, Mabrius."

"That's true," agreed Mabrius.

"What are the last reports of activity at Paupers'?"

"The patrols they beat back an hour ago. No activity for the moment."

"All right. Send the word."

Mabrius spent perhaps sixty seconds speaking into several different telephone receivers. Alarm units were released from Paupers' Field and began making their way back through the ruins of Cholm. Mabrius told those at the perimeter to ready still more alarm units, pending the situation during the night. The section leaders acknowledged this order but declared they would then have no men left to defend the Paupers' area.

"Understood," said Mabrius. "Acknowledge your orders."

He listened.

"Very well. That is all for now."

Scherer and a clerk carried Gadermann into Scherer's personal quarters. The small room was sealed inside the building, like a storage closet, lit by a kerosene lamp, maps strewn about on a chest of drawers and on some other furniture. Scherer swept some maps and other communications from the narrow bed and they laid Gadermann there.

"Stay with him," said Scherer.
"*Jawohl*, Herr General."

Freitag was shaken awake, or perhaps jostled or kicked inadvertently by the other men crowded in there, now rousing themselves as well. The gunfire had been audible for some time but he had slept through it—as had most of the others packed in here—until one of the men on duty had crawled in to actually rouse them.

He responded automatically, in a familiar trance of rote movements: pulling on his boots, buckling his belt, wrapping the length of cloth around his head and scrawny neck. They all slept fully clothed in there so it took only these few seconds of adjusting their garments before they were ready to crawl out the entranceway.

They had to crawl out, as there was no room to stand up in this blasted excavation; it might have been a potato cellar at one time, they never really knew. It was roofed over with scraps of corrugated tin and beams from the debris lying all over the place; then made shell-proof, somewhat, with packed-down snow and ice. A pipe rose like a periscope through the snow-banked roof, venting smoke, though it did this poorly so that the interior space below was always smoky, the men in there generally semiconscious from exhaustion—if they were not dead asleep—with the normal conscious surfaces of their beings further sapped by the lack of oxygen. They played eternally at damping the fire in the middle of their crawl space, trying to get the right proportion of heat and breathable air, never succeeding, yet fooling with it anyway in a kind of idling-away-the-hours fashion, like whittling, except it was never satisfactory because they could never get it right for more than a few minutes at a time, and had to endure the leaden-brained irritation of their comrades if they made it worse. Generally, though, a strange, somewhat disbelieving tolerance was shared by those trying to sleep in this crawl space and in many others like it.

Now shaken out of dreams or daydreams or catatonic boredom or absolute bottomless black sleep they dragged themselves one by one out into the cold, where they could stand up. They were dizzy, rocking around uncertainly, from these unpredictable rotations between sleep and not-sleep, here, in this place where they had been surrounded for weeks, in Cholm. Waking up into this. By now they were as used to it as they could be.

The savage cold had a bracing effect, not unpleasant at first; then shortly thereafter it would simply be too cold. They filed out collecting steel helmets, rifles, and grenades from a wooden framework of shelves and pegs in a snow alcove just outside the entranceway, so that these things could all be placed neatly in a certain place and not clutter up their sleeping quarters.

They stared dully at the spectacular fireworks arcing and spitting all over the town behind them, heard all the noise, though this seemed scarcely present, as it was such a familiar noise.

The Russians, of course, did not attack around the clock day after night after day, and often the men would stand up outside their crawl space beneath a black milky blanket of stars and space whose utter silence was also familiar. It was still there, above them and all around them, but tonight there was noise and the visual distraction of the fireworks and fire webs shooting over the earthbound roofs and ruins; they judged at once from the volume of fire that an attack was under way and waited to be told where to go.

Ohlsson and another NCO ushered them into a drafty aboveground ruin nearby where fires were going and men already on duty were gathered.

Those men were formed up into groups and watching the firefight with expectant looks. The men just roused from sleep were likewise organized and told to stand by, though thinking from the looks of things they would not have long to wait.

Freitag had returned to the perimeter from the center of town, from the GPU, just after dark. During the attack in the daylight hours he had seen the T-34 coming up behind them, seen the wounded Baer roll out of his saucer sled before the tank treads crushed it and then spat it back like a discus, hurling it somewhere, seen the jaeger who had been helping him with Baer climb onto the engine deck of the tank. The Russian springing up through the hatch had killed him with a pistol. Freitag was sitting stunned in the snow at that moment, staring at the crude surface finish of the tank's frontal armor only a few feet away. Sometimes the light of day had an ordinary effect on things that made everything appear utterly harmless. It was only a machine with the crude greasy painted finish of any kind of machine, stopped in the snow a few feet from him. The tank wheeled around on reversed treads, spraying him with snow and ice, and drove off toward the town center.

He just sat there. His red face was abraded from snow and ice, his helmet knocked off his head. Mechanically he walked over to where Baer was, helped him to stand, mechanically shouted at him to try to stand on his own weight. Baer was still screaming in terror but then he stopped. Freitag helped him over to the shelter of the nearest building and could go no farther, laying Baer on the icy boards.

There was no fire going in this place and Baer began to fade and Freitag didn't know what to do. Dully he stared out a window, window-frame, at the battle still going on at the snow wall a few hundred feet away. A tank blew up out there. Another tank drove back and forth in the distance, firing its weapons but not approaching, like a submarine lurking off some shore.

A terrible black depression began to paralyze him. It was all he could do to remain sitting upright. Baer lay beside him talking to himself, his face leached paler than Freitag's pale freckled face. Freitag began weeping, did not cry out but saw as he often did a mental picture of himself crying out and beating his head against the floor or the snow. There was a blackness to the light of day (which strangely, inside his head, became transformed to a terrible exposed naked whiteness), not the blackness of night but a blackness of the sick, feeble, naked sunlight that leaned right on him. He was ashamed of his helplessness with Baer dying right beside him but he felt so bad he was not ashamed.

Then all of a sudden he felt better, the fit leaving him more swiftly than it usually did. He wept again with the abruptness and strangeness of its departure but he still felt better. He felt fine. The cold savaging his hands and feet, creating hideous, bulging iron rods out of his smallest bones, seemed merely something he was eminently capable of dealing with, or at least enduring. He still did not know what to do about Baer. He got to his feet. He saw the fight still going on along the snow wall. Occasionally Russian heads and upper torsos rose up like surf shooting up from behind a jetty, some of them actually clambering over; he saw most of them being killed very quickly, toppling in dead lumps as if fallen from a much greater height, dropped off a cliff. He assumed a firing position and thrust his rifle through the window, feeling his innards beginning to collapse again when he could not get his frozen throbbing hands to work the bolt. He cursed and beat against the bolt and beat the bolt against the windowsill and when all was in smooth working order he calmly began firing at whatever targets he could see, feeling the cold brilliantly sunny wind of the steppe blowing through his tight red hair.

When things quieted down he hauled Baer out of the building. Baer made no sound. He had almost that peculiar terminated look now, but not quite. Some soldiers had harnessed themselves to a *panje* cart bearing other wounded. They stopped while Freitag struggled to lift Baer on board, which of course he could not do by himself, so that after standing in a stupor for a few seconds two of them stepped back to help. Freitag then harnessed himself with the others dragging the cart along; they dragged it along toward the field hospital at the GPU, staring with some interest at the tank treads imprinted perfectly in the snow that led them all the way back to that building.

By the time he returned to the perimeter the day was done; it was dark, and he had hardly slept at all in the smoky shoulder-high crowded space when he was roused again with the others in there. A few minutes later he was outside again, or rather standing in the aboveground ruin that was open in countless places to the outside and every bit as cold. He watched and listened to the firefight with the others there and waited to hear orders to move in that direction.

It felt like a new day somehow, even though he had hardly slept at all and the night was still hours before midnight. But still it felt like a new day to him, the bad things of the day before gone somehow, no longer leaning on him, and other things to come now. Someone told him about Kordts.

"Ah well, old Smiley is cleverer than he looks," he declared with terse jocularity. "I expect we'll catch up with him when we get over there."

"*Ja, ja,* we'll just catch it," said the man next to him.

"What a show that is," said Freitag. It reminded him of an ice carnival he had seen as a child, a bright memory from a poverty-stricken childhood, a happy time. If he was killed before dawn he would at least escape the sinking feeling that often came upon him in yet another of those bleary shrunken dawns. He flexed his nostrils, staring intently into the night. Behind them Ohlsson was called several times to the field telephone.

They were needed soon enough. They moved quickly in their small groups across the open stretches on the outskirts, pausing in the shelter of the first more densely clustered buildings, then moving on along the streets.

Brandeis told them several times to wait. Wait, wait. He shouted this as well to the two policemen behind the other weapon in the street, behind the dead body.

It was hard to wait. They watched in fascination as scattered figures grew in number and became a great mob. The street was narrow and the mob seemed to be surging up to them like a storm surge. They saw Russians stumbling and falling down against the sides of buildings lining the street, pushed there by the crowds of their fellows. They watched as the first tank rolled right over several men milling in front of it, they'd seen it happen to their own men too, today and on preceding days, the brief clench of horrified fascination evoked by that sight never changed. While other men kept stumbling and falling against the buildings, stumbling to get out of the way, stumbling against the piles of debris spilled out like vomit from the innards of almost every building, still more crowds of men surged up and out in front of the tank again and the tank did not persist in running them down. It idled, letting off a few cannon shots which rocketed up the street past the morgue-church and the police-ruin, striking other buildings or cratering in the street. They turned their heads, looked back that way, saw other groups of people, smaller groups who must be their own people coming to assist them, or else setting up other firing positions further to their rear along the street.

Kordts saw men moving in the alley behind them, thinking again that the Russians were going to come up the alleys into their rear. He shouted at Brandeis and grabbed him by the shoulder. Brandeis looked. In the yet-guttering flames of the police-ruin, in which the bodies of dead men were more clearly illuminated through holes burnt in the walls, they could see other shapes moving in the alley, silhouetted there. Kordts had his last grenade primed and could hardly resist the urge to fling it back there; what he'd seen in the alley at the beginning kept eating at his mind. But the four men visible in the flames were their own men, setting up a mortar, assembling it on its mount and leaning over range screws and then dropping shells down the tube in a single fluid burst of activity.

Kordts tried to screw the cap back into the grenade handle but his hands were too cold. He set it down on a plank with the cap dangling from its lanyard out of the hollow wooden handle. He wanted to just get rid of it but the mob was still not close enough.

"Well?" said Lockhart, the one at the machine gun, to Brandeis, Lockhart also seeing the mortar team in action.

"Just wait, boy," said Brandeis, who might have been Lockhart's age; both were younger than Kordts. "Steady now. You know the range, Lockhart. You could do this in your sleep by now. Don't get impatient."

"No, Herr Leutnant," hissed Lockhart. "I am not impatient."

His hand gripping the trigger and his other hand braced on the receiver were killing him. His tension had kept them warm or kept him from realizing how terribly cold they were but now he couldn't stand it any longer; he let out a barking sound and beat them against his knees, glaring at Brandeis and cursing him under his breath.

Brandeis placed his hand on his back, staring at the mortar bursts landing some distance back in the oncoming mob.

"It's all right. It's all right. Just a little further."

"Yes, yes, yes, yes, Herr Leutnant," said Lockhart, his eyes bulging. He made that barking sound again, clapped his hands together, gritted his teeth, heard his inner voice whispering to himself.

Yet canny enough, for all that. He'd operated this gun for days and days out on the perimeter; he didn't need the lieutenant to remind him of anything.

"All right, go ahead then!" said Brandeis fiercely, as if it were he consumed by impatience. "Fire! Fire!"

Lockhart fired. He was not able to grip the gun tightly enough to control the recoil. He screamed and then did grip it tightly enough, welding himself to the piece, firing burst after burst and knowing no more of his pain.

The Russians seemingly for hours—minutes, hours—had been moving up through some intermediate distance; now suddenly they were at some other distance, less than a hundred feet away.

Kordts watched it happen, the first wave of them blasted down like scaffolding all brought down with a single yank, yet peering more intently through this sight for any few who might still remain standing to rush the last few feet to their position. He saw a few, so did Lockhart; Kordts fired his rifle and Lockhart fired shorter bursts, and in the middle of the street the two policemen were firing and firing. Other positions across the street or further up the street were firing. The Russians recoiled yet were impelled forward again by other Russians behind them.

"Oooooooouuuuray!" they roared, screaming to gird themselves for their own slaughter, a strangely muffled screaming now in the racket of the heavy machine guns reverberating in the narrow street.

Kordts remembered the hand grenade, glaring about for any of them still close enough to kill; then he yanked the cap off and flung it out there, just to be rid of it. It exploded somewhere. He cursed himself for using up his last one but at least he didn't have to think about it now, knowing his own strange carelessness better than anyone and fearing he might set it off somehow. He fired his rifle, firing, firing, only occasionally seeing individual targets.

He was aware somehow that he was no longer cold, a hysterical gladness little different from hysterical rage. Mostly he was not aware of anything except what he saw.

He saw the dead piled in the street and then a second wave somehow coalescing back there . . . indeed like a wave, indeed like a wave, about to curl, break . . . as their officers formed them up to come on again. So that there was a pause, not all but most of the German gunners pausing as if in some symbiotic tidal response. Then they came on again. The first heaps of dead, the surging of the second wave up to the first heaps of dead, made for a perfect marker, all the German guns firing simultaneously without any signal from anyone, so that the effect was even more devastating this time.

The first tank moved up.

Now we're done for, thought Kordts, enraged at Freitag all of a sudden. He forgot it as soon as it occurred to him.

"Don't fire. Don't fire," hissed Brandeis.

The turret gun swiveled around. They all shrank back into the collapsed beams and were about to move into the lee shelter of the church wall when the shot cracked out, ripping just overhead and striking the burning police-ruin and passing through it, exploding somewhere.

The tank moved up till it was almost abreast of them. The two policemen picked up their gun and belts and ammo box and scurried back and were shot down by the machine gun in the bow plate.

"Fire. Fire," said Brandeis.

Lockhart fired, into the next wave that was surging up around the tank, roaring, "Ooooouuuuurayy!!"

He fired until the gun jammed. Brandeis gave no orders. He and Kordts and Lockhart and his loader picked up the gun and moved back against the church wall and set it up again flush against the church wall. About a minute passed while Lockhart cleared the jam, not daring to make that barking noise now, even though the uproar of other guns nearby was just as loud as it had been. When his fingers simply wouldn't move any longer he hissed something and his loader took over and finally cleared the jam and Lockhart forced himself to grasp the trigger again. The Russians were passing right in front of them, between them and the tank that was also parked broadside now right in front of them, rushing in their tight groups up the street. Lockhart fired into them as they passed by, all coming into abrupt view past the corner of the church. The range was point-blank. Almost every round that hit flesh holed instantly through it and ricocheted off the broadside armor of the tank, making a jackhammer clatter so loud that their hearing was gone, fused into some single un-hearing thing in their heads. Each of them thought they might be hit by these ricochets but Lockhart kept firing any-way. He kept killing them; the ricochets did too. So did the massed fire of other MGs set up further up the street. The tank moved forward again, out of their line of sight.

The abrupt cessation of the ricochet noise caused them to rock unsteadily, leaning against the church wall.

Kordts was out of ammunition. He went back into the al-ley to see if there might be a goat's leg lying around, or more grenades. The police-ruin was still burning and he was stupid to be standing in this light. He knew it and he stepped back and sat down under the collapsed beams by the alley, in the shadows there. It occurred to him that this would be a good place to stay, to just stay and stay. But it wasn't, not really; if this was the end, if this was the last night, then they would squirrel him out of here eventually and either shoot him where he stood or put him on the slow train to Siberia. He did not think he would freeze to death hidden in here as he had forgotten the cold. He couldn't think and for a moment just watched the Russians running on past up the street. Unthink-ingly he began to crawl through the beams back to where Brandeis and the gun crew were.

They were firing again, scything down everyone, or most everyone, as soon as they appeared past the church corner. One of them somewhere must have seen the muzzle flashes finally. Kordts saw a shape crouched low right at the church corner, flinging something at Brandeis.

With a strange resigned weariness he allowed himself to collapse like a sack right where he was, hoping the jumble of beams would absorb the blast. The grenade went off and af-ter an instant of white roaring silence he heard ghastly shrieks that also subsided almost instantly.

He did stay there now, stayed and stayed for some time. He

shuddered a few times, exhausted little convulsions. The jumbled beams of the outbuilding had blown down around him somewhat like a blanket, absorbing shrapnel, concussion, everything except the cold but he didn't care about that. He felt nothing.

By and by he groped through this mess, terrified of being discovered but he felt impelled to move anyway, he didn't know why, didn't think why. He came up to the church wall.

The sheet of blood there, lit up by any number of streaming lights near and far, lit up by the flames of the police-ruin behind him, seemed somehow to be oozing from the very stones of the wall, but it was just plastered there.

He looked to see if Brandeis or Lockhart or the other man was still alive but he couldn't tell in the darkness, feeling at them, they were dead, had to be. He lifted the machine-gun barrel; mangled, he let it drop. Then he picked it up again because it was still warm, gripping this warmth, lowering his face against it, weeping copiously. The barrel had been red hot and now it was perhaps as warm as a near-dead infant; he could feel the life ebbing from the living metal. He let go of it. The streams of tears were irritating against his face and he wiped them away, before they could freeze solid there and irritate him even worse. He stopped weeping, hardly aware that he had been. He was aware of the gash in his cheek for the first time since all this had started, tears trickling through it weirdly, pooling down under his tongue. He had a momentary feeling that the gash had torn itself much deeper without his realizing it, almost to the back of his head. His hand was too cold to feel anything and so was his face, cheek; he scraped his knuckles along there but gave it up, hardly aware of what he was doing.

He looked at the outline he recognized as Brandeis. Brandeis was sitting against the church wall with his head slumped forward, as if staring abstractedly at the ground. He was one of the few officers Kordts had liked somewhat, accepting this inconsistency as being perfectly normal. They had talked for a little while one time, at Lake Seliger, before it all came to an end there.

He sat down against Brandeis's body. The newly dead flesh was ice-cold but still less cold than the stone blocks of the church wall. Out in the street he could see a mass of Russian dead, almost as high as a low wall now. Gunfire blasted into it and shattered fingers, whole hands, pieces of heads, all frozen and shattering nicely when they were struck. A few of the Ivans persisted in clambering over all this, one of them getting his foot caught in the tangle of his frozen dead comrades, cursing in a disbelief that seemed the most recognizably human thing Kordts had witnessed all night. While the scene as a whole was only on a par with any number of other hallucinatory things he had witnessed these seven months. The cursing man was killed while trying to pull himself loose; all of them were killed anyway, whoever was still clambering over that mess out there. Then there came a few clambering back in the other direction, a few surviving to topple drunkenly down the other side, trotting off down the street, disappearing behind the corner of the church.

The first tank was killed by the usual methods.

The second tank in column was disabled by the somewhat unusual expedient of flinging Teller mines from a second-story window. Both mines bounced off the tank with a loud clang, landing in the iron-snow of the street and exploding there. The force was enough to snap one of the treads. The crew remained dutifully inside their vehicle, firing their cannon and secondary armament at the German gun positions further up the street. Their accuracy was hampered by the wreck of the first tank further ahead, partially blocking their field of fire, but they continued to fire at whatever muzzle flashes they could see.

This constituted a serious menace. Several of the machine-gun crews were killed by this cannon fire. Other crews switched position, a hair-raising enterprise with the Soviet infantry so close upon them, setting up again behind the wreck of the first tank or in corners along the street.

The effect nonetheless was of a massed battery of machine-gun fire, like the multiple guns mounted aboard a destroyer-type aircraft. The storm-surge of Red Army men coming up the street was met and bowled down. This happened again and again. From the more open and outlying areas near the Policeman's Ravine, the entire assault force had become funneled along this street that grew quite narrow here in the small center part of the town. The Russians advanced like a piston of flesh sealed tightly in its shaft; the similarly near-solid piston of massed metal parts flung at them from the other end of the shaft, from the German machine guns, broke them and shattered them. The Russian attack at length seized up and died. But the assault regiment was followed through the breach by other regiments from an entire fresh division that had been transferred to the Cholm sector, and these regiments too advanced into the street behind the waves of their predecessors, behind the bodies of their predecessors, on and on into the night.

The street became so crowded that men who were killed had no room to fall down, but were borne forward between the shoulders of their still-advancing comrades, until eventually slipping away somewhere, dragged down, trampled underfoot. Dead men and men who were only wounded were trampled underfoot, beneath the boots of hundreds of other men, beneath tank treads, it didn't matter.

Their breaching of the Policeman's Ravine had succeeded due to clever planning. It was the bane of the Red Army that after a certain point in any attack, even one so cunningly conceived, all organization would be lost. Mid-rank officers were poorly trained and their men still more poorly trained. Better-trained units might have flanked away from the death-funnel of the one street into other streets and alleys. They had the advantage of numbers, were equal to their enemy in stubborn courage, and might have rolled through the small blasted heart of the town along parallel streets and all through the tiny alleys. Their enemy could not have massed enough fire to defend all these arteries.

But initiative lay only with the higher-ranking commanders far to the rear, in the ice-wastes of the Russian camps beyond the perimeter. Initiative, like a limited resource, had been spent entirely at the point of breakthrough, at the ravine. There were no communications with the forward elements. In this respect the Russian commanders in the rear were no better off than the leaders of a medieval army, who after a certain point could not communicate, direct, redirect, or do anything at all; the lower ranks as primitively trained as any medieval army quickly became a mob and came on like a mob, again and again along that single street, artery, death-funnel, piston-shaft.

In fact it was the German alarm units that had taken advantage of the surrounding streets. They had been cut up but not entirely shattered by the ambushes laid by the various Soviet infiltrators, here and there, here and there. But the infiltrators had been dispersed in a dozen smaller firefights and the alarm units had kept their coherence, by men who were trained to cohere into functioning organisms even as small as three or four surviving men. In any case only a few of the alarm units had been cut up that badly. Those few, and the others in better shape, worked their way along surrounding streets and through debris-filled yards and alleys and entered buildings from the rear that faced along the single street where the Soviet assault was channeled.

In effect that was what they did, though it was not so simple as that. Men killed or were killed, in encounters with those infernal parties of infiltrators who had wrought such havoc right at the start and who were still roaming around everywhere.

But at length many of these buildings were occupied and the Germans from windows and doorways fired point-blank into the flanks of the attacking masses funneled along the one street. Or tossed down as many grenades as they had carried with them, in their belts or pockets or in gunnysacks, even more devastating. Or, wrought up wildly as if they were carrying out some juvenile prank, tossed a pair of Teller mines from a second-story window, bouncing with loud clangs off the armor of the tank below.

With its tread run out the tank was immobilized but its crew remained dutifully at their guns, firing. The men at the second-story window now flung grenades down, which exploded ineffectually against the tank. They threw more down. At length the tank crew could not stand this rain of concussions, reverberating inside their immobilized hulk. Their commander was knocked unconscious and the rest of the crew baled out. Freitag had already used up all his grenades. He delighted in the opportunity to use a goat's leg he had taken from a Russian they'd killed upon first entering the building. It was a delight. His rifle was propped against the wall beside the window and he fired the goat's leg down at the fleeing tank crew.

"Good! Good! Good!" shouted Bosstig, the man next to him.

They felt the ecstasy of just killing. It was not joy but the ecstasy of a vacuum where for long moments, even hours, they were no longer aware of their intense physical misery. They did not feel the cold or in moments, pulses, when they did feel it it simply didn't matter. They brushed their paralyzed, inadequately gloved fingers against hot gun barrels for a touch of warmth, trying not to burn themselves but not too careful about it. They would know that pain later. Freitag exhausted the disc-magazine of the goat's leg in a few seconds. This was the first chance he'd had to use this weapon and he wanted to keep using it. His comrades continued firing from the window or lobbing grenades. The vacuum-ecstasy of not suffering, of not feeling sick at heart, was indescribable, and then to be able to kill so indiscriminately, in this miserable godforsaken place, was a joy in itself. Fuck you fuck you fuck you fuck you. They were transformed, and perhaps subliminally frightened by it, as deeper down they knew it was all a fraud; but for the moment they didn't give a damn.

Freitag looked around hurriedly with his flashlight, dashing, stumbling down to the first floor where they'd left a few Russians dead, looking for another disc-magazine or just another goat's leg. He couldn't find one. He cast the flashlight beam around for a few seconds longer then shut it off, not wanting to be alone for even a moment longer. Was he aware that he felt better somehow, released of something, at night, even on such a terrible night as this? Yes, of course he was, even though he had no time to think of it or know anything about it. He went back up to the second floor where the others were, grabbing up his rifle propped against the wall, intently aware of something, something, his lips flexing, nostrils flexing. Later, in his official account to the High Command, Scherer would record that this night was the worst of the entire siege; even the May Day barrage and subsequent assault at the very end did not come this close to finishing them all. Long before night's end he had begun to receive reports, by runner or by wire-links still intact, of the slaughter taking place along Church Street—that was its designated name on the situational maps they'd drawn up. But the Russians had never gotten this deep in such strength into the town before; the perimeter was stripped of men. Any follow-up assault, at the ravine or still worse at Paupers' Field, would sweep everything before it. And there was still no artillery support from the outside. If they survived the night they would then come upon the day with the perimeter inadequately manned and still no artillery support from the outside.

Scherer had all night to ponder these fears. He got on the radio to the outside, several times, and each time heard that still no shells had been brought up to the artillery positions, those ten miles away. But by morning all was quiet. Quiet had already descended in the darkness, in the hours before dawn. Sporadic gun bursts, killing a few last Russians who had not yet been killed or fled the town, had mostly subsided still some hours before dawn. There was time to take stock; there was time to absorb things in a mechanical stupor, for Scherer and every other man. There was time to send men back to the perimeter, where no attack came in the morning anyway. The wounded were tended to, walled-off inside their suffering, while the dead were more companionable because they, like the unwounded survivors, could feel nothing at this point. German losses in such frightfulness had been fewer than what men might have thought. Russian losses had been about what they had seemed, to all those witnessing the Russian attacks during the night. Shortly after dawn Freitag was back at the perimeter with the rest of his people. He stood in the dawn-light outside the log-beams and banked-up snow and ice that covered their crawl space, sleeping area, with the pipe rising through it, still venting faint wisps of smoke.

Back here again, he thought.

The simplest phrase would have some profound significance attached to it. He was too tired to think and so this significance was absorbed wholly through himself, through his body.

Or what thoughts he did have at this point were like sparks

flaring erratically off some frayed circuit. In fact he could
see them inside his head every so often, little white flashes,
just barely noticeable. He was in no way surprised by this
and all the rest of his surroundings seemed as ordinary as
they ever did.

He was terribly hungry and thirsty though mercifully too
tired to feel it; but he knew he was. In the aboveground ruin
nearby there were fires going in oil drums and men brewing
some filthy liquid, coffee or tea, men looking at each other,
looking at nothing. He knew he could pass out on his feet but
felt he should drink something hot before he did this.

He shuffled inside the ruin, which was too shattered and
open to the air to really have an inside.

It was scalding hot, weak tea; good, because weak tea was
better than weak coffee.

Strangely, because he hardly felt more awake than before,
he began talking loquaciously to people nearby, slurring his
words somewhat. Feeling more himself despite his fatigue,
and all the rest of it. People next to him grunted or said nothing; and a few like Freitag talked in erratic bursts, interrupting each other.

Speechlessness settled over him a minute or so later. He
stepped back a few steps, so he could rest his back against a
wall of the ruin. But it was too cold, so he stepped back up to
the flaming kindling splayed out of the top of the oil drum,
nearly stumbling into it. He grabbed the shoulder of another
man warming himself, who kindly helped steady him.

NCOs had to tell people to get some sleep, to crawl down
into whatever places they slept in. For many of them seemed
to prefer remaining in a stupor on their feet, for whatever reason, feeling some strange urge to absorb something into their
still-waking minds, they were too tired to know what. The
morning light maybe, which cast an ineradicably cold ordi-
nariness upon everything. But that would only be part of it.

When he felt he could hardly bear to stay upright any
longer he shuffled over toward the snow-banked crawl space.
Other men were still on duty, behind the snow walls, elsewhere. The shape of things was ordinary enough but somewhat bent, bending. A few men in their long grey greatcoats,
partially swaddled with white bedsheets like packages im-

properly wrapped, stood near the entranceway to the crawl space, their entire quiet shapes bending slightly though they stood quite still where they were. They looked like devils, or maybe devils lurked inside them and nodded in and out on the vague rim of perception, peering out of ordinary eyes at a landscape, standing their ordinary sentry rounds at the entrance to the pit.

To have to go down into that crawl space again, and then come out of it again a few hours later, into this same place, here, day after day after day. When would it end?

He felt an urge to vomit; he didn't know why; he didn't feel sick. Then it passed. Even his depressing vision of the crawl space did not weigh him down as it normally might. His mind was bent with strange fancies that he scarcely noticed.

The air was very fresh on his face. He noticed that because he didn't notice the cold. He noticed that the dawn sun, just above the horizon, did not cast out the sick black naked exposure that he often saw at this hour, a dismal exposure blacker than any night. But he noticed it didn't look that way this morning; it gave him pause, and he thought of staying awake, aboveground, a little while longer, drinking some more tea.

By God, the idea appealed to him. Then he trembled, not from the cold, but from realizing that this curious lightheartedness was not to be trusted. He trembled but refused to acknowledge that it would evaporate in a moment or an hour.

Again he gagged, not quite vomiting. He didn't know what it was.

He stared at a bony copse of trees just to one side of the horizon sun. One of God's clean sculptures he saw—out there somewhere, outside the perimeter, outside the town. The trees stood in the early light probably a mile or more away. He stared on rubbery legs, staggering a little but persisting until he'd seen enough of it, whatever it was. He clapped one of the devils on the shoulder, muttering, "Heh heh heh," and the man looked back at him with a faint grimace, nodding slightly. Freitag removed his helmet and hung it on its peg, unslung his rifle and set it back in a recess between pegs. He collapsed to his knees and drew the blanket back and crawled inside, into the fetid dark, which was both clammy-cold and clammy-warm.

He made out Kordts in there and crawled among other men to lie beside him.

Kordts was staring into the dimness above his own face.

"Eh, Smiley," Freitag said, saying a whole slur of things inside his mind but unable to speak them out.

Don't call me that, thought Kordts, half-asleep, drifting half-asleep an inch or so beneath the surface of his flesh. He made a second effort and managed to say it out loud.

"I know. I'll remember," said Freitag, lying tight beside him, between him and another man, in the low crowded space. Kordts was disconcerted for a moment when Freitag flung his arm around him, gripping him tightly there; but it was all right, thought Kordts, dully stroking Freitag's arm.

Kordts had been sinking and sinking into black sleep for a while, yet still unable to sleep. Yet Freitag speaking to him, or the effort of him speaking to Freitag, slipped loose some last mooring pin and he fell deep, deep into sleep.

Erika was beside him, though he could not see her. And if she spoke to him he could not hear her. But it was they together and not he alone who looked out through some forest that sloped gently down to some lake or sea in the distance that they could not see. They knew it was there though, like something long familiar. Dark shapes drifted up around the edges of whatever this place was, but were not intrusive somehow. His contempt for them was so immaculately profound that he was almost not aware of them. Things convulsed him but he stubbornly ignored them, even deep in a dream where he could not exert his will. There was noise, noise of air in the treetops, roaring quietly, rising off the sea in the distance.

Chapter Five

The following is a brief account of the actions of the police unit before it was flown in to Cholm.

At first a curious procedure was tried. They were linked together in pairs. There seemed to be some purpose to this bonding, though it lasted only a few minutes. What purpose would that be?

It didn't matter. A number of other procedures were tried later, as time went by. Obviously such a system could never be perfected. That would be too much; and it was too much to begin with. It was just a question of making it easier somehow. If such a notion could ever apply. Making it go more smoothly, would perhaps be a better way of putting it. They understood that much at least, understood from their own experience.

At first a curious procedure was tried, with each man of the team leading away one individual from the large group assembled in the clearing. Each man of the team would lead one individual away, or prod him along, usually down a little path through a thicket to another somewhat smaller clearing. Hardly even a clearing. Just an open space among the trees, become a place because they had made it into a place.

All this took only a few minutes. When each man was done he came back up the path to the assembled group and led away, or prodded along, another individual. Again this took only a few minutes, or even less, once things really got under way. But so many trips back and forth along the little path; altogether, it took a long, long time.

Thus it seemed a curious procedure; it was much too slow, really. But it was only like that the first few times, the first few days; they had to get started somehow.

Linked in pairs, each team member and whoever he chose. I am my brother's keeper. Such rough humor did not arise till sometime later on, after the initial shock had worn off; but then, inevitably, it did arise.

Actually there were a few NCOs who stayed out by the larger group, who did the choosing. So each man going back and forth along the little path did not have to think about that.

Men were chosen first; though of course all of them would go by day's end. But it seemed only natural to choose the men first, if only to ease the team members more gradually into the task.

As the day went on though, some of the NCOs began choosing women and children, even though there still remained quite a few men with the assembled group. There was not really any sudden cunning to this change in tack. Any NCO, after all, in any military unit or similar unit, would find that a great part of his job would be devoted to dealing with personnel—which essentially meant dealing with them as smoothly as possible, so that any task or operation, in the barracks, on the drill ground, in the field, could be carried out as smoothly as possible. Obviously discipline was an essential, no doubt the foremost, element of this smooth-dealing. But there were countless other little things an NCO would learn or intuit, sniffing out potential sources of friction or mishap before they arose and instinctively organizing or reorganizing things so they could continue to proceed smoothly, or as smoothly as possible.

This would not entail anything so drastic as deviating from orders given to them by their commanders. The spirit and letter of the orders would still be carried out; but no order ever covered every little nuance that might arise.

Thus, while it seemed only natural to start by choosing the men, they began to realize as the day went on that it would not do to leave a great mass of women and children until the very end. To finish off a long and unnerving day with a great mass of women and children at the very end would not do somehow. Why not? Because it would just be better not to do it that way; and they realized this about halfway through the long operation and so made slight, spontaneous changes, randomly starting to choose a child here or a woman there to accompany each team member down the little path, working them in gradually so to speak, even though there still remained a number of men waiting with the larger group.

The team members were covered in gore, in blood and brains and sticky little flecks of bone, from shooting each chosen individual in the back of the head at point-blank range. That too was something that would have to change, though figuring it out today would be too complicated; some things would have to be figured out later on.

As the days went on some team members began to fall out because they could not stand the gruesomeness of the work. Their minds could not stand it or their stomachs could not stand it; either one, or both. Some of them told themselves they could stand the killing, but maybe some other method would be better.

There was a commander and several other officers, with several determined enthusiasts among the latter, though all of them were for the most part quite responsive to these problems. They felt a certain force filling their own guts, had felt it right from the start, and were more than usually responsive to the experiences of the men under their command. Other methods were tried as time went on.

I am my Jew's keeper. Rough humor arose, was bandied about, certain jokes staying in circulation even after certain specific procedures were abandoned, such as that first procedure, in which each team member had been paired with one individual, down the little path, and then another, and another, and another.

The commander felt a certain great force of responsibility, knew he would feel it, and then felt it still more deeply as time went on. At the very beginning, the evening before the very first action, he had addressed his men and indicated that any man unwilling to participate would not be obliged to do so. Some resource within him had guided his words, because he wished to make it absolutely clear he was not making this offer just for show. Men unwilling to participate would remain with the unit and perform other duties; they would not be ostracized, scorned, or punished.

He dismissed the formation to allow each man a little time with his own thoughts. He assembled the men again an hour later and repeated what he had said. A half-dozen men stepped forward. Perhaps they did not believe they would not be ostracized, scorned, or punished. Or perhaps they did believe it, because they wanted to, and they wanted to trust their commander or did trust him. In any case they had made their decision.

The commander displayed no rancor, either subtle or overt. It was not the kind of offer one makes to a band of gallant souls, offering any of them a way out but not really expecting them to take it. No, he had been quite sincere.

These half-dozen men were released from their obligation—or, to be more precise, the obligation was obviated before ever being conferred upon them. They were assigned to other duties, and not necessarily menial or degrading ones. Within any unit anywhere any number of routine duties need to be carried out.

These men were joined, some days later, by other men who did some killing at first, but simply could not stomach it.

After a week or two this weeding-out process had pretty much finished itself. The remaining were those who could stomach it, or who thought they could not but did not have the nerve to admit it, or who relished it with a vengeance.

It was found that the first half-dozen men never changed their minds. On the other hand, some who had stopped for a while, after the first killings, began to participate again some weeks later, gradually infected by the ordinary sunlight and blood of this alternate universe; which, like any universe, was only there, after all. And having this much fundamentally in common with any other universe, it inevitably began to seem not so alternate or unfamiliar. Vomit and horror, vomit and horror.

Emil Hausser had not been telling the truth. He would know this and admit it freely to himself. Perhaps he would have admitted it freely to Kordts, or to anyone, if he had survived a little longer and run into Kordts some other day.

He had been getting at some kind of truth though, even while letting it pass through his lips in a bald-faced lie to some stranger from the infantry on a thirty-below-zero night (and there would be other nights still more cold than this). He thought somehow that it would make a difference, and that it did not matter in any way. His mind did not contain these two opposites; it contained nothing anymore, except himself. And even saying that much would be making it too complicated.

He had shot them at point-blank range for several days, at the edge of those ditches at several different locations, where the bodies had piled up, and up, and up. Then he had fallen out, along with other men who had fallen out at about that time.

It had nothing to do with his stomach. He had a pretty hard stomach it seemed. He had not felt sick or queasy. Perhaps there had been a few odd moments when a red tidal wave of disgust had thundered through his entire being, but what of it; even among the haters and wild-eyed enthusiasts, a red tidal wave of disgust might thunder through their entire beings, during a few odd moments, during the long, long hours of a summer day.

But he had not been physically sickened by the gore that had gotten all over his face. A few days later he had simply decided he did not want to do this anymore. Even when entirely unspoken, there remained a certain invisible pressure from his comrades. But he felt he could rise above that; felt it with a strange clear matter-of-factness. He did not want to do this anymore. He said this to an NCO, just to hear himself say it, and then to a junior officer, both these men staring at him somewhat stiffly and unconcernedly, twitching their heads a little. Meaning—all right, go tell it to him then. So he went to the commander, whom he could have gone to directly though he had chosen not to.

He had thought of saying he was sickened and having terrible nightmares—he had had a few, it was true, though still more like dreams than nightmares at this point—as it seemed easier to say it that way. But he had seen already that the first half-dozen men who had refused, who had taken the commander at his word, had indeed not been scorned or ostracized; and so he felt able to say he just did not want to do it anymore.

Nothing is ever permanent. Promises kept since the dawn of time may be broken at any moment. Maybe the commander would have grown irritable or contrary in spite of his earlier guarantees, upon seeing still more men wavering after those initial few.

"Very well. Go report to . . ." so-and-so, with the cook's crew or woodcutting crew or vehicle maintenance fellows.

Months went by. Time is relative.

They were in Poland, and then they were in Russia.

Sometimes there would be a week or longer between actions, during which time they would be assigned to normal security duties, patrolling, or whatever. Or they might relax in temporary quarters, with the rough humor that had grown more common by then. The gaps between actions made it somewhat easier to adopt a normal routine, with the actions themselves becoming somewhat more normal, one task among various other tasks.

There were more facts than these facts. Little details of their daily lives, routines, the things they said to one another, the subtle differences between the men who killed and the men who did not; differences that the commander had long feared might critically fracture his unit and cripple its ability to function as a whole organism, as a unit. Perhaps in some inscrutable region or cell of himself he had secretly hoped this would happen, right from the very start; but it never did happen, never. Inevitably there did arise vague undercurrents of scorn or ostracism over time, but never very much; and the very little that there was made it very clear how little that there was.

The men in his unit remained bonded together in their curious way, in whatever way it was, even those who refused to kill and those who kept right on killing, killing, killing. For all those months it never changed, and the critical, ugly fracturing of morale that the commander had feared never occurred.

It was a mystery, and there came a time when it occurred to him that it must be part of God's plan for his men to be divided this way. It was for this reason that he had been given the strength at the very beginning, to offer any of them who wanted a way out to take that way out. He had feared that over time the killers would start refusing to associate with the other ones, or vice versa; and yet he saw how this was not happening, how they still lived shoulder to shoulder with each other, in Poland, and later in Russia. It was as if all of them were performing some necessary role, profoundly different, divided, though they might be, and that the operation, this endless, months-long operation, was meant to be conducted in this way.

While it occurred to him that this must be part of God's plan, he could never bear to articulate it to himself in quite this way. For he knew it was a sick, horrible blasphemy, and he could never quite bear to articulate that to himself either. He saw it in the sky, these assertions taking shape invisibly up there. A number of his men and officers were becoming quite terrible drunkards as time went by, and this seemed not part of any plan but only something even more inevitable than that. In other units—it mattered not whether they were SS or mere policemen—even commanders would become quite terrible drunkards. But the commander of this particular outfit, in which Emil Hausser was serving, did not take that path.

There were more facts than these. More facts may be gathered, made more explicit, as much as need be, facts pinned down like insects on a board. But the facts begin to quail, begin to not want to go on. Facts begin to shrivel up like living souls before a fire, before something corrosive and consuming, which may be thought of as a kind of anti-language.

Months passed. They were in Poland, and then they were in Russia.

Chapter Six

They could no longer bring the dead into that one church, as too many Russian dead were jammed up against the door, frozen there. It would have been necessary to blast them apart, or use pickaxes on them; either way, it seemed too much somehow. So they carried their dead into other churches the morning after the attack. It had become a habit by now, that no one thought of breaking.

About ten policemen survived from the police-ruin beside the church. But their unit had been larger than that, and other groups of policemen quartered in other buildings, who had fared better during the night, came to help carry the dead away from the place where they had been ambushed.

They were laid on the floor of another church, beside infantrymen and whoever else was at Cholm, fallen last night at Cholm. Emil Hausser was not found till later in the day, off by himself among Russian dead, among piles of junk, in the alley. So he was one of the last carried into the new church, and thus laid on top of the pile, at least for the time being, he was.

It was quiet throughout the day, except for a few shell bursts, Russian gunners outside the city hoping to catch men tidying up, after the night. In fact Scherer did insist on tidying up the ravine sector, just after dawn, with the one reasonably fresh unit he had left, comprising seventeen men. But within half an hour it became clear they could not take back the Policeman's Ravine. So the enemy had that much, after all the long night. He resigned himself to pulling the perimeter back still further. During the day scattered survivors continued to come in from the ravine, men who had been out there all night in their little outposts, after the Russian attack had swept past them. But a lot of others had been lost last night, lost for good, out in the deep snows of the ravine. The day was long, with those few shell bursts now and then. But otherwise it was quiet.

A few days later it was quieter still. There would be days like that, when no attacks came in or shells came in, before they started up again on some other day.

Kordts, Freitag, Bosstig, Krause, a few others were playing poker in their crawl space, even Ohlsson joining in with them today, tired of being in there as always but it was the only place warm enough to play cards. But as nothing was going on the day was long and peculiar, and they could go out later to stretch their legs for a few minutes in the cold, perhaps running errands to other parts of the town so they would have some other warm place to go to.

It was like a Sunday, a quiet Sunday in the winter. Occasionally there were days so quiet that the siege seemed to have been abandoned; there was no noise, there was no sign of movement or any sign of an encircling army, out there in the white emptiness beyond the snow walls. Such days were long; even short winter days were long. Sometimes Kordts would speak to the close blue sky, as if it were a being he was addressing, asking to be delivered from this place. Help me to get out of here. Help us to get out of here. The two ways of saying it passed interchangeably through his mind. The sky seemed to speak somehow, the shifting blue dyes that appeared when you stared long enough at the winter sky; but it spoke to itself, not to him. It did not seem peculiar, conversing with the sky. Anyway, to describe it in that way would be an exaggeration, making a man seem a little touched when he was nothing of the sort. Nothing seemed peculiar when it was only a few odd thoughts passing through your mind, in the midst of some day. Other men held their own conversations, and then it passed and they returned to waiting, or to whatever business they were attending to. The roof of the crawl space had started to sag down on them. He and some other men went to collect some planks to shore it up again, later on.

By April little had changed, other than the look of the land, now melting everywhere.

The thick snow walls that had been their only protection from enemy fire were now melting. The few strongpoints still holding on the outskirts of town had to be pulled back, because the only protection remaining was amongst the stone rubble of the town. But most of the other strongpoints were already inside the town now; the perimeter had shrunk that far. The defenders held positions a few hundred feet out from the GPU, but the GPU was effectively in the front lines. Not just roving tanks but squads of Russian infiltrators worked up to the place almost nightly, lobbing grenades. The Germans were now too few to man a continuous line and could hardly stop the Russians from coming and going as they pleased.

Little had changed. The situation had seemed impossible in January and thus could hardly be said to have gotten worse, even though it had, marginally, day by day and week after week, and now nearly one hundred days of this had gone by.

The lifting of the abominable cold had eased people's suffering but not done so much to lift their spirits, as the warming weather seemed to activate regions of fear inside their minds that had grown nearly numb over the endless frozen weeks.

Would the Russians grow more determined, better organized, with the change in season? Would this bring the end?

They had no point of reference, no rational grounds for knowing if this might be true or not. Only a vague foreboding. . . .

In a way fear was also activated by hope, hope that with the change in the weather their own people on the outside might somehow be able to break through to them. Fear and hope were closely linked, incestuous feelings.

Despair was obstinately countered by the simple inertia of having held out for so long now, for so many days that they no longer had any real sense of the time passing. It was a blur that seemed to have gone on forever and would continue to do so; on the other hand, a man might remember some little thing that had happened back in December or January, before all this had begun, which might for some reason seem to have occurred only five minutes ago. As if they had all been blacked out or delirious over all the intervening months. This peculiar sensation especially would become more noticeable once the siege was finally lifted; but that was still to come, and being still to come none knew in April if it would ever come. Gloomy despair—depression really, though this word was not so common back then—alternated with a kind of dull stubbornly confident inertia as one day irrevocably succeeded another; these two moods did not so much alternate as swim confusedly together, inducing a sort of dull mundane craziness though at least it was not like morale entirely ebbing away. As always every man felt these things in his own different way within the confines of his own self. April is the cruelest month.

Scherer, exercising command amongst the groans of wounded men, might have heard Kordts babbling loudly from time to time on the second floor of the GPU. For the second time Kordts found himself confined to this accursed building, though in constant delirium he was not so much aware of it now. The wicked gash had never healed properly and in the rising temperatures had become infected. For a while it had itched terribly, sometimes in deep regions of his mouth which he could never quite locate with his probing finger, driving himself half-mad scratching at it. Maybe that was how it had gotten infected. Also they had been dragging dead Russians about for a few days, as the melting snow uncovered the dead heaps and the defenders became unnerved to see how many there were. No one thought about trying to clear off all of them, nor even bury a single one of them; but a few places in front of individual strongpoints and around the entrance to the GPU were cleared away as the stench grew.

So maybe that had done it, some filth wiped off a dead man's belly. He had no idea really. As the fever grew worse it no longer mattered and his mind wandered all over the place. When planes roared overhead he kept thinking he would be flown out and he conversed with Moll, who had already been flown out months before, assuring this invisible comrade that they had their ticket home now. Moll was in a state of terror, his own hopes of being flown out suddenly paralyzed by the sight of one of the JUs being shot down by Russian flak only moments after it took off down the icy landing strip. It burned in the deep snow beyond the end of the strip and they saw that no one survived. The aviation fuel sheeted up in panes of fire as hot and clear as the atmosphere was cold and clear, shimmering over the wreck.

"Oh Jesus God," said Moll. For days he had suffered such pain from his frostbite-mangled hands and feet that he had been barely able to keep control of himself. His groans had punctuated the entire hundred-mile retreat from Lake Seliger to Cholm and Kordts had heard them for that entire distance, though Moll must have some fortitude to make it that far without collapsing and being left as others had been.

He had grown worse at Cholm and when he heard he was to be flown out his eyes had glared about feverishly with hope, still groaning all the while because he could not control himself. The surgeon had almost decided to amputate his feet when word came that Moll was on the roster for the plane.

Two JUs had come in that morning. The first one now lay burning in the distance and full of dead men.

"Come on, Moll," said Kordts. "They won't get two in a row."

"I can't. Take me back to the field hospital."

The second JU was still on the ice strip with engines idling loudly. People hurrying to board, wounded men shuffling as quickly as they could—for the strip lay under enemy fire— paused to stare at the burning mess in the distance. Through the greenhouse cockpit windows the pilots stared expressionlessly at the burning mess in the distance. Healthy men bearing wounded on stretchers lay their burdens down, not knowing what to do.

Russian gunfire picked up again and this pause in activity lasted only moments. Louder bursts of gunfire came from defenders around the strip trying to keep the enemy clear.

"It's your lucky day," said Kordts. "Just come on. You'll be in Riga in half an hour."

"No!"

But Moll had little choice, as he could not run away. He tried to roll off the stretcher which they had set on the ice and Kordts, enraged suddenly at arguing over the bastard's good fortune while they were under fire all this time, kicked one of

Moll's feet. The pain paralyzed him and Kordts and Freitag were able to roll him back onto the stretcher and they set off toward the waiting plane.

Freitag, who had a more positive effect on people anyway, tried to keep him calm for the last few minutes as they waited their turn, Moll's turn, under the boarding hatch.

Then they handed him up to the aircrew and hurried away from the exposed ground.

From the shelter of a snowbank they watched the plane take off. The roar and shriek as the pitch was cranked up to full throttle, deafening; the furious gunfire from the defenders during these critical moments, also deafening. The plane flew over the still-burning wreck and slowly gained altitude and then slowly disappeared into the deep clear sky.

Three months later Kordts continued to loudly reassure Moll in the heat of his fever on the second floor of the GPU. He did not exactly remember kicking him but still felt some pang of remorse and spoke to him a little more kindly. Kordts needed to reassure himself as well, convinced as he was that he was now getting on the plane along with Moll, and the dazzling flash of the first plane going down kept repeating itself in his fever, the burst of heat seeming to come right up under the skin of his face.

Then he would forget all about that and his mind would wander to something else, or he would lapse into black exhausted sleep.

He would wake up and know exactly where he was and his slashed-up cheek would be itching again, yet the infection was so inflamed that he could not scratch at it without causing himself agony. The medical people were giving him drugs to bring down the fever and the infection, and whenever they did not he rudely demanded them. There were scores of other hurt men lying about and his rudeness had little effect, other than to keep his spirits up in some strange way. He couldn't care less about suffering stoically, and it felt better to be angry. At times he felt ashamed of himself but this came and went. He no longer really felt depressed or afraid and didn't really care about anything any longer, except that he didn't want to lapse into depression and fear again, which always seemed very close at hand. Sometimes other people lying

nearby told him to shut up; sometimes he might say something morosely clever which might bring a faint grudging
laugh from someone, a thick wheeze. Anyway he was not the
only one complaining or babbling and it was not with the unnerving, contagious fear of some of the others. Normally, he
was never so talkative; it was the delirium, the putrid flame
eating at the inside of his mouth. Talking made it worse but in
his frame of mind suffering in silence was intolerable. Much
of what he said was incomprehensible.

He would hear planes flying overhead and this would trigger the business with Moll again. The planes he heard were
not flying in or out as the strip had been lost to the Russians
months ago. They continued to fly over Cholm and drop supplies by parachute, which now mostly landed outside the remaining five-square-block perimeter. The Russians fought
savagely to take possession of them, not so much to deny
them to the defenders but because they prized the goods contained in the supply bombs. The Russians themselves were
nearly starving much of the time and had almost nothing in
the way of medical supplies, though the defenders in their
own predicament were scarcely aware of this even after a
few prisoners said as much.

Then sometimes Russian deserters came over to their
lines, who said the same thing. It made a strange impression
on the defenders, to see men deserting and coming over to
their tiny encircled perimeter. How bad could it be out there,
if men were willing to desert and come over to them, trapped
like rats inside this place? Scherer ordered food distributed
to them, and set them to carrying supplies and ammunition
from one part of town to another, to the different strongpoints, and the Russians obeyed with a strange sunny grate-
fulness. Was it sincere? It seemed to be; but who really
knew. . . . Few prisoners were taken anyway, and some of
them were shot in unobtrusive corners by men who followed
their own grudges rather than Scherer's orders. The deserters
also were few, but still they continued to come over, now and
again, as the weeks and months went past; and these men
wandered freely about the town, with no guard set over them,
eating what the defenders ate. Nor did Scherer refuse food to
the few civilians left inside the town. The last hanging had

been months earlier and since that time there had been no more shooting into the backs of his soldiers.

In night dreams or sick shifting daydreams Kordts revisited these events, like different rooms opening briefly in his mind that he might revisit now and again. He remembered one hanging on a clear razor day, and another one, when clouds had come in driving snow around the intense stares of the condemned. This had been the last one, he thought, after Baer and the jaeger sergeant had been shot. The low clouds came in like solid things, too dead and grim even to bear snow, but then finally snow began to blow around them just before the five people were dropped from the platform in the main square. They had it coming to them, he thought, and if any of them were up there by mistake, well by God all of them were in this cold evil place by mistake anyway, and all just as likely to die sooner or later. For one who so clearly despised the war, he felt strangely little pity for civilians. Many of the defenders and most of their stubborn enemy were hardly more than boys who may have hated their own suffering but accepted it as part of the incomprehensible course of things, just as they accepted their jobs and difficult routine destinies in civilian life; war was not a normal everyday thing but when it came then it became a normal everyday thing, and most only accepted it and resented it in a normal everyday fashion, and in such dire circumstances as these even kept up their courage with ordinary obliging stoicism. No matter how bad things got, weaklings, after all, were only faggots, no different than it was in civilian life, though they were all reminded of these truths more acutely out here. Kordts was not a weakling nor did he really have much political conscience about anything; he just had a clear kind of anger, an occasionally witty fellow though he did not say a whole lot normally. He was almost thirty. In fact the draft of the early years had swept up a great many fellows his age; it was only later in the years ahead, after they had all been killed or wounded or frozen, that the army would become a vast clearinghouse for even more ignorant teenagers or old men over forty.

On the platform was a miserable-looking hag, maybe not so old but just ugly. "Motherland!" she screamed into the driving silent snow. The man standing next to her looked like some entirely innocuous peasant, no crafty-looking devil at all but seeming to ruminate sheepishly upon his mistake of getting caught, as if he were standing before a country judge for some foolish offense such as raiding his neighbor's chicken coop. And now blandly and sheepishly accepting that he would die for it.

Next to him stood a boy perhaps thirteen years old. It seemed that these Russian children starting from about age six all looked the same, more honest and sane than their elders yet still wise to things somehow, oddly capable-looking in a way that you never saw in German children or in any other children Kordts had ever seen. Yet inevitably they must at some point become mad or cruelly devious or half-witted when they grew older, as Kordts had never seen adults in this country who in any way resembled their children.

Scherer was there, morose, remorseless, a captain taking it upon himself to quell mutiny once and for all. Kordts had no idea how these people had been caught; the first time around there had been sniper-scopes and radio equipment, and maybe it was the same again, but he didn't know.

The hag looked as if she was about to speak again but the executioner dropped them and they dangled. The snowfall swirled around them and shrouded them, as if they were to be interred in this vertical position.

On the platform, the scaffold, was already nailed up a placard bearing the pronouncement of their crimes and a stern warning to others against any future crimes. The defenders, the Germans, were so used to seeing notices of this kind in their homeland, not warning of penalty of death necessarily but simply notices of regulations concerning every conceivable kind of human activity, posted on street corners or in train stations or on the walls of factory machine shops or barracks or lavatories, or in fine print on the papers and passbooks they all carried, that they never really grasped the loathing these notices evoked among the natives of the land.

The lettering was always perfect and the list of restrictions that could incur penalty of death was always highly detailed. It was the clerical precision of it all that was the most German and thus the most revolting, these placards somehow becoming the embodiment of the German presence and more provocative than the Germans themselves. If they had simply hanged people without posting these regulations everywhere it might not have stirred so much outrage.

Later, not at Cholm but elsewhere, denuded bodies of the conquerors would be found with similar notices meticulously carved into their naked backs. The conquerors never really put it all together though, as such carefully crafted mutilation was only one small variation in an amazing range of different mutilations practiced by the vengeance-addled natives and soldiers of the land.

Snowfall, blizzards, strange patches of light up in the sky backlighting circling JUs. They had to fight to collect the supply bombs one day, in the Lovat River. The frozen surface of the river was the drop zone. The ice was covered with fallen snow and the Lovat was like a naked valley threading through the town, a voidlike sunken white zone bereft of the black ruins and wreckage and shattered trees that lay everywhere else.

The bombs floated slowly down through strange patches of light and then further down into gusting snowflakes billowing up or falling from no one knew where. Small groups of defenders scurried out from their own bank hoping the snowfall would obscure them from the Russian guns which commanded much of the bank opposite. The bonesaws rattled out overhead to give them cover while they tried to drag the bombs back as quickly as they could.

Freitag pointed out one parachute coming down into a little cove and they struggled toward that place where they would be less exposed to fire. But to get there they had to clamber over a little thumb of land sticking out from the opposite bank and as they did this they were taken under fire anyway. They lay in the snow. Both of them had suffered frostbitten feet on the march from Lake Seliger, still unhealed, and to lie in the snow was hard to bear. Only tension and frenetic activity could make you forget the endless cold and the endless pain. For many minutes they lay in the snow with bullets coming close by. They were tense but they could no longer move. For a while the force of adrenaline continued to augment their circulation like a kind of pulsing body-suit that insulated them from the intense physical suffering. But as they continued to lie there the adrenaline wore off and they felt the throbbing in their feet and the cold everywhere.

They began to weep. They listened closely to the rattle of the bonesaws and during a prolonged burst they both moved off again. They grunted from the pain as they put weight on their feet again and both staggered at once, not quite falling, shambling down the other side of the little thumb and into the cove.

A lone Russian was there cursing at the supply bomb and pounding at the lid with a bayonet. They rushed him and stumbled over the blowing folds of the parachute but still had their weapons in his belly before he could react. Freitag took the goat's leg propped against the supply bomb and Kordts took the bayonet. Kordts then tried to unlatch the lid but the latch was frozen or seized up and he commenced cursing at it and pounding and prying at it with the bayonet. The Russian stood there and snorted through his nose, a quiet involuntary spasm from a man otherwise petrified. Kordts began weeping again as he had been a few minutes before.

"Never mind opening it," said Freitag. "We'll just pull the whole thing back to our side."

Kordts cursed and said it was too heavy, though perhaps it wasn't. They both looked back toward the white highway of the river to see if any of their people were coming up to help them. They couldn't see around the end of the cove; the snow was blowing harder and they couldn't see much anywhere. Kordts began beating at the hatch again, enraged, frightened, in pain, and frustrated—obsessed with the idea that if he could get the lid open he could steal a package of cigarettes from the innards of the thing and have a smoke to calm himself. A stock of cigarettes was always loaded in these things, always.

At last he got it open and peered inside. But there were different bags and boxes and he couldn't make out what anything was. His innards were boiling with near-hysteria and he no longer felt the cold.

"Let's go, Gus! Let's go! The Ivan will help us pull. Come! Come on!"

Kordts clenched his teeth and widened his eyes, feeling his own idiocy. Freitag was shaking his shoulder and Kordts looked about to see that Freitag had already cut the chute away and it was blowing slowly toward the river, flopping like some kind of disembowelment tossed aside from a killed beast. The Russian was holding one of the harness lines, somewhat less frightened-looking. He took one last glance and spied an oblong carton wrapped in brown paper and pulled it out, fumbling, throwing the wrapping on the snow. So he had his cigarette and now Freitag had to have one too. His teeth chattered with the thing in his mouth and he inhaled deeply and got them to stop. He felt sane and relaxed and somewhat diffidently observed this wave of sanity passing through him just as the other things had passed through him a few seconds before. They both looked around with cannier eyes and saw no sign of their own people or other Russians. The snowfall was shielding them pretty well.

"All right, let's go."

"You're a stupid bastard," said Freitag with relief, almost admiration, as he had long had trouble putting his finger on what it was he liked about Kordts. The Russian held part of the harness and they took up the rest of it.

"Here," said Kordts.

The Russian took the proffered smoke and relaxed still further, equally from seeing that he would not be killed on the spot and from seeing that he would be able to have a smoke. A lifetime passed by almost tolerably during ten or fifteen seconds of satisfaction.

Kordts saw the dull relieved smile on the man's face and thought how amusing it would be to shoot him in the belly with the smoke dangling from his lips. He had felt particularly depressed all day even before this had started and he hadn't the slightest urge to kill anyone. But he could not help it if such thoughts passed through his mind.

They could no longer see their own side of the river but the distance was not that far. Apparently the rest hadn't forgotten about them after all. They had pulled the bomb almost to the other bank when shadows appeared and now ten men hurriedly dragged the thing toward the perimeter. Snow was falling. Kordts looked around and saw the Russian running away, seeming almost to swim. Kordts stood holding the harness and said nothing.

"What are you doing?" said someone.

Someone else saw the Russian now and shot him down a little way off, out in the river.

"So. Maybe they're not so eager to join up with us anymore," another man said.

"No, I think Kordts scared him," said Freitag, not believing this but muttering it with a laugh because he felt like it.

The man lay out in the falling snow, a body, a log, anything at all, soon to be covered over.

The incident was insignificant, as were their comments. They hurried on, then had to toil hard to get the supply bomb dragged up the bank on their side. The bank was high and steep; it took almost as long to do this as all the rest of the operation. Kordts and Freitag were given a few hours off duty for their efforts. The manifests inside the supply bombs accounted for everything down to the last piece of cracker and Ohlsson reprimanded Kordts for breaking into the cigarettes. Then he sent him on his way and no more was said.

For weeks then his feet had gotten to where he could hardly feel them, a relief of sorts except for the nagging worry that he might be crippled permanently. All of them worried about that, their feet, their hands, noses. Even the genitals of some of them, and they were among the most pathetic cases. The slash in his cheek distracted him from his other suffering. When the weather grew warmer in April he began to feel his feet again and it was not pleasant.

The worst of it passed after a few days, but then his feet began to itch like his facial wound. Unable to scratch his face without torturing himself, he took out his frenzy by clawing at his feet. He continued to do so while laid up in the GPU, scarcely aware of what he was doing much of the time, like a madman endlessly repeating some obscure compulsion. It was gratifying to feel long shreds of his skin peeling away, clinging under his fingernails, as other men found it gratifying to endlessly crush lice and fleas between their thumbnails. Just to have his boots off his feet was a great pleasure; he could claw at his feet whenever he wanted to, which was seemingly all the time. In feverish moments he would stare at his feet like a man finding mysterious patterns in tattered wallpaper, which they much resembled, mottled red and white and yellow in vague blurs of color, and the peeling skin hanging off them. His toenails grew at odd angles like bad teeth and he also enjoyed peeling an entire nail away from time to time; he was observing one day that he had six of them left when someone spoke to him.

"Nice scar. You must be the one they meant."

Kordts didn't understand a word of this, partly because the accent was strange, but also he was dazed. He recognized that he was being spoken to and that it wasn't Moll or himself talking to Moll.

He peered at a seemingly healthy man sitting on a stool by the wall.

"My face is killing me. Give me some more of that morphine or whatever it is."

"Ask the doctor. He told me you were the worst complainer in here."

"Nonsense," said Kordts. "I just like to shout at him, that's all. It isn't whining."

He didn't know if he believed this but he didn't like being accused to his face. He could only remember a few of his tirades, but those few he could remember well enough.

"The wheel that squeaks gets the most grease, eh?" said the stranger. A Latvian accent, that's what it was. It came out sounding like the kind of gibberish Kordts was used to hearing from the other semiconscious men around him.

He stared at the man for a moment, then said, "*Ja, ja,* and that's nonsense too. With the medical profession it's just the opposite. The wheel that squeaks the most gets tossed in the corner to die. They take vengeance on complainers, I know it. I just don't care. My face is killing me. So you're not a *sani*. What are you doing here?"

"Yes, for days my bowels have been running down my legs like a river. Still, it isn't so bad, I suppose. They've got me watching for Ivans out the windows."

The Latvian had a goat's leg set across his knees. His knees were bare, his legs were bare. His only garments seemed to be a finely tailored greatcoat and a soiled shirt underneath it.

"Yeah, they had me doing that. . . ." Kordts couldn't even remember how long ago it was, the first time he had been laid up in this place. It seemed like a long time ago. "The first time. I was still able to stay on my feet, that time."

"I left a trail of shit all across the room, ha, ha, but I got one. Just yesterday."

Kordts heard this clearly but he didn't know what the man was talking about. It hurt his face to keep up conversation and he let it pass. The man's rubelike singsong reminded him of a Swede. The Latvians sometimes seemed like hayseeds but they also seemed less distressed by this ordeal than the Germans, which gave them a certain cockiness. Maybe it was just because they hated the Russians so much. Or because they were used to living in these stinking winters.

"Nice coat," mumbled Kordts.

"Hm. Yeah, yeah, nice."

Kordts was studying the man's almost foppish overcoat and his peculiar direct way of staring back at him. His mind went blank. He was tired and wretched.

"Yes, you know, your company sergeant told me off. Can you imagine it? He said it's unmilitary to wear a coat like this. Does he want me to hang it in a closet and have someone steal it? I had it made specially in Riga when I got my commission. I was a lieutenant in the Latvian army and a German sergeant tells me it's unmilitary. To hell with him."

Kordts laughed in spite of himself. It was good to have someone to talk to for a few minutes and he wished he felt better. But it was hard to think of anything.

"Well, that's the way they are," he said finally. He didn't know which company sergeant the man meant but he could imagine it well enough. He said, "You've got shit on it, you know."

He would have laughed again but a wave of nausea swam across his face. He would not have known before this that a man's head could feel nauseated just as bad as his belly, or even worse.

"Ah, yes, well." The man raised the goat's leg and flicked nonchalantly at his coat, though not touching the faint shit stains on the tails dangling behind his legs. The man had a kind of naive princely dignity which Kordts might have found ridiculous or maybe even enjoyed, depending on his mood; but he was fading away again and he couldn't think anything about it.

One day he roused himself to peer through one of the boarded windows. Some of the other less badly hurt men were peering out also. It was another bright day and Kordts was so used to the dimness in the place that he could only blink for a moment. Then he saw some men out in the square and he noticed Scherer down there, the bearded general, having a lively talk with a man in a white helmet and white snow-cape. They looked like Arabs, the defenders did, a bunch of sheiks running around in flowing white robes, and some of them with their snow-capes banded up around their helmets like burnooses. A lively talk down there, yes, they really were on to something; it was startling. Suddenly Scherer put his arms around the other man and embraced him, thumping his hands on the man's back, and the other one had tears running down his cheeks, his face red. He was a grizzled, lantern-jawed old fellow; he looked almost older than Scherer. My God, thought Kordts, it's over. That must be it. Look at them. My God, they must have got through to us.

He tried to concentrate, looking around at the others in the foul second-story room, hesitant to speak.

"My God," someone else said.

"What is it?"

"Has help come?"

"They've lifted the siege."

"No."

"Ah, Jesus."

A murmur of voices, men crowding around the windows, scarcely believing what they were saying, the words repeated as they were passed from one set of lips to another. Someone roared with laughter. From deeper back in the dimness an indescribable moan came from a straw pallet; it wasn't anguish, it was indescribable.

Yet it was all for nothing. It turned out to be only Captain Bikers.

"For God's sake, you idiots, it's only Bikers. Don't you recognize the man?"

"Who?"

"Bikers. Captain Bikers. The siege, the siege, the devil take it. We'll be cornered here till Judgment Day."

Some of them knew this Captain Bikers, who apparently was only another one of them. The captain stood speechlessly down in the square, staring at Scherer with tears of joy—it looked like that—shining on his face. They could see that the Knight's Cross was dangling from his neck on its long ribbon, hanging in the folds of his snow-cape like a religious medallion. There came the sound of clapping and a few ragged cheers from down in the square.

Ah God, thought Kordts. Yet the man's expression in the bright sun was so remarkable that he could not help but be moved. Scherer also looked very strange. Kordts felt another wave of delirium, letting go of the brief dizzying surge of hope yet scarcely aware of it.

The other wounded too seemed to come to their senses before disappointment could really befoul their minds. Probably none of them had really quite started to believe it; and then it turned out to be something else, after all. Yet it was a strange sight, Scherer clasping the man in a bear hug, beaming at him like . . . like you couldn't say what. . . .

A week later Bikers was killed, only a few days before the end.

That night—not after Bikers had been decorated by Scherer, Kordts could scarcely remember when that had been—but after his conversation with the Latvian, he awoke to see this same fellow standing over him, his face illuminated in ragged cracks and fractures by a sudden burst of light from outside the boarded window. At first Kordts could not remember when he had seen this man before; then he did remember as the man lifted the goat's leg and fired a burst out between the cracks. The noise struck like a knife working even deeper into his cheek and he jerked his head aside moaning, blinded from the muzzle flash.

Kordts was frightened and thought he had better pull himself together, but he could not do so right away, nearly gagging from the pain. There were two thumps against the window boards that he knew instinctively were grenades tossed from outside; quickly two sharp cracks followed against the wall of the building below. There was shouting and now other armed men were in the room with the Latvian firing down at the street below. Light from another flare pierced into the room; either the Russians were lighting up the building or more likely the defenders were trying to light up the Russians who must be crawling around outside. In the ghastly light he caught a glimpse of the Latvian jumping over wounded men and running to another window, his funny coat swinging from his shoulders and his naked legs the same pale shock color as everything else in the room. He fired again from another window where two or three other men were also firing. A bonesaw blurred out from somewhere below and grenades went off in a blur of crumps and flashes. The room went dark again except for gunfire—light, streamers, multicolored things. Kordts thought of trying to move but he did not know where to go. Then his head was roaring and all he could think of was to try not to vomit.

The other sick and wounded, all of them in there, were mostly silent. A few other men tried to rise, to flee to some other part of the building or to see just what was happening.

Kordts was staring at the ceiling and felt that he was awake again; so he must have passed out for a moment. A few seconds, he didn't know. He saw that the Latvian was standing over him again, peering below but not firing. It was quiet. Kordts was about to say something when metal-shrieks and then explosions shook everything. The window boards flew in and the Latvian was somewhere in the middle of the room, screaming; others began screaming.

Kordts tried to crawl away from the now open gaping window. He had vomited and now felt this mess against his palms and tasted it in his mouth and knew, prayed, that he must feel a little better. He kept crawling. Something was burning, the roof, it was something overhead. *Sanis* and other people with flashlights came into the room and began trying to take out the wounded, on stretchers or sheets, or just carrying them. There was shouting from those still in there unable to move. Kordts knew he could move and so forced himself to his feet and with sudden energy lurched out into the hallway. The whole place was in an uproar. Heavy artillery, it came in again and the building shook again. He saw flames somewhere overhead, beams silhouetted, smoke from burning and the cordite reek just as strong.

"Watch yourself!" someone shouted, and Kordts didn't know who was being shouted at.

He could think only to get away from the flames and staggered down the stairs jostled by other people also descending. On the first floor he was met by a strong gust of air and gaped in disoriented fascination at the jagged mouth where the main entrance had been. He could see figures beyond out in the square. He curbed his immediate urge to flee the building realizing it might be suicidal. As for staying where he was he didn't know, but he just stayed where he was. There were still people inside running about in all directions, or striding with fiercely shouting calm. Suddenly he did not feel so bad and he crouched beside a collapsed mess of plaster and wood next to the stairs, ready to move again if he had to.

A door opened onto the first-floor corridor. Kordts stared warily but then didn't pay it too much attention with all the other commotion. A man walked past him. With dull shock he saw it was a Russian soldier. The Russian disappeared somewhere down the corridor. Kordts shrank back under the stairs and tried to remain still but he kept squeezing his hands against his forehead and then clasping and unclasping them.

Chapter Seven

5 May 1942. The one hundred and fifth day.

Two hundred miles north of Cholm, along the Volkhov River Front, it was not the Germans but the Soviets who were encircled. The Red Army was not well-enough organized to supply tens of thousands of men by airdrop. Even if such a thing had been attempted, it is likely that the transport planes would have been shot down in great numbers by the few German fighter planes in that area. As it was, a few supplies were parachuted haphazardly into the Volkhov swamps, a pittance for men whose brains were beginning to turn black from starvation.

As it was, the Soviets had one supply artery in a forest clearing—actually a series of parallel fire lanes—just west of the Volkhov River. This was the only way in or out for the men trapped in the Volkhov swamps. It was a miserable and hopelessly inadequate "road" jammed with derelict Soviet equipment. The Germans called it the *Erika Schneise* (which has no direct translation in English, though a timber fire-lane best conveys the idea).

The Germans had cut off the *Erika Schneise* at the end of March, thus completely encircling several Soviet armies. The German forces too were desperately weak though not starving. But the Russians fighting desperately had managed to reopen the road and keep it open through the month of April. It was not enough. The *Erika Schneise* was a mud track cut up by nearly nonnegotiable bogs, a tiny capillary that must feed a body of tens of thousands. And so the Russians continued to starve.

The Germans attacked again in May, through the insect-teeming bush-forest-swamp they called *die grüne Holle*—

the green hell—of the Volkhov. Even in English this phrase
has a familiar ring to it, popularized in films about explorers
lost in the Amazon jungles. The Volkhov was in fact a worse
place. Only two months earlier it had endured the polar temperatures that had swept across northern and central Russia
during one of the worst winters ever known. Now, in May,
the green life had come up in a sick lush explosion, and the
crazy trees and bushes grew among wide-spreading bogs
that erased almost every vestige of dry land. The drowned
earth became a vast ovary spewing out insects by the bil-
lions. The Germans waded about in mosquito netting draped
from their faces to their chests that made them look like
aliens stalking through a primeval world. The Russians had
no such niceties and were eaten alive while continuing to
starve.

Finally the dismal capillary flow along the *Erika Schneise*
was reversed. The Russians could not be supplied and so the
trapped men began to escape, skeletons fleeing through the
fever-growth back to their own territory on the other side of
the Volkhov. When the Germans attacked in May they succeeded in cutting off the *Erika Schneise* for the second and
final time. It took another two months, until the beginning of
July, before the last of the enemy were killed or taken prisoner in those remarkable swimming forests. No one there
would ever forget this place, just as almost no one in the outside world would ever know of it.

Almost everywhere else, however, it was the Germans who
had been encircled during the course of the Soviets' winter
offensive along the entire length of the Eastern Front. They
had been surrounded at Cholm, and they had been surrounded at many other places. When before had a great army
been under siege in so many different places, across a front
that stretched for thousands of miles?

South of the Volkhov swamps, receiving the spated flow
of the Volkhov River, lay Lake Ilmen. South of Lake Ilmen
lay Demyansk. Around Demyansk ten German divisions
were cut off and besieged concurrently with the siege at
Cholm. This area was much larger than Scherer's one square
mile perimeter in the Cholm rubble. The Demyansk pocket

was a small nation covering nearly a thousand square miles, though likewise under attack from every direction, and likewise supplied ceaselessly from the air by the long, low-flying strings of JU-52s. At least these planes were always able to land and take off at the Demyansk air strip, which lay secure deep in the heart of the siege ring. An attempt by Soviet parachute units to seize the airfield in a surprise raid failed miserably in the blizzards. Meanwhile, on the outside, an undermanned German relief force had been attempting for months to break through to the Demyansk pocket. On 20 April 1942, Hitler's birthday, they succeeded, crossing the flooded Lovat River in rubber boats and linking up with the exhausted defenders.

At Cholm meanwhile, Scherer's men, their numbers by now reduced to a few thousand souls, continued to be supplied by parachute drop. At last two antitank guns were dropped within Scherer's tiny perimeter. Most of the supplies continued to drift down outside the siege ring, greedily anticipated by the Russians.

The Lovat River also flowed through Cholm, which lay in the middle of nowhere about seventy miles southwest of Demyansk, which also lay in the middle of nowhere. The Russians besieged these places with enormous armies that they could barely keep supplied in the desolate land, and so the Russians also suffered terribly.

In fact by 5 May, and perhaps for some weeks before then, they were just about at the end of their tether, having tried ceaselessly, horribly, and unsuccessfully for one hundred and five days to reduce the German stronghold at Cholm. For all these months the nearest point of the German main line had been only ten miles away, yet there had simply been no forces available to break through to Scherer's garrison. Hitler had ordered Scherer's people to hold out to the last man, as if the fate of the nation depended on them, yet Cholm was a tiny and probably doomed place that lay at the very bottom of German relief priorities, which were already stretched to the breaking point at so many other embattled places across the seemingly endless country of their enemy.

On 5 May only a single assault gun, one of the turretless tanks that often performed more critical service than tanks, was on hand to support the relief column—smaller than a regiment—to Cholm. They struggled through a peculiar landscape. During the month of April the spring thaw had come, a yearly occurrence in Russia that nonetheless was one of the world's more momentous climatic events. The entire country from the Black Sea to the Baltic was bogged and flooded, this ordeal following immediately upon the more familiar terrors of the Russian winter. No movement was possible at this time, though in fact some movement was attempted by both of the brave, determined, pigheaded combatants. The Russians attempted to supply the Volkhov pocket along the flooded *Erika Schneise*, failing utterly. The Germans attempted to break through to the Demyansk pocket beyond the flooded Lovat River, and they succeeded in this only at the cost of heartbreaking spiritual and mental suffering to the men involved. Meanwhile, at Cholm, there was still no attempt made to break through to Scherer's men across the endless mud fields—fields of mud, seas of mud. . . .

Yet by 5 May the thaw had ended, the mud had at last dried and hardened, and so the relief column escorted by a single assault gun had struck out across a peculiar landscape. In only a week or two the spring growth would erupt here, yet on this day the land remained utterly barren, the trees naked, the sky naked, the ground naked. The snow was all gone, and the flooding was gone, and the mud was gone. The relief column struggled forward across a hard brown plain, raising cold dust in temperatures that were still cold. On this day the land looked as stark as the surface of a deserted planet, and the trees looked lifeless as if they had always been that way, and there was a kind of grim ugly purity to all this, as if the earth were only some solid counterpart to the pure, dull sky above. The scene looked permanent somehow, dust and hard earth spread out thus forever, even if it was a false permanence and the land would be wild with green life only a week or ten days later. But this was the way it appeared the day the siege was finally lifted.

An understrength company from Scherer's garrison broke out of the town to link up with the relief column. A few months earlier the Russians would have smashed such a paltry operation within hours. But they, even more so than the

defenders, were at the end of their tether and could do little
to stop the two groups from linking up out on the brown
plain, along the road to Cholm.

The last Russian attempt to end the siege and terminate the
defenders had been on 1 May, May Day. They had fired off
almost all their remaining stocks of artillery shells in a
tremendous barrage that had inundated the town with dust
and nearly leveled the last solid structure remaining, the
GPU building. The GPU trembled in its cracked foundations
and the roof began to burn. The front face of the building
collapsed, burying the entrance, exposing the rooms inside.
Bikers was killed in this barrage, the man Scherer had embraced outside Kordts's window a month or so before. After
the barrage the Russians came in with their last men and
their last tanks, and the defenders held on for the last time.
By comparison it seemed almost quiet, five days later, when
the relief column crossed ten miles of dusty ground and
made contact with the company Scherer had sent out. It was
over now.

But it was never over. Cholm was only one name, one tiny
place. There were others. There had been others, there were
others, there would be others to come.

Fifty miles south of Cholm stood Velikiye Luki, ancient
stone town. The Lovat, forgotten river of sorrow, flowed
through this place as well. The Russian counteroffensive had
surged up to this point, its deepest penetration into German-
held territory, and back in January Velikiye Luki had nearly
fallen, just as Cholm and Demyansk and other places had
nearly fallen. Velikiye Luki, however, was never entirely
surrounded, though it had been touch and go for many
weeks.

As at Cholm, desperate frozen nearly broken men with no
winter clothing had retreated from all points of the compass
into Velikiye Luki, hounded and frequently overrun by the
Russian offensive, which was in fact the single largest counterattack against an invading enemy in the history of warfare. The disorganized units and demoralized stragglers from
the front lines were met here by parts of the 83rd Infantry
Division, which along with a number of other divisions had

been transferred from France to the Eastern Front in January to help stem what appeared to be an impending catastrophe. The 83rd was obliged to disperse its regiments over a wide area, as there were no other available units to hold this territory. Thus, while one regiment was stationed in Velikiye Luki itself and fought back the Russian spearheads right on the outskirts of the town, the other regiments were marched out to smaller villages in the outlying wilderness. One of these villages was Velizh.

The Russians surrounded this place and for three weeks in February part of 83rd Infantry Division was trapped in Velizh. It was the same cruel scenario as everywhere else, a great frozen fugue derived from only a single theme. At last a relief column broke through to the defenders of Velizh at the end of February, and so the ordeal of these men was of shorter duration.

But time is a misleading concept—or relative, as we say in modern times. To be surrounded for three weeks in subzero temperatures with Russian tanks constantly breaking into the middle of the town and driving the perimeter back and back upon itself was to endure a peculiar and irrefutable eternity no different from the one at Cholm. Velizh, though, was one of these miserable ramshackle places built almost entirely of wood, if one must visualize it there. The defenders were burnt out of one shoddy wooden isba after another. The wounded were kept in one of the few stone buildings in the town center, in the cellar; and as this place was less massively built than the GPU at Cholm, Russian shells sometimes drove through right into this cellar, with terrible results.

Then after three weeks of this another of the 83rd's regiments broke through to Velizh, and the siege was over.

The experience of time being relative, one might say that the three-week siege of Velizh was hardly different at all from the three-month, three-and-a-half month, siege of Cholm.

The only undeniable difference was that on 27 February 1942, the relief column fought its way into the first black burnt-out snow-drowned timbered houses of Velizh and the ordeal came to an end, while simultaneously at Cholm the ordeal continued to go on and on.

Even so, around Velizh and Velikiye Luki, the violence continued very much unabated, going on and on like the winter itself. Then spring came, the mud came, and it continued still. Even after the siege was lifted, the supply road to Velizh was precarious and very much in peril, flanked for long stretches by deep forests heavily occupied by the Russians.

In the spring the men of the 83rd set about operations to clear out some of these forests. On Easter Sunday the Kamenka Wald was taken in a bitter fight. A few weeks later, on 5 May, Sergeant Schrader and his platoon were engaged nearby in the Kasten Wald, a generic term meaning "Box Forest" that was used to identify small patches of woodland all over northern Russia. They were more or less box-shaped, a few square miles in area, a space large enough to hold many unknown terrors, which the Germans nervously anticipated whenever they approached these trees from the more open and barren terrain outlying them.

Generally they were not taken under fire during their approach. To avoid detection by the German artillery spotters, the Soviet bunkers of earth and heavy beams would be emplaced some hundreds of yards back into the forest, well-camouflaged there. The Germans were much afraid of these woodlands. A sense of danger is founded in some ways upon a sense of orientation, and in familiar, open country one generally has a sense of where danger is coming from; in the deep woods this sense is lost, as the men could be taken under fire from anywhere at any time, from very close range as often as not.

Also, one tended to get isolated in the thickets. Schrader's platoon of fourteen men was not operating alone but they had lost sight of the other platoons advancing on their flanks. Schrader had enough to do making sure that no one in his own crew strayed out of sight. Some of them still wore whitewashed helmets from the winter, as if even now they anticipated one last snowfall. It was not unlikely. But mostly it was because a few were lazy bastards and their white helmets stood out like little ghosts head-high in the green scraggy pines. Schrader knew this was his own responsibility but his platoon had only been told of the attack an hour before the start-time and so now here they were.

When the firefight started his men sank as one into the undergrowth. Schrader could only see the two or three nearest to him. The groans of whoever had been struck were loud and full of terror. Another man crawled up to Schrader to say who it had been, plus another killed instantly. Schrader cursed, hating it in here as much as any of the others.

Some moved among tree roots and tried to make themselves small. Others in a frenzy, a rage, were firing back, though their bolt-action rifles were next to useless for laying down a field of fire when no individual targets could be seen. Schrader had the only Schmeisser, and Krabel a goat's leg, and they fired a few bursts at waist level into the gloom, hoping to keep the concealed enemy's heads down.

It was impossible to know anything. Some of them began flinging grenades though they still could not ascertain how far away the gunfire was. But it was better to hurl out as much metal as possible; there was always the chance of hitting something, or frightening the ambushers away, or at least preventing them from firing back for a few moments.

It was the machine-gunner who had been wounded and now still cried from somewhere in the thickets. Someone else carried the 34 and the belts up to where Schrader was and he took it upon himself to man the thing, handing his Schmeisser to someone else to use.

He was firing. Ten or twenty seconds passed. He said, "All right, cease fire! Cease fire! Save your ammunition!"

Schrader let off a few more bursts with the machine gun. Then he laid off and an unnerving quiet fell like an ax, except for the hurt man. In these few minutes they had probably already exhausted half the deadly metal they carried with them. Hopefully the other platoons on their flanks would be drawn to the scene. For a few moments a keening silence pierced their ears like noise itself; and there were the strange moaning sighs of the pine boughs in the breeze or any gust of air, like silence moaning quietly in the all-around of the atmosphere up in the treetops. Then they heard another racket from some other part of the forest, gunfire, grenade crumps, the same business, off in the distance.

The Russians directly in front of them began firing again. Schrader had a better idea of where they were now, more or less. About a hundred yards away, and as long as his men stayed under cover the danger was not as great. Unless, of course, there were other guns even closer now waiting in silence. He cursed automatically, thinking and observing all the while. He called Krabel over.

"Crawl up a ways and see what you can see. If you can take care of it yourself then take care of it. Otherwise come back and tell us where it is."

"Why these jobs, Rolf?"

"Do you want me to hold your hand?"

"Sure, why not."

Schrader had no patience for making light of things; Krabel would be putting himself in danger, so he could make light of it if he wanted to. They were interrupted as some of the others began to fire again. Schrader let them fire.

"Take as many grenades as you can carry. Here."

He gave Krabel two of his. The man next to Schrader feeding the belt drew out two of his, though still keeping one for himself.

"All right, all right. That's plenty," said Krabel. He spent a moment finding different places on his person to secure all the explosives. He tightened his belt. He moved off holding the goat's leg with his other hand free.

"Tell them he's out there," Schrader said to the man next to him. "Aim high."

Schrader fired a few short bursts, watching where Krabel had gone.

The undergrowth was a pale hysterical green, as yet growing only sparsely in days and nights that were still cold. A few white flowers, trillium. The lowest pine branches hung low to the ground, like archways sagging from great age and decrepitude. The Russians had ceased fire and Krabel felt a quiet clench of fear around his entire person as he moved. About a hundred yards ahead, about what Schrader had estimated, it all came into focus. The way a confused green tangle stretching deep and yet depthless in all directions will suddenly focus into a discrete and recognizable scene, once recognition comes. Krabel bit his lips. The thing, now that he saw it, was oddly visible with the trees around suddenly seeming spaced a little further apart. It was a low mound covered with some new growth but also racks of dead branches and other debris. Somewhat to his relief the occupants of the bunker began firing again and he could see the muzzle flashes.

He collected himself for a moment before he began to work his way up and around it. From behind came the gunfire of his own people. He withdrew a stick grenade, clenching it and then setting it down, wiping his palm against his trousers and then gripping it tightly again by the wooden handle. The bunker was about fifty feet ahead and when he had advanced in a crouch and sometimes on hands and knees about half that distance, he was fired on from somewhere else close by. He could hear branches snapping and in a spontaneous panic he hugged the earth and flung the grenade as far as he could in this other direction. The instant it left his fingers he knew he had forgotten to prime it and instantly he withdrew two more and primed them and flung them after the first. He was still lying flat on the ground and they did not land very far off. The twin concussive waves blew over him.

The bunker gun was still firing and the gunfire from the other place picked up again. He shut his eyes—he had to for a second because his fear had turned the woods into a blur again. He opened them and nervously dragged his fingers across his cheek. The crotch of his trousers was damp, a normal and scarcely noticeable occurrence. With a deliberate flex of his jaw he unclenched his teeth, licked his lips. He studied what was around him, patience straining against the anxiety that blurred everything, until he began to recognize the way he had come. He began crawling back in Schrader's direction.

Chapter Eight

Schrader and Krabel, the rest of them . . . they would have lost all track of time. Sometime in the middle of the day. Or perhaps it was still morning.

It was early morning fifty miles to the north, when Kordts walked out. On 5 May he walked out of the skeleton of the GPU just as he had walked out five days earlier, the day after the roof had been set fire to, during the terrible night when the Russian had walked past him in the corridor. The Russian had disappeared into the darkness and confusion but Kordts could not rid himself of his fear, even when he saw a few of his own people moving in and out of the blasted main entrance or coming down the stairs. He stayed where he was through the night, through the shellfire, crouching in sickness and fear within the stairwell. At last at dawn he saw more people moving about and he sensed that no more Russians were inside the building. The shellfire had diminished. Still he was afraid to move and he had to tell himself he was being irrational before he could get up, fighting back the fear of being fired on if he startled someone. He walked out slowly toward the growing light of day beyond the entrance. Another man walked by him and went up the stairs and he began to relax. There were people out in the clear early light of the square and he walked out through the dangling womb cavity of the entrance.

There was no more snow. It had been melting before and now it was gone. There was no more mud. For weeks there had been mud in the streets, the streets nothing but mud. Now that was gone too. Now the street was dusty and there was dust carrying in the air . . . strange for dust to be carrying in the dew-heaviness of the morning. For an instant the

dust smelled even cleaner than dew might smell, and then he
was assailed by a sickening waft of death. He had become
used to bad smells, lying for so many days in the second-
story wards, but this overwhelmed him. The people out in the
square seemed to be ignoring it, but he had to back through
the entrance into the building again, feeling nearly pushed
there by a mass of putrid air. Lucky for him. It was then that
the shelling started again, the opening salvoes of May Day.

After so many months it was hard to judge anymore, if this
was the worst he had endured at Cholm, the worst any of
them had endured. The shellfire went on all day without in-
terruption, the GPU struck again and again as it had never
been before. At last the entire front wall collapsed. Kordts
was crouched in the stairwell again and felt his death descending upon him. His eyes were closed but he remained
conscious in disbelief, opening his eyes in further disbelief
after a while. He was able to crawl out from under collapsed
beams and planks. The entire forward face of the building
was exposed in a kind of ghastly diorama to the outside
world. He could see the Russian tanks out there; they were
the largest moving things and the first things to catch his eye.
They were near to the GPU but not quite right next to it; beyond the collapsed front wall was a field of craters, some of
them twenty or thirty feet deep. Men crawled about in them,
appearing and disappearing in smoke. They were German.
Wounded men who had lain on the second floor for days and
weeks, lying next to or near Kordts himself, now lay at the
bottom of these craters, having fallen out or been blown out
when the building collapsed.

Kordts was ambulatory and throughout the day was only
intermittently aware of the agony in his face. He was aware
of it when violent blasts of air and grit struck his face, his
cheek seeming to rip and flap like a flag. Thus he nearly
passed out several times. But he never did and was otherwise
too distracted by the shelling or other wild bursts of activity.
He had no weapon and somebody gave him one from a dead
man. He didn't see any use in a rifle and began to look for
grenades among other dead, though once he had collected a
few he thought of little except trying to stay low, although
there seemed nowhere to go, nowhere to hide. The GPU was

opened up, disemboweled, and seemed to offer no shelter at
all though men continued to look for it among the ruins; so
did Kordts, with little hope now but he did not know what
else to do.

Part of the second floor still remained. Survivors among
the wounded screamed for help from up there. Those who
could move at all had long since fled. Even while the shelling
continued parties of men tried to rescue the others trapped up
there, trying to carry them off to other nearby ruins, cellars,
shell-holes, anywhere. It was a nightmare, too noisy and confusing to really register on Kordts's or anyone's mind, except
in certain ways.

Scherer moved his own command post to another location,
from which he could reestablish communication with the
other sectors of the perimeter, leaving Bikers in command at
the GPU. Kordts knew nothing of any of this, though he did
see Scherer at some time during the day; he saw the general
and some other men doing something for a moment and that
was all he could remember. The day was long. It was the beginning of May and already the days were long in the northern world. Kordts had been kept out of the light of day for a
long time and the light was ongoing and everywhere, infernal with dust and vibrations. Beyond the crater-field individual men were taking on Russian tanks. A few antitank guns
that had been dropped by the JUs during the last days fired on
the Russian tanks. All of it, the entire day, was like the last
convulsion, the end of everything, dust choking the besieged
tombs of the pharaohs and burying them forever.

Yet it was only a day, and then the day passed into night.
The worst of it was over by then. Then the night passed into
the following day. It was quieter. And so they might think
that it was only another terrible day that had just passed, and
that the siege would continue to go on forever. They could
not think it was the last day, or the last days.

It was the evening of the following day, the day after the
May Day attack. The evenings were very long now. To Kordts
it seemed to have happened suddenly, the enormous extra
hours of a day. Men working in shirtsleeves, digging out
trenches that had been caved in and shoring them up with timbers, shattered tree limbs. Piling up blocks and debris to make

firing steps or higher parapets. Or looking about for wounded
men after yesterday, or finding the dead—German dead—and
collecting them for burial in a shell-hole; that was what
Kordts and his small crew of injured comrades were doing.

In May the dead were no longer carried in and laid in
frozen stacks upon the floor of a church. No, not any longer.
The thaw had come and gone.

A sobering task. Often the bodies in field grey would be
found alone or in twos or threes amongst larger scatterings of
Russian dead. The Russian dead would also be taken care of,
later—piled up and burnt, that is—if the lull in the attacks
lasted long enough to allow for this. Today had been quieter.
Shellfire, but less of it; not like yesterday's deluge. Still, shells
would come down not infrequently while the men worked,
adding more dead and wounded to the dead and wounded they
were already looking for, raising more clouds of dust. The sky
was dusty but it had a certain loveliness, in the evening, in the
strange long hours of warm air, of warm sunshine. There
would have to be a certain loveliness to any scene where there
was not terrible cold or knee-deep mud, even among the dead
and the ruins, which they were so used to anyway. But it was
not cold, and the filthy mud had dried up a week or two ago.
And the dust had almost a certain gentleness to it, suspended
inertly up in the quiet sky, or small eddies blowing along the
ground in a slight breeze, lifting up, settling down.

Large numbers of blackbirds chattered in wrecked trees,
as if there had been no violence here, or else it must have
happened a long time ago. Yesterday. What was yesterday?
Yesterday was tomorrow maybe; if the Russians attacked
again tomorrow. Today was quieter. In the days to come
numbers of other birds would arrive—large flocks of doves
sometimes, gathering about the shell-holes outside the town
where the churned soil had exposed seeds, things to eat, eyeballs for the crows, though mostly it was the tiny vegetable
parts turned up by the shelling that the large flocks would be
after. These other birds had not appeared just yet; there were
only the small blackbirds singing, chattering, in the wrecked
trees this evening, occasionally taking off and wheeling
about en masse in frightful reminiscence of the black shell
bursts of the day before.

Strange, that men working would see the birds explode from the trees and duck nervously, look about nervously before resuming what they were doing. But then again, any small noise or unexpected movement would jump their nerves that way.

They tried to steer away from the places that smelled the worst, hoping not to spy one of their own men among piles of rotting flesh, piles of the enemy for the most part. Anyway those were not yesterday's dead, which had not yet acquired time to stink. It was the older foulness that stank, and there was plenty of it around from weeks and months past, polluting the dusty spring softness of the evening.

Every so often shots would ring out, sniping, and the men would crouch down in shell-holes, behind blasted walls, glad for the opportunity to cease what they were doing, to stop working and just sit there for some minutes, their nerves ragged all the same, unless they were lucky enough to just be too tired, beyond all that, nothing.

A sobering task. Severed limbs. Viscera. Looking for bodies whole enough to be pulled out for collecting at a few designated places. There were eight men with Kordts in this detail, this crew of walking wounded, a few of the stronger ones pulling a cart about. They would take turns with a quiet democracy whenever something particularly hideous had to be dragged out of the stones. The sergeant overseeing this work limped along with the aid of a cane; he wasn't strict, more like an equal among the rest of them; the democracy of wounded men maybe, or maybe it had more to do with the work they were doing, humbling them all, more or less. They spoke little, occasionally let pass a few sick, quiet jokes, humor dry as the dust, matter-of-fact.

A Christly sky, thought Kordts, looking up at the quiet evening sky, raising his eyes from the drab littered earth. He didn't know what this meant; the words just passed through his mind; but he knew a Christly sky when he saw one, and he heard these words also just pass through his mind with almost a dim smiling flicker. He just looked up there for a moment. The warm low distant sun was shrouded with dust, so that it was not too bright to stare at for a moment. It was quiet. Shells had been falling, but the day had been long, and it seemed that no shells had fallen for a while now, for a half hour or maybe an hour. He recalled a few days from back in the winter, entire bright days that had passed by out in the snow walls, days without the slightest sign of activity, no shelling or other gunfire, as if the siege had been abandoned. And so it was quiet now but it was hard to think of the winter now. The winter was gone.

They worked back toward the interior of the perimeter—an oxymoronic locale, as the perimeter was so small now. There was really no place that could not be sniped at if an infiltrator managed to crawl in; it was not that hard to do. In many places there was no need for infiltrators; Russian snipers could sit at their leisure behind their own lines and see almost from one end of the siege ring to the other. So it was a dangerous and perhaps senseless task they were performing, risking themselves to find people already dead. But these Germans liked to find their dead if at all possible; it was something they did. Men, many of them pretty certain by now that they would not survive their long stay in this town, still had some odd wish that they would be found and put under the earth in some particular place. Such desires were confused, influenced by memories of simple and dignified birch bark crosses marking thousands of graves elsewhere in Russia; though they knew well enough that most of the dead here would be dragged together and tumbled into mass graves, into shell-holes and ditches. The time for niceties was long past, or else would come again in some unattainable future, attainable only in dreams.

But even Kordts did not rebel too much at this pointless-seeming work. He was apathetic and scatterbrained. His face, as badly infected now as it had ever been, did not bother him as much. Absentmindedly he saw some kinship between the living rot in his cheek and the dead rot they sorted through in the stones. And they did find a few who were not dead. Over the course of the day they had found and rescued several men who had been buried alive. They, the wounded crew of this detail, did not have the strength to clear much debris away; the sergeant in charge would start shouting, brace himself, and wave his cane in the air, and other men nearby would come over to help.

The faces of the unearthed men would be black with shock; their eyes empty yet granitic-looking, impenetrable for hours afterward. They were badly hurt too and they were taken away, to other shell-holes or cellars now open to the air, everywhere the wounded had been dispersed to after the collapse of the GPU building.

It was evening and they had covered as much space as they dared, within the siege ring. The dead out on the perimeter would have to stay dead where they were.

They circled back toward the GPU, approaching this ruin from the rear. The roof was gone and they could see through second-story windows up into the sky, through the several white stone window frames that still remained. Empty, rectangular sockets, eyed with the empty sky. They saw a few silhouettes of men still moving about up there, revealing themselves for only a second or two. They came to where they had left their weapons propped against a few foundation blocks in the lee of the building. They left their spades and picks propped against these same blocks and gathered their weapons, waiting to be told where they would be posted for the night.

Kordts saw Freitag, working with some other men to clear out a trench that ran from the GPU to somewhere out there . . . to other small strongpoints out there. He thought it was Freitag and peering more closely he saw that it was him; he hadn't seen him in over a month now. Still alive, Kordts thought mechanically. It occurred to him that Freitag was the only one left, out of the small group that had survived the walk from Lake Seliger to Cholm back in January. This notion popped into his head yet it also occurred to him that he didn't know if it was true or not; and he didn't have the energy to remember if anyone else from that group was still alive here, in Cholm. He remembered Moll being flown out, way back at the beginning of it all; but for the moment his mind could go no further. He looked at them digging out the trench and didn't see anyone else he recognized. He sat in the gaunt lee of the building and watched Freitag without the energy to go over and speak to him. In a minute, maybe. . . .

He sat there side by side with the other men of the burial detail, a few of them also staring dully at the activity in the trench. Freitag looked like a street urchin, his hair matted with dust, digging industriously, talking with a certain odd loquaciousness that Kordts could hear from where he was. They worked in their undershirts over there and looked like a crew of men repairing a railroad. One of them was leaning against the forward pile of the trench, steel helmet on his head, peering out toward wherever the Russians were, wherever they might be, a stick grenade in one hand, resting it against his knee. A few others lay sprawled in the bottom of the trench, off duty, trying to get a few minutes of rest, looking like the dead who were not dead, sleeping there, resting there, while the rest kept working a few feet to one side. Sleep, thought Kordts. One of these sleepers stirred where he lay, rolled over in the dirt, undershirt filthy, his face shaded by a filthy tunic crumpled over his head. Kordts stared at all this so listlessly that he might not have existed, his eyes no more than camera lenses with no soul behind them to receive or understand anything.

Freitag had noticed him and was shouting over at him. Kordts nodded and raised his hand. He started to say something but he couldn't shout that far; his face hurt too much to speak louder than a slurred whisper. He grinned stupidly and shook his head and pointed at his festering cheek, Freitag squinting back at him, probably not understanding. He set his shovel against the trench wall and started to make his way over to the building. One of the sleeping men sat up and shouted at him. Freitag looked back; then Kordts could hear them arguing. Stupid bastard, he thought. A dull disgust adhered to his lips, like a crust; no doubt it was there already. Ignore the bastard, he thought. Freitag was saying something heated. Kordts closed his eyes and the witless middle-distant yammering lulled him to the verge of sleep. A shell roared down. He heard it. He sat in the lee of the building and did not stir a muscle except for his belly muscles hunching up. It exploded. The earth shook, the stones shook, not too violently. He watched dust drifting slowly over the trench, drifting out from someplace nearby. The sleeping ones in the trench got up and the ones already working crouched down. The one with the steel helmet who had been looking out from there lay stiff, contorted. Not sleeping. The stick grenade

still dangling from his fingers. The one who had been arguing with Freitag now rolled this man down into the trench, at
the same time issuing a few more words to Freitag, whom
Kordts could see disappearing down the trench in the other
direction, scowling back angrily.

It was like the beginning of some dream. As if he were already asleep. He was sitting there still, against the foundations of the GPU, it might have been only an hour later, when
a hand shook him awake. It was dark. Kordts got up slowly
and picked up his weapon and followed the man into the inner holes of the ruin, defenders of Cholm. Loose things dangled from the window frames or other blasted gaps like
exposed nerves hanging down from broken teeth. They set
up to pass the night.

And so another night passed. A few days later it was over.

Kordts awoke from ugly sleep, festooned with nightmares
like disgusting lanterns hanging from the top of his mind. He
was still with this team of ambulatory wounded men, and
some of them also awoke beside him, still defending this
same eviscerated building. His cheek, maybe starting to heal,
had become infected all over again from the blast and dust
swirling about on that one day, May Day. But he could walk
and, the situation being what it was, he was a fighting man
again. He was almost beyond caring, though sadly a man
never reaches a point where the pain begins to desist and the
present goes away. On 5 May he did not walk out through the
main entrance, as it no longer existed; he walked out through
some part or other of the skeleton, seeing men standing
about and talking out in the dusty square just as he had seen
them five days before. He felt himself running in a nightmare, going nowhere, the same things repeating over and
over again, but he was entirely conscious and ill-tempered at
the advent of another day and paid these strange thoughts
only scant attention. There was something about their demeanor out there.

He skirted about some shell-holes, or crawled through
them. The same dust and the same force of rot hung everywhere. Many of those he was looking at out there were talking loudly or staring about crazily and strange sensations
suddenly passed through him, though he paid little attention

to these either. He had not seen a German armored vehicle in months and when he caught sight of the thing parked out in the square an instinctive paralysis froze him in his tracks. But then he seemed to walk right on through it, out of it. He walked on rather carelessly over there, beginning to understand now, maybe.

"What is it?" he said to the first man he came to.

"It's over."

"You're joking," said Kordts.

"No! No! No!" cried the other man hoarsely.

Tears came to Kordts's eyes which he tried to pinch away with his fingers, he didn't know why. A strange day had begun.

PART TWO

The Train

Chapter Nine

The train steamed through summer hills, normal passenger service of the Reich, city to city, the cars crowded with people.

All was as it had been before and as it should be still, everyday life, the twentieth century proceeding onward for a dozen centuries. The summer sun fell on green hills, steeping them in quiet as fruits would steep in subterranean jars.

The train passed through. Villages came and went. Stone places, stable, foundations settling inch by inch into the earth for centuries. And then larger places, towns and cities. These were still more astonishing, for they were filled to the point of bursting with people, all walking about or riding in trolley cars, ordinary and familiar.

The air raids had begun, but to this point there had been very few of them, and most cities had never seen the heavy bombers nor heard them either, droning overhead, nor heard the endless wails of the air-raid sirens; not yet. This was the era just before the beginning of the great air raids, and so everything was still unchanged. This was what the soldiers noticed.

The civilians seemed strangely unconcerned, almost as if there were no war. It was as if war and the fear of war had ended with the conquest of France and the expulsion of the British back to their miserable pigheaded island, two years before, and the feeling of relief and gratitude this had produced seemed still to persist. What was happening in Russia was an enormous and barely comprehensible thing that seemed as far away as the Pacific Ocean, which they read about in newspapers.

Deep down they might have worried, but this was too abstract and their worries were more mundane affairs related to their jobs and families, drinking and eating, going about their daily business.

Hitler—even while consumed with bringing war to distant regions of the earth—paradoxically fostered this notion that the war was essentially over, so that the German people might feel tranquility and also gratitude for his endeavors; and his people tended to believe this because they wanted to believe it, even amidst their own doubts.

There was a certain degree of food rationing. The British fleets blockaded the German ports while the U-boats blockaded the British ports. Nobody liked this, but all in all it was not that bad. Certainly it was nowhere near as bad as it had been during the first war, when the nation had nearly starved during the blockade then. The weekly newsreels sometimes displayed charts produced by the ministry of Herr Goebbels, which indicated how much more meat, fat, dairy products, and grains the average citizen was receiving than he had received during the starvation days of 1917 and 1918.

Apart from the rationing there was little to complain about, and seemingly much to take pride in. Millions of people, men and women, rose in the morning and went to work and then came home in the evening, and at night the great factories were mostly silent; as yet there was no round-the-clock wartime economy or other related travails.

Thus war was elsewhere, but the homeland was not at war. The soldiers observed all this.

Kordts and Freitag rode on the train, always a gay form of transportation aboard regular passenger cars rather than the straw-filled boxcars that had taken them to Russia. Beer was served and they drank as much as they wanted. They were on leave and frequently drunk and nobody seemed to take much offense. Officers, at least those who had served in the East, tended to look the other way or else were preoccupied by their own drinking; only once in a while did civilians look down their noses at the unruliness of people like Kordts and Freitag.

And even these two men, on leave from the foreign war, did not let themselves get too carried away. They were German and at least in their native towns and cities were not prone to excess.

They enjoyed themselves as much as possible, in part because they realized there was no real satisfaction in it. They drank and relaxed and tried to forget about that.

There were a lot of military personnel on the train, but most were on leave and scattered about among the even larger numbers of civilian passengers, who mostly treated the soldiers with quiet respect or sometimes with franker admiration. Those who thought the war was madness, or by now degenerating into madness, usually did not blame the soldiers, the young men, for what had happened. They kept their thoughts to themselves and went about their normal lives as other people did. The soldiers didn't mind being admired, though often it was strange and unsettling. There was much about being on leave that was strange and unsettling, though as best they could they tried to look to simpler pleasures. Alcohol, and much sleep and food; and then women, though it seemed women were still harder to get than they should be, though they would flirt more openly now. Most of the soldiers had forgotten how to deal with women or were too young to have ever learned it, and two weeks on leave was not long enough to learn anything, unless a woman simply gave herself without much in the way of complicated rituals. Sometimes that happened and a lucky man might bask in the glow of it, something to take with him back to Russia and shield his mind for a while from the dull and fearful existence there.

There were other soldiers on the train, not front fighters but those still stationed in the homeland or somewhere in Western Europe. These men tended to look like clerks wearing uniforms.

Married men would fuck their wives voraciously for a week or so, expelling pent-up energy; both husbands and wives starved for this, and then suddenly it would wear off, before their leaves were over. Somehow it didn't matter and they kept on eating and drinking and taking long walks in detached, almost dreamlike states through their hometowns or out in the country, staring curiously at things. Some were able to sleep in deep exhaustion throughout the whole time, while others gradually found they were not sleeping very well.

Kordts was not married but he had a girlfriend. Both he

and Freitag were from working-class backgrounds. He had a powerful attraction to this woman and when he came back she shared his feelings. That was good, almost intoxicating, like a powerful antibiotic cleansing sickness. Perhaps this would be a strange way of describing the force of love, but the deeper force of shock would alter the effects of other things that a man felt, or at least cast them in strange and different lights.

The ordeal at Cholm had had such a profound, untranslatable effect on him that he could hardly say he felt sick of it all anymore, the war, the officers, the military, even though he still was. But it was all too much somehow, and maybe that wasn't so bad for a while. His leave had begun earlier than Freitag's, a sick leave for his ugly face. But back home in a clean hospital the powerful drugs had worked pretty quickly, leaving only the scar. The relief in his face was almost as good as being away from the front lines, especially with a woman to see and no putrid hurt to distract either of them from that.

She had been very endearing about the wound; he had hoped she would be, known it really, but it was good to be with her and know it for sure. It felt so good to make love in clean, quiet surroundings that it purged a lot of things out of him, and he was certain he would carry this feeling back to the East with him. If he had to be killed he would just as soon not have to bear so much foulness around in his mind. To die with a few good memories . . . maybe his thinking was addled, but during those long weeks at home it seemed that a man could hardly ask for anything else—better to die with a few sweet memories at twenty-eight than to toil onward toward seventy. If Kordts had really thought about it he might cheerfully have conceded he was cracked, but he didn't really think about it, he didn't feel like it, and he simply accepted strange notions ticking in the back of his mind. At least, by God, they were not as unpleasant as he might have feared.

In fact once he got out of the hospital and went home he felt very good for a few weeks. Everything was beautiful and remarkably quiet and he seemed to absorb it all through every pore of his skin. It all took him by surprise somehow, and unlike some other men he was not troubled by too much dread as the days slipped away and the time to go back came nearer. Each separate day was like an island, a powerful fortress in fine weather. He felt stronger, less afraid and less hateful. It was fit and proper to go through a long terrible thing and then be rewarded with food and drink and a woman's love. He would never have said as much in just this way but he felt it regardless. In truth he was lucky to have such a woman.

The quiet of the town was remarkable, surrounded by heavy industry yet he hardly noticed this. He liked to take her in the middle of the afternoon; it seemed the full light of day always aroused him the most, then he would lie beside her in bed and listen to the strange little sounds of things in the quiet, and feel her listening as well, or dreaming her own daydreams, their minds drifting together and apart in the comatose dreamy haze after so much fucking. He felt it this way with her, and maybe it was really so. When they talked quietly, not too much, in bed it seemed it was so.

He lay in the half-light of the full light of day, light filtered through the windows of a tidy room in a house. He heard strange little sounds in the quiet. No shooting, no yelling, no brusque and businesslike commands, no cursing or crying out. No explosions, nearby or far away. No deep, deep rumbling through the earth.

He had always pictured it as a busy town and indeed he could still hear hammering and noises of other machinery from the factories off in the distance. Yet these sounds did not intrude upon him and they only formed a kind of agreeable background that punctuated the quiet and made it more palpable. The bells from the streetcars were also like that. Really, it was better than hearing birds sing in the trees; he had heard birds in Russia, the war had not dispersed them.

Sometimes he would get up and look out the window and expect to find the town deserted, or almost deserted. As if the little noises he could hear were no more than isolated things like the creaking of shutters or leaves and papers scuttling in the breeze through an abandoned city. The factory noises merely indicating some small, residual population tinkering away at something off in the distance.

So it was odd when he looked out the window and saw large crowds of people walking along in the streets below. He would have preferred that they weren't there. But what of it . . .

"Gus."

"*Ja.*"

She was gazing deeply at him. He leaned against the windowsill. For the first few days she had called him August, though he could never remember her liking the sound of that before, but she seemed to want to say that. A twitch came into his mind and he wondered if she'd been seeing another man, but her touch was so complete that he found he could hardly really care. Then it was Gus again, as she and most people had always called him. The town was not as bourgeois and stuffy as some places; he felt that, though he'd never traveled much, except to war zones.

She said his name several times, as if she enjoyed the sound of it; and it pleased him too. He thought he saw tears about to well in her eyes again, though she was smiling. She was sitting in the bed and he left the window and came back to bed with her. He could not get enough of her nakedness; it was like a mild yet continuously fine intoxicant, as if he were a boy again, not yet twenty, as if both of them were not. She put her fingers through his hair, monotonously touching him there. He placed his hand and arm under her breasts, a little plumper now than he remembered; he had noticed this over these days, closing his eyes to think of them sometimes.

She had her fingers woven in his hair, clutching at it sometimes, her face partly hidden against his chest. He felt wetness from her eyes against his chest, a faint damp there, not tears running down. She began to fill in the quiet with a few words, telling him of what she had been daydreaming while lying there after fucking, speaking quietly, lazily and abstractedly listening to her own words coming out into the air, both of them lazily listening. It was a daydream where nothing happened, only a small landscape that she described, filled with a pure, comatose light. It was a forest filled with tall trees that sloped down gently to a wide lake or sea, which she sensed was there but perhaps did not see. He too would have daydreams of this kind while lying beside her, afterward.

In fact he was startled to remember that he had had this very same dream, of a tall, spacious forest sloping gently down to a wide lake or sea, after that one long terrible night at Cholm. They had noticed this in years past, Kordts and Erika, sharing dreams and other curious images in their minds as if a kind of telepathy existed between them. Neither of them much believed in coincidence, in an unknown guiding hand, but they could not deny how often this had happened over the years; and so it was just another one of those things they both took delight in, with each other.

"I dreamed that too," he said, feeling strange superstitious impulses but brushing them aside.

"Yes, yes," she said, quietly stroking him. It had happened so often over the years that they did not need to make much comment on it anymore. Perhaps it was not such a delight, if Kordts remembered the circumstances when he had dreamed that dream; but he didn't dwell on it now. Rather he noticed a certain stiffness in her fingers as she stroked him, a reluctance that communicated something else to him entirely. He set his teeth together, set his hand on her hand.

"Oh," she said, laughing shyly.

She was a hesitant person much of the time, not forceful, but still very deep, lending a quiet mystery even to mundane things which he might never otherwise have noticed. It was love that made him see her this way, this was true; but he had known her for these years and noticed that most other people also reacted to her in this way. Her abstractedness would sometimes be an escape or release from worries and fears that closed in on her, and sometimes it was not escape at all but only paralysis induced by these fears; but other times it was only what it was, reverie, quietness.

He felt her teeth in his skin, in his chest. He reached down to grip her hair, to stroke it violently, but suddenly she drew her head away. She sat with her back turned to him, staring somewhere in the room. Her spine was stiff. Her hair hid her face. A few moments passed and he stared somewhere too, not really seeing anything.

She looked back at him, a strange nervous brightness in her eyes, smiling shyly.

"Let's go for a walk," she said.

They did this on most days, later in the afternoons.

It seemed to be worse on her. He could see her anxiety growing more marked on the last days. She did the best she could, though she could no longer drink beer with him without becoming possessed by something bad. She had a confused way of saying things but he mostly understood her quite well; it was a long time that they had known each other. Maybe they would both be relieved when this was over, but if so then neither of them would say it and neither were they entirely certain about reading it in each other's minds.

He wondered if her anxiety or loneliness would drive her to see someone else, or he wondered again if this had already happened. But his general feeling of relief and renewal was so curious that foul suspicions meant nothing to him; he resented nothing, he could feel her as he had always felt her.

He was right—he would find that all this would go back to Russia with him and stay with him for a while. And then quite suddenly it would wear off, and in the vast torn-up fields outside Velikiye Luki he would feel betrayed and filled with a nervous resentment toward everything. He should have known that this would happen, probably would have known, but during this strange leave he refused to think about it. It was enough of a curiosity that he could live in the present moment during these passing days; but that being so, he simply walked away from moments of speculation or foreboding, sometimes laughing faintly to himself as if he had gotten away with something.

The train took them back, swaying, whistling, traveling at a high rate of speed. Or so it seemed, if only because the train that had carried them home from Russia had traveled so slowly, and had stopped for hours at every depot. But this was still an ordinary German train. They had another several hundred miles to go before their transfer to a military train, somewhere in Poland or East Prussia. They steamed through green summer land with smoke from factories drifting quietly over it, here and there.

The truth was they were among a select few. On the Russian Front hundreds of thousands of men awaited their turn to get away from that place, if only to go home for a few weeks; they waited and waited and for many leave was never granted or else it was canceled, because there was one crisis after another out there and no men could be spared.

The first trickles of leave would begin, allotted to a few lucky men, but then others waiting their turn in the rotation would find this wait stretching indefinitely for months into no foreseeable future. They remained in the mud behind the thick belts of barbed wire, behind their guns, peering at some impenetrable patch of woodland in the near distance where the Russians lurked.

But for the defenders of Cholm it was different. There was no parsimonious trickle or allotment. All of them, every man who had survived with Scherer to the end, were granted a long leave back to Germany. Even the survivors of the police unit were posted home for a while, before being sent back to Russia to resume the operations that had been so rudely interrupted by their months-long ordeal at Cholm. The Cholm fighters were famous individuals. The public and the newspapers and above all the Party knew this, somewhat more so than did the men themselves.

It was a good publicity gesture, made feasible by the fact that there were, after all, only a little more than two thousand men still alive at Cholm on 5 May. Such a small number could all be sent home in one fell swoop of benevolence. After what they had gone through they deserved it, and the Party wished to show the German public that the long-suffering heroes from the East would be treated in the manner they deserved. For the Cholm garrison this was feasible; whereas it would not have been feasible to send home one hundred thousand men at a time from the larger-scale nightmares at Demyansk, or at RSV, or at Sevastapol, or in the Volkhov swamps, or along the Donets, or along the Mius. Such larger groups of men, or almost all of them anyway, had to remain where they were, out there in Russia.

But if it was special treatment the Cholm men were getting, then it was special treatment they had earned, with their
own blood and endurance and despair and psychotic terrors
and frozen suffering. They deserved a rest and they got one.

Then they boarded the trains and steamed back once again
to the East.

They were both glad they had waited until the last day to see
Moll. That day being yesterday.

Freitag had wanted to do this sooner but Kordts had put
him off, being preoccupied by his woman and his peace of
mind and hoarding that like a miser. In fact he felt strongly
connected to those he'd been with out there, just as most of
them did; but his subdued rage or contrariness would always
get the better of him in strange ways, and even when he was
feeling good it was no different. Or maybe especially when
he was feeling good, because he needed to feel this like a
starving person needed food and nothing better get in the
way of that.

Then he would be better prepared to go back there, he
thought, to go back out there and endure for another six
months or five years.

He was no different from thousands of others, really, who
felt these same cravings and satisfied them or tried to satisfy
them; it was just clearer to him somehow, the way a scientist
studying a certain field of research might come to recognize
certain primitive essentials of a thing, and separate them out
from other extraneous parts. Not that Kordts was overly ana-
lytical, fogged with the complex mantras of analysis the way
so many of his countrymen were prone to be. To some degree he had been that way when he was younger and more
full of himself, but now he saw more intuitively into certain
things and just seeing it was enough that he didn't particularly care whether he was right or wrong or how much he really understood; at least his mind was less cluttered up. He
tried not to argue or impose himself on people and only
wished, in vain, given the climate of the time, that they
would treat him the same.

He had ridden the trolley with Erika out into the country,
on the day he was supposed to be a special guest at a gather-

ing in town honoring the Cholm fighters. As far as he knew
he was the only Cholm fighter in the town—maybe there
were a few others, but he didn't know—and he hadn't
wanted any part of it. Still, seemingly irresistible forces
would tend to push even a contrary sort of person toward
simply going along with this business for a few hours. But
Kordts managed to resist, at least sometimes he did, as on
this occasion for example.

His obstinacy had not gone over well but what was the
worst they could do to him after all, those peasants? Not that
much. And whatever it was he would gladly live with it. He
knew they wouldn't send him to jail or to a camp and barring
that he really didn't care. A penal battalion? Ha, ha, he
would think. No, they wouldn't do that either. He was taking
advantage of his special status and he knew it but so be it.
He had not told Erika what day it was but then it had slipped
out somehow and she had gotten nervous, even while they
were picnicking and making love out in the hills. He could
hardly blame her and on the ride home a little cold sense had
settled into him, realizing she would have to deal with the
embarrassment and she was not as good at dealing with that
as he was; most people weren't. His parents too—some
kind of embarrassment would fall to them as the result of
his selfishness. They were good about it, better than he deserved really, but he knew he owed them an apology and said
as much later that night. To Erika too, when they were alone
later—suddenly feeling exhausted and half-mad in ways he
could not even describe; but it was difficult for her too and
so he thought of her rather than of himself. She had that effect on him. Over the years he had grown to be considerate
of her in ways that he was with few other people. Maybe this
consideration would have eventually rubbed off on other
people as well; but the era was not a good one for nurturing
such developments.

It was somewhat easier to get away with this kind of be-
havior in a factory town, if only to a degree. He was regarded
as rude and ill-bred; for a middle-class fellow the repercussions might have been more ominous—it was easier for the
peasants to sniff out subversion in a clean, polite environment. But if a middle-class fellow had worn the Cholm

shield on his sleeve they probably would have let him get away with it too, after perfunctorily telling him off and filling the air with vague and sinister threats. Kordts didn't know; he only knew that when the Party officials came to his parents' door the next day he had stood up to them with his usual truculence. It was only then that his father had become angry, angry with him, and he realized again that he was just making things unpleasant for his family. In '45, in the twilight, he might have been hung from a tree; if not at that precise moment then pretty soon. But it was only '42, and the weary Landsers were just beginning their long desert march to that horrible city on the Volga.

Kordts meanwhile, on hero's leave in the homeland, had calmed himself and allowed himself to be spoken to by both his father and the Party officials in thus and such a way. Then his father, trying to accommodate these men while retaining some semblance of dignity, said it was the wound that was having a bad effect on him, worse than anyone had thought at first. Except for the scar Kordts's wound was fully healed and the peasants had listened with a polite, vicious, oily lack of sympathy. Still, it was probably the smartest thing to say under the circumstances. Finally even one of the peasants seemed to have second thoughts, as if it would be more agreeable to all to find some positive way to get out of this, at least when the matter concerned one of the celebrated Cholm fighters. They said firmly that the matter would not just be dropped but at least they had left then, leaving the impression that perhaps the matter would just be dropped.

Later his father had really vented his anger, and as they were both drinking Kordts had shouted back, though it was tempered with a certain hidden approval of the way his father had managed the whole thing. His father had gone on and on though, violently drunk—not an unusual occurrence in this neighborhood, but unusual in this family.

The day they had ridden the trolley out of town they had got off at a rural station. They had picnicked in a field somewhere and then later walked further up into the hills, where they had stopped to rest on a long green slope. Erika sat with her legs curled under her, her back, her spine, erect in the curious way that she had. As if she was trying to stretch her muscles or settle some discomfort in them. Or as if, maybe, she was trying to sit up straight to see something far away, down the long green pasture to the forests below, down to the valleys and other hills in the distance. Though her eyes were closed much of the time, and she felt the sun on her hair and forehead like a hand of air and warmth stroking her quietly there. She would sit in such stillness as if in a dreamlike serenity, yet also stiffly somehow.

When she opened her eyes she stared abstractedly at the cows down at the bottom of the pasture, a small group of them in the shade at the edge of the trees. Some were down in the grass with their legs curled under them, some stood in stillness, unmoving while the leaves of the trees blew in the breeze above them. Every so often one would walk through the grass a few feet, and then stand drowsing in stillness again.

Before the war they would often come to places like this, far away from things. She was timid in many ways, which irked her somewhat, though generally she had come to accept it as part of her nature. She stayed close to home most of the time, and so it made her happy when Kordts took her to someplace farther away from everything, like this. Most of these places stayed in her memory long afterward, and she reckoned without thinking about it that this place would stay too, in her mind.

Kordts lay beside her in that heavy-lidded sprawl that he would have, a posture which often struck people as insolent, and she knew this because they had told her so. She dismissed them as busybodies and was at odds with herself because it perturbed her all the same, made her uneasy in some way she could not put aside. She was often surprised that he did not get into more trouble than he did, wondering how he managed to steer clear of it. She had known him for all this time and yet this was still something of a mystery to her.

But it mattered less, up on a hillside like this. It mattered not at all. That he was going to die out there was unbearable to her; and so she had somehow become resigned to it from almost the day the war began, as the only way she could go on. But this resignation had an unreal quality as well, and she had begun to distance herself from it for some time—and thus, to distance herself from him as well. This involved other secrets. She wanted to confess to him, as a way of easing her conscience, but she dreaded what might result from this. Deep down she believed that he would understand, or that maybe he would; but still she could all too easily imagine him reacting with great violence. She always sensed his sympathy but this would not prevent him from lashing out in some implacable fashion, with that terribly direct, almost lazy manner that he had when he was terribly aroused. She had seen this a few times, years before.

These things were harder to escape from, even on a distant hillside. But she could not dwell constantly on it, she could not or would not. She closed her eyes and the rays of the sun bathed her quietly, as if falling upon some underground sea, within her mind. Her childhood was very vivid to her; she felt it had never left her. She plucked at stems of grass, she stared down at the small structures of growing things or the dried intricate husks of dead things, the smallest parts of the land, beneath her hands. The cattle browsed down below. They had talked and joked quietly for miles, walking up here, or fell silent when they felt like it, silent now, Kordts staring somewhere across the land. She knew he could sense her unease and was puzzled by his unconcern. He seemed to be in the grip of some deep relaxation, the way other people would be in the grip of their nerves, their worries. She felt better to see it but it was strange all the same. He had been on leave twice before and she did not remember this. She could not pretend to know how a man ought to react, after being out there for months and years, and then coming home for a time. She had tried to imagine it but she couldn't, and so she simply accepted whatever way that it was, or else different ways for different men. All the same there seemed something almost unnatural about his contentment; finally she had asked him about it, in bed, in the house in the town down below.

"I know it," he'd said. "It is strange. I suppose I'll take what I can get though."

This had come out easily enough, but he'd seemed reluctant to say more, almost superstitiously so; and that at least did not seem unnatural to her. She had her own superstitions, things she did not believe in but which possessed her anyway.

The shadow of the Karlsberg, a small mountain that was the highest place in the area, lengthened down toward them in the late afternoon, down the long pasture. She moved out of the shadows a few feet and settled herself in the grass again, where the sun still lay. The day was warm, late afternoon blending into evening for hours and hours, high summer. The shadow of the mountain, the tall hill, came down very slowly. Bees hummed in the sunlight at the edge of the shadow, among small flowers that grew thickly like the grass. Lesser hills and valleys lay below, undulations rising just enough to hide the wide coastal plain beyond and the sand-pines and heaths that spread to the sea. The sea seemed nearer in the hazy light of summer evening, as if the coastal plain were itself the sea, just beyond the hills. A few tails of smoke rose from factory chimneys, hidden down there in the land somewhere.

Kordts sat up, leaned forward, leaning into the sunlight where she was. He touched her for a while. She responded abstractedly, and he looked more closely at her. She wished he would take her. Just to be touched by him unsettled her with the same horrible knowledge, but when he took her she could still escape, with him, into some last delirium that still remained pure. It was the last uncorrupted thing, the most important thing, though not enough to make up for the rest of it. She pulled down the straps from her shoulders and he took her. He gave out a low growl, growling and grunting in one loud continuous sound like a sound that issued from every pore of his skin. She tossed her head from side to side and moaned and moaned, gasped, louder than him. The thrumming sound of him controlled a deep force while she gasped uncontrollably, louder than him, until he cried louder still. Then they both twitched separately in the grass before lying still as the coma folded over them.

The peasants had their measure of spite after all, to no one's surprise.

When notice came that his last week of leave would be

canceled he had only two days of leave still remaining. He'd been home longer than most of the others anyway, longer than Freitag; because of his inflamed face he'd been shipped out only a few days after the siege was lifted.

He got in touch with Freitag and said perhaps now would be the time to go see Moll.

They got on the train and stopped off first at Torgau. In Torgau there was a military prison with a bad reputation known to everyone, but Moll was in a hospital somewhere else in the town, or out in the countryside as it turned out.

So it took them a while to walk there and they didn't have as much time to visit with Moll. Perhaps it was just as well. He was the only other survivor that they knew, who had gone into Russia with them a year ago. Almost certainly there were others, but on the retreat from Lake Seliger to Cholm the division had gotten broken up into tiny bits and pieces and they no longer knew who else was alive or where they were.

Torgau was a rather forbidding town, but the hospital on the outskirts was surrounded by deep green lawns and flower beds. It overlooked a bluff where the country fell away in a quiet haze.

The staff saw the bronze shields on their sleeves and treated them with deference, or almost with deference, as it was beyond doctors and other hospital personnel to really treat any outsiders that way unless they were other high-ranking officials. An administrator in a fine suit spoke to them admiringly with a few pompous words, as if he were an officer complimenting his men, a barracks officer anyway, speaking with lofty politeness in order to hide his own feelings of intimidation at the sight of these two men from Russia—one who still looked young and naive even if he did wear the bronze shield, the other brutally scarred.

But then once through the administrative areas nobody paid them too much attention. The nurse who guided them through the corridors was respectful but also genuinely friendly. They liked that. Freitag especially, as he did not have a girlfriend to see at home and had been compensating with youthful confusion by soaking up the gazes of every woman he saw or that saw him. By now Kordts had begun to

see that Freitag was a rather talkative and sociable fellow,
something he had first noticed at Cholm, of all places. In the
weeks before the invasion, and then for the first six months
out there, Freitag had been subdued and almost sullen in the
way that Kordts generally was, seemingly one of the odd fellows of the platoon and the company; but maybe that was not
his real nature.

Cholm, of all places. Freitag said, "You know, I wonder if
Moll received one of these. Maybe we should put them in
our pockets."

Freitag tapped the bronze shield with his finger. Kordts
might have acquiesced but it was an odd thing to think about,
and then they were there anyway.

"I don't know," he muttered indecisively. "Let's just see."

The friendly nurse herded them over to a sterner-looking
woman at the door to one of the wards.

"We are honored," she said, as the administrator had said.
"Normally we do not allow visitors here, except for relatives
of course. But I see Herr Gart has made an exception. Please
be considerate and speak quietly. Some of these men are
quite disturbed. Ten minutes should be sufficient?"

"Ten minutes?" said Freitag.

"No, no, of course you can stay longer, but I suggest that
that should be adequate. I will be outside here."

Kordts had noticed already that the place was different
from the several hospitals he had been in. They had seen
none of the horribly wounded, no amputees sunning in
chairs out on the lawn. They had seen none of the shocking
things that even soldiers, who had seen the sickening origins
of such things out on the battlefield, found hard to face when
they visited a military hospital. The place did not have the
normal foul blood- and fluid-reek of physical dismember-
ment and violence and cloying anti-infective agents in the
air. The place did not have all the normal things that Kordts
had seen himself in several hospitals, been amongst, been so
glad to get away from.

She took them in to see Moll and then left them at his
bedside.

"By God, you look all right, Moll," blurted Freitag. "It's
good to see you."

"You," said Moll, almost shouting, as if snapping awake suddenly. He gaped. "Freitag. Kordts and Freitag."

At first he was delighted to see them. Even Kordts.

"You kicked me pretty hard. By God, I remember that. Thanks. Thanks for getting me out of there."

Kordts felt relieved. He smiled and laughed and scratched at his face.

"And you took one too," said Moll, staring at Kordts's cheek. "Christ, what a mess that was. Cholm. The newspapers are full of it. They let us read them."

He noticed the shields.

"Let me see. Let me see that."

Freitag unpinned his and Moll inspected it, turning it over. They noticed his hands now. There wasn't much to notice, they were mottled and somewhat scaly but they looked all right, and he had all of his fingers.

"Nice tin," said Moll. "Heavy."

"Bronze," said Freitag.

"Bronze then."

"They'll give you one too. Everyone who was there, even if they were flown out. I read that."

"*Ja,* maybe I did too. The devil with it. What do you think, Kordts?"

"Nice tin," said Kordts. They all laughed. Kordts bit his lip, laughing quietly, mindful about not making too much noise. He said, "*Ja.* Cholm, anywhere. They should have given you something for dragging yourself back from Lake Seliger. That was worse, really."

Moll became more subdued. He asked about some of the others, yet suddenly it seemed he was making an effort.

"How are your feet?" said Freitag finally.

"They're better. I thought I would lose them. I just wish they would let me out of here. But they keep telling me I'm not fit to leave." He lowered his voice. "Some of these *Kerls* around you are really batty. They're quiet now, but at night I hear the craziest things. I was a little that way myself, I'll admit it, it doesn't matter to me. But that was months ago. I just want to get out of here. It's so damned dull. Otherwise I'll just start up myself again. I can walk all right and they won't even let me outside."

It was strange, and they didn't quite know what to say. Ten minutes, thought Kordts, as about that much time must have gone by. That was strange too, even for the usual routine. He said, "Well, we're on our way back. We would have visited you sooner but we didn't want to ruin our leaves by visiting one of these shit-holes. Eh, Moll? You're damned right. I was in Lublin for weeks and then I was in Leipzig for about that long. Not to mention goddamned Cholm."

"What about Cholm?" said Moll.

"The hospital, the GPU. I don't even know how long I was there anymore."

Kordts shook his head, dazed all of a sudden, realizing he had raised his voice, he didn't know how loudly. To hell with it. Moll and Freitag didn't care.

"So what about it?" he went on. "If you're sick of it here you can come with us. These hospital people can't match up with the Ivans."

"Jesus Christ. So you're on your way back? Sure, sure, take me with you. Except I'll never take another winter. Never. Not out there. I can feel my feet dropping off just to think of it. I do still have them, you know. Look." He drew back the bedcovers. His feet were there. They were ugly but they were both still in one piece. "Send me to Africa. Send me to France. Now that's the place to be, by God. Or Africa, I don't care. Hell, some of these other crazy bastards, they've lost their feet or their toes or fingers or what all and they're crazy to boot, but I can get about fine. I can't take the cold, it's just that one thing, but I've already been through enough, just like you, it doesn't mean I can't fit in somewhere else. By God, it's good to see you, just to see somebody for God's sake. The days just last forever in here, especially when you start feeling better. I'm not the only one. It's the cold. Some of these other people are as fit as I am, they look that way to me anyway, and they say they're all right too. Maybe a few of them are a little cracked, but I don't think all of them. It's just that one thing they can't face, but that's no reason to keep people pent up like this. I don't have those nightmares anymore, except sometimes I do because I'm so bored. I start to feel it again, I'll even start crying again; we all did during the very worst of it, didn't we?"

There would have been something shameful about Moll, except that he seemed to refuse to accept his shame, and somehow he conveyed this feeling to Kordts and Freitag very well. He was right, they had all been crying, constantly in tears, during the very worst of it, the cold, the cold, the unspeakable thing. Moll was sitting up straight and then he sat back. The wildness had come over him instantaneously and then just as quickly he was himself again. "I know, I know," he said, staring hard at Kordts and Freitag, and then staring just as hard into space between them. "Well, you'd be going on too. Think of it. I just want to be outside talking to normal people. There's some in here who are all right to talk to but I'm fed up with it. Never mind. Tell me about the rest of it, how you got out and all. Reading it in the papers is nothing."

They didn't know what to say, as it would have taken hours or days, if they could even bring themselves to dredge up all those experiences, even to share with a comrade who had been there too.

And then ten minutes had gone by. Actually it must have been longer, the stern-looking nurse had been at least that considerate. But then she was at Moll's bedside again, wearing the look of someone not to be argued with, of a master sergeant who actually ran a place while the men in suits sat in their offices. Actually she looked more formidable than a master sergeant; Kordts recalled his own stays in hospitals. Well, he supposed they weren't all so bad.

"What is all this?" he wanted to ask her, about the strangeness of the place, but he didn't.

This time Moll was startled, and then angry.

"Ten minutes? What are you talking about? A man can't even chat with his friends in this place? If people are going mad it's just from staring at the damned walls."

"You are worked up again, Herr Moll. Otherwise you would be grateful to be allowed outside visitors at all. Herr Gart personally allowed an exception for you. And it's been longer than ten minutes, because I personally have allowed your friends to stay a little longer."

Moll stared and his lips moved uncertainly, like hands

groping about in the dark, taken aback by these cool and efficient declarations of generosity.

"Well, I don't care," he said finally. "Let them stay longer then, Frau All-Powerful. Oh, for God's sake, nurse, we Russia boys just need to chat, eh? We're like pigs in a sty. We need each other's company for a bit."

She glared at him with a look to signal that she would be back to see to him later. Then she turned around and walked with her certain dignity back through the beds, calmly telling Kordts and Freitag to follow her out.

Moll had been speaking more to Freitag before, but at the last moment he grasped Kordts's sleeve and whispered to him, "Euthanasia. Hah, you remember? They're going to start that up again, start with all the cripples. I'm serious, Kordts. I've had months to think it through. Get some kind of word to the outside for me, thank God you showed up here."

"For God's sake, you're not a cripple, Moll," he said in his normal voice; it was too much trouble to whisper. But this made him feel badly, as if he were just brushing Moll off. He lowered his voice a little and said, "Listen, I don't blame you, I'd be half-cracked too from this stir-crazy setup. They'll let you out in their own sweet time. I don't think there's anything wrong with you either. But you know you can never tell anything to these fools. They make all the rules."

"No, no, you don't understand."

No, Kordts didn't understand; what was there to understand? Except that being cooped up in here was making Moll neurotic and who could blame him? Hospital staffs kept a tighter rein on their little domains than anyone. He didn't know what he was thinking; in his mind he was already walking toward the door, part of some deeper and crazier impulse to just flee, to flee in a rage yet to flee like a coward away from it too. The nurse was over there looking back their way. Clearly she wished not to have to come back to speak to them a second time.

"What is it?" said Freitag.

"I don't know," said Kordts.

"What is it, Moll?" said Freitag, nervous under the old bitch's stare but not wishing to just march off like that.

Suddenly Moll got out of bed and Kordts realized he'd
been wondering all along if Moll could actually walk, if
maybe there really was something wrong with him to just be
lying there. But he could walk and he walked down the aisle
with them. The nurse started forward but then held her
ground, waiting for them to come to her. And all the other
beds in here, occupied by men only a few feet away, staring
at them or else lost in their own worlds and showing no interest. It was always strange like that when you visited someone
in the hospital, as if the particular bed you were visiting were
mounted on a little stage surrounded by vaguely interested
spectators. Usually someone else would be talking, grousing
with the person in the next bed to pass the time, or groaning
or wanting something for God's sake, but they were all so
quiet. Sedation maybe. As if the three of them and then the
nurse were the only people here. In a few confused seconds
he could only half think any of this and later on he would not
sort it out much better either.

Moll walked up to the door with them but was no longer
saying anything. He had an upset, entirely sane look on his
face, as if he had made a conscious effort not to babble these
bizarre things. He had been a big man before and he was still
big, trailing blood and black pus behind him through the
snow, dragging himself with terrible, agonized, and often
highly vocal fortitude through the snow between Seliger and
Cholm, showing more courage than any of them really, even
though Kordts remembered becoming nearly unhinged with
the unforgiving loudness of the man's pain. Christ, all of it,
all of it. How had they ever managed to save his feet? It was
a miracle, now that he thought about it, but he'd been too distracted. Doctors, doctors, the evil and the good of all human-
ity in one profession . . . He hated it when his thoughts
rambled chaotically like this and he shut his eyes and shut
off whatever was in his mind, bumping his leg against one of
the bedsteads.

Moll said, "Thanks for coming, boys. I'll be all right.
When I get out I'll raise a fuss, just see that I don't. I think
that's why they're keeping me in here in the first place, just
to spite me. All right then. To the devil with you."

He shook their hands, gripping them tightly on the upper

arm with his other hand, and they both gripped him that way too. Moll's eyes were red.

Suddenly Kordts very much shared Moll's anger but he had a terrible urge to leave this place and he didn't want to make a scene, even a short one. It was an effort not to say something though and he was glad when Freitag did.

"You treat these fellows all right, do you hear? You have no idea what they've been through, no idea at all. They ought to be treated like gods, and that's the truth. Actually I think you do have some idea what they've been through. You must. So you just treat them all right, you hear? When the war's over we'll be back, and that's the truth too."

The nurse was unflappable and she even looked a little sad. But only a little.

"All right, *mein Herren*. Yes, I understand a little. Please find your own way out." Then more sternly again, but with a strange sincerity, "Our thoughts at home are always with you."

Freitag muttered something vulgar when they were a little way further down the corridor.

They walked back toward the grimmer parts of the town. Kordts felt hysteria rising in his throat and Freitag would be no different. But it was an entirely normal sensation, like being in a good mood or a bad mood or no mood at all and they simply walked on through it. Nightmares followed behind them, following them but keeping a respectful distance during the daytime.

"Treated like gods," said Kordts, shaking his head. "Where did you come up with that?"

"Well. I don't know. They should be."

Kordts was not in a mood to laugh but he laughed anyway, they both did. He was wishing they hadn't come here at all but it was too late now. Impulses were twisting through him and now he regretted not telling off the nurse like Freitag had done, telling them all off in that place. But it was too late for that too.

They needed a beer. They always needed a beer and now in particular they needed one. There was still a little time left at the cafe by the railroad station.

Kordts wanted to put it out of his mind. His mind was still

very much on Erika, so he thought of her instead as he lowered his lips tiredly into the big mug. At the last she had been crying, trying to turn her head away but crying too visibly to conceal it. Kordts had felt rotten that this had made him feel good, but he knew that it did and there was no help for it, as if such uncontained emotional displays would help bind her to him across a thousand miles of distance, too far for anything to remain bound, he knew. But it was something to remember anyway, as long as it was genuine, as long as it had all been real. They could never hope for too much out there, while their women remained at home.

But he could not stop himself from talking about the other thing with Moll, and Freitag talked about it even more, a young man exposed to injustice like a bush growing by the side of the road. The problem was they still weren't quite sure what to make of it all, apart from some kind of obvious rottenness.

"What was he talking about, euthanasia?"

"So you heard that, did you?" Kordts said.

"What is it?"

"What is it? You're an ignorant screw-turner. How old are you anyway?"

"I just don't know a lot of words. I dropped out of school to help my damned mother, what do you want?"

"Your damned mother," said Kordts mechanically. He felt no desire to explain anything but he couldn't think of what else to say except to explain it.

Freitag looked at him suspiciously. "I've never heard of that."

"So, you're young," said Kordts. "It was years ago and it was quack talk even then."

"So he was just talking craziness back there?"

"I don't know," said Kordts. "Yeah, of course he was. Not even that. I think he was just angry at those fools and he's got too much time to think, locked up like that."

Kordts felt pretty certain about this. If he felt doubt too it was only because anything seemed possible anymore; but he knew it was nonsense. He could barely remember it himself, he could remember the archbishop talking back to Hitler about it, before the war, and then nothing had come of it. He thought so anyway.

"Thing is, Adolf used to say so many crazy things you couldn't keep track of them all."

"He used to."

"Well. Now he's got the war to run. Or something."

"Oh," said Freitag. "I see."

He didn't see, though he was absorbing it with interest. Kordts no longer knew what he was talking about and only wanted to talk about something else, or be quiet and drink, tired of Freitag's queries. The whole subject had nothing to do with anything and at this moment he could not bear to have something on his mind that had nothing to do with anything, unless perhaps it was to daydream about half-dressed women on a desert island.

He pulled the bronze shield from his sleeve and set it among the wet mug rings on the table, tapping on it with his fingernail, turning it over and back, sliding it back and forth a few inches as if it were a coaster. His mind went completely empty and he was not aware that he was faintly smiling.

"Stop doing that. Stop it, will you please?"

Kordts looked up.

"Hm? Ah, all right." He put it back on his sleeve, he said rather too loudly: "*Jawohl*, Herr Oberfeld! Ah, just think, we'll be saying that again in only another day."

The train came and left with them aboard.

PART THREE

Velikiye Luki

Chapter Ten

Ancient stone town.

The blocky white towers, pitted and broken up but still there, still there, were visible across the wide green expanse on the outskirts where the relief company was moving up.

They advanced across a green acreage of cabbage, unruly and unkempt, though the invaders had tried to restore some of these fields for their own food needs. Truck gardens staked out amidst shell craters. They moved on further through a thick sward, uncultivated and perhaps it had never been, grasses rippling as if trying to follow the movements of clouds overhead. Ankle-high, calf-high mostly, they moved through it in widely scattered lines, and it would take a skilled observer to see just what kind of formation was moving up. But it was only a company. The landscape would make large groups small and scattered groups even smaller. The lines remained within hand-signal distance of each other, scattered to minimize loss, though they still had several kilometers to walk before they entered the direct-fire zone. But there was always the threat of a sudden barrage. *Feueruberfall*. Up ahead, where they were going, the barrage fire was already much more concentrated.

The day was not overly hot but the wide-spreading force of sunlight was potent in mid-afternoon. Overhead great clouds were set at anchor in the deep blue sky. They moved very slowly, the entire celestial harbor moved as one, drifting very slowly overhead. Day after day in Russia they would see sights such as this, weather that would be rare and memorable back home; but here day after day such spectacles drifted slowly overhead, with light falling between the clouds and scattered everywhere up among them. Mid-afternoon. They walked slowly on across the open land until they came to the *rollbahn*.

Here the lieutenant looked at his watch and raised his hand. Stop. They stopped in the slightly elevated lee of the *rollbahn*, white dusty road.

Some of them looked back toward Velikiye Luki, which they could still see in the distance, buildings rising on the horizon yet still small enough.

The werfer battery was over there and the first shrieks came within seconds of the lieutenant looking at his watch. The shrieking of the rocket battery was like the roar of adrenaline itself, enough to sublimate even fear for the duration of the salvo. They all felt this, no matter how different they were from each other during other moments.

Even shirkers and men who had long since been reduced by fear to barely reliable baggage would feel their spirits rising, if only for twenty or thirty seconds. Because they could not help it. It was like a force of nature, the intensity of this noise. Morale boosters, the rockets, when unleashed from their side, or crushers, when released from the Russian side.

It was only noise, a certain highly peculiar kind of noise. And then the effect, of course, was also terrible.

The salvo consisted of thirty or forty rockets fired in quick succession. This quick multiple shrieking had a cumulative though highly compressed effect upon the senses almost like a multiple orgasm, if one may describe something accurately though also crudely. Long successive digits of shrieking smoke arced up into the sky, which they watched intently passing overhead. Simultaneously with the muzzle blast of each rocket came a noise still more peculiar, like a metal spike being driven deep into some equally hard object. A ringing kind of noise, occurring in quick successive blows in the manner of all the other noise. This noise was peculiar because no one could understand what caused it. Peculiar also, that it should be so audible within the much louder roar of the rocket engines, carrying for miles out to where they were.

The salvo landed about a kilometer ahead. Where they were the earth trembled faintly a few seconds later. Or it seemed faint only because they were used to it; the tremor was still violent enough. The shock wave passed through, dissipating from point of impact. Even at this distance they were left momentarily deaf. The storm parties up ahead, who had already crossed the *rollbahn* hours ago in morning mist, would be deafened for a minute or longer. Likewise for the Soviets assembling to counterattack at the zero point, all the Reds in that neighborhood not killed instantly by the blast.

Dazed by the first salvo, the men of the relief company were less aware of the second salvo as it now also passed overhead. The NCOs kept their eyes on the lieutenant and at his signal they led their men in quick dashes of threes and fours across the slight elevation of the *rollbahn*.

They advanced more hurriedly now during this interval when the enemy up ahead, and his observers, who might still be scanning their own area, would be stunned. The racket of other kinds of gunfire began to supplant the aftershock of the rockets. Still they breathed somewhat easier when they reached the shelter of the birch woods. The little birch woods. These woods were not quite so dense as the heavily infested forests, the fear forests, which many of them remembered scouring out several months earlier.

The storm parties had also passed through here those hours ago. The lieutenant was expecting someone to meet them here, to guide them up the rest of the way. They waited for a few minutes, used these few minutes to catch their breath. The lieutenant cursed but could imagine well enough what might be happening up ahead and did not think about laying blame on anyone. They would just have to find their own way forward. The NCOs knelt around him under the birch trees and they all looked at the map, which they had studied closely many times during the preceding days. They had not only committed the terrain to memory but had practiced the whole operation in the hinterlands back of Velikiye Luki.

So when one of them took two men up to find the lane staked through the minefields it did not take them too long. When they came back the rest of them got to their feet again and they all moved off in single file through the thin white trees.

A body lay across their path.

The lieutenant recognized the dead man as somebody

from Schrader's platoon. Perhaps this was their guide. The man had been shot through the head and lay neatly in the middle of the narrow lane staked out through the minefields. The birch leaves quivered all about, quivered as they always did even on the most peaceful of days. Well they had already found their path and if there were snipers about they had better move through here as quickly as they could. The lieutenant signaled and the men in single file kept on going nervously past the dead man. The little leafy woods were only slightly torn up and the sunlight roared peacefully around them, the roar of fighting sounding closer and closer.

In fact the man was no guide sent back for them; he had been killed in the dawn mist when the storm parties were still making their own way forward. They had been relying on surprise and at this first shooting thought they had been discovered. A head shot, too nice to be only a random bullet. But it must have been that; they'd waited in the mist and nothing else had happened. At this place they could hear a Russian harmonica being played, faint and dead-sounding in the mist but still audible enough. The *Iltis Stellung* (polecat position) lay only a few hundred yards ahead. They'd kept on going and stormed the place at first light with the enemy still entirely unaware.

Almost ten hours ago, that had been.

The relief company was almost there when they ran into Schrader and a few of his men coming back along the mine lane. The noise now was so loud that it was difficult to talk. Schrader looked terrible, they all did, and the effort required to raise his voice loud enough to report anything seemed to visibly depress him. He collected himself and continued shouting, pointing up ahead, and the lieutenant of the relief company listened intently and stared up ahead. The commanding officer? Schrader shouted again and pointed up ahead again. The lieutenant nodded. He clenched Schrader on the shoulder and then began shouting instructions to his own NCOs.

Besides Schrader's platoon the storm company had consisted of four other platoons plus supporting weapons squads. The weapons men would stay up at the *Iltis*; the rest of the storm party would also stay in position as they had done since dawn, supported now by the relief company that would in fact relieve no one except for Schrader's people.

Schrader, hard as he was, was in shock and there were only five of his own men coming back with him. Two were badly wounded and needed to be carried. Then there were three badly wounded men from other platoons who also needed to be carried. And then a *sani*, who told the lieutenant that some would die if they weren't brought back quickly enough. Which were they? The *sani* coldly and hastily pointed them out.

The others, bad off as they were, would have to stay until more people could be spared to carry them back. The lieutenant gave Schrader three men from his own company. This was generous, probably contrary to the spirit of his own orders—every man would be needed at the *Iltis*—but Schrader was a respected NCO and the lieutenant was taken aback by his appearance, and by the awful shape of some of the others with him. These were not wounded; these were dead men, unless they could be brought back to where help was.

But that was all he could do or would do. Already his attention was focused on the uproar only a few hundred yards ahead. Two other *sanis* had come forward with him but he told them to stay. That was it, his own people were taking casualties now, cries of pain in this unending din. He had no more time for Schrader, having enough difficulty keeping his own thoughts in order.

A low devastated ridge rose above the birch woods, the now more and more shattered birch woods, up ahead. The ridge protruded like an erupting sore, strewn with torn-up barbed wire, littered with bodies that were often more or less invisible among the chaos of other debris, except for a few hung starkly on the barbed wire, mortar bursts peppering the site repeatedly and then larger caliber stuff sometimes shaking it.

It was a long way back, a long shocked march. Shock was natural and the three unwounded men were not exactly incapacitated by it. They could speak, though just barely, and their movements were robotic though also slack with exhaustion. But they could react out of instinct or experience if they had to. They were not taken under fire again though, except for a few shells falling, Russian stuff rather aimless in this area or else shortfall from their own guns in Velikiye Luki. This by itself would be enough to unnerve them, but they were already so weary, their senses clogged by what they had already experienced during the day.

They passed the dead man lying in the mine lane, Schrader barely able to absorb that it was one of his own, so many hours ago that had been. They stopped in exhaustion before crossing the *rollbahn*. No one ever wanted to cross the exposed *rollbahn* and they would have just stayed where they were for a while, half-dead, but then they forced themselves to go across because of the plight of the wounded.

Shambling men crossing a road. From this slight dusty elevation they could have seen almost everything spread out to the front and to the rear, the city away over there, but they weren't really looking at anything.

It seemed to take forever. And they only covered half the distance. About halfway back they were met by another small party with horses and two wagons. They set the wounded on the ground and could barely lift them up again onto one of the wagon beds.

The Spiess was there with the wagons, Hasenclever, the old NCO who served as administrative pooh-bah for almost everything that went on in the company, and who rarely entered the forward trenches, much less ventured out beyond them. But he was there and he had brought a liter of beer in one wagon.

Schrader and Krabel and the one other unwounded man drank deeply, though it seemed to have little effect on them other than to assuage their thirst. That was enough. Then they drank deeply again and after a minute felt their nerves settle a little, settle down like lead, which was about what they needed really. The *sani* also drank a little. Then the three men from the relief company were given some.

These last three were disgruntled, seeing that they were no longer needed and would have to go back up to their unit at the *Iltis*. They fell away to one side and sat in the grass, talking amongst themselves. There was no one to order them to go back there, Hasenclever not being their own Spiess and not knowing what their own officer would have told them to do. But one of the wagons was still going ahead anyway and there might be trouble if they didn't go back there. As they had not been in action yet they could not legitimately bear the dull defiance of shock or exhaustion and none of them was devious enough to think of some other excuse. They talked about it senselessly though they knew already that they would go back; but they would rest for a few minutes first. They were still very tired after all, from helping carry the wounded this far.

Schrader had been hardly aware of these three all along and when they set themselves off to one side he completely forgot their existence. Hasenclever went over to talk to them. He did not bother asking if they had any other instructions.

"Escort the second wagon back up to the *Iltis*," he said.

They stared at him, not knowing who he was but seeing his rank.

"*Ja,* Spiess," said one. "We're already on our way. Except we just needed to rest a minute."

"All right," said Hasenclever.

They climbed onto this wagon, which normally they might have walked alongside of, as it was a target. But they were tired. They would dismount, or think about dismounting, once they got up to the *rollbahn* again.

Hasenclever took the other wagon with the wounded and headed back for the rear. Krabel and Schrader sat in the wagon with their legs dangling over the side. One of the men who lay right next to them surely bleeding to death had lived side by side with them for many months, a man whose habits and face were as familiar to them as their own. If they weren't beyond feeling they might have felt something about this, and no doubt would later. Earlier they had been speaking to the hurt man to keep his spirits up but now they were too tired to speak. The *sani* had given him morphine, easing his pain and also sparing his close acquaintances from the excruciating dull pointless embarrassment of having to attend to this hopelessness and listen to his screams and fear.

The other two terribly hurt men were from other platoons and they knew them too, though not as well.

The last survivor of Schrader's platoon, wounded too but not quite so badly hurt, was still up at the *Iltis*.

There were nearly twenty hours of daylight and the vast sunlit cloudscape seemed barely changed when they at last returned to the fortified positions of their own main line. By this time Hasenclever had told Schrader that he would be getting two of the new men who had just arrived.

"They're not green. They were at Cholm, both of them. Lucky bastards that they didn't show up here a day sooner. But maybe it's just as well, Schrader, two good men like that. You wouldn't want to lose them right away."

"You shit of a mother hen," Schrader said.

"No, Rolf, you misunderstand. I didn't mean it that way. I'm sorry about all this, Schrader. Anyway I'll keep them with me till tomorrow morning. They can report to you then."

"Makes no difference," said Schrader. He was listening but it was with utter indifference.

They passed through an opening in the barbed wire. As they approached the forward-most trench several men hoisted up a ready-made plank bed so the wagon could pass over the trench. The horse hesitated. Hasenclever flicked the reins and they went across.

"Look at Matlee," said Krabel. Schrader looked down in the wagon bed. Krabel was holding Matlee's hand. Schrader jumped off the wagon, walking slowly off somewhere, hardly seeing things.

Chapter Eleven

Scherer had been assigned to take command of the division a few weeks before. The details of the assault on the *Iltis Stellung* dismayed him greatly, but like the lieutenant of the relief company out in the field, he was aware of how things stood and could not really find fault with the regimental commander directly responsible for the attack.

He would have liked to find fault with somebody though, if only to dispel nervous energy and frustration.

Like his own men at Cholm, Scherer had been given a long furlough back in Germany. He might have been feted as a national hero, and indeed the press hailed him that way. His professional acquaintances also complimented him with a mixture of awe, jealousy, and genuine admiration. Only a few of these men had heard of Scherer before, and even they did not know him well.

And Hitler of course knew nothing about Scherer. He knew his name—everyone who had followed the siege over the course of these months knew his name. But that was all. Scherer had already been awarded the Knight's Cross, dropped by parachute in one of the supply bombs that had made it into Cholm, the same method used to deliver this decoration to the teary-eyed, emotionally overcome Captain Bikers, who had been embraced by an equally emotional Scherer and then later killed during the siege's final days.

So Hitler's invitation to Scherer to visit him in the Reichskanzellei in Berlin was not for an awards ceremony, but understandably Hitler wanted to compliment the general personally and talk with him man to man.

The problem was that these cordial receptions for heroic

frontline generals were not always going as Hitler expected
them to. Only a few weeks earlier he had had a similar reception for General Seydlitz, whose corps had broken through to
the small nation of German troops surrounded at Demyansk
and finally lifted that siege. Like Scherer, Seydlitz was perceived as a national hero by press and public. But his personal interview with Hitler in Berlin had been a chillier
affair, with Seydlitz voicing numerous complaints about
conditions at the front, above all indignation that his men
were not being given some rest after successfully completing
such a grueling, even nearly impossible, operation. Those
present in the Reichskanzellei, and especially Seydlitz himself, had been struck by Hitler's manner of listening to these
complaints with visible indifference, with polite but visible
indifference.

In fact Hitler was not indifferent but simply masking a
strong surge of irritation. He spoke politely and with a rather
distracted manner, as if so many other urgent matters were
pressing upon him, which was true enough. But more than
that his demeanor was only a diplomatic guise to hide his annoyance with the complaints of these army generals. Seydlitz was a hero and Hitler did not wish to muddy the occasion
by coldly dismissing the man, though he had to restrain himself from doing so. He had already vented his rage upon a
number of other less heroic generals during the course of
that endless, terrible, and nearly disastrous winter. He had
genuinely wanted to congratulate Seydlitz and hear inti-
mately about the exploits of his corps, perhaps as a tonic
against his growing ill-feeling toward so many of the army's
other upper-level commanders. Instead Seydlitz's complaints, and his direct and barely respectful manner of voicing his complaints, had only aggravated this ill-feeling even
further. Hitler's vague politeness on this occasion was not
evidence of distraction but of a conscious effort of will not
to put the man in his place.

In effect, though, Seydlitz was put in his place. He was
sent directly back to the front, to Demyansk, where his soldiers awaited him in their own prolonged agony.

Then a few weeks later that tiny fly-speck at Cholm was finally relieved, and it was Scherer's turn to be summoned to

Berlin. Already Hitler had brusquely canceled the publicity tour organized by Goebbels and other Party officials, which would have sent Scherer on a whistle-stop junket across the nation, shaking hands and being feted as guest of honor at any number of parades or ceremonial dinners. Inevitably there would still be a few of these events, but the idea of these cool-eyed generals receiving too much adulation from the public was beginning to eat at Hitler's craw.

The meeting with Scherer went better than the one with Seydlitz. Scherer at least did not voice any complaints. How could he, when he and every other man of his beleaguered crew had been rewarded with long leaves at home? And he was no more than the commander of a security division suddenly thrust into prominence, a general in name only—when you got right down to it—though now of course he would have to be promoted.

At the reception Scherer was correct, polite, duly respectful, and even beaming with the incomprehensible urges of his own inner glory. But even with this happy fellow Hitler perceived a certain diffidence, and in a perverse sense the very fact that it was not as marked as it had been with Seydlitz only irked him the more.

Scherer was beaming because he could not help himself, but paradoxically he also rigidly bore the long frozen cruelty of the siege in his demeanor because he could not help that either. The spirits of dead men rose up behind his eyes, staring out even while amiable and modest words issued from his lips. It was true that for months he had been embittered by the scant, even miserly help delivered to him at Cholm. He had nothing but praise for the pilots of the supply planes who had kept them alive, but all the same the failure of the powers-that-be to deliver any kind of heavy weapons to his garrison until the very last days had struck him as pathetic. He knew also that the siege could have been broken up much sooner if any kind of determined effort had been made by German forces on the ground. Only ten miles, only ten miles away for all those months!

But who was at fault? Hitler? The army group commanders who had diverted German forces to other crisis spots during the winter and left Cholm to endure alone? Scherer was

anything but highly placed in command circles and didn't
know if it was anyone's fault; he really didn't know, and had
not come to speak to the Führer face-to-face with any kind of
ax to grind.

Anyway, the very hopelessness of his command at Cholm
had redounded all the better on him. He might reflect back on
his own judicious command decisions, he might reflect on
his months-long tenacity and the tenacity of his soldiers; but
even so he honestly could not say how they had survived
through it all, and a certain element of the miraculous still
resided within him that seemed to dispel petty grievances or
misunderstandings.

Scherer still wore the famous beard. Bearded or not, on the
whole he looked little different from a typical, not overly distinguished Prussian-style general. Scherer also had the curious trait of looking markedly different with his spectacles on
than without them. A general might wear reading glasses
from time to time and you would merely dismiss his appearance then as an uncharacteristic anomaly. But Scherer's eye-
sight was not that good and more often than not you would
think of him as a bespectacled man. He was short and looked
almost elfin, someone who did not inspire a great deal of seriousness, a man of high rank but who appeared nonetheless
as someone on the lesser fringes of command and command
decisions. Yet he also had the tendency to do without his
glasses much of the time—no doubt he was aware of how he
looked with them on—and immediately a deeper seriousness
would emanate not only from his eyes but seemingly from
the entire structure of his face.

What to make of a man's face? Idiosyncrasies, idiosyncrasies . . . just as with a beard; idiosyncrasies or else illu-
sions, superficialities . . .

But Hitler did not give himself over to a close examination
of Scherer's face. It took only a few glances to see things that
displeased him. Even when looking directly at the general
his eyes were somewhat glazed over by his own inner suspicions and preoccupations, loftier concerns that were for him
alone and which a mere general of lower rank could not intrude upon. If he glanced into Scherer's eyes from a few feet
away and still perceived a certain diffidence there, it perhaps

had not much to do with Scherer's attitude toward Hitler. It was perhaps the diffidence of a man suddenly become independent and self-reliant in ways he could barely understand—though by now Scherer had accepted this change within himself and it almost seemed as if he had always been this way. People who suddenly come into their own late in life—or really at any time in life—have little ways of fooling themselves into thinking that deep down they had always been that way, always. And who is to say that they are wrong, that they are even fooling themselves at all? No one knows.

Still Hitler had come to certain decisions after the earlier meeting with Seydlitz, and he had intentionally allotted himself only ten minutes to speak to Scherer. Of course he could have stretched this out or done anything else he wanted to do, and after Scherer had been ushered from the room he wondered momentarily if maybe he could have spoken to the man a little longer, warmed to him a bit.

But no, no. He was not going to belittle himself by thinking about personalities, especially not those of these old-guard army bastards. They had already begun to let him down, as secretly he had always known they would, and they would have to show him a great deal more respect before he warmed to them again. He was not one of these pompous Prussian asses; he did not demand respect, but only expected it as the sole leader of a resurgent nation. That did not seem too much to ask for an Austrian visionary who enjoyed a pleasant little chat as much as the next fellow.

But he had already thought through much of this even before now, and he had little difficulty putting Scherer out of his mind and getting on with whatever other business lay ahead on this day, and then the next day and the next. He was distracted because he was consumed and had been operating at this level for years now. It was May of 1942 and already places like Cholm and Demyansk seemed to belong to past history; on the maps of his war rooms the name of Stalingrad was already encircled with grease pencil.

So it was that Scherer returned to the East in July, decorated, honored, and just promoted from brigadier to major general. This time he was given command of a true fighting division, the 83rd Infantry, still holding positions around Velizh and Velikiye Luki.

These places were not very far from Cholm, which still stood in German hands only fifty miles to the north. On a Russian scale of distance, the towns seemed to be almost next-door neighbors.

Scherer was dismayed to see that German strength in this area was about as inadequate as it had been when he left Cholm. His own division was scattered over a front of more than twenty miles—a situation so extraordinary that it would have elicited strong protests from him; but he knew that the other divisions on his flanks were equally spread out. Dispositions such as these would have been suitable for keeping rebellious natives at bay in some remote colony. And perhaps the powers-that-be in the Reich still considered this to be the current situation in many parts of Russia—though Scherer could no longer conceive of such ignorance. Von der Chevallerie, the corps commander in Vitebsk, discussed this with him when he first arrived; it wasn't really ignorance, he said, it was rather the high command willfully keeping their collective heads buried in the sand.

"You're splitting hairs there," said Scherer. "It's still the same thing."

"Yes, I agree," said von der Chevallerie, an overweight but rather debonair man whose mannerisms seemed to fit his gallant-sounding name. He had come from France in January, along with the 83rd and several other divisions assigned to him; by now he had fully experienced the exhaustion, the anxiety, the shoestring fashion in which seemingly every operation had to be conducted. "The other thing is the big push that's started in southern Russia. It seems three quarters of the army has been sent down there. And then Demyansk is still sucking in resources like a great cesspool. We can be thankful, Scherer, that at least in our own neighborhood things have quieted down over the last few months. I'll leave it to your operations officers to go over that with you. I don't mean to sound overly optimistic, understand, but any kind of respite at all at this point is a godsend.

"I've kept at the other divisional commanders to clear up loose ends while we have time to do it, by which I mean all these damned Russian nests overlooking our supply lines. By the end of winter we were grateful just to still be in one piece, but we need more room to breathe. I've had too many sleepless nights thinking about that and so have the others. I'm sure you can appreciate that."

"Yes," said Scherer.

"Congratulations on your new command. And welcome back."

Scherer smiled faintly. For him it was enough, at least for now, that he was to command a genuine fighting outfit. If his disorganized stragglers at Cholm had fought so hard in a bad place, then these men would too, he figured. Yes, they'd been through it all too, the Landsers in the 83rd.

After this meeting with von der Chevallerie a staff car drove him out from Vitebsk. Vitebsk on the banks of the Duna River was another shattered, mangled, pulped, pulverized, and no longer recognizable town, impressive because it had been a city housing several hundred thousand souls before the war, now containing a bare fraction of that population even with the German forces stationed there. Not a ghost town but a ghost city. It was an industrialized place silhouetted here and there by mangled cranes and great factory sheds, by solitary smokestacks surviving gaunt and strange above the razed debris of the surrounding heavy plants, showing a somewhat different presence from the ancient medieval stone of Cholm and Velikiye Luki. But amidst the rubble that it had become it no longer showed that much difference. The car took him out via the river road along the Duna, where tall-windowed warehouses gaped hideously at the wide river. The subtle, open mouthed contortions of these buildings seemed to suggest that they had been laid waste and rendered paralyzed in the midst of the act of speech. Speakers require a listener and the wide river passing slowly below listened quietly forever yet also heedless. The water was low in high summer.

And then out into the countryside beneath the wide-spreading clouds. It was fifty miles to Velikiye Luki and along the way he would stop to visit another of the division's regimental command posts at Velizh. That was the southern anchor of Scherer's own front, while Velikiye Luki was the

northern. A whole alphabet using only the letter *V,* the ruined
places in this area of the Soviet Union . . .

Velizh rose up blasted from the crest of a small hill, devastated yet picturesque beneath the sky. The single sand road
ascended at a slight gradient up the small hill to the various
stone structures that still remained. A skeleton flayed of its
body, really, for all the helter-skelter wooden isbas that had
formed the bulk of the town had been burned to the ground
during the winter.

The regimental commander informed Scherer more
specifically about the kinds of problems von der Chevallerie
had mentioned. Local operations to drive back the Russian
strongpoints that were forever menacing the very few supply
roads.

"Yes, little has changed, has it?" said Scherer. "Listen
now, perhaps you have some schnapps. If not I've brought a
few bottles in the car. This is just a courtesy visit. I'll have
you and the other regimental commanders come up to divisional HQ in a few days, so we can all hash this out together.
For right now let's sit down and have a drink, shall we? Unless there's anything that can't wait. No? All right then. In-
troduce me to your staff."

They looked at Scherer appraisingly, warmly, very happy
to have a drink with him and sit a few feet from him in the
faintly altered sunlight of his fame and charisma. His
charisma had in fact preceded his person and now the colonel
and his staff wanted to see what kind of person he really was.
They were courteous and relaxed, cheerful, around tables set
in the sun outside the building housing the command post.

Scherer had the curious presence of a flinty-eyed yet actually rather amiable man who tended to speak as an equal to
his officers, not pressing the aloofness of leadership because
he felt comfortable among men and the ranks seemed little
stratified around him. Other generals would relax and have a
drink with their officers once in a while, but they still normally conversed with each other through these invisible
stratified layers. Scherer tended to dispel some of that, however. Again like a sea captain in close confinement with
long-term acquaintances—not friends but shipmates—on an
isolated vessel far off in lonely seas. One of the reasons his

star had not risen earlier in his career was that he tended not to stand out when functioning as part of a large organization, the army in peacetime being little more than a large and overly complicated organization. In war this arrangement still held true, but the organization tended to be broken up into smaller and more discrete bands of souls the closer one got to the sticking point, to the violence and the stress.

It was a short visit, the drinking of a few toasts, the introduction of a few new faces. He then drove on toward the divisional headquarters at Novo Sokolniki, a small, miserable though not entirely ruined town chosen for this site only because of its location in the middle of the division's zone, about seven miles behind the front lines. Velikiye Luki would have been a more appropriate place, but it was on the far northern flank, and in any case the Russians were still obstinately established right on the outskirts of this city.

The division being so widely spread out was irksome, not only from the standpoint of tactical weakness, but also because it made it difficult for Scherer to really exercise command, especially in the direct and intimate style that he had made his own at Cholm. In effect, one could almost say there was no division, but only three separate regiments operating out of widely dispersed strongpoints. It was difficult for him to issue orders without seeming to intrude upon the judgments of local commanders who knew their local situations day in and day out better than he did, who could only keep apprised via field telephone or time-consuming visits back and forth across the poor, dusty roads. With the front more or less stabilized for the time being this was not overly critical, but he could only wonder what lay ahead.

The attack upon the *Iltis Stellung* was another one of these minor, utterly savage operations to drive the Russians back from a commanding stretch of ground that overlooked the *rollbahn*. *Rollbahn*, main highway, was a term used with endless sardonicism in Russia because the *rollbahn* was never more than a dusty, frequently nonnegotiable track along which supplies must be carried. This particular *rollbahn* was the only direct link between Velizh and Velikiye Luki and Russian artillery spotters atop the *Iltis* were less than a mile away from it. To reroute traffic along the even more godforsaken roads back in the partisan-infested hinter-land would add hours, even as much as a day, to any journey between the two towns.

Worse still, the German main line was in many places ac-tually behind the *rollbahn*, with only a screen of outposts on the far side of the road standing between it and Russian infil-tration or worse dangers. Life for men in these outposts was unnerving (sometimes one can only use the first word to come to mind, even if it seems foolishly obvious), unnerving and also exhausting, because out in that isolated country they could never relax, even when very little was happening for days at a time. The Russian snipers or patrols or raiding par-ties were busy just frequently enough, or infrequently enough, that a man's nerves felt constantly nagged at by the need to stay alert, even when every other fiber of his being apart from that one faint little voice wished to surrender to a kind of monotonous stupor after standing watch and seeing nothing hour after hour.

The outposts were relieved every few days and the men coming back to the main line would be thankful for the end of some particularly loathsome chore. Meanwhile the driv-ers of vehicles along the *rollbahn* would feel an equal anxi-ety when passing through sectors hardly more secure than no-man's-land.

This disagreeable supply situation might have been termed intolerable in other wars; but people do get used to things even while continuing to feel discomfort and fear. The So-viet counteroffensive back in the winter had imposed this ir-regularity on the German main line and neither Scherer nor his predecessor had had enough forces at hand to advance the main line securely beyond the *rollbahn*. It was frustrating, even idiotic, because the whole situation would have been ir-relevant if there had been any kind of decent road network in the rear areas. But that was Russia. Frustrating, idiotic, mo-notonous, exploding with anguish at the end of infernal and unpredictable intervals of boredom.

Even now Scherer did not have enough men to do a proper job. But it was time to do something nonetheless. He had un-derstood von der Chevallerie perfectly well over in Vitebsk:

at the end of the winter they had been grateful just to be alive. But now it was high time to set things in order, somehow.

And so he knew in advance that the attack upon the *Iltis* would be made by only a single reinforced company. This was no good; a battalion at the very least should have gone in. Kreiser, the regimental commander in Velikiye Luki, could only agree, but where could he take a whole battalion out of the line without leaving the barn door wide open for the Russians?

Scherer insisted that at least one more company be brought up in the event of a Russian counterattack, which of course was inevitable. Kreiser bore the tight-lipped expression of a man who did not need to be told something was inevitable. But by now the regimental commanders had been operating for quite some time somewhat as Scherer had operated at Cholm—as masters of their own lonely ships. They were not as completely independent as all that, and they wanted to get along well with a man like Scherer, but they tended to hoard their own units in miserly fashion, never sure when some new crisis might explode upon them before help could be summoned from afar.

"Damn it," said Scherer, in the citadel, where Kreiser had his command post in Velikiye Luki. "This isn't just a show of force. That would be a sham anyway. If you're to accomplish anything at all you'll need more than just a company."

Kreiser said, "I would like very much to use more than just a company, Herr General. As you suggest, I'll scrape up another one to go in behind the assault troops."

The faintly accusatory tone behind this last comment left Scherer unmoved. As if he, Scherer, ought to have more people brought up from one of the other regiments or even from corps reserve in Vitebsk. Well, of course he should, but von der Chevallerie had no one to spare and neither did Scherer's other regiments. The *Iltis Stellung* was no more than a small festering pimple anyway, an objective that might easily be taken out by a single company. The problem was the hornet's nest that would be stirred up when the Russians responded.

Scherer said, "All right, Kreiser, I don't like this piecemeal approach any more than you do. Besides the *Iltis* there are at least three other of these hemorrhoids overlooking the road and the other regiments will have to deal with them. What's needed is a limited offensive to clear out all of these places at once and have done with them. Just to push the whole line forward for a mile or two would be a big help. But to do that would take a whole fresh division and no one else wants to give up a precious division. So we'll just have to take these nests out one at a time and I want you to use every man you can spare to do that. We're all in the same boat here."

"Yes, I know," said the other man.

Scherer had spoken this single phrase over and over again at Cholm and now out of habit he was saying it again. But he knew that more than old words were wanted and he tried to stick to the details of things. He was weary, weary with the formal manner he had to assume whenever he was forced to insist on something with his officers; it was alien to him and so it tired him. He said, "The area north of Velikiye Luki is a swamp. You know that better than I do, you've been here long enough. Take a company out of the line up there, even if you have only a few sentries left to screen the place. This whole area is a backwater right now, Kreiser, as impertinent as that may sound to you and me. Perhaps when the southern armies have finished up with their tour of the Caucasus then more people will be made available to us here. God only knows. I have confidence in you, Kreiser. Just make sure you have enough men."

This last was the inherent contradiction they had been talking about all along but Scherer wanted to reemphasize it anyway. The attack went in in heavy mist at dawn on 3 August. Kreiser's rehearsals had been thorough and the *Iltis* had been stormed with only slight losses. Often the Russians seemed to be slumbering in the drowsy summer, gathering strength for their own next series of blows (whenever that would be) via some mysterious somnambulism. But once poked out of their lethargy they struck back hard. Artillery batteries, for weeks so quiescent that German spotters did not even have them marked on their charts, now opened up to deluge the *Iltis* pimple. By mid-morning more than a dozen T-34s had appeared and these would be but the first of many more. Scherer had no armored vehicles to send up there and the men of the storm company were not expecting any. They had manhandled two small antitank guns up there and as soon as the *Iltis* was secured these were brought into position. But these 3.7 mm guns, doorknockers as they were called with great contempt, were next to useless against T-34s except at point-blank range, and so the storm troops must undergo the grimly familiar experience of having the Soviet tanks drive very nearly into their positions before being able to fight back. The 3.7s were no more than another of the many and various hideous tools of man/tank combat at close range and the storm troops now burrowed down in the captured Soviet trenches employed all the others against the tanks as well: grenade bundles, Teller mines, and various other explosives that must be laid upon a tank by a single human being climbing up and exposing himself.

As there was no other choice but to do this, to do this or be crushed or buried alive in their trenches, it became a superb way of creating heroes. Dead heroes or else those miraculously lucky. Truth be told, they had gotten rather good at it, and six hulks were smoking on the *Iltis* even before the relief company arrived. One of the 3.7s had been run over, squashed like a bug or like plumbing and the dead crew pulped underneath. A pity for those steadfast mangled souls but no one else much regretted the loss of one of those shitty demoralizing guns. When the Russian infantry got up into the trenches men started to be killed more quickly in various terrible ways. In one five-minute period Schrader lost more men than he had lost during the preceding six months, and the effect of this would hang about him for almost that long afterward, over him and Krabel and the few others that managed to get out of that one section of trench.

The werfer salvo was scheduled to come down with maximum possible effect, that is by the time in mid-afternoon when things had gotten truly desperate and at least twenty T-34s were assembling and ready to overrun the *Iltis*.

The blast of the salvo—the quick multiple deluge of blasts—had rendered the storm party nearly speechless, knocking some unconscious and more seriously injuring a few of them. Out in front of them several T-34s were turned entirely upside down. Others burned. Others remained motionless in the stunned aftershock, seemingly unharmed, yet they would continue to remain motionless out there for hours and hours. When these vehicles were finally recovered by the Soviets a day or two later they would find the crews sleeping quietly within, small trickles of blood dried around noses, ears, mouths, assholes (if they cared to look that closely), all of them stone-dead from immeasurable atmospheric forces.

After the salvo a few tanks drove drunkenly away, steered by perhaps one or two survivors inside. Finally the remaining crews who had been only stunned regained their composure and stubbornly resumed their attack upon the *Iltis*. But they pressed it with less energy now and withdrew at about the time the relief company appeared on the scene.

The defenders of the place had a short breathing spell, apart from barrage fire that continued to come down.

Then the Russians came again with more men and armor and the defenders were all still there—dead or alive—thirty-six hours later when Scherer at last ordered the place abandoned. Without more men the place could not be held. Perhaps even with more men the place could not be held. The Russian response had exceeded Scherer and Kreiser's worst fears; not since the winter had they displayed so much relentless energy.

Hasenclever, the old Spiess of the storm company, was out there again by the *rollbahn* with a dead wagon and a wounded wagon and several liters of beer, greeting these survivors as he had greeted Schrader and his survivors the day before.

A few days later Scherer was surprised to see that the storming and subsequent defense of the *Iltis* hemorrhoid had been mentioned in the Wehrmacht communiqué, praising the men of 83rd Infantry Division for their valiant effort. Yes, thought Scherer, it had been a valiant effort, and if nothing else he had a good sense of the fighting spirit of the men now under his command. He was in his headquarters in nearly the only habitable building in Novo Sokolniki, thinking this, holding the communiqué in his hand and staring at it with some pride.

In some ways he was already living in the past, where dead men were already dead—and it no longer mattered whether they had gone down in a useless display of fighting spirit or for some better reason than that. He felt their blood, he very much did, and he felt pride as well, a certain grim businesslike pride that in a sensitive enough man was strangely similar to remorse. Scherer displayed more emotion than most but he was not overly sentimental. In any case the operation had not been a complete write-off. The Soviets had been so maddened by the business at the *Iltis* that they had responded less violently elsewhere; storm parties from the other regiments had come about a mile past the *rollbahn* in two other places and were still holding their ground there.

Chapter Twelve

Klenner was an eccentric fellow, enthused with his own enthusiasms, older than most of the others. At some point he had acquired a corporal's stripes, though he never exercised the slightest authority, even upon the newest recruit; his manner was tutorial, if anything. Most of the men simply found him strange, though some were drawn to his energetic, workmanlike habits. He worked with the supply people in the rear areas but often he would visit the forward positions on his own initiative, bringing fresh vegetables. He distributed these fresh things to anyone he came across, officers or men. Gardening was his enthusiasm and he would enlist muddy Landsers, off duty, to follow him back to the rear where the gardens were, in those green shell-torn areas outside Velikiye Luki.

They all prized the things he grew, that spring and summer, because otherwise their rations were not so good, as in any army. He tended a small acreage outside the city; or you might consider it fairly large, if you knew that he alone had done almost all the digging in these plots, all the digging and caretaking. He had a few horses at his disposal, but often he would just harness himself to a small cart laden with manure, hauling this from the stables over to where his plots were. His body was lean from this hard work, his skin browner than so many others who spent too much time burrowed down in the trenches and dugouts of the forward line. He had helpers to help him from the supply battalions and cook's crews, but he did far more of the work than anyone else, and never chastised anyone for not keeping up with his pace.

So he didn't really need the assistance of any of the Landsers from the combat platoons, but still he would encourage them to come back and work with him, as if it were a kind of wisdom he was imparting. And there were enough who would follow him back there, into the sunshine, to weed and till for a few hours. It was peaceful there, most of the time. Apart from the *Iltis* operation, the front had been fairly quiet, during these warmer months.

Freitag had been up at one of the forward listening posts for ten hours. Duty in one of these positions was arduous, even while almost always dull and uneventful. But a man up there could not relax, and so upon being relieved he would always be stiff and tired. For the moment, though, Freitag did not want to go back and sleep in one of the dugouts, nor sit dully in those shadows and talk quietly or smoke or play cards. He did do that when he was empty and listless, or just had to sleep. Today he walked back that further mile or so, back to where Klenner was working.

There were a few other men back there too, hoeing or mounding soil at their own pace, while Klenner worked nearby with his own industriousness. Freitag worked and joked quietly with some of the others, among rows of beets and cucumbers, other things, clumps of manure and compost. It was peaceful. The countryside was large. Often they rested against the handles of their hoes or shovels, not because they were tired, but just to stand there quietly and absorb the satisfaction of seeing things growing at their feet, to smoke and stare about at the land without being threatened by fire. Klenner for all his continuous activity would sometimes join them, discoursing on growing things. The others would listen to him with interest but often he would talk on and on, his way of talking as compulsive as his physical energy, and so Freitag or some other man would listen abstractedly while letting their eyes wander across the land.

The land was marked, or anchored, by the city over to the right, white stone murky in heavy summer daylight. Then the cemetery, the birch-bark cemetery of one of the regiments, on the outskirts near the bank of the Lovat. Then the moorlands, with birch trees clumped around the greener places— though all was green during these months, with a good deal of rainfall this summer—and part of the horizon anchored by the railroad embankment leading to Novo Sokolniki.

The same clouds were up as were up almost every day,
their scattered masses spread far above serving also to spread
the landscape underneath farther and farther, giving scale to
the immensity and making it more forceful than it would be
on a clear day. Sunlight in deep, mobile shafts walked slowly
across the moors.

A man appeared at the edge of a forested area nearby, to
the left of the railroad embankment. It was Kordts. Klenner
looked up, saw Freitag studying him over there, and himself turned to watch, mumbling some words of approval or
curiosity.

"He should be careful out there," said Klenner. "Is he a
gardener?"

"Could be," said Freitag.

It was against regulations to wander so far afield, especially alone, though regulations were not always strictly enforced. Most men instinctively stayed near to the company
of others, but there were some who felt the need to wander
back from the dull confinement of the trenches when they
had the opportunity from time to time. Kordts was one of
these, walking off by himself into the hinterlands sometimes
when off duty. He had asked Freitag to accompany him once
or twice—stretch your legs, get some air, as he would say in
one form or another—but the regulations, and the reports of
partisans that were behind the regulations made Freitag
nervous. He had heard of no ambushes or murders this close
to the city, but you never knew. The moors were wide and the
forests scattered across the moors were deep enough.

In truth Freitag would have liked to wander off once in a
while. He was a good talker, used to associating with people
in close company, but he wouldn't have minded some soli-
tude for a few hours. If Kordts had encouraged him more he
might have let himself be persuaded. But Kordts, while men-
tioning it, had simply left it up to him; he seemed indifferent
whether he wandered about alone or in someone's company.

"You don't feel nervous sometimes, out there?" Freitag
had said one day.

"Oh. Maybe a little," Kordts had said. "Not so much
though. I've felt a little easier lately. Might as well take advantage of it while it lasts, heh? Ha, ha."

While it lasts. Freitag had guessed this to mean while his nerves lasted, before his nerves inevitably began to crawl in upon him, making him more reluctant to wander about under the distant sun-clouds. Freitag wasn't sure; maybe he was thinking of himself more than Kordts. A certain resigned glumness had gradually come over them all in the train, the nearer the train had brought them back to the front. You wouldn't expect much different. But Kordts seemed to have remained in fairly good spirits, even for some time afterward.

Beside him Klenner said, "Wave him over this way, why don't you? He needs to set his back to something useful."

"Ah. Maybe," said Freitag. But he raised his arm. Kordts was coming their way, slowly, in the distance, between the forest and the railroad embankment. He raised his hand to acknowledge the signal. Another man nearby said someone should let off a few rounds out there, to make him jump a little. People laughed.

Freitag felt the need to talk and suddenly he was describing at length to Klenner the garden plot he had tended with his mother, in the scrubby lot outside the large building where he had lived since childhood. He began to feel easier and more animated, explaining little tricks he had used to grow things in tired and scabby soil. Freitag did not even know Klenner's last name, calling him Fred as almost everyone did, as if it were natural to call a peculiar older non-com by his first name. Klenner never seemed to mind this and Freitag was taken aback when the man abruptly began berating him for being so full of himself.

"Be humbler," Klenner commanded. "It's unhealthy to be so full of notions. Listen more. It's all in the proportions. Soil is no different."

Freitag felt he had been talking agreeably enough and was somewhat insulted. He persisted in smiling in a friendly manner and tried to explain himself, but Klenner only glared at him and turned his back, stepping his shovel into the soil. He was shirtless and Freitag stared at his brown back and felt still more insulted. But he told himself the gardener was too peculiar to take all that seriously. He could not help feeling a little worked up but after a minute or two he just shrugged, swinging his shovel up on his shoulder, gratified when another man gave him a knowing look and nodded his head in Klenner's direction.

"Well, he's a funny one," said Kordts, too, when he came up a few minutes later, having a smoke with Freitag. Kordts was not inclined to do any gardening. It just reminded him of the trenches, he said. Walking was the only thing he could tolerate, walking or sleeping. He grinned crookedly. The grin seemed somewhat incongruous, set beneath eyes that often cast about with a dark fixation on the things around.

He walked back toward the forward positions, less than a mile away, though nothing whatever of them visible from this distance. Freitag stayed on a while, thinking he would take Klenner's measure by not being put in an ill humor, talking to him again if he felt like it.

Chapter Thirteen

A special service was held after the *Iltis* attack, on a green knoll. The divisional chaplain came over to the rear areas of 257.

He was not well-known to most men. The division was too large an entity. There had been chaplains serving in the smaller units in earlier wars, in regiments and battalions, dispersed that way to be closer to the men; but not in this one.

Only two companies had been at the *Iltis*, but men from throughout the 257th Infantry Regiment could be found now, in the grass, around the green knoll. They sat with their knees drawn up; or they sat with their knees curled sideways under them, supporting themselves with one hand or leaning on an elbow.

Only a few, in a small semicircle close to the chaplain on the crest of this small elevation, were actually kneeling.

Only a few, too, were even facing in the chaplain's direction, or listening to him at all; his voice did not carry far. They might listen to the sound of his voice but be unable to make out his words.

Most of them at the bottom of the knoll sat with their backs or their sides turned to him, if only because it was more comfortable facing that way, and they stared off into the distance or at individual stems of grass at their feet, resembling men lost in their own thoughts on a hillside far away from anyone, or men resting during a pause in a long march, finding a few minutes to look about and let whatever thoughts pass through their minds.

There was no disrespect in these seemingly too relaxed attitudes. They came here, sat here around the knoll, only if they wanted to. His voice might carry out to them like a small stream, individual words appearing and disappearing, if they even heard anything at all apart from the faint tick of sunlight in the grass. But to be here around the knoll served to focus their minds in certain ways, which was the purpose of this or any service, really; focusing a certain kind of silence or other force within themselves, where the dead rose quietly past their own solemn, still-living spirits.

He stood there before a plain wooden bench, upon which was set a crucifix and a few sacramental objects. He wore a military uniform with a purple cloth, his only vestment, draped over his shoulders. A few feet to one side tall green bushes grew across the crest of the knoll and ran down one side of it. Bushes and small trees, hardly more than saplings. It was like a small wood, small but lush now in the northern summer, and the short grass where the men sat was also lush. The elevation was just high enough, breezy enough, to be above the mosquito swarms that clung in a particular miasma to the lower-lying fens or that infested the innards of any region of woods or forest. They needed only to wave their hands about once in a while, or brush their fingers against their cheeks, or twitch their heads; no comical or violent slapping, or only a little.

The knoll was about as high as the *Iltis Stellung* had been. Those who had been at that place might have been reminded of it, seeing the knoll stripped of its grass and saplings and mulched with bodies and metal, barbed wire, with the debris of violence that tends to lose all particulars, becomes only litter, a mess, smoking or smelling.

Yet the knoll was too typical of the landscape for hundreds of miles in any direction to be too closely associated with any specific place, maybe. It was quiet and the clouds walked far overhead, and broad columns of sunlight walked between the clouds and across the earth's surface.

Freitag watched Fred Klenner, still with some interest. He'd still had little luck in talking with the man; though having finally given up on it, it no longer bothered him particularly. He'd been out in the gardens again in the early morning and achieved the response of a few grunts from Klenner, disconnected ramblings that seemed almost civil, though the man still eyed him with suspicion; Freitag had no idea why. Klenner was made uncomfortable by anyone who talked as much as he did, or almost as much, as Freitag did, but Freitag had no sense of that.

Klenner knelt the closest of anyone to the chaplain, a little apart from the small semicircle of men around the bench altar who were also kneeling. Freitag saw Klenner's lips moving and occasionally he spoke loudly enough that his voice carried down to the other men scattered across the lower part of the knoll. Some would glance over their shoulders when they heard Klenner, but only for a moment, and most remained absorbed in their own thoughts, sitting and staring abstractedly with a peculiar geometric force at right angles to the direction the chaplain was facing.

Klenner listened closely to everything the chaplain said, though he seemed almost to be monitoring him as well, a sun-dark man closely eyeing this earthly religious figure, Klenner in his strangeness seeming to hover there, though he remained kneeling.

Freitag looked up the gradual slope at him for a few moments, over the shoulders and bare heads of other men seated around him, then fell back into his own thoughts, sunlit, sun falling on the grass nearby. He stared at the lush scrubby bushes, this growth growing perhaps twice as tall as a man, that ran down one side of the knoll. Men sat ten or fifteen feet away from the edge of it, a border area to the insect realm in there. The sunlight moted slow mosquitoes among the leaves and small branches. There were a few white birch trees among the other little trees in there, with leaves trembling in any breeze, blinking, shivering, like a being about to materialize.

To stare at anything like this became part of the service itself, for him and for other men; it was natural, and he recalled staring at stone piers in a church during Sunday services as a child, or at light in the windows, as a child and as recently as a year or two ago. Clouds passed every few minutes overhead and brought shadows like robes of darker light, trailing quietly across the land. His mother was quite religious, or at least in her own mind she was, though it tended to come over her in irregular fits of church attendance and religious talks; probably most of her drinking acquaintances would not know this side of her, except for some of the men who would live with her and Freitag for a while.

He was cheered to see Kordts arrive. He was standing there suddenly, nudging Freitag's thigh with the toe of his boot. Freitag grinned and said something. Kordts stood with his hands on his hips, looking around like someone who had unexpectedly come upon some gathering in the countryside, this gathering. He looked strangely serene and Freitag felt a vague stirring of envy, though he might have thought himself serene enough for a few moments here, or something like it. Kordts stared about lazily yet intently as he would do, his face sun-dark though not with the permanence of Klenner's face, a few reddish gleams on his cheekbones that would fade away after another night's passing in the trenches.

He settled down on his haunches, nudging Freitag in the shoulder with his hand as he had nudged him with his boot, whispering that he had seen a ration of beer being brought up, a few barrels, a little way from the knoll. "Oh," said Freitag. His eyes brightened with this news. A few other men nearby raised their eyebrows, grinning crookedly, nodding at Kordts or to themselves with sudden relaxation. A few observed Kordts and Freitag together, or they noticed the bronze shields on both their sleeves. Dark bronze shields gleaming dully in the light, still dark. Kordts stretched out and lay full length in the grass; there were other men who lay on their backs like this, knees drawn up, staring at the sky, some with their heads resting on a comrade's knee. Kordts already felt pretty easy, beer or no beer. He put a stem of grass in his mouth, took it out, scratched his face with it, absently outlining the scar by grazing the live skin on either side of it. A small rim of sun peered over a tall cloud passing far overhead.

He felt a hand on his shoulder and looked up. "Schrader over there," said Freitag. He was pointing. Kordts sat up. Schrader and Krabel stood in a pasture a little way from the knoll. Kordts looked at them for a moment, about a hundred feet away. Then he looked at the grass beneath his legs, closing his eyes again.

Freitag had looked around for them earlier, noting their

absence; there were quite a few men here but he thought he would have seen them if they'd been here. Krabel hunched down, tentatively on the balls of his feet, then sat cross-legged out there. Schrader remained standing and Freitag drifted back into his own thoughts, glancing here and there, at Klenner, at the chaplain, at the dark bushes, at nothing, noticing a few minutes later that Schrader had gone.

Hasenclever and Goff, the commissary corporal, had set up the beer keg a little way from the knoll, and tapped it to see that it was in working order, getting their taste of it. It was an exceptionally fine day and a taste of beer assured them that this was so. Wide clouds and wide bands of blue sky drifted over them in a strangely invigorating procession.

They were surprised to see Schrader and Krabel come by and Hasenclever asked if the service had ended so quickly. They hadn't gone there yet, said Krabel. Schrader said nothing.

The beer was to be dispensed after the chaplain had said his words, but Hasenclever invited them to go ahead if they wished, still feeling solicitous of Schrader and wanting him to feel at ease. Schrader did not look as hostile as he had a few days earlier; Hasenclever reflected that it had been a poor choice of words on his part, but he hadn't intended it that way and Schrader must know it. Schrader seemed to acknowledge this in his way, though he made only a few barely audible comments, drinking his beer and staring into the distance.

"A little fortification won't hurt, eh?" said Krabel.

Schrader nodded.

Both of them but he in particular felt pulled toward the little knoll by some tide, which they knew they were resisting. But it was not a steadfast resistance. Rather they let themselves be pulled a little way, then braced their feet for a few moments, drinking their beer and feeling the tug of that tide that they would give in to again in a minute or two.

Schrader looked at the beer-foam on Krabel's long dragoon mustache and thought back to Velizh, where in a three-week frozen siege they had still fared better than during a five-minute span a few days ago. He could not think about this directly, or would not. Velizh had been terrible anyway; for they had only just arrived in Russia, without any chance to become acclimated to the winter. There must be some other word than winter for what that had been. But he did not think about all this directly either, not really. He saw the beer-foam on Krabel's mustache and remembered it dipped white with milk. They'd found a cow in a barn buried under snow, the animal so distressed by undernourishment and shellfire that it would not give milk. But they had kept it alive through all those weeks and when the siege was over they finally coaxed it into giving a little milk. A little milk, from a cow in the winter silence that came after the siege was lifted. They'd been fond of that animal, indeed they had, grudgingly though she'd given up what she had. But it was all a fine gesture of generosity, as far as they were concerned. Krabel would wipe milk off his mustache, but always a few white beads would cling there to freeze.

He remembered these few little things in less time than it would take to describe them to a listener, and they disappeared from his mind and were replaced by other things.

They drained their cups and dangled them from their fingers and walked closer to the little knoll. Though in walking it felt rather that the forward movement of their feet was bracing them slightly, against that dull steady pull. They stopped again about a hundred feet away from where all the men were gathered on that small elevation, with that green summer thicket running across one side of it. Now that they were here that faint tugging sensation disappeared and they felt they could either stay or leave as they pleased. Krabel stayed and sat down cross-legged in the grass, removing his pipe from his pocket but simply holding the bowl in his two hands without lighting it. Schrader stood beside him and stayed a little while, then walked off again.

Chapter Fourteen

Kordts and Freitag sat at the entrance to Kordts's dugout. It was night. The nights were cooler now. So were the days.

Freitag was strumming his guitar, an instrument he played with skill. Kordts dimly remembered seeing Freitag sitting in a corner of a barracks building, almost two years ago now, strumming at what must have been this same guitar. Then he could not recall seeing it again until they were on the train together, coming back here. The boy must have left it at home, that first year out here. Too much marching then, to carry such a bulky and frivolous bit of gear halfway into the Soviet Union and then half that distance back again, marching, marching, through the low clouds of their own dust, and through mud and rain. And then that endless stopover at Cholm, that frozen place. Kordts tried to imagine Freitag or anyone playing a guitar during those black nights in Cholm, but he couldn't picture such a thing. Maybe a little music would have helped them through all that a little better, but he still couldn't imagine it. Ah, that was it, he thought, their fingers would have been too damned cold; even in the warmest of those wrecked buildings it was still cold all the time. So it actually made sense then, didn't it?

He made some kind of unascertainable noise to himself, within the confines of his nostrils or some brief flex of his belly. It was scarcely even a noise, just some kind of bodily thought that had no words or pictures attached to it, only the presence of his own self sitting in dim acknowledgment of something, he didn't know what.

Any thought about that cold would actually seem to lower his body temperature by a degree or two, and why shouldn't it? It had done so at chance moments in high summer and so fleetingly he felt it again now at the end of summer, outside of some other ruined town.

Just now though, in the cool quiet night, even while he felt a chill passing through the core of his body, he still did not feel the glass-iron feel of frostbite within his fingers. No, he didn't feel that. But he could remember it, and he was surprised to note that the memory of some physical sensation should be every bit as vivid as some visual memory inside his head. He would have sworn he had heard or read somewhere that human beings have no memory of pain, apart from the fact of it having occurred—but no sense memory. Well, more nonsense, he thought, or maybe he had just misunderstood the whole idea. Because he could remember that pain in fine detail—how the frozen outer touch of the air would set it off, but how the worst of it came from inside the hands, all the little bones transformed into iron rods that seemed somehow to expand into the flesh, that agony. Though he felt briefly the overall chill of that unnameable god—that thing, whatever that whole experience had been—he did not actually feel the hideous rods again inside his fingers. But he could remember how that had felt, as clearly as the face of his own mother.

He had remembered all this often enough over these last months that it made no particular impression on him now. It had just happened to occur to him again, something about Freitag's guitar, of all things. His train of thought wandered on and around like everyone's did and he could no longer recollect some stopover along the line from only a minute earlier. Anyway there was no need to dread anything just now; there would be plenty of time for that in another month or two.

"By God," he blurted. "I wonder if they've still got old Moll locked away like that?"

Freitag looked up in the darkness but only shook his head slowly, as if this gesture were still keeping in time with his music-making. Kordts had become used to the boy's loquaciousness by now; over these recent weeks he had seen too that when he was strumming his instrument—actually he never seemed to strum it, he really played the thing—he would become more self-absorbed and tend not to respond to interruptions with his usual energetic chatter. Almost all the men liked hearing him play and on different nights he had been more than willing to entertain them, laughing and talking in his way, seeming quite himself in this way of spreading cheer. In the trenches and dugouts there was no privacy anyway; but he had told Kordts once or twice that he really preferred to be off playing by himself somewhere, and Kordts could see it now, in the darkness.

In the darkness there was light barely visible from Hindenburg lamps lit behind drawn blankets or makeshift doors, coming from within the various dugouts. Kordts and Freitag sat on a firing step in the trench just outside. And there was the starlight of the night, remote yet intense with its unchanging presence, whenever a man might wish to ponder it; and so many hours did they have to do it, living in these trenches, day, night, day, night. And then there was the intermittent shock-light of flares sent up by men on duty in the different forward emplacements up and down the line. They all shot up flares with the utmost regularity, to see what was out there in no-man's-land and dispel their fears of being crawled up upon and murdered, to keep their nerves steady but also maybe to pass the time somehow—long black utterly dull hours on watch—sending up flares at about the same intervals as a man might allow himself a cigarette, to keep his nerves steady and make the time pass. Except they couldn't smoke on watch—a highly disagreeable kind of abstinence—with any orange pinpricks glowing within an embrasure liable to draw a clean head-shot from the other dark over there.

Some men would smoke anyway—in moments of discomfort and gloom no longer caring whether they were shot or not, or given some filthy punishment if an officer happened to discover them—but still they were careful, bending low in the darkness to light the weed, ducking to inhale, holding the smoke down low by one thigh.

The Russians over there were not in the habit of sending up flares all the time, as if the darkness were their ally. It was the kind of superstitious rot one builds up around the faceless enemy, maybe. Maybe they weren't so well supplied with the things over there, or trusted to their hearing or night vision or whatever it might be. On a day-to-day basis the Germans probably fired the flare pistols more often than their normal weapons. The waning August days had been quiet outside Velikiye Luki. At night the flares arced, burst, fizzled into blackness again, giving the illusion of some kind of on-going activity within the nothingness below, like sparks sent flying out from some constantly whirring bulk of machinery. But there was nothing really, only the men gathered silently in trenches and dugouts.

Another man joined them.

"How can anyone sleep listening to that rot?"

"It's a damned lullaby," said Freitag. "Well, why didn't you say something sooner?"

"Ha, ha," the man said. "No, I was just joking. Nothing can stop me sleeping when I want to sleep. But I thought I might sit out here for a few minutes."

It was Heissner, a man given over from another company to help replenish Schrader's losses. He wore glasses but had a kind of sculpted-looking face, brutal-looking, Slavic maybe, high cheekbones. He was another working-class Landser with a sly mouth who could outdrink them all when drink was around. Given over on such occasions to rude, working-class opinions, whatever they might be. Jews, bosses, draft-evaders, various assholes. At first Kordts and Freitag had looked at him as some kind of loudmouthed fool, the kind of man they had seen often enough in their own neighborhoods at home.

Or perhaps Heissner had been put off at first by the other two, who were unnerving—or at least Kordts was—unde-servedly famous, and who had the habit of spending too much time together, as if the others weren't good enough for them. Schrader and Krabel had been acting that way too of late, but no one blamed them for it. So Heissner had found himself in the odd position of keeping company with the replacements—the raw ones, that is—and understand-ably irked at being separated from his old crew in the other company.

The thing was, it turned out he wasn't such a disagreeable

fellow after all. Though rough-spoken he was considerate and easy to get along with in most ways, a corporal who was probably better suited to the extra stripe than either Kordts or Freitag, who now wore this stripe as well. After a while they'd seen, also, that maybe he didn't take his rude loud-mouthed opinionating as seriously as they'd thought at first.

"Well, damn it," said Heissner. "You didn't have to stop."

"Shut up then," said Freitag. "You broke my train of thought."

"Train of thought? Just play, man."

"Maybe I will, maybe I won't."

"Ah, you're just like my own little brother. What do you think, Scar?"

Kordts laughed quietly.

"I don't know. I think my own brother was a little afraid of me. I feel bad about it sometimes. I'll make it up to him, if we ever get finished out here."

"Hell, you don't want to finish just yet. You've got one sleeve still empty. Maybe you can pick up another bit of bronze. Maybe I'll get one too this time."

Kordts was no longer so troubled by the urge to glare with overt hostility at certain people. Heissner's rattling igno-rance was not quite so offensive somehow. He had an odd kind of decency. Having experienced an instinctive wave of loathing upon first meeting the man a few weeks earlier, he was warming to the pleasant idea that maybe he'd just gotten it wrong. At a glance Heissner would give off all the not-so-subtle signs of being a bully, a stupid fool echoing all the coarse cruelty of other stupid fools. There were enough like that around. But unaccountably Heissner had turned out to be not so bad. More and more Kordts would grow weary of the deep, inscrutable principles that seemed to have been planted in his spine from the day he was born; being wrong about something, maybe even everything, was beginning to bring him a curious sense of peace.

Maybe he was just fooling himself. For the time being he didn't care.

"Just don't call me that."

Heissner shifted his feet in the darkness.

"What? Scar? Oh. You don't like that, eh?"

"No. It gets on my nerves," said Kordts. He said this matter-of-factly.

"Well, that's fine by me then," said Heissner. "Heh, heh. Those new men say that all the time."

"That's all right. I'll talk to them if I feel like it. You know, Heissner, you're ugly enough they could call you that even without one."

Heissner laughed. Freitag shook his head and laughed. A shock-light burst overhead and the three of them sat white and exposed in this illumination. Freitag picked up his guitar again.

"So what about Scherer then? What's Scherer like?" said Heissner. It was the first time he'd talked to these two at length. He was thinking maybe they were a little more approachable after all.

"Oh for God's sake, just let me play," said Freitag. "I'll tell you all about him some other time."

Heissner looked at Kordts and Kordts shrugged. The flare went out. The light was gone in a kind of black burst as instantaneous as when it had first appeared. Freitag hesitated a moment, still dubious about Heissner interrupting, then commenced upon the guitar again.

At times they would hear harmonicas being played from the other dark over there. Not tonight, but from time to time. They were seated far enough behind the forward emplacements that they felt secure enough, as secure as they could ever feel. In any case, music-makers tended to be left undisturbed on either side of the shell-torn ground in the Russian nights. Maybe all of them out there felt less evil upon hearing any kind of music. Or maybe they felt that evil would descend upon them if they tried to take out a music-maker, though if such a superstition existed it was entirely unspoken.

Schrader came. For some moments he was there, leaning against the trench without saying a word. All of those who had arrived after the *Iltis* had barely formed an impression of him one way or another. He said little and frequently seemed to look right through them. They remembered other sergeants they'd had to deal with and could think of worse ways to be treated. He'd told Kordts and Freitag right away, before the extra stripe was officially conferred, that they were his acting corporals; but having made that clear and parceled out the raw men between them he'd had little further to do with them.

Freitag just kept playing. Maybe Schrader was only listening, like the others.

Some minutes passed. Then Freitag set the guitar down carefully, staring into space.

"How are you then, Schrader?" he said.

A flare went up, some distance away, throwing only a greater starlight upon them. Schrader looked out there. Then it was dark again. When Freitag stopped playing the stars were somewhat brighter overhead, very still.

"Well enough."

He sat down beside them.

"I split you up so the new men would be with someone who knew their way around."

"Yes?" said Freitag. His own dugout was a hundred feet off to the left, where his own group was huddled down or on watch.

Schrader said nothing.

Freitag said, "I'm off to the chicks as soon as I hear a peep."

"You are a chick, boy. At least until I see otherwise. I've seen you bent over that thing. A shell could land on your head and you wouldn't notice."

"As if anyone would," said Heissner, laughing quietly.

"Ah now, don't scare me, Schrader," said Freitag, suddenly the temperamental younger brother again. "We'll get along, you'll see. Just say the word and I'll go back."

"I already did," said Schrader.

In truth Freitag had made it his business to do things properly with his little group of men, which maybe Schrader had observed by this time. He was off duty and his annoyance carried invisibly in the dark as he picked up the guitar and stood up.

"Well, you're both pals, that's fine," said Schrader. "I'll pack you both off to the homo farm."

Heissner laughed uproariously. So did Kordts. They could not see Schrader close his eyes in the dark, smiling ruefully

to himself, something of his own making impinging upon
him and he grit his teeth. He had not said anything the slightest bit amusing in many weeks. He squeezed his face with his
hands, opening his eyes, staring at nothing.

At length Freitag also laughed quietly and walked off.

Kordts had many dreams of Fortress Cholm and he dreamed
another one later that night.

He was looking out a window from inside a small room.
The room was very dark and very cold, but in the mercy of
the dream he did not feel the cold. The room was dark because the sunlight framed by the perfectly square window
was so very bright, so very bright. The winter light was all
outside and within the room there was none. He was there
somewhere within the room and by and by he moved
slowly—or rather the dream pulled him, for he did not stir at
all—closer to the window, until he could almost rest his elbow on the peeling sill.

An unnaturally large head slowly appeared in the window
frame, much larger than his own and blocking his view of
anything beyond. The head seemed mostly teeth as the lips
had rotted away, and the nose was a glistening, pulpy, can-
cerous red and black from frostbite and sunburn. He did not
have much sense of the eyes but he could see that this head
was watching him quietly. Still, he somehow just expected it
to pass on by the same as it had appeared, some fellow passing by outside on his way toward the perimeter and the maze
of the snow walls.

When the head did not move Kordts became irritated. He
did not like being stared at but more than that he was upset to
have his view blocked. He himself was directly behind the
window now and this face was only inches from his own. He
could not speak in the dream and in a sullen explosion of
anger he delivered a sharp backhand blow through the open
window that knocked the fellow down to the snow outside.

That was better.

The momentary fit of anger rose straight up his spine and
seemed almost to lift the scalp from his head and it nearly
jolted him out of sleep. Instantly there followed some terrible feeling of remorse and selfishness, as well as some deeper

feeling that was connected to all of it, to everything. This too caused him such uneasiness that he nearly awoke. But now that he could see out the window again he remained in the dream and observed a scene along one of the snow walls a short distance away, where Freitag was saying something to him in the frozen noon silence. He, Kordts, was out there listening to Freitag and he was also behind the window in the dark room. The man Heissner laughed loudly, either at his side in the room or out there by the snow wall; he was somewhere but Kordts could not make out where he was.

Dead men wandered around with shapeless flesh that seemed to moan, as if shapeless matter made its own peculiar sound that was like moaning. They wandered around like tanks, which made no sense, but then they would bump into things out there and this seemed to make sense to him.

In all that terribly framed brightness the details of Freitag and himself and maybe a few other living people remained oddly murky, not blurring exactly but somehow he could not focus his attention on them. Something kept lifting away and after a while the dull anxiety or frustration this produced caused him to awaken.

He heard frogs roaring and smelt rain and earth in the deep darkness. The scent of rain or mist gave him a vague satisfaction, which he absorbed for a few moments. He was lying next to another man, he could not remember who. He lay on one of the wooden plank beds set into recesses in the dugout, where four or five men would sleep side by side like articles in a cupboard.

The earth trembled faintly a few inches above.

He was stricken by foreboding, a sense of omen. Maybe it was a good omen but the feeling of it was unpleasant all the same. That other stupid nickname Freitag had dubbed him with at Cholm had annoyed him even more . . . he remembered saying as much only that one time and Freitag had kindly desisted without another word. Maybe that was when they'd started getting along; it seemed that way. And then tonight the same thing had happened with Heissner . . . kindly desisting without another word. He knew some of the newer men called him that behind his back and he could not deny a certain grim virile satisfaction, stupid he knew but it was of no importance anyway. But it caused him a marked distress when somebody called him that to his face, and he didn't know why.

Smiley. Scarface. The idiocy. But he recalled the one time with Freitag so many months before and this other time only a few hours ago and it fit together somehow. Telling a man to stop it and he kindly stopped it without another word. Of course it didn't mean anything, but it felt like it meant something and he didn't like this feeling. No, he didn't like it at all, even if he interpreted it as a good sign. But he didn't give a damn about interpreting it; it just reminded him how stress, paranoia, and superstition had come to infuse his entire being in ways he could never have imagined a year or two earlier.

Signs, omens, for the love of Christ . . .

A terrible uneasiness took hold of him, a chink pried open in the inexplicable shell of unconcern that he had carried about for several months now. It had nothing to do with the dream; he dreamed things all the time and many of them were far worse. Dreams almost never bothered him; the sick horrors he viewed in some of them seemed perfectly natural and understandable, by God if they didn't.

No, it was lying awake like this that bothered him, when he felt vague ugly forces pulling on him, pressures seeming to suck on invisible atmospheres inside of him. He fingered the scar, the thick node at the corner of his lip, something familiar there at least. From experience he knew it would be better in the morning, this uneasiness fading in the daylight the way dreams themselves would fade for other men.

He had no idea what time it was. But as they never had enough time to sleep then dawn could not be far off. In the blackness inches above his face the earth trembled faintly. But that too, at least, was familiar.

And Erika too was familiar, the most familiar, even from as far away as this. He reached down and took hold of himself. But he was tired and simply lay there, utterly still. He brought his hand up and laid it on his chest, still thinking of her.

Schrader crawled along the trench, stunned. Adrenaline kept him going, away from what he had just seen, from what had just happened. An overwhelming fatalism, not quite despair, almost kept him calm.

He came near the mangled remains of three men, the gun crew it must have been, the crumpled shield partially covering them. The bodies were pulped together so that the three heads seemed to belong to a single body. The three faces were distinct though, each with its own peculiar screaming rictus.

Krabel was there. He was crouched under the T-34 that straddled the trench, and like Krabel it seemed to have appeared in that spot instantaneously.

No, that couldn't be right, thought Schrader. Always these damned T-34s. The tank had been hung up over the trench for long minutes, minutes like hours.

Schrader thought that the other men had been following behind him, what remained of them, but now he saw they were in front of him, past Krabel, the rest of the platoon. The T-34 hanging across the trench formed a kind of low gateway, like a culvert, through which he could see the rest of the platoon in the blowing smoke and dust and sunlight on the other side.

Krabel leaned back against the trench wall, the top of his helmet grating against one of the treads of the T-34, and now Schrader could more clearly see the others beyond him. They were calling for him, he could see it, though like Kordts he could not really hear anything in his dream. He could but he couldn't.

It was the same when Krabel spoke to him. He couldn't hear him but he could understand him somehow. They need your help, said Krabel. They're dead, replied Schrader. He could not bring himself to say this aloud, but somehow Krabel understood him, just as he had understood Krabel. I know it, I know it, shouted Krabel, but look at them, will you.

He could see them in the trench on the other side of the T-34. Viscera from one or several held them, all entangled in some obscene, connective-tissue, spiderweb. He could see it in their faces, beseeching him, they needed his help.

What can I do for them, mouthed Schrader.

Even in the midst of the dream he was struck by the

strangeness of his tone of voice . . . his voiceless voice . . .
for he seemed to be talking not like one of them, but like a
disinterested observer who just happened to be passing by.

No, no, it was not like that at all, not like that all. Nothing
could be less disinterested than this savage, passive, uncertain horror that he felt; the force, the weight of the dream
suddenly sank from his head deep down into his guts.

In response Krabel looked back there uncertainly, lowering his head a little to peer beneath the bulk of the tank. He
didn't know. It seemed that hours passed while they stood
there, discussing what to do, becoming more and more brutalized by the hot sun leaning down into the trench.

The others began to move about, the expressions of need
on the dead men growing more confused, seeking help from
Schrader, from anyone; Schrader could barely understand
what they wanted anymore. A head lying by itself in the
churned dirt beseeched him with weary patience, eyeing him
for long minutes until the eyelids drooped slowly from exhaustion. Yet it was all less horrible in the dream somehow,
even though in the dream he clearly remembered that all of it
had been exactly so, exactly so, that day.

Chapter Fifteen

The changing seasons always brought apprehension.

Usually there was good reason for this. Improving weather could mean an attack; worsening weather meant living in filth. But in and of itself a change in the force of weather induced mad longings that the men observed within themselves stoically or halfheartedly, longings of any kind being brutalized by monotony and random death.

Thus longing became a kind of apprehension. The weather changed as if the clouds were to say, What now? What next? Though often it was nothing; they had been stuck in these barely changing positions outside Velikiye Luki for almost a year now. But any change stimulated certain things within themselves, recalling things from earlier years . . . from normal life, so to speak.

There had been a great deal of rain in the latter part of August, which was unfortunate as it only reminded them of the heavier rains still to come in the autumn, which they remembered from the year before. At first it was good to be sheltered from the sun for a while, as the endless summer daylight leaning into the trenches grew unnerving, something from which there was no escape, a hot force of monotony that tended to expose all their dim anxieties. They were in a vast land but often there were no horizons, because they lived deep in the trenches; and there was something disturbing about standing in the bottom of a trench and seeing the same blue unyielding thread of sky above, hour after hour after hour.

Men needed some shelter and at first the rains provided this. But there was never any kind of moderation with the weather in this land. No brief, easy showers or calming mist.

The rains came down heavily for days on end and their positions became filthy running gutters. The discomfort of rain and stinking mud was more elemental than the weird psychology of the endless summer sunlight. They felt more at home in their misery and in the simple desire for this sodden misery to come to an end.

They grimaced cheerfully in this endless discomfort, thinking at least there might be a reprieve from combat for a while.

But it was unfortunate that they could only look forward to long months of worse mud and worse rain, because autumn was always like that in this country. A nice savage attack on dry ground, taking a nice bullet on dry ground, would be preferable really. And then after that there would only be the winter.

So they didn't know what they wanted, but as they never got what they wanted and had no say in the matter it was of no consequence.

For a few weeks there was a calm window of better weather in September. The mud dried out a little; and the nights grew longer, which provided another kind of shelter from the endless sky.

But now it seemed there really would be an attack after all, and they felt their nerves slowly tighten, slowly tighten. In their confusion there was opportunity for much discussion, debates in which a man would take one side one day, the other side the next, not knowing his own mind anymore. If only they could be sent home for a while; when would the damned leaves be granted?

There wasn't much to discuss about this last issue, because they were all of the same mind about that. So they discussed the other matters in greater, more peculiarly ignorant detail. Some were so unnerved by the monotony of their existence that the idea of moving on was not so bad, superseding their normal dread of an attack. They were terribly antsy, some of them, and an attack could be no worse than the raids and patrols and daily shelling that killed them anyway. There was something about living in these ditches that fogged their minds, made them desperate to breathe and move about, even at the risk of a quicker death.

Then there were those who had given up forming opinions about anything and who looked with scorn on those who insisted on discussing things. In scorn of rumor they would invent the most preposterous rumors: von Manstein has landed in Vladivostok and is advancing along the Siberian railway to take Stalin from the rear. There were also those who had grown so used to listlessly staying where they were that it took an effort even to imagine any kind of change, an effort that they mostly did not make, participating in these discussions about the coming unknown only to pass the time, absorbing a few days of dry and tolerable conditions in September and not thinking about anything. They did not have scorn for rumors; they were beyond caring. Except, if they really had to think about it, they would rather stay where they were than become cannon fodder for some restless general's ideas about something.

Men became possessed of several different selves, as they shifted both anxiously and listlessly back and forth among these things, these tight yet ephemeral forebodings.

The notion of an attack was not just idle talk. After almost a year of manning these sparse outposts in Indian country, this seemingly forgotten sector that straddled the vague boundaries of Army Group North and Army Group Center, they suddenly saw new units beginning to arrive. Some had armored vehicles and they all seemed to posses a great deal of heavy artillery. Von Manstein's name was bandied about, in a more serious vein now, the general from down south who had just finished hammering the great fortress at Sebastopol into submission. The Crimea had been finished off and now all those divisions down there were free to make trouble elsewhere, and many of them seemed to be arriving in their own lonely stretch of central Russia. They had seen the newsreels in film showings in tents and little houses to the rear, or in the old stone buildings of Velikiye Luki; they had seen the titanic railroad guns and mortars that had pulverized the twelve-foot-thick casements of Sebastopol. They could hardly imagine that such enormous guns would now be used in their own neglected countryside—to fire at what? Swamp, steppe, meadows dotted with little birches?

No, a few know-it-alls declared, the big guns were going

to Leningrad, to take out Leningrad in an iron rain just as Sebastopol had been taken out. Leningrad, which lay almost as far north of where they were as Sebastopol lay to the south.

But why then were so many of these veterans from the Crimea appearing in their own sector? And what about von Manstein? Von Manstein is on his way to Leningrad. No, others insisted, von Manstein had set up shop in Vitebsk with von der Chevallerie. They talked in circles but it was true, one thing at least was true—there were more men and heavy weapons in their area, and that could only mean one thing, von Manstein or no von Manstein. The divisional front was shortened and Scherer was able to relinquish the distant outpost of Velizh to another division, consolidating the regiments of the 83rd more tightly around Velikiye Luki itself. They gave their trenches and isolated strongpoints over to other men and moved to other trenches closer to the city, or even inside the city itself, where the names of the doomed were etched invisibly on the ancient white towers above their heads.

Through September and into October they waited to attack. But there was no attack. This could only be because the attack was still to come, and so they waited still. The filthy rain and filthy mud came in October, worse and much colder than it had been in August. This time of year seemed unending and so they began to think only dimly that the attack must come after the endless rain. Those moved into Velikiye Luki were gratified to be sheltered by dry buildings, at least part of the time anyway, as the rest of the time they still lived in exposed positions guarding the edge of the town, with the Russians still as close by as they had been before. Kordts looked at the Lovat River many times and shook his head, exhaling quietly. The Lovat ran wide and turbid in the autumn rain and looked nothing like the meandering white void he remembered from Cholm. But all the same, it was the Lovat.

Leningrad was not attacked either, which they were hardly aware of as it had nothing to do with them. They began instead to hear about Stalingrad, such a peculiarly evocative name that they began to think or barely hope that perhaps the war would be won down there, a thousand miles to the south, without their ever having to go over to the attack again or do anything again, except to stay as they had already stayed around this ancient white town. The white stone force of the old towers became grim or merely meaningless beneath the close-hanging, unending autumn rains.

A few of the Velikiye Luki strongpoints were built within familiar landmarks around the town, and called by those names. The Felt Factory, the Friday School, the Red House.

All the other strongpoints were named after German cities. Breslau, Bayreuth. Preussich-Berlin. Hamburg, Bremen. Bromberg, Stettin, Kolberg. Wien I, Wien II, and Wien III. Regensburg, Ulm, München, Nurnburg, Innsbruck, Augsburg, and still more.

Each was held by about a company, either in the fortified point itself or in trenches nearby. Reserves were close at hand, quartered in the solid old houses, with cellars further dug out and reinforced by their occupants.

Observers were posted in the upper floors of buildings in the near vicinity of each strongpoint, in less obvious structures, less likely to draw fire. For their long-range binoculars were equally as important as the heavy guns whose fire they directed.

The strongpoints were in low buildings, often with their second stories razed, taken out, unless they were of truly formidable construction—the Felt Factory, for example. And then those built into houses were stronger than any house, the walls becoming like shells or facades, though they might have been strong enough to begin with. But further work was always done, and the men were very thorough and meticulous about building things, layer upon layer of earth, sandbags, beams, blocks. Their enemies were always astonished by the high degree of artisanship the fisheyes displayed in even temporary positions, as if they were possessed by some curious, compulsive devil of craft and design—even homeliness, if you considered the little curtains that often hung in bunkers, the lovingly crafted bits of furniture, little knick-knacks set on shelves or hanging from the walls as if a support army of doting grandmothers followed the fascist dogs on campaign. To the Russians such charming features would evoke uproarious mirth, not to mention a certain degree of jealousy and confusion; and there was also avarice, for such idiotic knickknacks also suggested there might be real treasures lying around, cheese and tinned meat and chocolate, schnapps, God only knew what, and as often as not they would find these things too.

Usually, though, such luck only followed upon an overwhelming attack that sent the fisheyes reeling all to hell, leaving their good things behind. The Russians hated it when their enemies were cornered but refused to surrender for weeks or months, for inevitably all the fine tasty things would be consumed by the end of that time. By then the surviving Landsers would be as starving as the Russians usually were, and barely a few crusts of bread would be left on the nicely fitted homemade tables. It angered them considerably, for after a siege of weeks or months the Russians would always have taken horrible losses, and to find no booty after such a murderous ordeal was trying indeed.

Such was war. Velikiye Luki was about to die, in long stages.

To return to the matter of the strongpoints. These were not temporary of course, the occupying regiments having had almost a year to make them what they were. They had to be strong, given the relative scarcity of heavy weapons, not to mention armored support, which troubled almost every German infantry division. There were antitank guns in Velikiye Luki—the utter lack of which had made the long stand at Cholm so seemingly inconceivable—and the newer 5 cm and 7.5 cm PAKs had begun to displace the useless and despised 3.7s. But still there were not enough of them.

A look at a map of the town would have pleased any German operations officer with an eye for design. And perhaps the officers responsible for the layout were indeed pleased with themselves. For each strongpoint named after a German city had been situated so that it more or less corresponded to where the actual city would have been located on a map of Germany. Thus, for example, Strongpoint Hamburg guarded the northern approaches to Velikiye Luki, hard by the east bank of the Lovat; then, correspondingly, Stettin and Brandenburg lay further to the east, and at the easternmost tip of the perimeter stood Bromberg, named after a Prussian city near the Polish frontier.

Likewise, in dense clusters along the southern perimeter were the Bavarian and Austrian city names: Ulm, Regensburg, Innsbruck, the multiple complex of Wien. And so on.

The Wagnerian Bayreuth was isolated somewhat further to the south, outside the city limits near the Felt Factory, and so would be one of the first to fall.

One might deduce some practical effect from this. Scherer, set up in his headquarters some miles behind the front at Novo Sokolniki, would not be caught off guard by the coming onslaught. But the Russian blow would be of such terrible magnitude that Velikiye Luki would be cut off and surrounded within the first twenty-four hours, with Scherer able to communicate only by radio with the regimental commander trapped inside the siege ring. The radio reports would take on a doleful pattern, and without referring to the map Scherer would be able to visualize where and when the multiple Russian thrusts were the strongest, upon receiving each report bearing the names of fallen cities.

Bayreuth has fallen. Bromberg has fallen. Innsbruck has fallen. Stettin was surrounded earlier this morning but is still holding. Hamburg is under fire from twelve T-34s but is still holding.

So on, so on. This would unfold shortly, and would last for months.

The practical effect of such a layout would have been greater if Scherer had been able to offer any help. But there would be little he would be able to do. He would be on the other side of the looking glass this time, able to do nothing except listen to the radio and issue instructions back into the darkness.

Chapter Sixteen

On one of these days before the end began Kordts was playing chess with Schrader in one of the deeper recesses of Hamburg. There was light from oil lamps and then some kind of daylight filtered in from somewhere. The outer light was murky, the grey skies remaining grey. It was cozy enough where they were though, after their fashion. They smoked and drank water out of tin cups and stared at the board. Krabel sat on a comfortable-looking bunk bed in a corner, smoking a pipe, sometimes watching their progress, sometimes not.

"Where are we going then?" said Kordts.

"Don't know," said Schrader.

"I thought Hasenclever told you about things."

"Well, yes, he told me we were moving out of the city again. Where to I don't know. Maybe back to where we were before. Or maybe not."

"Ah, I'd already heard that much," said Kordts.

Their quarters were better in the city and they were somewhat put out at the prospect of having to leave so soon, after having been rotated in here only a few weeks before.

"From what I heard," said Schrader, "von Sass is a bit of a nitwit, or maybe just inexperienced, I don't know. So maybe Scherer feels better having 277 inside the town, instead of out on the wings somewhere."

Kordts stared down at the board, as if to judge whether such dispositions could be made sense of there.

Two seventy-seven was the regiment commanded by the Oberst Freiherr von Sass, who had arrived from a desk job in the homeland a few months ago, replacing Kreiser, the former commander. In spite of their words at the time of the

Iltis attack, Scherer had thought well of Kreiser and been sorry to see him go. Von Sass was a spit-and-polish man who had yet to prove if he was a nitwit, though so far his lack of understanding of conditions in Russia had not inclined his people to think the best of him.

Schrader and Kordts's company belonged to 257, one of the other two regiments, now rumored to be heading out again into the dismal landscape.

"I think," said Kordts, "that if that Freiherr wants to get acquainted with things then he should be stuck out in the marsh somewhere. I've heard he's got himself a fine office at Sing-Sing. Why should we have to go back out into that shit just so he can keep shuffling papers behind a desk? Two seventy-seven's already been inside town for a whole damn year."

He blurted this out in a confused rush after a long silence, so that Schrader did not quite catch all of it. Kordts had just moved a piece and Schrader was puzzled by the man's intuitive grasp of the game.

"Let me think, will you? You're a devious one, aren't you? I thought you said you never played this game."

Kordts shrugged, scratched his scar, trying not to smile.

"I played a few times when I was younger. Ten years ago at least."

"Hm. Interesting," was all Schrader could think of. He had been obsessed with chess at one time and entered a few competitions during his earlier years in the army. Not with great success though; obviously he didn't have the knack for it, the vision or the knack (he had been disappointed then, though after a while he had simply come to accept it, skill at chess being no different from musical talent or athleticism), and he had played only occasionally since then. All the same he was surprised Kordts could keep up with him, even beat him as often as not. Schrader knew that much of this came from not paying close attention the way he would have years ago, but still there was more to it than that.

Every so often Kordts would make a boneheaded move— these were the games Schrader would win, or else he would let Kordts take the move back so the game could go on without being a waste of time. Kordts did this often enough (as did Schrader, for that matter) that he did not appear to be a

ringer, leading Schrader by the nose with false modesty. But
the rest of the time he would make moves according to some
strange scheme which was irritatingly successful.

Schrader was not really irked though, but rather curious.
He had felt little curiosity about anything for a long time,
thinking diffidently of late that maybe he was beginning to
snap out of that, though still not wishing to ponder it much.
A few times during these recent chess matches he had paused
to consider Kordts as if he had never really laid eyes on him
before.

Which was not entirely true. Kordts tended to evoke odd
suspicions in people, Schrader being no different, though he
had not previously bothered to articulate to himself just what
these suspicions might be. Kordts was one man out of
twenty, for one thing, and Schrader no longer wished to
know any of them very well.

But he did find himself remembering long midnight hours
spent studying chessboards a few years back. He reached out
and made a move. He said, "So what's your secret?"

"Lines of force," Kordts replied, as if he had been waiting
all along for someone to ask him.

Schrader pulled his cigarette from his lips and spat on the
floor.

"There, you see. You have given it some study."

"No," said Kordts. "No, I haven't. It's just what I see on
the board. It's about the only thing I can see, for that matter."

"What do you mean, lines of force?"

Kordts pointed down with a few vague gestures.

"Diagonal lines. And two perpendiculars. Fields of fire, if
you will. For Christ's sake, I don't know anything about
chess. I just keep my attention on what I can see. It's all I
can do."

Schrader wondered if the man was pulling his leg. Kordts
would make remarks as dry as sand sometimes, impossible
to know if he was serious, some inscrutable joke whose
meaning lay beyond reach within a desert wasteland.

But at the moment he seemed to be speaking straightforwardly.

Lines of force, mused Schrader. This seemed not some

kind of game theory but something too obvious to make any sense of. Maybe there was more to it than that. Maybe he would ask him again later. If he felt like it.

"Ah," he said, no longer concentrating. "Come over here, Ernest. What do you think?"

Krabel remained where he was, cross-legged in the dim recess. He said, "It seems you're dealing with a general, Rolf. So you must think like a general, eh? You set up your fields of fire, and after that you move your pieces around without any idea what you're doing. Isn't that what you said, Kordts?"

"*Ja*," said Kordts.

Schrader looked at Krabel and laughed quietly. "All right, good. Thank you."

"You're welcome," said Krabel. He sat a few feet away in dimness and pipe smoke.

"So you're a general in disguise," said Schrader.

"No," said Kordts. Terse once again.

"You're a troublemaker, aren't you?"

Finally Kordts reacted a little. His eyes narrowed and the corner of his mouth narrowed into his scar. But then he seemed to smile with a dim satisfaction.

"Yeah, maybe. But how would you know? I've never made any trouble for you."

"Good thing too," said Schrader.

Krabel looked up, setting his pipe aside.

Kordts's eyes narrowed again. As if he'd been caught out at something, off guard, when he'd hardly let any vicious remarks pass through his lips for months. And more than that. His eyes narrowed further into a familiar hatred, not really directed at Schrader but at all of them. It was coming to an end, he thought. He'd been feeling it of late, not terribly surprised. It was that strange shell of well-being that he had been hard-put to understand, but it seemed it was beginning to wear off anyway.

"If you want to be personal," he said. "There's plenty of other people around who don't like authority. So what?"

"I don't know, to tell you the truth," said Schrader. "And I don't want to know. That's the best way, Kordts."

Schrader was struck by the sensation that he did not really know what he was saying. He'd had no intention of putting the finger on Kordts. Or if he had, it had caught him un-awares as much as the other man. If they were sent outside the city again then maybe there would be another *Iltis*, and they'd all be dead in the smoke. Dead, yes, let's hope so, to make everything so much more simple and quiet. He hadn't really been thinking *troublemaker*; he'd been thinking sur-vivor, though with an odd ring to the word.

But Schrader like most of them had no belief in survivors; survivors were only those who survived. A sick horror passed through him that he absorbed as coolly as if it were news of the field kitchens coming up.

"Never mind. The watch is almost up. You, go out and see what Hasenclever wants. Show him the way in here."

They'd taken over Hamburg from one of the companies of 277, only two days ago. When Schrader spoke the others looked toward a narrow slit where they could see Hasen-clever coming up out in the murky, rubble-torn street. He'd yet to visit Hamburg and would have to be shown the way in, the entrance nearly invisible at the bottom of a rubble-choked alley.

"Never mind," said Schrader again, to the soldier he'd just ordered out. "I'll go talk to him myself."

Schrader went out into misting rain. He passed between sandbags stacked so high that they resembled inventory de-posited in some rear area depot. He threaded a maze of barbed wire, passing men at intervals in smaller rubble-forts gathered listlessly around a heavy machine gun or a mortar. After months of quiet, Russian activity had begun to pick up again in recent weeks, and now scarcely a day went by with-out some dramatic incident somewhere along the city perimeter. In this part of town the Russian lines were not quite so close by and they were listless and bored, playing cards or smoking listlessly, one eye always cocked toward the dull drifting weather out there, where the enemy was, and where the weather endlessly was. Or one eye cocked toward the approaching Hasenclever, who as company sergeant tended more toward mother hen than martinet, but even so.

Schrader emerged among buildings that were not quite whole, not quite wrecked. Such was the town at this time. North of Hamburg, and north and east by the Lovat, outlying houses had been razed to create fields of fire. Hasenclever was coming from the city center, from the direction of the citadel, which they called Sing-Sing.

"So, Schrader. What are you doing out here?"

"Getting some air. I saw you coming. What's the news?"

"News worth hearing for once. We're staying."

"The regiment's not moving out?"

"No, it is moving out. But 5th Company is staying here, with 277. Don't ask me why, because I didn't ask Gebhardt. Who ought to be coming up shortly himself. Anyway, I thought you'd be satisfied to stay put here for a while. I understand 277 fitted up Hamburg quite nicely."

"Yeah, it's not bad," said Schrader slowly. The idea of good news and bad news was another thing that had become foreign to him; except maybe this was pretty good news. Maybe so. "They're not going to take it away from us again, are they?"

"No, we're staying in town, and as far as I know Hamburg is ours for now. So I thought I'd better come up and see the place after all."

"Well, stay a minute and I'll show you around. Have a smoke with me. Weather's filthy."

Hasenclever did not ask why Schrader would prefer to stand outside and smoke in the filthy weather. He accepted a cigarette and they smoked in drizzling rain, mist that was drifting a little more heavily into rain. It was not so bad really, because inside the town there was not much mud. That was the main thing. They solemnly absorbed whatever comforts were granted them, just as they grumbled when they were taken away.

"So that means we'll be under von Sass's command," said Schrader. "Have you seen him?"

"Just a little while ago. Gebhardt asked me to come along to the citadel. He'll get used to things, I suppose. I saw the way the officers were looking him over when he talked. Maybe he noticed it too. Anyway, you know how it goes; we probably won't see too much of him."

Schrader shrugged. To stay in dry quarters would be a worthwhile trade-off for an unknown quantity in von Sass. Sing-Sing, about a mile away down the riverbank, seemed a remote enough place for now.

He had soon forgiven Hasenclever for his ill-chosen words after the *Iltis*, though he had hardly been able to speak to the man for some weeks afterward. The name of that place passed through his mind as if printed on a sign or little piece of paper; for he could still hardly bear to hear his inner voice think the name out loud. Over time he would more purpose-fully remember Hasenclever coming far out into the field with liters of beer on the wagon bed; so that whenever he saw Hasenclever approaching from a distance he thought of beer, and could almost taste it. Like now, in fact, and even this imaginary taste was all right by him. Maybe after all that he would have lost his taste for beer too. No, not damned likely. And if they stayed on in the town, beer would be more readily available too.

He looked up to see two other men approaching in the dis-tance, following some way behind Hasenclever during these minutes. One was a battalion commander of 277, whom Schrader saw raise his hand to the other man and then turn off onto a side street. The other one still coming up toward Hamburg was Lieutenant Gebhardt.

Hasenclever looked down there.

"Well, we needn't stand out in the rain. He'll find his own way. Let's go inside."

They passed Kordts and his little group now coming out into the rain. Schrader alerted him to the lieutenant's coming up and told him to point out the entrance. Kordts responded with a passing nod. He couldn't make much sense of Schrader's odd remarks from a few minutes before—apart from their obvious grains of truth—and morosely felt it was hardly worth troubling about. He was disturbed and as he led four men out into the rain he distinctly felt things caving in on him, or something of his insides collapsing from within. Schrader had nothing to do with it and he gave no more thought to Schrader. The little group passed through the bramble thickets of wire and passed other little outlying forts where men were beginning to coalesce more tightly around whatever weapon they served, inside small dugouts, to get out of the rain. He had forgotten Gebhardt almost as soon as Schrader spoke the name; now he glanced disinterestedly into the city but could see no one coming. They went on to Freitag's position and relieved Freitag's little group.

Freitag was standing outside the dugout—hardly more than an alcove of rubble and sandbags—in the rain, as if he were intent on being young and stubborn about something, refusing to let the elements budge him. Freitag was not all right. Neither was Kordts. And say what you will about the others. Freitag greeted his friend with a burst of hearty nervous cynicism, which by now Kordts had gathered was his way of showing him friendship and respect. By now Kordts had found it agreeable to no longer have Freitag by his side all the time, because he needed as much of his own aloneness as he could amass among the enforced companionship of all of these other men. Still he smiled and muttered a few barely comprehensible rude remarks and placed his hand on Freitag's shoulder.

Kordts settled his men around the heavy MG in the alcove. He did not like being in charge of even three or four people so he was brusque and businesslike, no longer offering them much of his wit because it no longer suited him. A few minutes later he stepped out into the rain and with dim-witted amusement found himself standing in it just as Freitag had been doing moments earlier. So it goes, he thought with a faint smile. From his greatcoat he retrieved the letter from Erika and with his own peculiar stubbornness watched the rain weep spottily on the single sheet of paper.

He had read it through already and thought it might cheer him up again. But the feeling . . . just "the feeling," as he thought of it . . . was so powerful that he couldn't concentrate and he couldn't fight it. It was no use that he had seen it coming, felt it coming, for a while now. That it made too much sense to really be true was no use because he knew it was true all the same. The shock of going through all that at Cholm had led to the equally profound shock of being rewarded at home with the solace of her body and everything about her that deeply filled him, and with no murky unhappiness or anything else bad that could happen between a man and a woman. A reward fit for a hero indeed, and a fortress-like feeling of relief and good and distinct memories that had carried over for months afterward. How could he have been so stupid? But he hadn't been, not really. He was thinking delusion, and fraud, and such things, even though no words fit that he knew; and he was thinking maybe it hadn't been a delusion anyway, maybe it had been real enough, that contentment . . . it was just that it was over now. He had been much aware of how strangely well he had felt and now he was every bit as aware that it had all worn off, all worn off, and that was all there was to it.

In a way it seemed a natural process to undergo, shitty but perfectly natural, so that he could hardly begin to understand the fog of evil and perversion, the utterly twisted nature of deep shock itself, that hovered around it all.

That deep shock could feel good for four or five months now seemed a twisted and perverted thing. By now he was used to any manner of craziness but he felt terrible all the same.

Her letter had cheered him a little and so he tried to concentrate and read it again. He got past Dear Gus and a momentary wave of sanity passed through him from somewhere. There, that's better. He read on, savoring the words as he had savored them before. She wrote of how hard it was to write, not because of the war, and he knew it was because she had always felt shy and awkward about putting her thoughts on paper. He had always known this, probably because she had told him so years ago, though he could no longer remember for sure. Her letter did not wallow in the cheerfully degrading and adoring pornography that had filled his own letters to her, a lot of them anyway, though she did say some things that made him happy. And she was sorry for being such a poor writer because she liked getting the letters from him and didn't want him to be upset and stop writing.

It was true that it was odd to see her thoughts written on paper. It seemed she was too shy and natural to put herself on paper but he liked seeing her words all the same, especially a few of the things she said, which he reread several times.

He read the letter through and felt a little better but he continued to feel some deep mad pressure inside himself. And so to hell with it, he thought. He wanted to cry out and instead only imagined himself doing so, and what kinds of awful incomprehensible impulses pass behind the tired almost expressionless faces of all kinds of other men?

He didn't know. The rain was turning to sleet. He looked for Gebhardt again and did see him this time, though some distance away over by the main strongpoint, somebody else guiding him in through the sandbags and choked little alley.

Stubbornly he persisted in looking for something to cling to, something inside himself that he thought must be there, because after all it had been there until recently, hadn't it? And maybe he would collect his thoughts better if he just ducked into the alcove and dried off with the rest of them, or even better just put it all out of his mind. But he couldn't let go of it, whatever it was, and he was bedeviled by the foolish notion that if he stepped away from the spot he was standing in it would all evaporate. Which would be just as well, and so to hell with it; but still he didn't move.

He stared unseeingly at the rain or sleet forming and unforming on the rubble and other filth at his feet. A few events from back in the summer and early autumn continued to swirl in and out of his mind. In fact he could hardly focus his thoughts on specific events or incidents, for the strange spell that had been cast over those months was inside him, not related to the world. He concentrated stubbornly and he saw colors of daylight most clearly, as if these were the illuminated stains and dyes of his own curious well-being back then. The weather, of all things. Yet he had seen it, he had really seen it, in the summer clouds roaming day after day through the large fields of sunlight overhead, above the rain-green expanses outside the city. How unconcerned he had been for a little while there, an emptiness inside him (empty of stress and resentment) that had seemed like a kind of fullness, fulfillment. Well, he must have been cracked, but even so he remembered the feeling as if he could almost taste it.

He could no longer taste it—feel it—but as he concentrated he could still see it somehow, clouds and sunlight eddying through his mind. He had seen the force of nature inside Russia and been struck by it, and no doubt thousands of other men had been struck by it in just this same way.

Even the year before, during the first months of the invasion in the summer of '41, he had been struck that way, but always the feeling then had been polluted by fear and exhaustion, by the gradual sucking away of all creature comforts into the animal existence of the winter. Polluted was maybe not the right word, he didn't know what the right word was.

He didn't know, he didn't know. It was a feeling; it wasn't knowing something. August Kordts, cantankerous and narrow-eyed, might have understood it better if given years, decades, who could say . . . more time to absorb it and understand it, this feeling that he had never associated with his own personal nature before, not during the war, not before the war.

But there was no time. Time was up. He felt little surprise and hardly disappointment. He just felt sick and it seemed to make not the slightest difference whether this had caught him by surprise or not. He remembered long peaceful hours roaming the hinterland back in the warmer months, walking here and there by himself, entirely unconcerned that he might be murdered by the different bands of murderers who also roamed the scattered forests behind the front lines. He remembered the generous impulse he had had for a little while, to share this unconcern, asking Freitag to wander about with him a few times beneath the far-spreading weather. But Freitag hadn't wanted any part of it. So be it then. His train of thought wandered here and there or even came apart completely—while he stood there in the rain outside Strongpoint Hamburg staring fixedly at Erika's rain-spotted letter. Standing in the rain just as Freitag had been standing a few minutes earlier, he thought again, and smiled faintly and stupidly again, shaking his head slightly.

There had been a few raids early in the autumn, when he had followed Schrader and the rest of them out of the trenches, out into the Russian fire, not apathetic but still unconcerned that he would surely be killed at any moment. What of it, the weather was nice, it seemed a good day to go. . . . Could he really have been possessed that way? Sure, why not, why not . . . He remembered muttering to Freitag the same things he always said, but with a sort of dazed lightheartedness, Freitag staring at him curiously; the same day Klenner had been killed, Klenner the gardener, he remembered suddenly.

Klenner had brought some green things up to the forward positions; he must have known an attack was about to go out, but the fellow seemed to live in his own world, his own scheme of things. The officers and NCOs tended to humor him, humor him by just ignoring him, mostly. *Ja,* Fred, just set those things down for the time being. Most of the men, Kordts included, tended to ignore him too, though a few would gravitate toward him with an odd respect. Someone, Heissner maybe, had asked Klenner if he wanted to go along, since he had already troubled himself to come all the way up to the assembly positions. The start time was only minutes away. He was only joking, Heissner or whoever it had been. Klenner knew it too; he was not so strange that he couldn't recognize a dry, tight little joke. A crazy idea, Klenner had retorted, a bearded, sun-dark, older fellow, a rear-echelon eccentric, speaking with the same unassuming yet somewhat evangelical directness with which he tended to speak about growing things or whatever else. Who knew what got into him that day—people just did things sometimes. He had only minutes to think about it. Schrader had caught wind of it and the look on his face had said no, no foolishness; but he said nothing and only looked at Klenner, at all of them, and then turned his back to say something to Hasenclever or one of the lieutenants, Kordts couldn't remember, someone looking at his watch. He couldn't remember either if Klenner had been carrying a weapon; he would have had no reason to. He hadn't seen him get killed, hadn't seen anyone bringing his body back either, though he heard later that it had been.

What all this had to do with anything he didn't know; the vividness of the scene came on him so unexpectedly that he completely forgot all the confused ramblings in his head that had led up to it. Only the sick, collapsing feeling remained, reenveloping his innards so forcefully that he forgot about Klenner as well. A spasm of mindless energy caused him to dart forward a few steps, away from the sheltered alcove where four men were clustered dully around a machine gun. Get out of this blasted rain, he thought. He turned around to duck back under there with the rest of them, staring at the letter clenched in his fist, thinking of tucking it safely in his pocket but it had gotten so wet he was afraid he would damage it.

A distant concussion rapped against the back of his skull. Almost like some jokester skulking up and swatting him there. And so he went down. How he could have failed to hear the incoming roar he did not know. In spite of his self-absorption he could have sworn he had been listening all along, somehow. There was no time to scuttle back into the alcove. He saw the shell bursts coming along the street like black wet trees sprouting full-grown. He crouched deeper, he groaned or sobbed, clutching bits of rubble till his hands bled.

Chapter Seventeen

The operator handed the telephone to Scherer. The room was crowded. Some listened; others were too busy to do so.

"Is that you, von Sass? Yes, that's hardly the word for it. First give me a report from your end."

Scherer listened.

"All right," he said a few times. He said, "I'll get to that. Finish your report."

Finally he said, "I see. Bayreuth gone. All right. All right then. Do everything you can to hold the Felt Factory. Take men from the east end if you have to. Yes, Bromberg, if you have to. Now listen carefully and I'll tell you how things stand.

"To be blunt, von Sass, it is not good. You will probably be cut off by the end of the day. Both regiments outside the city have caught hell and the first order of business is to reestablish a main line before they are pushed back any further. Every available man is being sent to the wings to shore things up there. As I see it, it won't be enough at this moment to prevent the enemy from encircling you in Velikiye Luki. But if we can maintain on the outside then a relief force will be sent in as soon as possible. Now that may take a few days. Are you with me so far?

"Yes. All right. All right. Yes, I have no doubt they're already squeezing you pretty badly. But the wings will have to be held first. Meyer has already been surrounded at," he looked at the map, tracing the railroad line out of the city with his finger, "at Goruschko. That's just to the east of the railroad line. But the railroad line will be held, I'll see to that. Now go back to the Felt Factory. What is the situation there again? Yes? All right, good. If we can clear the situation out-

side within forty-eight hours then we'll try for the linkup at
the Felt Factory. That's right on the rail line. Yes, yes, I know
the line is still open at this moment. I'm sorry but I have no
men to send to you right now. You must understand that any
attacks against the city at this point will be only diversionary
affairs; they'll be fully occupied on the outside until they can
close the circle around you. We'll do what we can to prevent
that but, as I said, the prospects are not good. Meyer's situation is desperate. I'm sending the armored train in to you to
take out your wounded and sick. Take care of that as quickly
as possible before the line is cut. If the train is trapped inside
the city it will be useless to us all. Have you got that? All
right, yes, I'm getting to that.

"Our dear colleagues have obviously anticipated the departure of von Manstein's divisions from this sector. But a
number of his units are still nearby and they will be called
back here, I'll see to that personally and there will be hell to
pay for anyone who says otherwise. Most of them are already boarding trains in the rear, yes, it's Stalingrad, I know,
I know, but I'll have them turned around if I have to send
men to block the tracks myself. In any case it will be at least
twenty-four hours before they can be brought back to the
combat zone. I'll be calling von der Chevallerie in just a few
minutes and I'll talk to von Manstein too if I have to.

"That's all I have for you right now. No, one more thing."
Cholm, he thought. Cholm . . . he had been thinking this
both consciously and subliminally for some time now.
"You've got one of those special observer detachments with
you, is that right? Major Redde, yes, that's him. He is to set
up direct radio communication with the artillery regiment
outside the city. You will have fire support, all right? Have
him concentrate fire around the Felt Factory; Ivan's southern
spearhead should be nearing there very soon. Other developments I'll leave to your discretion until I say otherwise. Yes,
that's it for now. I regret this rude introduction to our life out
here, von Sass. You sound well. Either myself or Major Metzelaar will be speaking to you every hour. I'll have a sched-
ule arranged the next time I contact you. All right, goodbye,
von Sass."

He handed back the receiver. Other operators had other calls waiting for him. Is it Meyer again? Scherer wanted to know. No, not Meyer, there was only radio contact with Meyer any longer.

Scherer said, "Tell everyone I will speak to them in a few minutes. Hold the lines. Now get me von der Chevallerie."

He had already spoken to von der Chevallerie as soon as the first reports had started coming in. He had also spoken to him during the preceding days when the signs of what was coming had become irrefutable. Von der Chevallerie had been in complete agreement and had also been working hard at his end in Vitebsk. But now was the sticking point, Scherer thought, and while the call went through he curled his lips against his teeth and braced himself for what he was sure would develop into a serious argument. The first of many, if it had to be that way, though he desperately hoped it did not. For he knew von der Chevallerie was his ally and if he had to raise his voice it would not be to him but to the whole of High Command East, if he could get his voice to carry that far. Von der Chevallerie would have to help. He knew only that he was not about to let von Sass sit in Velikiye Luki as he had sat at Cholm, while help was sent everywhere else but there. No, not this time.

Von der Chevallerie had been standing by in Vitebsk throughout the morning and less than a minute had passed when the operator handed the receiver back to Scherer. He wasted no time. He said, "Have you spoken with von Manstein?"

"Yes, it's all right, Scherer. Thank God he is a fellow who can decide things in a hurry. Two divisions, or major elements of them anyway, are heading back to you immediately."

"Thank God for that." Scherer grew visibly smaller, a wave of relief pulling his inner gravity downward. He looked for a chair, sat down.

"Yes, I like von Manstein all right," said von der Chevallerie. "A bit of a cold fish, but what of it, eh? Damned shame he's leaving, is what I say. Stalingrad, for Christ's sake. Goddamned Stalingrad. Anyway he's turned two of his divisions back on his own authority. The others he must take with him back down south. He told me he'll fight for us if the High Command doesn't like it. I believe he will."

After the initial good news Scherer had stopped thinking for a moment. He shut his eyes and pressed one hand against the bridge of his nose.

"I'm sorry, Herr General. Did you mean, what is it, von Manstein intends to stay in our sector?"

"No. In fact he's already left. I meant only that if High Command tries to overrule him he'll fight it, stonewall them, whatever it takes. He's detached two of his divisions, ehh, 20th Motorized and 291st Infantry, to come to your assistance at Velikiye Luki. Von Manstein's not someone to leave people in the lurch, I'll say that for him. But he's already gone. Stalingrad, eh Scherer? Goddamned Stalingrad."

"Yes. Yes." Scherer was having trouble collecting his thoughts again. He had braced himself to make a great deal of noise, and now that it wasn't necessary he was trying to think all at once of all the other issues that were still critical.

"What about armored units then? Does 20th Motorized have any?"

"A panzer jaeger detachment, I believe, or *Sturmgeschützen*. Not enough to do the job, in all likelihood. Eleventh Panzer Division is east of Vitebsk, they're not part of this von Manstein business. I've been trying to get hold of Wohler to release at least a battalion over to you in Velikiye Luki. That should provide a suitable force, along with Manstein's two divisions. I'm sure he'll agree to that, if he hasn't thought of it himself. He's been placed in command of the relief force."

"Who is that? General Wohler?"

"Yes, Wohler is in command," said von der Chevallerie. "And your 83rd will also be placed under his command. So we won't be talking much from now on, Scherer, you and I. Sorry to say. Wohler is still in transit somewhere so I can't put you in touch with him, but he'll be calling you within a few hours, I should think. Get back to me if he doesn't. Is there anything I can do before I ring off?"

Von der Chevallerie would be out of the picture and he must be asking this out of courtesy.

Scherer said, "You might try to get some people ready in

case Wohler gets turned around again. They're capable of anything up there, you know, they might decide to send him off after von Manstein. You never know."

"Yes, I've already thought of that. But he will be coming, Scherer. Von Manstein gave me his word."

Scherer tried to imagine the scope of von Manstein's authority, but he had no sense of it to the extent he could give his word about anything. One could never give one's word within an endless chain of higher commands. But hadn't he given his word to von Sass only minutes earlier? He couldn't remember. To the devil with it, thought Scherer, imagining but not wishing himself at Cholm again, cut off from all higher authority, out there, out there.

"All right. Then I will expect to hear from General Wohler. Every hour is critical up here."

"I know it. Don't hesitate to call me back if you don't receive word very soon. Good luck to you, Scherer. Good luck to all of you."

Hours later Scherer would think that he should have thanked von der Chevallerie for all he had done, or all he had tried to do. It would have to wait for some other time. In another week, in another month.

At the moment he still had calls waiting from his other regimental commanders, the ones in the sleet and mud outside the city that were currently being hit very hard. The main thing was that help was coming now; he was about to make this announcement to his staff when he was interrupted again. The radio operator this time—that could only mean Meyer at Goruschko.

Meyer was the senior surviving officer of a group from 257 that had been cut off within hours of the first blows. They were in a wasteland of mud, sleet, and—with the temperature dropping—swirling snow some miles south of the city. They had been fighting to keep the Russians from overrunning the railroad but now they were surrounded and other groups would have to be brought up to hold the railroad embankment.

Many of these other groups too would be splintered, cut off, and surrounded out in the winter moonscape of the land, over the next few days, and almost all of Scherer's energies would be devoted to keeping these men alive and somehow coherent, in lines or strongpoints or any kind of positions at all. This would have to be done before he could even begin to contemplate sending relief to Velikiye Luki itself.

This was what he had tried to explain to von Sass inside the city earlier in the day. Von Sass had accepted the situation calmly enough, either because he was made of sterner stuff than Scherer had previously suspected, or because he was still too inexperienced to grasp how desperate things were on the outside. He was still calm, or sounded like it, when the city was cut off as predicted later that night. The call to Scherer in Novo Sokolniki took place over the radio now, as it would week after week from now on, on into the darkness.

By now General Wohler had been able to telephone Scherer. It was not some treacherous fantasy—the relief divisions were indeed on their way. Upon being informed of this, von Sass replied over the radio: "That is good news, Herr General. I may report also that Strongpoint Bayreuth was retaken in a counterattack only an hour ago. Elsewhere around the perimeter the Russians are amassing stronger forces, with many tanks, by the hour. So far there have been no further breaches in the line. Major Redde has set up a firing plan with the artillery regiment. The fire around Bayreuth this afternoon was delivered with admirable precision."

"Very good. Bayreuth is in our hands again? All right, good, von Sass. Now what has happened to the armored train?"

"The train left several hours before the tracks were cut at 1830 hours. I expected it to be back in Novo Sokolniki by now."

"Damn it then," Scherer said.

He waved Metzelaar over. "Find out where the damned train is." He spoke to von Sass again. He asked von Sass to recite a list of his reserves of food and ammunition and a detailed accounting of his defensive deployment. Scherer already had a pretty good idea of these things. He listened to the tenor of von Sass's voice, which still sounded as smooth and controlled as a voice from the homeland. He was tempted to give von Sass independent command inside the city as of this moment, but he did not want to make a critical mistake by misjudging the man. The pressure on von Sass was still nowhere near as violent as it was elsewhere, that is to say at almost every other point outside the city.

This would change over the coming days, with the violence to become distributed with equal and overwhelming horror at all places and all times.

Meanwhile, a thousand miles to the southeast, a thousand miles away across alternating weathers of bitter snow or muddy snow, of great slush-choked rivers or iron-frozen creeks, across fir forests bowed with snow or across vast scrubby deserts blown clean of snow and then covered again by snow-blowing east winds, lay Stalingrad. It was 26 November. Stalingrad had been surrounded exactly a week earlier.

Throughout this week the great industrial city, the great serpentine blasted wreck along the banks of the Volga, had begun to exert a force like a magnet throughout all the East, in fact throughout all of occupied Europe.

Velikiye Luki, a small, previously rather picturesque provincial seat, threw out a much weaker magnetic field.

And so Cholm again, thought Scherer.

Except that he was on the outside this time. It was a fact, and apart from that he did not know what else to make of it. He was exhausted and it was only the end of the first day, except that from now on there would be no day and no night, which he knew.

Cholm was in the past and it seemed fraudulently restful and quiet there, beneath the frozen arc of the Cholm sky, but only because it was laid to rest in the past and gone forever.

There was no end to the first day and thus it had gone on long past midnight when reports came in that the railroad embankment was under heavy attack. The snowfall was a blizzard by now and the T-34s could hardly be seen and how the Russian drivers could even begin to orient themselves at night in such filth was a mystery but they were there. Drive on by compass heading alone, thought Scherer, into blowing impenetrable darkness, until they bumped up against the railroad line. Crude but effective. He remembered the chaotic armored attacks at Cholm and hoped the defenders along the

embankment might profit equally from such confusion to de-
stroy the tanks one by one, the Russians stalling there with
their usual poor organization. Surely they could not mount a
concerted attack in this weather, even if they did find the railroad? Perhaps this was only wishful thinking, as he had had
no good news all day and all night except for the news about
Wohler's divisions coming. News of even one success somewhere might allow his nerves to settle down enough to give
him an hour's rest, which he badly needed but all his
thoughts and plans seemed pressure-forced to the very top of
his skull and the possibility of even a few minutes of sleep
seemed nonexistent. The radio reports from Meyer's group
trapped beyond the railroad had ceased coming in hours ago
and he feared the worst. Meanwhile the defenders along the
railroad itself were using flares and even searchlights to see
the tanks before they were overrun but the driving snow did
little except throw the light back in their faces. Once again
the antitank guns there were forced to wait until point-blank
range to take the enemy under fire; the new guns there reported success after success yet still there were other reports
of gun crews being rolled over in the swirling dark before
they could see their targets. He had sensed already during the
preceding days that things would be different this time and
now he knew it. No pigheaded, repetitive attacks against a
single predictable point but attacks everywhere at all hours.

Worse news came in from a nerve-shattered captain along
the embankment whose name escaped him; the man reported
that reserves Scherer had sent up hours before had been all
but obliterated by a rocket barrage in the dark. This seemed
inconceivable to Scherer and he asked the man to repeat
what he had said. The man had gone back to see the dead
himself, many dead, many dead. That the Stalin Organs
could even find a target in a midnight blizzard let alone hit it
seemed more like witchcraft than bad luck and any legitimate rationale seemed inconceivable. Partisan bands sending out radio reports to the Russian batteries? He had never
experienced anything so finely organized from their side and
doubted that was the answer or anything else he could think
of. Stubbornly he asked the man to say it again, cursing him-

self, thinking already how exhausting it would be simply to pick up the telephone and call von der Chevallerie again after all.

For he was using up his own reserves and how soon Wohler's divisions would arrive he did not know; maybe not soon enough. Next in line south of the 83rd's front was a Gebirgsjaeger division attached to von der Chevallerie's corps, and Scherer instead decided to place a call directly to the commander of this outfit. A good man, very good, no dilly-dallying; he said he would send a battalion up to Scherer without waiting for von der Chevallerie's approval; yes, he'll approve it, by God, said Scherer, and the other man agreed, yes, he will.

With that promptly settled Scherer knew he should ring up von der Chevallerie in any case, but his mind was nearly seized up with desperate contingencies and he wanted no more telephone conversations with anyone for at least fifteen minutes, if he could manage that. He left Metzelaar to monitor the lines and stepped outside the claustrophobic nerve center that had been set up inside nearly the only habitable building in Novo Sokolniki, stepping out of the single room he had not left in over twenty-four hours, out into the drifting dark.

He could see the snowfall drifting diagonally, like a single white sliding panel, through a few lights glowing at the train station. Hardly a train station . . . simply the place where the trains would stop. The armored train was there. It had pulled in at last some hours before, around midnight, having barely made it out of Velikiye Luki before the ring closed there. The unaccountable delay had been caused by partisans blowing up the tracks en route to Novo Sokolniki. The tracks had then been repaired in the dark under fire; a courageous effort to have made it back here at all, Scherer thought. The guns on the train would be needed but the train could not be sent back into action until daylight. Good enough, good enough. A surge passed through him, some unidentifiable surge of emotion or nerves, nearly disorienting him. He did not wish to speak to the train commander just yet; and then the wounded, the wounded.

Through the slow drift of light and snow, through the steam discharged from the locomotive, he saw the stretchers being unloaded, stretchers or else merely bundled shapes, and such shapes being laid down and spread out in the falling snow on the platform.

And no shelter . . . they didn't even have any shelter there. He stifled an impulse to go over there, among the wounded. He sagged finally, his shoulders sagging, and he reached back with one hand to find the log wall of the headquarters building, to rest his back there. He leaned against it for a moment and then made himself stand upright again. He began groping through the pockets of his greatcoat. Tobacco. The silver cigarette case Hitler had given him in the chancery office. He smoked, knowing he should remain within earshot of Metzelaar and the telephone lines, knowing he should send somebody else over there, to do something about that miserable scene on the platform. But he began walking over there himself; somehow it was the easiest thing to do now.

Chapter Eighteen

Kordts was unconscious for a day and semiconscious for part of another.

When he finally awoke it was to an unending din. He listened and felt it and looked at activity around him in the dimness. His skull felt as thin as an infant's, flexing with every vibration or seeming to. There was a great deal of dust and grit in his face, which he wiped at automatically while becoming more and more aware. More dust and bits of things fell on him and he blinked it irritably from his eyes, impossible to do, his eyes weeping, he wiped them with his hands but they too were covered with grit.

At length he reached for one of the curtains hanging from an upper bunk and mopped his face.

To touch any part of his head made him groan, and he groaned. But the noise, the savage, bending pressure of the noise, was worse. It was less painful against his face than against the back or upper part of his skull and so he lay down again facing upward, shutting his eyes whenever he saw dust descending.

In truth his head hurt so badly that there was no way he could position it that could make any difference. He had no memory of anything and it did not occur to him to think where he was, thinking automatically that he must still be inside Hamburg. He was there in fact, having been carried in from the rubble outside two days before.

Then he did remember something and he panicked. He remembered how very bad, how very bad he had felt, and he felt now this badness crashing down inside him like a wall collapsing, and this sensation was so overwhelming that the terrible uproar all about seemed scarcely to matter. What is going on? he managed to think, and he felt so bad that he did not care if it was the end or not the end.

He fought hard to stem this panic, which so strangely had nothing to do with whatever was happening all around him; the brain-guts of his body remembered it from two days ago when all had been still and quietly raining.

He thought of a talisman and recalled her letter, breathing easier for a moment but then panicking again when he groped through his pockets and could not find it. There it was then. It was crumpled inside his fist and he unclenched his fist and batted at the paper till it was smooth enough to see that it was her handwriting. He exhaled, set his hand down beside him, then raised it to his eyes again to make certain he had really seen it.

A talisman, good-luck thing because it was more than just the fact that it came from her. A talisman was important, no matter what it was or who or where it came from. Things started to fit together according to superstitious patterns that had been growing more familiar for months and this very familiarity eased him somewhat, in a cruel and cynical way. He had contempt for all that even though it was childishly and ineradicably inside him, superstition and contempt for superstition being present in equal and familiar parts that tended to embrace or neutralize each other, or else merge into some more indescribable presence.

The panic was dispelled and feeling more himself he arose and seemed to understand everything at once before he saw it. But he saw it too, within seconds.

A few minutes later Schrader had him by the collar of his tunic, pointing with his other hand out through one of the slits, embrasures, in the concrete. Schrader said a few things and repeated them and Kordts grasped this as the words repeated yet again inside his head, himself mouthing a few of them. Then Schrader was gone.

The other man beside him was dead and Kordts, aware of what was happening but having been unconscious for so long that he was still somewhere between there and not there, kicked him aside and drew back the bolt on the machine gun in the slit.

"Are you ready?" shouted his loader, a man from his own section whose name he could not remember.

"Goddamn all this," said Kordts, drawing back the bolt again as he was seeming to have to do everything twice. Kordts had pushed the dead man onto the ammunition belts coiled on the floor. The loader now shouted as he attempted to free the belts by pushing at the corpse with his boot and then having to bend down and drag him out of the way.

"Are you ready?" shouted the loader again.

Kordts nodded, tight-lipped, and commenced firing.

The noise was always worse for the loader than the gunner and so the loader swiveled his head back and forth with gape-mouthed idiocy as he fed the belts in, that being the only way to relieve the pressure of the tremendous hammering. The blurring quick-fire of the 42 was appalling and hypnotic to watch. The first burst arced out toward the razed buildings by the Lovat bridge that they had helped to raze sometime before, whenever that had been. The two T-34s were closer than that and he adjusted the gun, firing several short bursts until he had a better feel for it. He then fired a longer burst and the gun began bucking uncontrollably.

"Don't do that," shouted the loader, Hornstritt.

"Be quiet," said Kordts. He knew it would buck and wanted to gauge how long he could fire before it would do so.

"Goddamn it, once it starts it won't stop," said Hornstritt.

Kordts ignored him and fired shorter bursts until the gun settled down again. With dazed interest, with wild and detached interest, he watched the fire-sheaves striking several of the Russians riding the first tank. The others scattered. Still raining out there, he thought for the first time. An anti-tank gun fired from some other embrasure close by. The report cracked like a rifle and Kordts felt the flex of his skull. His vision went red but he fought it off and felt nothing more for minutes, hours, whatever it was. The armored shot gouged a skull-sized piece of plate from the turret and the tank backed up a way, leaving a group of about a dozen men exposed to Kordts's view and he fired again. He did not really see how many he hit but only that he had the target and he fired about a dozen short bursts until there was nothing visible but smoke and rain. He was staring as if down a tunnel only a few yards wide and when Hornstritt shouted and beat on his shoulder he grunted and swiveled his head and saw other Russians approaching behind the second tank. The tunnel-vision swung as his head swung, the gun barrel also; he fired again.

"That's it, that's it!" the other man shouted.

Kordts ceased firing as the platoon came into view. Where are they all? he thought senselessly even as he was looking at them. Krabel emerged from a crater where the first tank had backed up to, as if he had been waiting there. So. A few of the Russians nearby raised their heads as Krabel climbed onto the tank and Schrader ran past catching all of them with one burst from his Schmeisser. Not just Schrader, the others too, firing at a distance of only a few feet and then going to ground still more abruptly than they had appeared. All except for Freitag, addled fool, rising with smoke-wreathed solemnity like a sentinel or Red Indian from a pile or rubble—that was all there was—and firing, firing at something with a goat's leg.

Krabel leaped down, his momentum pushing Freitag into the debris.

Long seconds went by, smoke, rain, no sign of movement.

Kordts and Hornstritt crouched down.

The Teller mine went up with great force and sent out a wall of air like a great quick sphere from the tank at its core. Kordts jerked his head back but experienced no pain in his head this time. Adrenaline perhaps pushing with equal and neutralizing force against the interior walls of his skull, he was aware of neither the one thing nor the other.

"All right now," said Hornstritt a few moments later.

"What day is it," said Kordts.

Hornstritt looked at him.

Kordts looked over at the second tank. It appeared to be rigged up in some peculiar fashion. He saw all of them now emerging from wherever they had hidden themselves and running off, saw that several had been in plain view but he hadn't seen them again until now. But they weren't coming back, they were moving off further away toward the Lovat bridge. He could not recognize any individuals now and he wondered how he had picked them out so clearly moments earlier, not wondering this but only noticing it pass through his mind, then leave it forever. Gebhardt, it looked like, the lieutenant, out there at the head of them. The second tank, the flame tank, spurted a long red jet of come and those nearest were flecked with blobs of devouring semen, shrieking, a horror.

They felt faint, Kordts, Hornstritt, the others watching from inside Hamburg. Still it continued, what was happening continued. Time, already blurred, disappeared, became no time. Whole personalities had been erased for days by stress and exhaustion and then at last the lives followed after them, extinguished, gone. The second tank (quite some time had passed by now) burned like an oil-field accident after the antitank gun put several rounds into it, and then continued burning on and on, as such an accident would do.

Kordts felt faint again. For a while he had trouble pressing the triggers of the gun as in a dream where you had trouble running and then this passed without his even really knowing it. When he saw them coming back, whoever was coming back, he laid arcing sheaves of fire over their heads and other MGs from outlying rubble forts did the same.

Heissner came in first and Kordts jerked his eyes away but then had to look again. His glasses were sculpted onto his face as if they had melted there, the lenses fogged, cracked, blackened, and Kordts could see no more than this in a glance that was all he could bear. Heissner was racing into the depths of the bunker and they all heard screaming and frantic banging commotion.

The rest came in more slowly, black, staggering, carrying one man; it was Krabel. Freitag was there. Schrader. Gebhardt. Seven or eight others. A few glanced at Kordts to see this man returned to the conscious world but had nothing to say to him. They slumped against the concrete, too tired to raise their heads and their eyes to look at anything must peer up at odd angles. Most stared at the ground or at some invisible place on a dead level. Freitag was there and he reached

out to strike Kordts's shoulder, barely managing to grasp
him around the neck with a few fingers and then he slid down
against the concrete with the others.

Krabel's blackness glistened more hideously than the
others'—glistened from the rain and sweat on his face, the
blisters on his face, and Schrader and another man were carrying him down to the lower recesses of the bunker from
whence screaming and shouting and violent banging of
things still came. It was Heissner and a *sani* shouting at
Heissner, trying to look at him.

Faces were fixed in hideous grins, more the wild gape of
eyes than the dead slack set of lips. There were some men
who must still be attending to things, Schrader for example
and also Gebhardt, who could be heard speaking loudly over
the radio. Or Kordts heard him anyway, perhaps none of the
others did. Kordts felt himself awakening as if for a second
time, things that had come into focus when Schrader first
grabbed him by the collar an hour or so ago now coming into
focus again. He listened to Gebhardt talking to another voice
issuing from Sing-Sing.

Then Gebhardt began looking around to collect people for
another counterattack against the bridge, the next platoon,
anyone else he could lay hands on. Kordts feared that he
would be recognized as a fresh hand and slumped down next
to Freitag.

"It's about time," Freitag said to him.

Kordts kept his eye on Gebhardt. Perhaps it would look
better if he kept standing by at the machine gun but he could
not make himself stand up again. To the devil with it. He was
part of Schrader's platoon and he would say so loud and
clear if it came to it.

But Gebhardt never spoke to him, and the others he had
collected now hunkered down to wait for a while, for the signal to go, their faces set more grimly than the crazed-looking
but otherwise almost expressionless faces of those who had
just come in. The wait turned out to last quite a while, seconds ticking out of no clock, pulse-beats maybe. Smoking in
taut forlorn anticipation while those who had just come in
smoked in individual voids of exhaustion.

A shout came from somewhere, a lookout.

"Scarface!" It was Hornstritt shaking him. "We must stay by the gun."

"Find a gunner," said Kordts.

Nonetheless he rose and resumed his post. The dead man he had kicked aside a while ago stared up at him from beneath the coiled belts and the cartridge cases expended everywhere. Dangling somehow in the midst of this was a length of chain, with rusted manacles fixed curiously to it. Kordts glanced out the embrasure, then glanced again at the inner wall to see this odd device but it was not there, or he could not make out where it was now.

He saw figures moving in blowing smoke a few hundred feet beyond the embrasure. Rain and cloudy black grease blowing over from the destroyed flame tank limited his field of fire to an unnerving wrecked area like a small stage. He felt the urge to shrink back and forced himself to fire when Horstritt was ready with the belts again. Now he could see nothing at all except for the smoke and the empty debris leading up to it and he felt quite naked. He glanced angrily at Hornstritt feeding the belts with his head well below the level of the embrasure. The gun was cunningly equipped with a scope that could be rotated below the level of the barrel, to allow the gunner to lower his head, except Kordts could not remember how to work it. He had been taught once, taught in fact with mind-numbing repetition, a skill that he had never since put into practice and he was innately clumsy and forgetful with mechanical things. When Schrader and his group had first gone out he'd been still too dazed to even think of it; thinking angrily that the bastard Hornstritt should have pointed it out to him, now he kicked at Hornstritt and shouted at him to adjust the scope.

Hornstritt shrugged his shoulders with a kind of weary patient disrespect and reached up to fiddle with the screws. Gunfire came from nowhere, from the nearer wall of smoke and Hornstritt was hurled ten feet back with a hole in his head. The crouched rows of men all about stared dimly at him. Scarface, thought Kordts with insane righteousness. Now he didn't know what to do and felt bizarrely exposed and alone among fifty or seventy other men. Gebhardt was in a corner talking with Schrader and another platoon sergeant,

Schrader stricken-looking, muttering things to Gebhardt that Gebhardt was having trouble hearing, Schrader at length raising his voice in an automatic way, not quite looking at Gebhardt or the other man.

Kordts slumped down beside Freitag again. He saw Schrader looking at him and then Schrader went below.

Gebhardt was on the radio again requesting artillery fire, which he must have demanded land only a single calibration hair in front of them as this was where it came down less than a minute later. Wet choking dust blew in through the slits and through every other aperture; the other gunners now shrank back from their own viewing posts. A tornado exerted great force against the walls of Strongpoint Hamburg, as if to make violent room for itself against every structure around.

Whatever Gebhardt was shouting must be audible only to the other platoon sergeant standing right beside him; this man's face paled and he looked warily at the crouching stonily frightened row of his own men.

Gebhardt headed for the entrance to the rear and when the platoon sergeant began addressing his people they looked at him with fear bordering on refusal. Gebhardt must want them to go out into the bombardment, some mad plan that only he could see clearly and no less mad for that. The sergeant was angry not just with his men but with Gebhardt; as he saw the looks on their faces his own look grew more to resemble theirs.

"Goddamn it!" he shouted inaudibly, though the word-contortions of his lips were startlingly clear. "Hasenclever! Hasenclever!"

Hasenclever came from somewhere; he and the platoon sergeant headed for the entrance. But Gebhardt had already come back into the forward part of the bunker, yelling that they follow him, his face white with anger and perhaps also with shame at the reckless audacity of his idea that he could not think of reconsidering; he had a picture of something in his head and he would not let go of it.

"I don't need your advice, Hasenclever. Not now."

The platoon sergeants would have been better suited to give Gebhardt advice; Hasenclever was not there to give advice but to plead with him, however he might think of this or say it.

"Herr Leutnant!" Hasenclever shouted, shouting with his own peculiar authority but also beseechingly.

"Now you listen to me, both of you. Those gunners can hit a Jew's mark and you've seen it for yourselves. We'll take cover out in the rubble and when the fire lifts we'll be in on the Ivans before they know what's happening. We'll have at least a fifty-yard head start if we're out there already when the fire lifts. That's it, I'll only say it once, now bring your men out with me."

This to the platoon sergeant whose jaw seemed to dangle loosely; he stared at the lieutenant and walked stiffly to his men. The certain measure of truth in what Gebhardt said seemed outweighed considerably by the horizontal rain of force shaking Hamburg. More than one man thought that if anything happened to the lieutenant within the first few seconds of their going outside then they would simply bolt for the rear, for whatever other buildings or structures stood further back. For they were going outside. The osmosis of their training and of other indivisible habits made refusal impossible if not quite unthinkable. A few rose angrily while others rose stiffly with almost disinterested expressions of horror, as if futilely willing themselves to leave their own bodies. Making a show of checking weapons and straps and grenade bundles, as if this had not already been done.

Gebhardt did not quite lose patience as he saw they were coming, still ashamed of his own audacity—he looked piercingly at the faces of men momentarily to be killed, maybe—but not about to relinquish it.

Then suddenly he lost his nerve. He strode up and began shouting about the unmanned machine-gun post. He was standing directly over Kordts but not looking at Kordts directly. Kordts in spite of himself silently gestured with one hand to catch Gebhardt's attention; a jerk went through the lieutenant's body as Kordts pointed out Hornstritt in the middle of the floor and the other dead man tangled among the feed belts.

"Well, then get another crew over here. Where's Schrader?"

"Here."

Schrader had gone somewhere and now he was back. He said, "They can't see a damn thing out there till the fire lifts. They'd just catch it standing there."

"Use your brain, Schrader! Just have two of your men standing by when the fire lifts."

Schrader nodded with his lips curled back into his gums. Yes, by God, the damned lieutenant was right and he wasn't using his brain; he had emerged from below after checking on Krabel's black body and been struck to see Gebhardt losing his nerve, momentarily or for good.

"*Los! Los! Los!*" Gebhardt shouted at the men of the other platoon. His nerves were still dissolving but he was going to lead them out anyway. They all went out, stumbling in the entrance as vibrations shook them.

Schrader knelt in front of Kordts. Kordts looked curiously at this face only inches from his own.

"Get back on the gun. Freitag, load."

Schrader raised his head to the embrasure and then quickly lowered it, having felt the wall of force against his face and seen absolutely nothing. Irritably he pulled the gun down, surprised it hadn't been wrecked already, and dropped it on Kordts's lap on the floor. It was heavy; Kordts winced and said something. Yet only moments after Schrader had pulled it down the barrage lifted and the three of them, Kordts, Schrader, Freitag, set the gun up into the slit again. With dull nimbleness Freitag swung the scope down. Kordts stared at him and then set his right eye against the rubber eyepiece.

"Well. It's broken," he said. He was too tired to even acknowledge his normal instincts of refusal and he simply stood up and took hold of the triggers, peering out dully as he had peered out an hour before. Thick dust made a thick wet mist that was still easier to see through than the blowing black oil from the flame tank, which must have been blown out by the barrage, the wreck hissing faintly now. He could hear that hissing noise clearly and all remained quiet for a few seconds longer before every gun in Hamburg including his own let loose in support of Gebhardt's foray.

The Russians in front of Hamburg were already largely in bits and pieces and this time Gebhardt made it all the way to the Lovat bridge and established a forward perimeter there. This would bring him the Iron Cross a few days later, followed by a grave in shallow debris a few days after that.

In the night, weapons teams and a second platoon and engineers were sent out to Gebhardt. Schrader's people and the antitank gunners and other weapons teams remained inside or immediately around Hamburg with Hasenclever left in charge there. Gebhardt's radio by the bridge had been destroyed and a runner came back to tell Hasenclever to radio a report about the bridge to Sing-Sing.

Von Sass was pleased and asked to speak to Gebhardt; when told he was up ahead he congratulated Hasenclever and emphasized the importance of holding on to the bridge.

"Yes," said Hasenclever, "but the lieutenant has already ordered them to set charges there."

"Yes," said von Sass, "it's the right thing to do in the event of an emergency. But one must think positively and hold there if at all possible. A relief force is coming and the bridge may be vital to us."

Von Sass was not thinking clearly, or perhaps thinking too much, as Hamburg was on the north side of the city and Wohler's group would be heading for the Felt Factory on the south side. But wisely or imprudently he judged that any bridge should be held for as long as possible, pending God knew what detours or deviations might skew the days ahead.

Hasenclever had only the vaguest sense of this, though they had all been notified that relief was on its way the day before. Von Sass's voice was smooth, perhaps too smooth, but it tended to have an ameliorating effect on Hasenclever all the same. He thought only of his own little acreage and that they should have more men sent up here; he thought it was not his place to ask such a thing of von Sass but did so anyway.

"What is Gebhardt's situation?"

Hasenclever peered out one of the slits, though the quiet—the relative quiet—informed him more. He could only reply that the enemy had not begun any countermeasures yet, not liking to say this as he could sense it coming with every quiet palpation of the night.

"All right, Master Sergeant. Reserves are standing by. I'd send them up directly but I must keep them in a central location now in case the lid goes up elsewhere. Well done for you out there. Tell Gebhardt to come back to the radio and speak to me if he has the opportunity. Better yet, send another radioman up there to him."

"*Jawohl*, Herr Oberst."

Hasenclever felt better, if only because von Sass had spoken to him as straightforwardly as to any officer. Small intuitions cannot be diagnosed too much for truth or falsehood; if they calm a man's nerves for a few moments, then that is at least something. His nerves were not any more used up than anyone else's but already he was mulling the prospect of command if Gebhardt did not come back and no one else was sent up from the city center. All right then, but he did need a smoke. Or half a smoke, he thought resignedly, as they were having to think about cigarette rations now and not smoke the tension up like fiends. Willpower, abstinence, tension. So be it. Carefully he broke one in half, tamping the loose shreds back into the one half before setting it to his lips, being more careful still with the remaining half that he lowered gently into his pocket.

A man raised a match and Hasenclever said thanks. He drew one puff, lowered the glowing tube out of sight behind the concrete, and peered out the embrasure. He then stepped aside and took these short minutes to finish the smoke, his mind whole with a stillness—just as the terrible roaring noise had been whole a few hours earlier. When he finished he dropped the butt and peered out the embrasure again.

He glanced at a man and signaled him with two fingers to come over, telling him to go up to the bridge with another radio.

"And be careful. There's only one other one and that will have to stay here."

He was still looking out the embrasure a few minutes later when the flare went up. He cursed as the radioman and another man sent out with him went down heavily in the debris. He could see them crouched out there in the great white light. Then blackness followed with its own extinguishing burst and he listened intently and heard them resume moving again. When the next flare went up he could see them no longer, though he could perceive the movements of others over by the bridge before they too vanished like startled night animals. There had been desultory Russian harassing fire toward the bridge throughout the night, but at this moment nothing started up again and the shock-light of the flare seemed to intensify the silence. The sizzling incandescence hung high and floated slowly over a powerful emptiness. The flare light rendered countless small darts falling, the soft rain falling.

In such light as this a man from the Volkhov River Front would have looked out at the single road or street leading to the Lovat bridge and seen, rather than an urban rubble-field, a devastated clear-cut in the forest, the *Erika Schneise* or *Dora Schneise* or some similar broad somehow ceremonial hallway cut through the endless forests of the Volkhov. For the razed rubble-field in front of Hamburg had somewhat the chaotically annihilated yet ultimately uniform aspect of such forest clear-cuts, tangled roots and convulsed stumps similar enough in the lowering shock-light to depraved lengths of metal pipe and tumbled concrete blocks all spread out there, all of these things during a long intent glance as uniform yet individually distinct as ten million grains of sand.

And the skeleton of the bridge over there just so, and the road leading through the debris-field of stumps or stone blocks just so, and the one tank on the left and the ghastly flame tank on the right just so.

The flare went out.

It was quiet but as far as Hasenclever was concerned it could never be quiet enough for him, forebodings or no forebodings. In fact he could hear them working faintly over at the bridge, just as he could hear men conversing faintly close by within the confines of this place. The Ivans would get busy again whenever they were ready to, that was all there was to it.

Freitag, having hardly moved at all from where he had been sitting earlier in the day, said, "You didn't miss much. They shelled us. Bombers came over. Today . . . today was the worst so far."

Kordts, to whom he was speaking, grunted.

"It was snowing like mad. Then today it started raining again."

"Snowing," said Kordts.

It was damp and cold, with a pervasive stench of cordite and burnt oil, but the cold was not bitter. This could only be in a relative sense, of course, but that was how it felt to them—Cholm during the previous winter being their true idea of cold, of the unspeakable beyondness of what cold could become. The reek of death, out there especially, was not yet so strong and the slow drifting rain was washing over it; so far it was.

Finally Freitag grew more animated.

"*Schweinhund! Schweinhund!* Heh, heh. Schrader was going to have you carried back to the field hospital but I persuaded him not to. I remembered all you said about it at Cholm. He listened to me, eh? So I guess he listens to me now. Anyway, anyway—"

Freitag put his fingers together then drew them apart. Two other men were manning the machine gun now and he sat almost in the same damp outline against the concrete that he had made sliding slowly down, during the day.

Kordts was barely listening, as his head had commenced throbbing again and would not stop. He was continually grinding small bits and pieces of things into his palms to distract himself, palms which, inexplicably to him, had already been raw and painful when he'd first come-to down below.

"Anyway," Freitag went on, "I know you're a stupid ass. The field hospital took a direct hit yesterday. So for certain you are."

Kordts did not know what to say. "A direct hit?" he muttered.

Freitag jerked his head back as if to rap it against the concrete but stilled himself and rested it gently there.

"It's a disgusting place. I remember when you said that to Baer. It's a disgusting place, you'll like it there, heh."

Then he laughed more loudly. If only he wouldn't talk so much, thought Kordts. He didn't want to speak but he had to interrupt him for at least a second or two. So he said, "So you saved my hide then."

"Well. It could be. They said thirty men were killed. You

would have been all right though. But I knew you'd hate it
there anyhow."

"I would," agreed Kordts. It was the most thanks he could
make himself say. It was only that none of it was immediate
enough right now. The field hospital? Yes, he had said that,
hadn't he? Disgusting place. His thoughts vaulted starry
voids, vaulted strange blank voids and then somehow descended upon the Cholm GPU. But he didn't care and the
picture vanished quickly. A spasm passed through him and
he forced himself to say, "*Ja,* good job. You stupid pimp.
Thanks for thinking of me. Thank God for everything."

He smiled in spite of himself now and thumped his fist
dully against Freitag's knee. Having forced this through his
lips he felt a little better. And Freitag stopped talking now.
Kordts shut his eyes and again saw something, himself,
vaulting through starry voids yet arriving nowhere. The sensation was unexpectedly pleasant and he continued smiling
faintly and shut his eyes for a number of minutes. His head
hurt less for that long and then when it hurt again he opened
his eyes.

He saw Hornstritt, whom no one had moved, and realized
dimly that he had gotten the man killed. For a number of
weeks, up until these last few days, there had been less
killing and fewer dead men. He felt a shiver of guilt—that
was all that came—and then no more came. Krabel was still
alive and at some point a *sani* and two bearers brought him
up from below and bore him out past Freitag and Kordts, into
the darkness, toward whatever now remained of the field
hospital. Schrader glared fixedly at these men as they went
out but otherwise would not budge. Then almost as soon as
they were gone he bolted out the entrance after them, and
then he came back a few minutes later and sat down again.

Heissner walked about somewhat maniacally, now and
again smiling broadly in spite of himself, in spite of the pain
he was in, staring myopically at anything, talking gruffly to
anyone at all. Someone, the *sani,* had pulled off his wire
frames. The wire-thin white silhouette was stark around his
eyes and the sides of his head, bizarre-looking as was his
whole demeanor. The wire-rim silhouette was in fact not really white but blistered and pus-ridden, but it looked a

strange white in the greasy blackness of his face. The others could not help but look at him. Sometimes they would see peculiar things that they would not forget. His eyebrows and eyelashes were nearly gone. But his eyes were whole. He could still see.

Angrily Schrader told him that if he'd been paying attention he could have gone back with the *sani*. As he still couldn't see well enough to make his own way back in the dark, nor maybe in the daylight either, Heissner shrugged, taking the news in stride.

Chapter Nineteen

One could become weary, during the bombardments. For lack of distractions. The ever-present fear of a direct hit during such shelling would eventually wander off somewhere, like a person in the audience leaving a dull and endless theater performance. Except there was nowhere to go to. So the fear would become submerged, or even almost shut off, by sheer boredom, by the slow passing of the hours that in their way exerted a greater force than the most powerful high explosive. Like a person in the audience falling asleep or half-asleep, never permitted to leave, gazing dully at one place or another, with only a dull tension remaining coiled deep within his intestines, that was also never permitted to leave.

There was raining and shelling, raining and shelling, and long hours of winter darkness.

There are times during a storm at sea when a small crew on a small ship have done everything they can do, lashed everything down, set the rudder to keep the bow pointed into the waves. And with nothing else to be done they go belowdecks to wait it out. The first man to circumnavigate the globe alone, in the early 1930s, spent the worst typhoon of his experience beneath a reading lamp in his bunk, turning the pages of a novel by Balzac. It was all very boring, frightening, boring. From time to time he would leave this claustrophobic space and go above to see the storm. It was too awesome to really look at, and his sailing craft too tiny. He would go back below and continue reading until he could not stand it any longer, try to sleep for a while, then read again. This went on for three days before he was dismasted and must crawl out of his lethargy to cope with this disaster.

The officers tried to keep them at work rebuilding the

wreckage of their strongpoints, rebuilding sandbags and beams. But when the shelling became too intense they could not do this. Only a few might carry around things to read among their belongings, or stored in a nook in a bunker. Anyway it was hard to concentrate on something like that. Either because it was worse than a storm at sea, or because they could not concentrate among the strange silent presences of their comrades close by . . . some of them on the verge of hysteria, though it was always like that. Wounded men too, and dead. They might manage to pass around a frontline newspaper. Sixth Army at Stalingrad had been surrounded by the Russians. Von Manstein was leading a drive of panzer divisions to relieve Stalingrad. How interesting. Goddamned shit. Filthy mess. Shut up. Goddamned shit. Nothing. They would have preferred just to smoke and stare into space but the cigarettes were almost gone. And when disaster came, the mast snapping in a lonely typhoon, or a direct hit upon some manned position, they must crawl out of their lethargy to cope with this, cope with the wounded, scarcely reacting to the new unlucky dead . . . the wounded were worse; being still alive, it was difficult for even the most hardened man to completely wall himself off from their agony.

The enemy shelling was of an intensity they had not previously experienced. As if the war had entered some new phase. And so it had. Or endgame, as far as these men were concerned. But they still had hope that the relief might break through. How could they know anything? Anything beyond the most immediate concerns and scraps of bread, fetid air.

The weather was cold and foul, rain-snow-sleet-rain. It was not the Arctic shattering of the first winter. The clouds were foul and low, very close to the earth and to the wreckage. Kordts saw the black sunlight of Cholm encased in cold below the realm of measurement, the air of space. He saw Cholm in a scene of strange proportions, a bright scene within a deep black outline a few inches high and several feet long. As if he were viewing Cholm through a pillbox embrasure. Well, they were still inside Hamburg after all, peering out the slits in the concrete; maybe that was all it was about. What of it? Vibration, dust falling, lamp flames trembling. A glance out any aperture would show clouds rolling like smoke, smoke rolling like clouds, a grim wet lowness that seemed an exact mathematical opposite to the Cholm infinity. He remembered days at Cholm that were so unnervingly cold and bright that he could almost reach up to touch the rim of the sky; but that was the senseless and paradoxical infinity rim, not this filthy hanging murk. Shells exploded in the wet rubble of Velikiye Luki, black sprouts erupting toward the low-hanging sky. A few times the roof of clouds was raised up enough, cleared up enough, that air support could come in, Stukas howling, Stukas howling. They watched this as some kind of show within the heavy weight of the hours, some even cheering to have some kind of excitement and those were their own planes up there. Also, the Russian batteries would cease firing. They began to see the pattern of this and would thus be able to emerge from their mole dwellings for a few minutes to watch the planes better, or just to stretch their legs. A cognizant Russian commander might have resumed the artillery fire at a precise moment and caught half the garrison standing outside their damnable strongpoints watching the skies above. But the Russian guns remained silent so as not to betray their positions. The Stukas were destroyers from among a large pantheon of destroyer-gods, both Teutonic and Slavic. The garrison could see the planes but usually not precisely where the bombs were falling, as the targets were out in the land beyond the outskirts of the city, out where the Russian guns were. The Stukas would be overhead for ten minutes, fifteen at the most. Then they were gone; and the guns on cue would resume the barrage.

The JU-52s would come in too, landing supplies at a strip in the city center, and this too made him and Freitag think of Cholm. And when the JUs began dropping supplies by parachute they knew the strip was no longer usable and this too made them think of Cholm.

Then for three or four days, now the first week of December, the artillery fire diminished somewhat. They might guess the reasons for this; but the officers again kept them busy shoring up their strongpoints, shoring up everything, and there was enough debris lying about that it could have been shifted back and forth forever. They worked hard out in the open with less metal flying about, focused on these tasks, a good thing perhaps though such hard labor made them still more bitterly hungry, nuisance bursts meanwhile continuing to land at various points around the town.

Chapter Twenty

The day before the Russian assault resumed the men in Hamburg were waiting for a supply column to come up. Food and ammunition were brought up from the landing strip in the city center. The men were hungry and waiting. They dared to think of cigarettes, knowing that at least a few cartons would be brought up.

They were weary of their surroundings inside this place, Hamburg, which had been comfortably set up by 277 now gone to ruin, smoke-blackened, wet. Beams dangling, tins lying about, little tables overturned, idiotic little curtains soiled like dishrags, expended cartridges lying everywhere like a kind of brass sawdust, irritating underfoot.

An old plaque on an interior wall was ornately carved with the word *Heimatstadt*. More year-old leavings of 277. Hamburg was where 83rd Infantry Division had been raised, and many of the men from all the regiments were from that city. No one noticed this plaque anymore. Though inevitably many of them would think of the name of their strongpoint from time to time, and think of a great north German city laid like a kind of template upon the place where they were, though such reflections being little more than scarcely heeded reflexes by now. Names have their own peculiar force and if they had been holding out at Regensburg on the south side of the perimeter, a Bavarian town where none of them hailed from, then that name too would have carried its own odd, evocative, meaningless ring.

None of them were immune to this, even the most cynical or weary. They were a sentimental race, like all races, yet more so. Christmas was coming. Low skies hung, sometimes moving, sometimes hanging still. They were hungry and wondering when the rations would arrive.

The Lovat bridge was outside, and to the squads and platoons in tiny rubble-forts and pits out there, Hamburg was "inside." So they took their turns out there during those hours and waited to be relieved by other squads or platoons, when they could go back inside.

The damp cold helped to weigh down the stench of the dead, and a number of the dead had been roasted by the flame tank, so that they did not give off too much. The stench was not all-pervasive, and so they had not quite become inured to the great rotting gusts that carried up to them sometimes, a man grunting and lowering his face inside his tunic, shutting his eyes.

The greater sterilizing cold would be coming within twenty-four hours. They did not know this. Likewise the Russian drum fire would be coming, coming again after this hiatus of three or four days, though they awaited the resumption of this with every passing moment.

Kordts looked up at the sky, which moved slowly and was unchanging. Except that he had just felt the first raw touch of cold, the bite, upon one side of his face. His scar, dull and plasticky, never really felt cold but it seemed to convey cold like a network of veins to healthier tissue. He looked at the sky, and could make nothing of it; heard planes droning somewhere. Small scattered bursts of firing from everywhere and nowhere. In fact there was still a great deal of noise, always, but with the lifting of the drum fire a few days ago the noise seemed confined to the surface of a large invisible dome hanging above any given point, with lesser noises and other sensations quieter and more discrete below it.

Freitag was with him—they had been sent back to look for the supply column—and Heissner, whom they were leading back to the field hospital by the airstrip.

It was difficult to find one's way in the destroyed city. Reference points were destroyed or so changed that they were disorienting. At night it was nearly impossible to walk any distance without becoming lost. Even in the day things outside one's immediate vicinity—Hamburg or some other strongpoint—looked unfamiliar. Though they were in a city, they were like city folk acclimating themselves to finding their way through the deep woods, not quite able to perceive the odd landmarks that lay shattered and twisted all around them. Things instead of assuming some recognizable shape dissolved into a blasted sameness.

A man used to living in the deep woods might enter a small place in the trees that would look like nothing at all to a traveler passing through, yet to the woodsman this small nondescript place might be as familiar to him as a room in his house, in anyone's house.

They had been making their way along a path—a route, which consisted in part of streets, in part of alleys, in part of passages through collapsed houses—which they thought they knew, with the Lovat River as a landmark a few hundred yards over there to the right. At times they could make out Sing-Sing off in the distance on the other side of the river, which also helped to orient them in a general sense. Russian shells fell there in an uninteresting fashion. So, thinking they knew their path, they came to a small intersection and looked around and saw they had no idea where they were.

"What is it now?" said Heissner, whose vision had gotten worse.

"Let's sit down," said Kordts.

"Are you lost again?"

Heissner said this in his gruff, accusatory fashion. He was sour now, his upper face disturbing to look at.

"Nah, nah," said Kordts.

There seemed no point in sitting down when there was nothing left to smoke, as sitting down reminded them of this. But they were tired and sat on three blocks.

Kordts had the best feel for places—for terrain and the existence of things in certain patterns. Or he thought he did, and he was unsettled because he was sure they were not lost, that they had passed through this very point at different times over the preceding weeks. Yet he could see nothing of it; it simply wasn't there.

And then suddenly, it was there. It was an odd sensation that caused him to twitch his head. For he had not suddenly spied some landmark that he recognized. No, it was just there all of a sudden, like a photographic plate sliding into his head.

"All right, I see where we are now," he said.

"Well, the next time we run into somebody we can ask directions," said Freitag, as if he thought Kordts was merely being optimistic.

Kordts looked at him and smiled faintly, not bothering to repeat what he had said. He did know where they were now, but was content not to move off again for a few minutes. Something awful was gnawing at him and he grimly absorbed the way Freitag had made him smile and he nodded faintly to himself.

"Well, to hell with you," said Heissner.

"Find your own way then," said Freitag.

Heissner cursed at him and then laughed quietly. Even now Freitag was somehow amusing to him.

Freitag was generally well-liked by people but often he did not like the fact that they found him funny. He was uneducated but blessed with natural intelligence and a probing curiosity about people and things, about certain abstract mysteries of life that his comrades tended to find amusing—or at least Freitag's way of talking about these things struck them that way. He was an unschooled but remarkably gifted musician, though he wasn't vain about that. He enjoyed drinking and a wild laugh as a way of relieving his deep seriousness, not quite aware that it was this last thing that made people grin at him more than anything else. He had a few irritating qualities, his excessive talking probably the main one, yet he was one of the few people in the company that no one resented for one reason or another, almost as if he were a kind of mascot.

Of course this last thing would have peeved him too if he were aware of it, and maybe sometimes he was. He was dying for a smoke.

Heissner's brief amusement changed to disgust as he remembered again that no more planes were flying out. My goddamned luck, he thought.

"Well, let's get going!" said Freitag, almost shouting. "We'll find someone."

They had earlier passed isolated groups of men along their way. Carrying messages or ammunition to one place or another, repairing telephone lines, working at rebuilding some structure, manning some artillery piece set some distance back from the forward perimeter. A town originally populated by one hundred thousand souls was now empty of all civilians. Six thousand men were still there in Velikiye Luki, almost all of them manning the perimeter, or clustered around the central points of the landing strip or the citadel. Whole neighborhoods of the city were devoid of life or any suggestion of life.

"It's all right, I know where we are now," said Kordts.

Though where the column with the rations was God only knew. But at least they could take Heissner to the field hospital. From there they could call back to Hasenclever and see if the rations had arrived. If not then maybe they could organize something else. It seemed workable.

Kordts pointed in an offhand way and they got up and went on between the deserted buildings.

They heard the shrieking. Falling in their tracks like rags with the stuffing knocked out. They had a sense of the sound of artillery shells, of how far away they might land. But the rocket noise was all-consuming and it seemed the rockets could land anywhere.

Panic-stricken—all three of them were—Kordts caught a glimpse of the smoke trails and saw they were going somewhere else. The blast was audible to them and to everyone else in the city and the shock-wave passed through like an ocean wave rushing the shore.

"Ah, Christ, Christ," said Heissner. He could hardly see and had still to fight to calm himself after the other two had recovered their senses.

"It's all right," said Kordts, gripping him tightly by the shoulder. "It was nothing."

"Are you sure? Goddamn it. They're going to start it up again now, aren't they?"

Kordts and Freitag were thinking it too, glaring around for the best-looking shelter, waiting for all the other guns outside the city to start up again now. They took shelter in a cellar and stayed there for fifteen minutes or so; then nothing more came down and a strange nervous energy got them going again.

They found the supply column not long after. The salvo had come down much closer than they'd realized. They felt a hanging sensation in their bowels, as if they could feel the dangle of their own intestines, dangling in empty space.

With a strange uncertainty they began looking about for anything useful. The remains of the goods were more salvageable and they began putting things in their pockets; even Heissner did, who would pick something up and peer closely at it. Irritably he would ask Freitag to read him the label from something. Freitag found him a cigarette and Heissner quit looking about and sat down on some pile, smoking with his elbows on his knees. Severed limbs lay scattered here and there, as if they too had been crated up inside supply containers and then strewn all about by the blast. An arm or a leg might come off cleanly enough; there one, there another. Or a head. Torsos however trailed long yards of viscera across the stones; even so it was all only one thing or another, so much lying about that it was difficult for the eye to settle on one thing in particular; just as well, just as well.

A few other men now appeared from somewhere, looking about with dazed greed, hunger, yet they kept a certain distance from Kordts and Freitag and Heissner. The remains of the supply column were scattered over a wide area.

The upper part of Heissner's head bulged itself like some kind of rubble, an almost handsome kind of deformity rising from his cheekbones. His eyes peered out narrowly from within this face. The white wire-rim silhouette had disappeared within the folds of swollen flesh. Clear fluids weeped down; uglier fluids adhered more persistently around his eyes like ooze on a wall, unless he wiped it off with his hand from time to time.

"I'm too hungry to smoke. Find me something," he said.

Kordts and Freitag could not smoke more than a few puffs either, they were so hungry. They had found some bread and were looking for something better to eat with it, but they were so hungry they had to stop and sit down and share the bread with Heissner.

Heissner ate more quickly, less able to see everything lying around them. Kordts and Freitag chewed uncertainly in the middle of the slaughterhouse, gagging and spitting out a few morsels. But their pangs were such that they put them back into their mouths and kept on eating.

"We are the noble huntsmen of the plains," Freitag muttered. It was part of a song he would play sometimes. The other two did not respond. From time to time they would gaze at the other men in the near distance, and the other men would stare back at them.

After they had eaten as much as they wanted, or as much as they could stand, they lit up again; all of a sudden they were content and no longer interested in the littered remains.

"Ha, ha," said Freitag, not quite laughing, rather uttering this quietly. "Do you remember that supply bomb?"

Kordts thought for a moment.

"Yeah, sure," he said.

"You were going to have a fit. I can still see you pounding on that damned lid with your bayonet."

"You're right. I was about to have one," said Kordts. It occurred to him that he got a small pleasure from agreeing to something in the simplest fashion. He inhaled smoke, fine dead particles. My God, my God, he thought about nothing at all.

There were a few heads about; one caught Kordts's eye and it reminded him of some kind of stage prop. Mangled torsos on the other hand seemed more properly to belong to where they were, war, puke. He had an urge to go kick the nearest head like a football and was glad he was too tired to move. By God if he didn't feel that way though. A surge of hysteria rose up like a fountain and when it lifted from his head it seemed to yank at the top of his scalp before departing. He sat there stonily as if entirely oblivious to this, though he was not oblivious.

Freitag said, "Well, I suppose we'd better collect some more food so we can take it back up to the company."

Heissner laughed and Freitag gave him an evil look. Kordts felt a weariness as if he could no longer stand up straight.

"Can you stand it?" he whispered.

"Well. I don't know. What should we do then?"

"I don't know. Don't be idiotic. How much can we carry? Hasenclever will just have to send some more people if he wants to collect all this."

"We can carry something at least," said Freitag. The terse disrespect of his friend left him unhappy. This kind of disrespect had been going on for a while, it seemed. Even Kordts seemed to know it, for every so often he would make some friendlier gesture, though Freitag remained disturbed by it. How many friends could a man have in a tithe like this? But he consoled himself by thinking it didn't matter, as they would all be dead soon. This seemed an easier prospect to consider than his own uncertain place among the different places of other men. Instantly he felt better.

Heissner laughed quietly again, shaking his head.

Kordts said, "I've had this feeling for days, like some kind of hand is pulling on my scalp, right at the top of my forehead."

He stared at Freitag and rubbed the spot on his head with his knuckles. He had been doing this on and off for days, though no one else had taken any notice of it. At other times he felt—or merely saw this picture in his mind—a scalpel or razor slicing into that one particular sensitive place at the very top of his forehead. These two ideas seemed to contradict each other, he thought with morose self-absorption—slicing, or pulling. But that was what it felt like. He didn't mention out loud the other part about the scalpel or the razor. He could tolerate it when it just passed idly through his mind, but to think about it so clearly made him wince.

"It's from when you were knocked out those two days," said Freitag.

"No. No, it isn't that at all," said Kordts. "That was just a damned headache."

"That's all it is," said Freitag.

Strangely this had not occurred to Kordts and for an instant he thought maybe that was all it was, after all. But no, he knew that had nothing to do with it and he grew impatient, grimacing at the ground.

"I can't go through this again," he said. "I'm going to do something terrible."

"What? What do you mean?"

"I can't go through this again."

"You mean like at Cholm?"

"Yes. Like at Cholm," said Kordts.

"Come on now, Gus. My God, we're only crazed here, that's all it is. Isn't that right, Heissner?"

Heissner was looking at them but said nothing.

"Ha," said Kordts. He had never felt such a desire to put something into words before. For an instant he thought it might relieve him.

"I feel this thing, this pressure, just pushing at me from the inside. I can feel it right in my arms," he said, as if this were an unusual place to feel such a thing. And he rubbed his left bicep to show just where it was, though in fact he felt it everywhere on the inner surface of his body to one degree or another.

"Yeah, I know, I know. I feel that way too," said Freitag.

"*Ja*," said Kordts. Except he doubted that, but only an ass would argue about such a thing here, in this place. He was trying to explain something very specific and for an instant he felt a wild urge to argue in a rage and tell Freitag he had no idea what he meant. But Kordts hated arguing; he much preferred lashing out with some insult, or just beating the daylights out of somebody; getting into an argument always filled him with the desire to hang himself.

At last he said miserably, "Yeah, I know. I know you do."

"Scherer will be here in a few days. Think about it, man. They'll probably give us another home leave."

"Ah, my God," whispered Kordts. "Scherer can go to the devil," he said more loudly.

Now Freitag laughed, wild, disturbed-looking. He patted Kordts on the back.

"Yes, by God. Ha, ha. But all the same, he'll be coming. Or maybe he won't. Well, all right, all right then, Gus."

He laughed again, choking on cigarette smoke.

"For Christ's sake, let's get going," said Heissner.

The other two ignored him. Kordts had meant nothing about Scherer; he thought he would either come or he wouldn't come. It just seemed to have nothing to do with anything, though what this meant he could not explain even to himself. Some inchoate force reminded him of something. What was it? He remembered sitting at the little cafe table in

Torgau with Freitag, listening to all those questions about whatever Moll had been talking about.

He said, "I just want to shoot the officers. That would be a start anyway."

He'd felt the urge to blurt this out for a long time, just to say it out loud. That damnable months-long period of contentment had just kept it quietly bottled up inside him. So now he'd said it.

Heissner let out some kind of hissing or spitting noise. He grunted some incomprehensible words. He shook his head and said, "Well, Christ, if it's nothing more than that."

Kordts looked at him out of the corner of his eye. Heissner gave him back a vaguely dubious look, as if he could see normally all of a sudden.

"Well, there's only Hasenclever left," said Freitag. "You wouldn't want to shoot him, would you?"

Gebhardt had been killed in the shelling a few days before.

"No, I suppose not," said Kordts. He didn't mean a word of it, though he had nothing, or little anyway, against Hasenclever. No, another lie. He almost stood up. He did stand up.

"*Ja,* let's go," said Heissner.

Kordts walked out into the rubble, to nowhere. The other two followed him thinking he was going somewhere in particular.

Freitag kept talking. He was not really trying to make light of it all; he felt his own blackness; but there was nothing wrong with trying to snap someone out of the gloom.

"Too bad Belzmann isn't here," he said. "We could all shoot him."

"Yeah, that would do," said Kordts. He was satisfied to have spat it out of his system, though it hadn't made him feel much better.

"Would you go along with that, Heissner?" said Freitag.

"Sure. I suppose. Belzmann was a pig. I'll be damned if I'll get myself stood in front of a wall though. I'd be sneakier than the devil, you'd better believe that. You know what? You're nothing but talk, both of you. Let's go."

They were already walking, though aimlessly now. Kordts thought Heissner was right, which meant he was nothing but a spineless fool, and the pressure bulged inside him with full force again. Tears came to his eyes and then he forced them away.

"Where does this go to, Gus?" said Freitag.

"Nowhere. Nowhere."

Kordts did not quite shout this. He said, "All right, look, I'll take Heissner on to the hospital. Go on back to Hamburg and tell Hasenclever where this shit-pile is. He can send some people back to pick things up before some other bunch ransacks it all. You better hurry."

"All right," said Freitag. "But why don't you let me take Heissner to the hospital. I know how much you hate it there."

"No, I'll go. As long as I don't have to stay there. Heh. All right?"

For a dreadful second he was afraid Freitag was going to argue. What are you arguing about? he would have shouted back at him.

But Freitag only said, "All right, if that's what you want to do. So. I'll see you in a while. Take care of yourself, Heissner."

Kordts felt relieved and had to take a step backwards. Freitag was standing on the remains of a low wall, with a heap of debris sloping up to it like a gravel ramp. Kordts saw a wrecked city at the end of the world, a vast metropolis a hundred times larger than Velikiye Luki, in which a few people stood about talking to each other, their voices carrying strangely in the utter silence, one man standing on top of a wall with a pile of debris beside it, talking down to two other men in the empty street. Yes, that's what it was. He looked up at Freitag standing up there.

He regretted talking to him like a child sometimes but to express anything seemed unbearable. Even his usual stone-calm insults. Filthy swine. Stupid pimp . . . that strange language of comradely revulsion that Freitag had begun to pick up from him. Kordts walked up the debris ramp, grasping at a bent steel structural rod and pulling himself up onto the wall. He put his hand on Freitag's shoulder.

"See you later."

"See you later," said Freitag. "It'll be dark soon. Don't get lost."

"*Ja*. We'll see."

"All right then."

Freitag picked his way down the other side of the wall and began heading back.

A while later Heissner said, "You should be careful how you talk."

"Talk is talk," said Kordts. "Just like you said. You must have heard other people say those things. I have. Not just recently either."

"Yeah, yeah. But I know you. You really would. You just haven't done it yet."

"I think just about anybody would. Given the right circumstances."

"All right, whatever you say. I don't care. I don't think you're very careful though."

"More careful than you think."

Heissner had nothing more to say. He'd started to like Kordts a bit. But if he was going to do something stupid and get stood in front of a wall that was his problem. Like everyone he had grown to despise certain officers over the last few years but there were others he respected and got on well with; he could imagine drinking with them on equal terms if this thing was ever finished, and they pulled the tabs off their collars.

Christ, if I go blind I'll shoot myself.

He thought this blankly, as if he were not thinking it at all. Refusing to.

"Don't talk anymore of that crap, Kordts. I'm just worried about my goddamned eyes."

"Yeah, you brought it up again. All right. Never mind. It's not that much further now."

Kordts found himself thinking of Moll for some reason. Heissner was remembering Belzmann, one of their pig majors in 257, who was no longer around because all of 257 except for them had been moved outside of the city. Heissner did not wish to be a spoilsport and he had nothing against people who sometimes felt they must talk about shooting officers. Except it seemed to him there was both a sane and a crazy way to talk about such things.

Heissner looked like a difficult character and Kordts was not the only one to be surprised that he was easier to get along with than his appearance suggested. Still, Heissner would bristle if he thought he was being taken advantage of or being unfairly prodded into some shitty situation, speaking his mind quite forcefully at times even to officers. But officers or sergeants did not much feel the uneasiness dealing with him that would come to them almost automatically when sizing up a character like Kordts. Because Heissner, rough as he was, was still an organization man—or perhaps he did not think about it unduly, which by definition included him as an organization man—and his rudeness rarely seemed to convey some deeper disrespect; officers had a pretty good nose for sensing this. So they generally thought of Heissner as a reliable soldier (he was) and his roughness was often mixed haphazardly with a crude geniality that suggested he was basically an all right sort of fellow.

Months ago Heissner's first impression of Kordts had been of a weasely sort who would look down his nose at things. The Cholm shield on his sleeve had impressed him, but there was only so much stock you could put in something like that. Anyway it didn't matter, because over time Kordts had come to seem a little different from what he'd thought at first—he could sometimes make people laugh, for one thing. Apart from that, he really didn't know; but after a few weeks had passed Kordts was never hostile to him, and so he was not hostile in return.

Somehow to understand this much about a man, or two men, would make more sense in some other situation—out in the trenches beyond the city for example, earlier in the year, during the long months when events both violent and mundane would pass by day to day, a kind of life. Perhaps people's basic characters did not change during a siege like this, but it somehow made less sense to understand them, even when their lives might depend on each other. But maybe that is not the right way of saying it—perhaps the essence of the thing is that during a prolonged siege, during the "cauldron fever" of the siege, people became anxious and preoccupied in many strange ways, groping about sullenly and confusedly within themselves, putting up a brave front perhaps, but always distracted by listening to something in their inner ear, waiting for the other shoe to drop—this other shoe being either death, or the unknown day when relief would come.

So for the moment Heissner thought nothing about Kordts apart from what he already knew, whatever that was. He had every reason for his own concerns; a man need only look at his face. He tried to be optimistic but he was growing more and more worried about his eyes. He hoped it was just the swelling. He prayed that was all it was.

Kordts read his mind. It was not that hard to do.

"The surgeons will just cut you up on your head somewhere to relieve the pressure. Then you'll be fine. Just look at me."

Heissner looked at Kordts.

"That's your cheek. It wasn't around your eyes."

Kordts exhaled through thin lips and fell silent. They came to the landing strip cleared on an avenue in the center city, where the field hospital was. Suddenly there were people and vehicles about, like the denizens of some other city within the dead ruins of the larger city, gunners at their guns, supplies piled up in various places. Heissner had already been to the battalion aid station a few days back, been given some ointments, been told he needed the attention of a doctor.

They went to the building where the field hospital was. The edifice stood there half-demolished . . . the direct hit Freitag had heard about. In the half that was still whole people went in and out still going about their business; what else could they do? Heissner took this in. Then he looked over, tried to look over, at the landing strip nearby.

"Damned shit looks all right to me. Why can't they land planes on that?"

"It's a bunch of craters," said Kordts.

"So? Fill them in, goddamn it. All we've been doing is hauling bricks around the last few days."

They went inside. They had to wait. Heissner was given a ticket and they stepped back outside the evil structure to wait for a while. He had no worries about missing his turn. The wait would be long.

The day was short. Darkness had been above all day and now it was growing darker.

Kordts was in no hurry to return. It was good, better than nothing anyway, to stand around in different surroundings for a while. Things were a little easier now that he had bread in his belly. He and Heissner smoked more of the cigarettes they'd taken from the charnel field, puffing hungrily, refusing to ration themselves for a little while at least.

"What's that then?" said Heissner.

"Nothing. They'll be dropping more supplies."

"No, no. What is that?"

Kordts stared more carefully.

The planes were like specks of coal coming in in the dusk.

"Gliders," said Kordts.

"Gliders? What gliders?"

Specks of coal suddenly surrounded by powdered bursts. The Russian flak batteries commencing. People everywhere ceased what they were doing to watch.

There was a yellowish-white bar of light to the west, where the planes were coming from. Two JU-52s towed two gliders.

The gliders were released into the teeth of the flak. Still some distance away, perhaps outside the city, it was hard to say. No, there was Sing-Sing; they were passing right over it. The two JU-52s surged on ahead, released of their burdens, dropping parachute containers in a single pass over the landing strip. They pulled away to get above the gunfire, roaring. The gliders followed behind like shadows left behind in terror. Their silent approach seemed somehow to switch off all the other noise in the area, of which there was a great deal. The Russian flak belts ringed the city and commanded most of the sky directly over it.

The first glider went up like a moth set afire. They could see very distinctly the bodies, or perhaps still-living souls, tumbling out of it. Plummeting a short distance to earth. Then some kind of artillery piece, it appeared to be that, dropped like an anvil. The glider floated up, surged up, for a short distance, skin evaporating in fire. Still burning with a dozen little moths of flame the metal skeleton came twisting down, crashing a few hundred yards from the landing strip.

The second glider passed nearly through it, too close to the ground to maneuver. It came in.

It skidded, it bumped at the edges of craters, finally turning sideways. The skin was ruptured in a dozen places and the frame was humpbacked.

It sat there. People began running toward it. A few seconds later the men in the glider began to come out. They were well-armed and wore clean uniforms.

"I can't believe it," said Heissner. "You think they volunteered to come here?"

"I don't know," said Kordts. He stared over there. Some of the glider party went down to their knees once they were free of the wreck. Others stared back at the small already guttering flames of the first skeleton. Shreds of flame were still floating down, spiraling down slowly, back there. "I don't think so. They don't look like volunteers to me."

"Poor bastards."

"Yeah. Those ones that made it don't look too happy either."

"*Ja*. Well, they'll fit right in. For God's sake, they send us twenty men in a glider. What good's that going to do?"

Kordts shook his head. Already the glider party and other people that had rushed over there were manhandling an antitank gun out of the rear. People were cutting part of the skin away to make room to get it out.

Twenty men and one antitank gun then.

At Cholm that would have seemed like something. Here it didn't.

The show was over. Kordts told Heissner to break a leg. Then he simply said, "Good luck," reaching out to grip Heissner at the angle of his neck and shoulder; the two men parted. Heissner stared at the hospital building, then walked back toward the entrance. At the end of the building that had collapsed the wounded from a few days earlier still lay invisibly underneath the wreckage.

It was dark.

Tracers arced above the city and illuminated the low clouds, a vague whitish darkness that silhouetted the black crags of buildings on the ground. Down there it was impossible to see anything, except for the sky overhead.

He knew he would find his way back one way or another and was not concerned about getting lost. It might take him half the night, or all the night, it didn't matter.

He felt the need of company and stopped to talk to small groups of men clustered around small fires. It was much colder now. They were all damp and rotten from months of that kind of weather and now they tried to dry and warm themselves so they could face the bitterly worsening cold, which they knew would last longer than just the night. They looked above to see if the skies were clearing. They were. The vague white luminescence drifted slowly away. The sky was black with stars aching above.

They would give him directions, or try to. Anyway directions were almost impossible to follow in the night.

Many times he thought he was lost, knew it, and thought of settling down somewhere until morning came. But it was too cold and he kept going, stumbling, following streets that led anywhere.

The conversation with Heissner had made him feel better about that little fit of faggotry or cowardice or whatever it had been. Actually he had not mastered it, he had simply forgotten it for a while. Even better that way. He remembered it again and it no longer mattered. This and everything that had gone before this justified everything. He was a Cholm fighter who had spent one hundred and five days in Cholm and that justified everything. He was justified in talking whatever rot he felt compelled to spit out. He would do whatever he was going to do and it would be justified and if he did nothing, now or at any time for the remainder of his days, so would that be. It was all so clear that he hardly thought about it, really, and felt better to just keep on walking.

Around one little fire was a group of four men who wore silver half-moons dangling from chains around their necks. He had been walking, walking, and walked right up to them before he saw what they were.

They wanted to see his papers. He laughed contemptuously. That put an edge on them. But when he explained what

he was about they seemed convinced and invited him to
warm himself for a few minutes. He stood close to the fire,
staring directly into it.

"We heard those rockets come down this afternoon," one
of them said. "Stalin Organs. A nice concert for everyone in
town."

Kordts nodded.

The man said, "No use sending anybody back there. It
would have all been picked clean within an hour or two."

"Maybe so," said Kordts. "What can you do? I picked up
as much bread and smokes as I could carry."

He said this and groped about for a moment and handed
out a few cigarettes.

The headhunters smoked and Kordts looked closely at
them and they looked closely back at him. He felt heat rising
in his chest. He took a deep breath and looked up at the stars.
One of them said, "You sure you're not going to keep all that
to yourself and find a little hidey-hole somewhere?"

In a rage Kordts snapped his cigarette into the dark. Instantly he looked to see where it had fallen. He'd been waste-
ful with them all day and felt a pang of anxiety. But he
couldn't see where it had fallen.

"Eh? Answer me."

"Shut your damned mouth."

Now he was also angry at himself and he groped for another one in his pocket, gave it up, stared at four smokes dangling from four sets of lips.

"Listen, you, I've been walking all day and all night. I've
passed ten thousand hidey-holes. Have you got nothing better to do?"

"No, you listen," said one. He had a bad look and the other
three looked worse. "I said I believed you, but we can fuck
you all the same if you like. There are orders from von Sass.
Deserters have started crawling about. It's a big city all of a
sudden, eh? Lots of room for shirking little bastards. We
have orders to shoot, now."

"Well, don't let me stop you. You can share out everything
I've got on me."

A brick of silence encased them all, firelight passing over it.
Kordts felt a dim advantage. He said, "Where are all these

little bastards then? I've hardly seen a soul. Have you shot any yet?"

His confidence evaporated with this last witless remark, the words seeming to yaw out of his mouth as he tried to suck them back. He held his breath and felt his eyes narrowing.

"Why don't you just get going again. No. No, we haven't. We've hardly seen a living soul ourselves. But I think tomorrow we'll start looking."

Kordts didn't know what to say. He could not bring himself to walk off into the dark with his back turned to them. It's all right, he told himself, nothing but more hot air; but he couldn't bring himself to do it.

"I'm leaving," he said finally.

"Goodbye," the one said.

He went on, so disoriented now that he was not sure if he was still heading for the perimeter or going back toward the city center. For a while he walked back and forth in a frenzy of indecision, thinking that it would be right—and above all that it would do him good—to go back and shoot them where they stood. Why waste time with officers when those four would do just as well? No one would ever know anything about it and the temptation caused him physical pain. He bent over at the waist, stamping his feet in the cold. Only when he was certain that he had no idea how to find his way back to them did he start to recover himself a bit.

He snarled audibly at his miserable luck. He had walked all day and all night and he had walked pretty much all of that weird bulging pressure right out of his system; in other words he had pretty much forgotten about it, at least for the time being. And then to run into those swine. He cursed them for what they were but mostly he was cursing at his bad luck at having to be reminded of all that—whatever it was—again. Goddamn it, goddamn it, goddamn it.

Even so, it took him long hours to find his way back to Hamburg, and by then it had faded into just another stupid incident, set like an ugly little tile into some lurching, unstable mosaic.

They had much in common with their Russian cousins, Kordts and three million others did. They faced guns, and they had guns pointed at their backs. It had always been that way.

Hasenclever told him either he or Freitag should have stood guard over the remains of the food until others could have been sent back to carry it up.

"Yes, you're right, Spiess. And it's too late now, isn't it?"

Angrily he began dumping out everything he was carrying and then he simply pulled off his greatcoat and dumped it on the floor with everything in it.

"Yes, it is," said Hasenclever. "Which means we'll all have to go hungry now. Except I assume you stopped to fill your belly."

"Damn right I did," said Kordts. "So did Freitag. So did Heissner. So would you."

"That's right. And then I would have guarded it with my life so the rest of us could have our share."

"That's true," said Kordts. "If you'd been there that's what would have happened."

He genuinely despised his own incompetence; it was more than just defiance in his voice.

Hasenclever was tired and he'd already berated Freitag long hours before, when Freitag had finally come back in. He'd already sent some other people back but they were still gone; in the dark they'd probably never find the place at all. He was staring past Kordts at nothing. Kordts picked up the sleeve of his greatcoat and unpinned the bronze shoulder shield.

"Here, take this, Spiess," he said.

Hasenclever blinked. Without thinking he put his hand out and then instantly drew it back.

"Don't you dare hand that to me."

"All right," said Kordts. He clenched it in his fist and walked away.

And then Schrader. Schrader wanted to know how Krabel was and Kordts gaped at him. His innards were churning at great speed and so were his brain cells and he instantly thought of a believable lie. Instead he spat out the truth, which was that to look for Krabel in the hospital had never occurred to him for a single instant. He considered that he was a thoughtless self-centered bastard but instead of feeling ashamed of himself he only grew angrier at Schrader. Schrader looked at him in disgust and walked away, they both walked away.

A moment later Kordts was back pounding on Schrader's back.

"You could have reminded me. Eh?"

Schrader gave him a savage look. Kordts resembled him.

"Yes. I should have done that," Schrader said.

Morning came. The dawn light showed that all the ugly hanging clouds had disappeared. The morning sky was blue like a section of space cracked off and dropped down upon them. The drum fire commenced.

Chapter Twenty-one

They, the Russians, were tightening the ring, bringing in more troops and armor before the final assault, which would begin two weeks before Christmas. Scherer could see them doing this in his mind's eye, small details added by the reports from von Sass in the citadel. Not frittering their strength away in clockwork robotic assaults, the senseless mechanism that he remembered, but massing it before a single great exertion. During these waiting days the reports from von Sass were no longer hourly; they came in periodically throughout a day.

Scherer was not idle. For the time being he had less time to think about von Sass inside the city. In fact it had been that way right from the start; the pressure on the wings, especially along the railroad embankment south of the city, remained relentless. Now both his other regiments, 257 and 251, were fighting here, barely holding. This consumed almost all his waking hours. In the days before the litany began coming in from Velikiye Luki (Bromberg has fallen. . . . Stettin has fallen. . . . Hamburg has fallen. . . .) this litany would be well-rehearsed by similar news from outside the city: Goruschko has fallen, Group Meyer has been wiped out, survivors from Group Meyer have filtered back to other units still holding along the railroad; the Russians have breached the railroad here, at Botowo, and here, at Tchernosem.

He had nothing to send to von Sass. His last reserves were used up trying to clear up the breach at Tchernosem, about ten miles south of the city. Even some of Wohler's people had to be sent to this place, to secure any kind of defensible line from which the relief attempt could be launched, as well as to secure the flank of the relief attempt once it set out. Tchernosem, a small village like Novo Sokolniki, was annihilated, but the German line began to stabilize here, about ten miles south of Velikiye Luki.

At Novo Sokolniki—Novo as they called it—Scherer was also kept apprised of the efforts of Kampfgruppe Wohler. Besides the two divisions von Manstein had left him, Wohler was also using elements of the Gebirgsjaeger division of von der Chevallerie's corps. But none of these units had much material to work with. Very little armor, that was the main thing. A battalion of tanks had been detached from 11th Panzer Division, currently stationed east of Vitebsk in the more densely held sectors of Army Group Center. A single battalion, not at full strength (there was not a single armored unit at full strength in the whole of Russia) . . . perhaps thirty operational tanks, if even that many. Wohler and von der Chevallerie had arranged for this one depleted unit to be moved over to Velikiye Luki—the spearhead of the relief column, for without it there would be no spearhead—but even an optimist would barely dare hope that this would be enough. Not a division, not a regiment, but only a battalion. What great genius—Napoleon, or someone else?—had declared that victory always went to the side that could throw in the last battalion? Anyway, it was the last only for the Germans; the Russians still had more than enough to counter it with.

One might guess at a tragic pattern—that the great bulk of the armor had been sent south with von Manstein, tanks that would ultimately fail to raise the siege of Stalingrad, but which might have broken through across the shorter distance to Velikiye Luki. Such a tragic pattern might have appeased the gods and those who submitted to fate, or the justice of the gods. But this outlook would have been misleading, as even von Manstein's tanks down in the snowy southern deserts were very small in number; they would be fought off so far from Stalingrad that the three hundred thousand men beginning to starve down there would never hear more than the faintest rumor of their approach. Even the faintest of rumors in such a situation may be magnified into dull anxious hopes, but these rumors would be crushed for good after only a few days of existence.

The greater tragedy—or boon to the Russians, but the gods

much prefer tragedy mixed with faint sneering elements of farce—was that German armored reserves were at such a low ebb during these days. The true nadir had been achieved the previous winter—the first destroyer winter—and since then production rates and replacement vehicles had never really caught up. At this moment German panzer divisions were mere shells, entirely as fragile as they would be during the final hours in 1945. In 1943 production would grind massively forward, at a pace to keep the war going for another two years, with new destroyers arising in the pantheon in the form of Panther and Tiger tanks. But these would all arrive too late for von Manstein in the Kalmuck deserts outside Stalingrad, or for von Paulus and the three hundred thousand starving inside that enormous desolate perimeter; too late for Scherer at Novo Sokolniki, and too late for von Sass and the garrison trapped inside Velikiye Luki, ancient stone town.

Velikiye Luki was scarcely more significant than Cholm had been the previous year, an obscure nearly depopulated town out there somewhere, held by a small garrison out there somewhere. In the confusion of events Scherer was not aware that von Manstein had in fact taken little more down to the southern steppes than his own person and his headquarters staff. He had not withdrawn a critical mass of armor from the Velikiye Luki sector. He had simply taken command of a few underequipped panzer divisions already forlornly assembled in the Stalingrad area.

In all of northern Russia, from Velikiye Luki north to Leningrad, there was almost no German armor, nor had there been any for the entire year preceding. *Sturmgeschütz* battalions, equally underequipped, had formed the bulk of materiel for the offensive planned back in late summer that supposedly would drive the enemy away from Velikiye Luki . . . that long-anticipated offensive, now aborted and forgotten. To Scherer, used to seeing almost no friendly armored vehicles during his long tenure in the East, these low-slung reptilian tank destroyers had looked impressive enough, and indeed they still formed the bulk of Wohler's relief expedition. Actual tanks were only available in the form of older models, some even of Czech manufacture, which had been outdated since the French campaign in 1940, useless against T-34s, and still so few in number that their very uselessness did not make much impression. Scherer had never seen a Panther or Tiger tank, nor even one of the revamped Panzer IVs, so he did not have much basis for comparison.

To the north of Velikiye Luki an actual panzer division, the 8th, had been aroused from months of stationary warfare, fitful slumber, to form another relief spearhead to complement Wohler's group coming from the south. But what panzer division, the 8th? This unit had lost over ninety percent of its vehicles the previous winter and had never been reequipped. Throughout the summer and fall this division had been stationed at Cholm—Cholm, yes—and now fielded a few dozen half-tracks and doddering, oft-repaired tanks to strike south across the marsh-slush to Velikiye Luki. Was it in anticipation of this splendidly equipped armored force that the Freiherr von Sass had urged the defenders of Strongpoint Hamburg to maintain possession of the Lovat bridge on the siege ring's north side? Yes, perhaps so. But this handful of tanks would never come any closer to the siege perimeter than Scherer's own headquarters at Novo.

No, the only chance lay with Wohler's group coming from the south. Scherer had little time to think, that is to ponder anything. Otherwise he was thinking automatically almost twenty-four hours a day, issuing such thoughts in the form of directives to his regiments along the railroad or to von Sass inside the citadel. He may have been disgruntled for only a few minutes that he himself would not be leading the relief force, instead of General Wohler. The soul of Kampfgruppe Scherer for one hundred and five days at Cholm would not now be in command of a second Kampfgruppe Scherer to relieve Velikiye Luki. He felt he owed it to von Sass to do everything possible to come to his aid. But in fact everything lay in Wohler's hands now, and Scherer was too tired and preoccupied to think that the shape of events would not take on some other more fitting, more personally satisfying shape. From time to time he would think of himself at the head of the relief column, walking into Sing-Sing or the Felt Factory and being the first to shake von Sass's hand, or by God even embracing him as he had embraced Captain Bikers in the GPU square on a bright winter day. Yet such thoughts even while arousing a strange burning sensation in his blood would pass only fleetingly through his mind before disappearing into the matrix of events that would never be.

He had been placed under Wohler's command, but even in this respect he would not be part of the relief attack. In effect he was still operating independently in an entirely separate universe of battle, deploying every remaining man and gun to 257 and 251 along the railroad flank. This small universe remained violent and all-consuming, and when he toured the men in the bleak overcast void along the rails littered with Russian hulks he was much disturbed. They were nearly at the end and they looked worse than had his people at Cholm the year before. He spoke to them with the same disgruntled determination irrespective of shows of confidence.

It was not that he lacked confidence, but he made no undue displays of it, nor demanded any from the officers and men he spoke to. The situation was brutal and ideas of confidence seemed hollow, words of confidence even more so. He was by nature an optimistic person, but his optimism had nothing to do with the war, nor with the views he held about things in the world; it was only something he had been born with, or which had come upon him in his youngest days, influenced by God only knew what things in his youngest days—the care of a tender mother or father perhaps, though granted this can be only speculation about the origins of a man's disposition fifty-odd years in the past. A general can be optimistic in a domineering, chin-forward kind of way, or he can be optimistic because he has an unperturbed confidence that he knows what he is doing. Scherer had little of the former quality and quite a fair amount of the latter; but all in all, his optimism owed much to that "sunnier outlook" (as people tend to phrase it) that arises unaccountably in different kinds of people, regardless of time or place or circumstance.

This matter-of-fact, nontheatrical optimism had radiated from him, like a quiet core, for one hundred and five days at Cholm, and done much to influence his men there, soothing many of their fears in ways almost beneath their notice. As if the whole course of events there, month after freezing month, were only a kind of matter-of-fact process that must sooner or later turn out for the best—at least for those who still survived at the end. There were those at Cholm who worked alongside Scherer day by day and who maybe thought him naive, in those hopeless circumstances, to comport himself in that manner. Some might have aligned themselves with the dour, hard-bitten outlook of Mabrius, his second-in-command, the square-set colonel who had a good deal more frontline experience than Scherer did. Mabrius was no defeatist but simply saw things the way they were, and many at Cholm might have felt more comfortable fighting under his dour gaze—for how else could any human being look out upon the situation in which they found themselves? For in that situation, or even in a better one, the outlook of a naive man is almost always intolerable.

But the thing was, Scherer also saw things as they were; his sunnier outlook had nothing to do with that and did not hinder his ability to see things as they were. And so those men influenced or calmed in their fear and misery by his quiet optimism did not feel betrayed or deceived by the radiance of a naive leader.

It all added up, if only because it was all over with now; they had made it through at Cholm. And even those who had long felt doubt and dismay about the man might in retrospect see that they owed more to Scherer than they had understood during those days.

All that was some months ago now, and might as well have been a year ago or two years ago or five years ago.

The men of 251 and 257 holding on at Tchernosem (or, for that matter, of 277 holding on in Velikiye Luki) would have had little opportunity over these recent months to acquire an impression of Scherer one way or the other. The three regiments had been dispersed across all these miles of the front and Scherer had not been able to make his face well-known. The soldiers might bank some hope on certain established facts, on hopeful conclusions drawn from these facts—they knew he had somehow carried his men through that mess at Cholm and might think that somehow he would do the same here, at Tchernosem, or over there, at Velikiye Luki.

But they also knew this was only a hopeful logic that might mean nothing at all. The situation was very bad, at

Tchernosem, and Scherer saw it that way too, every time he
visited the feeble positions there, talked with exhausted and
feeble men holding feeble positions in a snow-waste.

The more cheerful aspect of his nature was shunted aside;
he knew it, and did not expect anything different. He was
tired and depressed—though too busy most of the time to
feel more than dull fitful bouts of this depression. (Had he
ever felt depressed at Cholm? Yes, perhaps a few times, during the worst days, or during the longest days in March and
April when it was becoming clearer and clearer that the
whole ordeal might never come to an end. But on the whole,
no, no, he had not felt that way at Cholm.) Any longer his
confidence was not what it had been. No doubt that had much
to do with his lack of control over the situation here. Over
von Sass's men in Velikiye Luki—no control whatsoever.
Yet the necessity of remaining in Novo Sokolniki, where radio contact with von Sass was somewhat better, also effectively diminished his control over events at Tchernosem.

And when he came up to see things for himself he saw
how bad it was at Tchernosem; the stark reality of the situation threw all the other elements of his inner nature into the
shadows, into some inconsequential corner of himself; his
confidence sagged when he saw how burnt-out these men
were and he knew he could offer them very little. He could
not lead them or comfort them when he was going back and
forth to Novo all the time, when von Sass's dilemma nagged
at him and distracted him and hung over him all the time.

His confidence sagged when he walked through the burnt-
out timbers of Tchernosem, another ramshackle wooden
place; after weeks of fighting it had effectively ceased to exist. But the ruins were at least something—or gave the illusion of being something—that he understood when he
toured the positions outside Tchernosem, in the snow-
wastes, where there was nothing. The nothingness was terrible and sapped his confidence, his spirit, in almost an
awe-inspiring way; and he looked into the faces of the men
out there and saw how the effect in them was greater still, far
greater. The wind blew from the east over a white nothingness scabbed here and there by scabby-looking patches
where the snow had blown away. The wind was coarse, the

snow coarse. A grey blackness to the east billowed high in the atmosphere, lit wanly with evil light, like a storm coming; but it was only the climate, blowing endlessly against them, nothing so particular that it could be called a storm.

In places there were trench networks, though pitifully shallow in the frozen ground, with the scabby articulations of barbed wire thrown out in front of them, and then the mines seeded out in front of the barbed wire, many rendered useless by drifting snow, or rendered useless because snow had blown off them and made them visible again. When not under attack the men were often at work re-digging and re-laying these mines, a dangerous enterprise somewhat like moving counters in a game, some obscure symbolism inherent in it all, ramified by the unnerving emptiness in all directions. The dead could not be buried in the frozen ground and so they too looked like counters or pieces now removed from the game, set aside here and there, stacked or laid in rows, as if to indicate the border of some field of play. It was rubbish of course and if some gestalt formed in the mind to suggest counters or games then this gestalt quickly crumbled and faded away into the rubbish that it was, leaving only a dreary, scattered mess out there, where the scattered lines of the two regiments were.

The heavy weapons that remained, PAKs and heavy machine guns, were set up behind their clearly articulated fields of fire, within the trenches or behind the trenches, or within shell-holes where no trenches existed; and these dispositions might be considered barely adequate. With adequate reserves and artillery at hand this wasteland might have served as an adequate defensive position. But there was not enough artillery at hand to create the necessary killing fields out of Russian breakthrough points, or out of their assembly points that would indicate another breakthrough forthcoming, today, tomorrow, the day after. And reserves of men needed to seal off these breakthroughs were culled only at the expense of men already defending the trenches, leaving positions critically undermanned for hundreds of yards at a stretch. So that the trenches often appeared empty, ghostly, like the weather-beaten leavings of some bygone battle rather than the dwelling- or dying-places of the current one. Men continued to move about here and there, so few of them it seemed, it always seemed.

Hateful as the place was—you could not be there without thinking constantly of the desire to be away from there—he would have felt more comfortable speaking to these men, looking them in the eye, if he knew he would be obliged to stay here too, or at least somewhere in the normal proximity of command, in a headquarters close behind the line. Novo was too far away, and the distance somehow dragged at the very sincerity in his voice when he spoke. He was not used to that, though he was having to get used to it, for good or ill. With a few regimental officers he would walk out among these positions and observe the men there looking back at him as a stranger; maybe they were bolstered a little by his reputation, but even so they looked at him as a stranger, and their spirits did not look all that bolstered either.

There was shelling and other noise. The emptiness diminished it somewhat, the impression of it if not the danger.

He saw that it was easier to defend a place if you had a place to defend. Cholm had been a place, a place for them to die or starve maybe, but still a place. Already he had been a year and a half in Russia and yet outside Tchernosem he seemed to see for the first time what it really was, and what it would be. The German army sown thinly like impotent seeds across a land, far away from towns and cities whose true insignificance was now revealed, horribly and unendingly though those towns and cities might be fought over.

Even before the crisis the regimental commanders—leaving aside von Sass—had been used to operating with some degree of independence. This was just as well—essential, in fact. But the commander of 251 was dead, and so was the next most-experienced officer, Meyer, who had been lost with his battlegroup weeks ago beyond the railroad. This left Materna, the former 1A, in command of 251. Scherer discerned Materna's ability to make do with the men he had left, to slice and dismember units into smaller entities to create reserves in some reasonable proportion to the frontline defenders, to properly select the cadres of men who would best be able to carry out the constant shoestring counterattacks that were the only hope at all of defending this nothingness, this no-place.

That was as it should be; at least until such cadres and groups dwindled to such small size that none of it mattered anymore. Two fifty-one and 257 both needed to be relieved by fresh troops, by a fresh division, but that was not in the offing. In the meantime Scherer had discerned that Materna's abilities were offset by his need to have his moves frequently validated by a commanding officer, by himself, in other words. Materna did what he could but he looked for reassurance whenever Scherer arrived. A man would want reassurance in a place like this, Scherer thought. But it was not a good thing. He did not want to imagine Materna paralyzed in a crisis while he was twenty miles away at Novo. Perhaps not paralyzed, he was not that inexperienced, but hesitant, not quick enough. While the Russians surged in like acid through cheesecloth. Or like a wave simply surging on through an empty ocean. An option was to make a single battlegroup out of 251 and 257, with Bark of 257 in command. But Bark's people were already too widely dispersed; to place him over 251 as well would be little better than inserting his name at the top of some meaningless organizational table.

Other ideas ramified like branching limbs.

Bark's 1A was a good man. He could be delegated to lead 257, allowing Bark to assume ad hoc overall command of both regiments, in effect taking over Scherer's own function. (While he went back to Novo to fret ceaselessly over von Sass in that damnable city. . . .)

Then there were the Gebirgsjaeger, two battalions that von der Chevallerie had transferred up here to Tchernosem. He considered combining one of them with 251 and placing the battalion commander over Materna's head, forming a smaller battlegroup while Bark still kept free rein over 257. Scherer had seen enough of the Gebirgsjaeger officers to think that he could place confidence in either one of them.

But he knew also that Wohler would be wanting one or both of the Gebirgsjaeger battalions, in a few days, perhaps even tomorrow, when the drive on Velikiye Luki began.

In the end he talked to Bark, in a bunker two miles outside

Tchernosem, built into a barely discernible white hillock, much like other undulations of the land thereabouts. He then informed Materna on his way back through what remained of Tchernosem. In addition to what he had already noticed about Materna, the man seemed only tenuously present anymore, within the haggard confines of his body. But he was not the only one. Some, officers and men, held their presence shrunken more deeply and exhaustedly inside themselves. Then those like Materna looked as if presence had deserted them, fled somewhere, their eyes flitting into musty corners of a miserable log hovel or across snowy horizons in the distance, like golem eyes.

He rode on the back of a half-tracked motorcycle to the rail-spur where the armored train was waiting, waiting to steam back to Novo Sokolniki.

He rode the armored train back to Novo, along the spur that branched off from Tchernosem where 257 and 251 were grouped either to stand for the duration or go under. He rode in the command car in the middle of the train and spoke with the armored train's commander, a specialist junior colonel whose job Scherer vaguely envied; he was too tired and preoccupied to know why. The man captained a fortified ship traversing the snowfields. The guns on the train, mounted in impressive cupolas that exerted a disproportionate force over the land, were badly shot up but had done much to support and sustain the staggering people around Tchernosem. Ammunition for the cupola guns had been expended, used up at the rate of a ship's boiler devouring coal, and the train was headed back to Novo to rearm. Even in the hinterland every gun-port was manned to keep partisan bands away from the tracks, should they appear. The train moved slowly, ponderously, an iron worm.

"Wohler will be set to start tomorrow," said Scherer. "I expect you will be sent over to support him."

The junior colonel, raffish as a U-boat commander, somewhat vain, nodded judiciously yet without particular concern, like a jack-of-all-trades used to being sent to one place or another, Scherer only a passenger aboard his own elongated iron universe. It was this that Scherer envied though still without articulate shape in his mind. The armored command car was somewhat roomier, less congested with fittings and gear of every kind, than a U-boat; otherwise the atmosphere inside this fortified chamber was somewhat similar. Plated slits offered glimpses of a gloomy nothingness outside. Neither man looked out at the landscape though, as if life aboard the train excluded the visual world.

The train would be able to advance only a short distance along the other branch line toward Velikiye Luki, up to where the Russians had blocked the tracks, but the guns to that point would be enough to help Wohler's group get started. Scherer reflected that this would mean the train would not be available—for several days at least, and probably more—to support his own people around Tchernosem. He was resigned to this. Von Sass and 277 inside Velikiye Luki were his own people too, though already a strange inexplicable remoteness was beginning to hum at the very back of his brain. He did not, could not think that the relief attack would fail, though it had taken Wohler's group over a week to assemble and it was still perhaps only a barely adequate force; diluted in the meantime by the necessity of spreading out to contain the ever-widening Russian ring around the city. Some elements of the Gebirgsjaeger and 291st Infantry Division, for example, had been taken from Wohler's core force to shore up the ongoing crisis at Tchernosem. Tchernosem, where he had just been—and the Gebirgsjaeger in particular had made a good impression on Scherer, and he felt a little easier, just a little easier, about that place now.

The train steamed into Novo.

Frozen men, the dead, lay in a peculiar rubble of statuary upon the station platform. Scherer did not like this. They would not have been left there to freeze to death. They would have been already dead upon being unloaded from the wounded car a day or two before, the *sanis* and every other man in Novo available to carry a stretcher tending only to the living, carrying them off to the field hospital in this village, leaving the dead to pose in arresting agony, or sometimes even tranquilly welded by the cold to the station platform or to each other.

Still he didn't like it and at the same time he realized, as he stepped down into the open air, that yes it had grown very much colder today, bitter, windy. No matter what else he had to do he would find a few souls to free the dead with axes and pickaxes and at least drag them off the platform. So that at least he and everyone else would not have to see them like this, so that at least the newly arriving wounded would not have to see them like this.

He saw Major Metzelaar waiting by himself on the platform in this blowing cold and knew it must be something important, yet he suddenly turned to speak angrily to the train commander. This man stood upon a small steel platform built over the coupling between the command car and one of the gun cars.

"Damn it, tell the engineer to pull up until the car with the wounded is abreast of the platform."

The commander was startled and craned his head out to peer down the length of the train. He said, "Yes, Herr General."

He disappeared into the command car to contact the engineer before the locomotive lost too much steam. A few dismal faces were peering out from another coupling several hundred feet further back. The *sanis* and bearers on the station platform, with stretchers held upright like furled and colorless battle flags, had already started to get down and flounder through the snow toward the back of the train. Scherer shouted at them to remain on the platform. Slowly the train squealed forward again, smoke churning from the stack and steam blowing sideways in a hot gale, crosswise to the bitter gale now blowing in from the east. Metzelaar remained standing where he was, at the edge of the steam, in the warmth of the steam.

"How long have you been standing out here?" said Scherer.

"Ten minutes or so," the major said.

"All right, what is it then?"

"Von Sass," said Metzelaar.

He handed Scherer a typed transcript of a lengthy radio message. Scherer read it. He said, "The Russians would have to start while I was off somewhere. What reply did you send?"

"That Wohler is starting tomorrow. I told von Sass that you would be due back at this time. He should be standing by."

Scherer looked at the message again. Some phrases had been underlined. Bromberg has fallen. Preussich-Berlin has fallen. Garrison wiped out to the last man. He set his teeth together, his breathing more measured. He looked for mention of Bayreuth or the Felt Factory but there was none. He saw that von Sass had moved his headquarters from the citadel, from Sing-Sing on the west side of the Lovat, to another location—identified as Barracks Complex—on the east side of the Lovat, where the greater bulk of the city was situated. The renewed Russian attack had commenced at all points— at all points, Scherer stared at this—at 0900 that morning. No, von Sass, he thought. *Schwerpunkt? Schwerpunkt?* But he would be speaking to the man in a few minutes. They walked, he and Major Metzelaar, with their backs bowed beneath the wind toward the headquarters building.

"How long has it been like this?" said Scherer.

"The weather? I don't know. It was like this when I stepped outside."

Scherer had been on the train for an hour and a half, a distance of seventeen miles, Tchernosem to Novo Sokolniki. The cold front had blown in over the slow-moving train, over everything now. They had acclimated themselves to the blowing wet, the dampness, with temperatures for weeks hovering just above and below the thaw point; now their bodies tightened. Snow hissed sideways through Novo Sokolniki. The place looked not so much wrecked by the war as abandoned for the last hundred years. There were vehicles parked around the headquarters building and other vehicles parked around the hospital building and various supply depots, which were often mere piles of goods spread over with tarpaulins. Every other structure stood like scrap on either side of a single icy road.

They went inside. Solemnly they both sat down at a table beside the radio operator.

Chapter Twenty-two

As the barrage intensified they became isolated. Field telephone lines were cut. Radio traffic was garbled. Runners were killed.

Different strongpoints underwent their own sieges. Wien I has fallen. Wien II has fallen. Bromberg has fallen.

Massive as the Russian assaults had become, they still had not enough force to attack every strongpoint simultaneously.

At Strongpoint Hamburg the radio operator said, "Locksmith reporting. Quiet for the moment. No signs of enemy activity."

But it was not quiet. The operator had to speak loudly. He said it was quiet because the shells were falling some hundreds of yards away, across the Lovat on the next link in the chain, on Strongpoint Bremen. In other circumstances this would have been considered a deafening roar, but the operator indicated an immediate circumference of quiet whose focal point was the spot where he sat inside Hamburg. He trembled even as he spoke, as did everyone else in there, including the dead. The foundations of every structure in the city vibrated continuously, as if the barrage had set off some deeper sympathetic tremor within the earth that would not stop. It was very tiring and induced headaches and other physical maladies, almost like a kind of seasickness.

In any case this was but a general condition, hour by hour; whereas in all likelihood the Russians would switch their fire in another hour or two and Hamburg specifically would be blasted, as it had been already at many intervals, sometimes more frequently, sometimes less.

But Hamburg had not come under attack for several days even after the Russians had resumed their overall assault against the city. Hasenclever was unnerved by this, as their position commanded the key point of the Lovat bridge. What were they waiting for then?

Time passed.

Time and violence were the dominant opposing—and yet also complementary—forces of a combat zone, the depth and breadth of both forces becoming heightened during a long siege.

Kordts and Schrader played chess a few times, in the depths of Hamburg. The games went quickly, because neither could concentrate. It was a diversion and not a good one; but neither was smoking or staring into space or trying to talk or play cards or monotonously clean weapons over and over again. They would be interrupted by fire or by an alarm or by Hasenclever wanting something or by some other thing; and they had to take their turns in the smaller rubble-forts that were outside, up by the bridge.

They were distracted also by a certain self-consciousness, to be doing this under the vaguely staring stares of other men nearby, many of them wounded. The foundations would tremble and pieces would fall off the board. They would pick them up and set them back if they could remember where; otherwise they would just set them back somewhere with a tacit resignation and continue playing, the game altered arbitrarily, but the diversion, such as it was, remaining the same.

They were distracted also by a certain antagonism, though this became more subdued over time. Schrader had been angry and remained so, though he considered that maybe he couldn't blame Kordts for failing to look for Krabel. Kordts was right; he should have reminded him. But why couldn't the bastard think of it for himself? He couldn't think clearly anymore and so he simply remained angry, and only fatigue and monotony made it less. He thought playing chess again might enable him to judge Kordts a little better, somehow allow him to abide the sight of him. But he found he couldn't think any more clearly than before and notions of judging the man facing across from him became pointless and dull; still suffused with moodiness, but he could not concentrate on that any more than on what they were doing. Kordts could have been anyone in the platoon, the company, passing time

until they were interrupted again. They spoke little. Occasionally Schrader would stand up angrily and simply walk
off, and Kordts would lean back narrow-eyed and watch him
with a kind of disinterested anger of his own, if such a thing
made any sense.

He wondered if Schrader was working his way through
something, toward some violent outburst or tirade. He didn't
much care one way or the other. His head still ached continuously. Often he would lean back and close his eyes till
Schrader said something to him. Sometimes he would fall
asleep entirely and wake up to find that Schrader had gone.
Amorphous thoughts and daydreams passed in darkness
through his mind, thoughts and daydreams weighed down by
anchors that dragged dully from his mind down deep into his
innards.

Hasenclever shouted down to Schrader and Schrader rose
and went up to one of the observation slits where Hasenclever was. Kordts leaned back against the wall, resting his
cheek against it, the least sensitive part of his head, and
thought he might sleep for a while. If it was some kind of
alarm he would know it in a moment or two. Tears welled up
in his eyes as they sometimes did; he paid little attention to
this. He opened his eyes and saw Freitag and another man in
a corner, staring fixedly into a Hindenberg lamp, as if they
were asleep with open eyes.

The radio set crackled and hissed like something left too
long on a stove. The operator leaned forward and reached for
the headphones.

In a fit of idle disinterested despair—despair spread over
too many hours and too many days, losing any specific
sticking-point of anguish—Kordts lifted his boot and tipped
the board over and spilled everything onto the floor, among
shell casings that had rolled down the stairs from up above,
among any other kind of litter that people had dropped or
that had been jolted down from walls or ceilings. This slight
action caused him some slight uncertain unease that he responded to by bending over and collecting the spilled pieces
and placing them all in a small pile in a corner. Other men
nearby paid only the slightest attention to this, looking at him
only because he was moving about and introducing some

small variation into the death grip of hours. He thought of Moll again and laughed faintly; it came out between a wheeze and a snarl. Two weeks now, or about that, as he was no longer certain how many days it had been. Only a fraction of those months at Cholm. He thought about this for a moment—not for the first time, of course—but it was too awesome to really contemplate; a leaden force within his bodily organs absorbed it but could not contemplate it.

He observed himself moving with a curious almost precisely half-assed quality, picking up the pieces one by one but then merely piling them at the base of the wall, not even troubling to set them back inside the little cardboard box Schrader used. Where oh where was it, the famous German thoroughness. . . . Fumes lingered in the depths of Strongpoint Hamburg. He took a few steps and he was standing over Freitag and Kastner, the Hindenberg flame sending up oily guttering spirals. The floor vibrated, not enough to send anyone off-balance; he did not reach out with his hand to steady himself but merely buckled his knees very slightly, so that he felt this vibrating force absorbed along the front of his shins.

"How are you doing?" he said.

Freitag shrugged, tried to smile. "I don't know," he said.

"*Ja, gut,*" said Kordts, feeling a certain iota of strength, a faint bending force, pass through him for a fraction of a second. "Ha, ha," he said, tacking the bronze shield on his sleeve with his fingernail. Freitag laughed faintly too, thinking he understood this little gesture, or something of it anyway. He raised his arm and glanced at his own shield, dark bronze glimmering in dark and smelly lamplight.

"Where are you going?"

"Air," said Kordts.

"We'll be going back to the bridge soon."

"*Ja,*" said Kordts.

He went up the stairs. He saw Hasenclever and Schrader and another platoon sergeant by one of the embrasures, peering out there. The radio operator emerged from below and brushed past and went over to where they were. Kordts listened for a moment but the rumbling from everywhere obscured their voices. He climbed a ladder fastened with baling wire to an interior wall.

What had been the second story of the building was now a chaos of rubble and beams and sandbags, much of it razed and left this way by the occupants from 277 earlier in the year. In effect the defenders had lowered the whole structure of Hamburg deeper into the earth over the course of months, taking out the upper floor while excavating deeper below ground. A few parts of the walls and the roof had been left standing at random, giving Strongpoint Hamburg a misleadingly wrecked and hollowed-out appearance from the outside. Russian fire had further pulverized the rubble up here, without—as yet—penetrating to the main quarters below. It was dangerous here and for some days observers had been stationed in other unoccupied buildings and structures nearby. But communications were becoming too difficult, runners too frequently killed or wounded, phone lines cut and line repairmen too frequently killed or wounded. Even so the observers remained at their posts out there, but now an observer was also stationed amidst the rubble on top of Hamburg itself.

A kind of corridor no wider than a man threaded the piles of debris up here. It led to an "office" at one corner of the building, like a closet or small garret, where part of the roof still remained. Two men, sprawled haphazardly along the corridor some yards from each other, had lain up here for some time. Kordts walked past them.

In the office Razlitt said, "What are you doing up here?"

"A little air," said Kordts.

Razlitt nodded sardonically, though understanding the need. The air was dank and bitingly cold but it was better air than below ground.

"I wouldn't hope you'd relieve me a little early," said Razlitt. "Or would you?"

"No," said Kordts. "I'll be going up again in a little bit."

He meant up to the bridge. He could not see the bridge, unless he crawled over to the particular spot where Razlitt was looking out. Instead he looked at the grey sunlight that poured dimly past Razlitt through several cracks and holes, into the dim narrow confines of the office.

"They might mean business today," said Razlitt. "They've had tanks moving about."

"Which side of the river?"

"Both sides. But at least ten of them on this side."

"Have you told Hasenclever?"

"A while ago." Razlitt pointed at the floor. "Like the master ringing his valet, heh, heh."

A phone box lay by his feet, with cable disappearing through a crack in the floor. Kordts eased up to look through a bullet hole or perhaps the work of a 20 mm shell. But it wouldn't have passed entirely through the wall of the building. The gouge mark left by the bullet or shell on the outside had been drilled through from the inside. More cleverness.

He still couldn't see much, however.

"*Ja,* that idea didn't work out so well," said Razlitt.

Kordts slid over to a wider crack.

"Careful," said Razlitt.

The rubble-field led up to the tangled girders of the bridge. Lovat bridge. Lovat River. Place names passing in idle talismanic fashion through Kordts's mind, as they had done at other times over the course of many months. Even elevated like this he could not see down into the river, would hardly have known it was there if not for the tangle of the bridge. He knew ice was forming there, though not frozen solid yet. He knew it from taking his turn up by the bridge perimeter every other day. Dusk was falling almost imperceptibly—as the short winter days were an ongoing dusk, low clouds hanging day after day, like a low corrugated roof that was part of the city itself. He and the others would go up after dark, and the ones up there now would come in. Tanks, he thought fearfully, though it was an absentminded fear as almost all thoughts and emotions would be over the course of time except when they were jolted violently on occasion by immediate incidents, terrors. Shells striking, or the beginning of another attack. . . . He wondered if they would come with tanks during the night, or if they would wait for daylight. Nearer than the bridge were the two hulks from a week or ten days ago, the one Krabel had destroyed with the Teller mine and then the other one, the flame tank. . . . Burned alive some day, Kordts thought, perhaps tonight, or in the morning. He was different from many men, in that he had no more fear of being burned alive than of being ripped apart by shells or bayoneted or shot in the face or belly. It was all the same to him. He feared, if anything, being buried alive, though he was able not to dwell on this, he was not sure how, as he had an active enough imagination generally. He had had this fear even before being buried alive in the GPU building during the May Day barrage, when the stairs and everything else had collapsed on him . . . though only for a short time, a few minutes, he had managed to crawl out of there under his own power. . . . Since then he had had the idea that he would shoot himself, if worst came to worst, though he hadn't had his rifle with him that time; and even if he had it might have been buried beyond his reach. But he didn't dwell on this much either, and thus managed to hold on to this clearly flawed belief. . . .

Perhaps he shared in common with many men the fear of death more than any specific way of being killed. Apathy, hunger, monotony, privation, as well as a certain unending quality to these several years, and also even now a kind of vague disbelief that any of this could be happening at all, had served to diminish this fear somewhat as well. He feared the cold, the cold as it had been last winter. Not just at Cholm but before then, between Lake Seliger and Cholm, when inner voices had screamed in agony within his skull, released through the wall of his flesh to the terrible outer air by an endless series of grunts and moans and hoarse disbelieving whispers, small pathetic noises echoed by Moll and Freitag and every other one of them.

Even so, what tough little faggots we are, he thought suddenly with a perverse, irreducible and unacknowledgeable pride. He knew somehow that she had betrayed him, Erika had, though this had never dawned on him at any particular time as somehow he had known it all along, since those days on leave, when his peace of mind had not been disturbed by one iota and had remained intact for months afterward. And when he began to feel sick of things again it was only because that peace of mind had worn off; it didn't have to do with realizing anything about anything. . . . He could hardly blame her, they had known each other too long, knew each other's temptations, spirits, deep abiding anxieties, too well. . . .

He heard tank motors now. He glanced at Razlitt and Raz-

litt nodded slightly. Kordts peered out across the distance
and could not make out anything until something moved. He
saw a metallic surface moving, blotchy and dull, whitewashed, more like a concrete surface, for the texture of armor plate resembled concrete as much as steel. It was the top
of a tank turret moving along, not approaching them but
moving at a right angle off in the distance, like the back of
some sea beast moving in a trough between ocean swells, between the erose walls of buildings blasted or still standing,
between piles of debris. He watched another one moving
along behind it, and when they both came to a stop he saw
the upper parts of other armored vehicles assembled in the
remains of what appeared to be a small industrial yard. He
tried to count. Ten or about ten, as Razlitt had said. Razlitt
was bent over, turning the crank on the telephone box.
Kordts's vague and often disinterested fear became a more
specific fear. A flash of heat, sweat, in his face, a curling sensation in the arches of his feet . . . He thought of moving up
there in the darkness, toward the bridge. . . .

The light changed and Kordts blinked. Razlitt had finished
speaking into the receiver. He said, "Get away. Don't stick
your head there when the sun comes out."

Kordts moved his head aside. Razlitt smiled wryly. A
shaft of sunlight came like a lance into the office, like several lances, through whatever holes there were. A roar came
from somewhere, followed by several more; the building
trembled.

"It's like a child poking a stick through a wall," said Razlitt. "He'll put your eye out. Snipers."

"*Ja, ja,*" said Kordts, issuing a dull explosive laugh at this
colorful notion like a horse snorting. He shook his head and
stared at nothing. More roaring shook the neighborhood,
over to the left somewhere. Careless movements . . . It was a
death trap up here. Observers in other structures nearby were
sheltered by the chaos of everything, the Russians not sure
where to look for them. But they would have Hamburg under
observation at all hours. The office was a snug and secret little place but eyes would be watching it all the same, perceiving what it was if any glimpse of movement was seen. And
the two men back in the sandbagged corridor, secure from

sniper fire, had been killed by mortar fire landing on the roof, random patterns peppering the roof and one or two unlucky shells dropped right into that tiny threadlike corridor.

"You can go below," said Razlitt. "If you draw their attention it's my head they'll pop."

Though he said this not too harshly, Kordts even so didn't like being spoken to that way, because he knew better, even if perhaps he had been careless for a second. But Razlitt was right and Kordts took no offense, thought no more about it. He knew Razlitt only slightly but had felt an instinctive liking for the man the few times they had spoken. His face did not seem too marked by the tension of the hours spent up here. Perhaps Razlitt was not tense. Unconcern could sometimes wind through a man at long last—surrender, if that's what it was—though he might remain cautious and canny. Perhaps it was almost worth it to spend a few hours up in this garret, away from the dull unnerving presences of all the others. Kordts's own tension, which at times a few days earlier had come over him like a paroxysm, pushing outward through every pore, harassing him with the nearly irresistible urge to do something, had faded somewhat; he really had no idea why. He felt a kind of gratitude, though he could not imagine feeling grateful for anything, but he did feel that somehow. . . .

He rested his head against the wall beside the crack he had been peering through, the shaft of sunlight so bright that it rendered Razlitt invisible on the other side of it. Then the area nearby roared and trembled again and he yanked his head back from the vibrating wall. Kordts turned his head and peered obliquely out through the crack, up at the sky, where the low clouds had opened momentarily to reveal a gash of pure invisible light, evening light darkly stained, invisibility leading up to the invisible beyondness that lay above all this. The building trembled a little more violently. The roar of the barrage, when not laid directly upon Hamburg itself, was like the ocean roar that you might find yourself listening to for a few moments and then not hearing for hours and hours. Though there were other times when it was like the agony of listening to a faucet drip through the night, when the intervals were such that it was impossible not to keep listening, anticipating when the next one would land . . .

A column of smoke boiled up toward the blue gash in the sky . . . about to blot it out, but then the clouds closed first, the low clouds blotting it out.

Some feet below, on the first floor of the building, Hasenclever and Schrader and the other sergeant still stood to one side of an embrasure, appraising things in suspicious tones. The low sunlight had been bladed through the embrasure and then its abrupt disappearance caused Schrader to glance over there, in the midst of speaking; then he turned his head back and went on, "No, I suppose it's not a trick. I don't have that feeling. Why should they bother with that now?"

"You can feel what you like," said Hasenclever. "Who knows what the bastards might be up to. They've got plenty of time between now and the morning."

They were talking about the cease-fire order that had just come through from von Sass's headquarters.

In truth Hasenclever also suspected it was not a trick. He suspected the Russians would wait until the next day, until noon precisely, when the four-hour cease-fire had elapsed and the terms of surrender had been rejected, as he and every other soul instinctively knew they would be. But he had grown sick of waiting for the Russians to resume their attacks against Hamburg and the bridge, days waiting while other strongpoints in the city were annihilated or were still resisting after being attacked for days. They had all heard the motors grinding out there, and Razlitt had rung up several times, and a runner had made it back in daylight from the bridge perimeter.

And then the radio operator had come up from below with the message from von Sass's command post, the message relayed to Hamburg and to every other point along the eight-mile perimeter. Effective at 0800 the next morning there would be a four-hour cease-fire. Further notice would come to indicate where the Russian parliamentaires would be conducted through the lines.

"What are you afraid of?" said Hasenclever. "That we'll rouse them up tonight if we hit them first?"

"Not at all," said Schrader, too tired to be afraid of anything or to take offense at any suggestion of it. Though he did think there was a good chance that the Russians would respond, if Hasenclever sent out his request for an artillery strike and it was granted. But he too was very tired of waiting and was indifferent as to whether this wait would end tonight or at noon tomorrow.

"I'm all for it," said Gipfel, the other sergeant. "I don't give a damn. Let them have it while there's still a chance."

Schrader waved his hand irritably, thinking Hasenclever was only confusing the issue because he couldn't decide for himself whether to make the request. He said, "Put the call through. See if they have any damned shells to spare."

Darkness was falling. Schrader thought it would come to nothing because the request would be turned down anyway. He began collecting his men for the night up by the bridge. He was right. Hasenclever went below and then emerged again a few minutes later. For days artillery pieces throughout the city had been nearly out of shells, with supplies dropped by parachute barely making a dent in the shortfall.

"This is what they said," said Hasenclever. "If the Ivans attack during the night we'll get as much fire support as can be spared. But they won't allot any ammunition except in the event of an emergency."

Gipfel smiled craftily. "Tell them they're coming right now. Tell them a dozen T-34s are already attacking the bridge."

Hasenclever stared blankly at him. After a moment he said, "No. No, we can't do that."

Gipfel shrugged, as weary and indifferent as Schrader. He began collecting his own platoon. The first flares were rising and their white bursts pierced the embrasure. A half hour later the Russians shelled Hamburg and the bridge perimeter heavily for half an hour. Schrader and Gipfel's men were already in position by then, out in the dark. There were casualties among the men they had relieved making their way back to Hamburg. The rumble of tank motors kept on for a while longer, then ceased. The rest of the night passed in silence.

Chapter Twenty-three

From von Sass/Fortress Commandant/12-12-42
Enemy parliamentaire received at 0800 in Barracks Complex. Surrender terms rejected at 1315. Barrage recommenced at 1400, unparalleled force. Attack by enemy bombers at 1600.

New main line on west bank holding against all attacks. Friday School Strongpoint in flames, must be abandoned. Main line elsewhere, especially south perimeter, still holding. Losses since renewed enemy attack 10 December—700 dead, wounded, missing.

From von Sass/Fortress Commandant/16-12-42
Bremen has fallen. Hamburg has fallen. Positions remain secure around Felt Factory.

From von Sass/Fortress Commandant/24-12-42
I feel it is my duty to give an unadorned picture of the situation. Russian storm troops of 100–150 men supported by masses of tanks and massed fire from mortars and PAKs have been attacking our critical points for days. The tanks stay out of range of our remaining antitank guns. One strongpoint after another has been systematically shot to pieces. Our losses are extraordinarily high and cannot be sustained if resistance is to continue. Today 40 men out of 74 in a section of the north perimeter were put out of action. The lack of ammunition for all weapons—howitzers, werfer batteries, mortars, antitank, heavy machine guns—will render us incapable of continuing the fight. Every effort must be made to send in more supply gliders with weapons and am-

munition. The New Year Square has been cleared for night landings. The performance of the troops can only be described as superhuman.

From von Sass/Fortress Commandant/26-12-42
Russian attack of extraordinary intensity. The enemy has succeeded in recapturing the forward strongpoint Bayreuth after the garrison fought to the last man. In addition he has broken into the main perimeter at Wurzburg and Innsbruck with heavy armored support. The strongpoint garrisons destroyed four tanks but were shot to pieces by others that had broken through on the flanks. Both strongpoints were lost; Innsbruck was retaken in a counterattack; Wurzburg impossible to approach as it has been surrounded by enemy tanks. Supplies of Teller mines and other close-combat materiel are nearly exhausted. Few antitank guns remain in action, so that the men are powerless against the onslaught of the steel giants. Reserves and materiel for a radical restructuring of the main line no longer exist.

The situation is critical. To this point losses in dead, wounded, missing—2000 men. Few and priceless heavy weapons are put out of action every day. Every man knows what the situation is and is fighting beyond the limits of endurance, facing heavy tanks without weapons. I do not exaggerate if I describe the situation as having reached the final phase. Every man will do his duty.

27 December.
  Novo Sokolniki.
  The few centers of activity around headquarters building, field hospital, and supply dumps, presented the aspect of an Antarctic research station. Wind-driven particles seethed across the emptiness. The railroad tracks were no longer visible beneath the snowdrifts. There were not enough men— and no longer any civilians nearby to be dragooned—to keep the tracks cleared. The armored train had been withdrawn to more populated areas in the hinterland.
  The remaining shambles of the town were strewn about beyond these few hives of activity. Pieces of wood, nothing. A few years earlier the American writer H. P. Lovecraft had

completed one of the great horror stories, in which a research team in the Antarctic had discovered the remains of a foul civilization at the edge of the Mountains of Madness. The wind blew.

The brilliant edge of space, terrible sunlight, had been visible for only a single day with the advent of the cold. Then more blizzards came. The temperature remained below zero. The snow did not fall but whirled horizontally for miles at a time. The cold remained. The blizzards were of a curious teething dryness, the wind blowing the snow like sand.

Inside the headquarters building one had the feeling of being cut off from everything, of being "inside," such as workers at an Antarctic research station would have for months at a time, daring to go out into the weather for only a few moments now and then.

Radio contact was erratic.

Scherer looked through the messages of the last ten days. Lamplight flickered. Inside it was warm and still; though one could always hear the wind howling, howling.

He was hardly able to feel anger anymore, as it had become part of the status quo that he could do nothing to come to von Sass's aid. The wind howled like the fates and Scherer and other men seemed paralyzed by the kind of resignation familiar to more ancient earthly peoples. They could not really abide that though, so they tried to remain active, more and more perfunctorily. Listening, sending messages. In fact he concentrated more on things that he could do, which revolved around the other two regiments at Tchernosem. With the train gone he could not physically reach them either, except by laborious and draining journeys by half-track, which he did undertake every two or three days.

If not for the hypnotic force conveyed by von Sass's words he would have moved his headquarters closer to Tchernosem, so that he could at least be close to something, on top of something. He considered that he should do this anyway, as he could offer von Sass nothing by staying at Novo Sokolniki. Nothing, that is, except radio communication, which was somewhat better at this place. But what could he say to von Sass any longer?

Help is coming. But he had said this too many times already. And so had General Wohler in command of Kampf-gruppe Wohler, maintaining his own radio contact with von Sass; even though Wohler's group had still made only limited progress. Time was running out. And he could no longer think of this either except perfunctorily, as he had already begun to see time running out over a week before.

The casualties. Dead, wounded, missing. Seven hundred within the first twenty-four hours of the resumption of the Russian attack on 10 December. Two thousand by the end of the following week. The garrison in Velikiye Luki was bigger and better armed than the group he had led at Cholm, but not that much bigger, and not that much better armed.

He considered that if he had taken casualty rates like this at Cholm they would have gone under there within three weeks. Over two thousand now, fully a third of von Sass's force. The Russian guns, the Russian guns. For a day or two when the skies had cleared and the wind had been right, he had heard that thunder like an expanding shell of force carrying over Novo and beyond. Louder even at this distance than anything he had heard month after month in the shattered GPU fifty miles to the north. Only that terrible May Day barrage, the day Bikers had been killed and the front of the GPU had been blown entirely away, could compare with the volume of detonations that he heard incessantly from the direction of Velikiye Luki whenever the wind was right; and even through the dense muffling of the blizzards he could hear it still.

The one message in particular, from 26 December, from yesterday, he had read over and over. Not that it was any more desperate than the others. But it had been so extraordinarily long, breaking all normal radio protocols. Through the ether Scherer could sense the terrible strain of a commander who had not been long enough in the East; yet he had sent back no reprimand to von Sass. Instead he had studied it and felt his lips working faintly and silently. Hardly a radio message at all; more of a narrative, to be studied in detail. "Steel giants" . . . Had he ever seen such a phrase in official communications before? He couldn't remember. But he could see it very clearly—or see them, the enemy infantry, working in close cooperation with their tanks and other heavy weapons, methodically reducing the strongpoints one by one.

He recalled the T-34s roaming through Cholm like a pack of dogs, shooting at anything, accomplishing little. He recalled the Russian artillery fire, predictable and idiotic. Bad enough, all the same; but he and his men had held. He recalled the waves of Russian infantry surging across the blinding snowfields, and he had had nothing at all except machine guns to stop them, and so they had done, butchering them out there beyond the maze of the snow walls.

Had it all been so easy then, at Cholm?

Christ, no. What madness. He knew the truth—an absolute truth so rare in a grinding universe of events—and to think that Cholm had been easy almost caused him to spit out a small gust of laughter.

In fact he did not even have that much reaction; it was too foolish.

They had held; that was all, even while no one had come to get them out. And Velikiye Luki was going to fall, unless Wohler's group broke through.

By now he no longer thought: If only I were there myself, in the citadel, if only I were in command there myself I would . . .

In fact right from the start such an instinctive idea had passed automatically through his mind; as only a kind of passing fancy. But that was all nothing.

He could see what would have happened to him and his men the year before, in von Sass's radio messages, if the enemy had operated then as they were operating now.

A few days earlier he had recommended von Sass for the Knight's Cross; approval had come back from Berlin in a very short time.

Still there was hope, because there was always that. A gambler playing a certain kind of game might turn over one useless card after another, knowing with quiet objectivity that the odds against him were growing longer and longer. And so the peculiar transition would not occur until the very last card was turned over, the transition between objective appraisal and dead dull surprise that it was all over now. Surprise not so much at the final course of events as at a peculiar emotional reaction, when all was over.

Until then there was always hope. Wohler's group was still struggling forward, into the wind, crosswise to the wind, crawling toward any possible soft spot.

Indeed, today, just this morning, one major change had come about. Though more so for Scherer than for von Sass.

Scherer said to Major Metzelaar, "It's time for him to report."

Metzelaar spoke to the radio operator. Without stirring from where he sat Scherer could hear them clearly.

Metzelaar said, "It's the weather. It must be that."

"Yes," said Scherer. "Try and raise him anyway."

It took a while. Finally they got through. Von Sass reported that the Russians had been jamming their frequency.

Metzelaar said, "Switch to . . ."

There was another wait while the operator adjusted the knobs, matched by von Sass's operator doing the same in the citadel. Or in the Barracks Complex now, the Barracks Complex on the east bank, where von Sass had moved to a few days earlier.

Scherer stood up. The radio operator nodded. Scherer walked a few feet to the other little table and sat down. The room was stuffy. He wiped at sweat in the hollow of his throat.

"Von Sass, this is Scherer."

"Yes, Herr General."

"Make your report."

Scherer listened. The city had been cut in two. There was one pocket on the west bank of the Lovat, still around the citadel. The other pocket was with von Sass on the east side of the river. In spite of this development the current report was briefer than many of those from previous days. When von Sass had finished Scherer said, "Who is in command at the citadel?"

"Captain Darnedde."

"Tell me his frequency. In code."

The operator jotted some figures on a slip of paper. He handed this to Scherer.

"All right. I will be talking to Captain Darnedde momentarily."

Scherer tried to compose himself.

"Von Sass?"

"Yes, Herr General."

Scherer listened to the static. He could hear the static and the sound of the guns. He heard other voices in the background.

"Do you remember Cholm, von Sass?"

"Yes, Herr General. I was in the homeland."

"All right, von Sass. Help took a long time in coming. But we made it through."

Silence.

"Yes, Herr General. Cholm will not be forgotten."

"Yes. You must keep that in mind. Remember Cholm. Remember Cholm, von Sass."

Silence.

"Yes, Herr General."

Scherer began to speak again. But instead he leaned forward or just slightly nodded his head. He pinched the bridge of his nose, forcing the tears back, only a few. He pressed his lips together. He said, "Von Sass, I have received orders today from General von der Chevallerie. Eighty-third Infantry Division is to rejoin his command at Vitebsk. Two fifty-one and 257 have been fought out at Tchernosem. They will be pulling out. The Gebirgsjaeger will take over their sector."

Scherer paused. In order to say these things he must speak somewhat mechanically.

"Are you still there, von Sass?"

"Yes. Yes, Herr General."

"You are now under General Wohler's direct command. I will recommend to him that you be given freedom of action in Velikiye Luki. As far as I am concerned that is a reality in any case."

Silence.

Scherer knew very well that it was a reality except for the one essential thing. And so it was not a reality.

Von Sass addressed this now. He said, "General Scherer, I

request freedom of action to break out of the city. I will request this of General Wohler."

Scherer said, "Understood, von Sass. I will make this rec-
ommendation also. You have done everything humanly possible. Understand also that General Wohler is not in a
position to grant such a request. The High Command will
turn him down, unless he chooses to defy their directives."

Silence.

Von Sass said, "Very well, Herr General. Velikiye Luki
will hold until help arrives."

"Remember Cholm, von Sass. Remember Cholm."

Silence.

Von Sass said, "Scherer. I must speak frankly with you.
The enemy is within two hundred yards of this bunker. Last
night infiltrators with hand grenades killed several of my
staff. At this moment . . . I last went outside ten minutes ago.
Six tanks were visible from the bunker entrance. You may be
able to hear the sound of their shells."

Scherer said, "Yes, von Sass. I can hear that."

"We will continue to hold. I can no longer estimate. Unless
help arrives within a day or two our position is hopeless."

Scherer was silent for some time. Invisible conduits carried
lead toward the backs of his eyes, toward other parts of him.

"I will be leaving Novo Sokolniki for Vitebsk this
evening. Elements of Kampfgruppe Wohler will take up position in Novo Sokolniki. I must say goodbye for now, von
Sass."

Silence.

"Very well, Herr General."

"God be with you."

"Thank you, Herr General."

Chapter Twenty-four

In looking to distinguish one thing from another, one attempts to see important differences. But all the same, certain similarities will remain. Some things will remain the same.

The Russian dead in front of the strongpoints, for example. Sheaves of machine-gun fire from the pitted embrasures cut them down in the rubble as they had been cut down in the Cholm snowfields the year before.

When the tanks were there the Soviet commanders saw fit to have their men work more closely with the tanks. Often with good results. The tanks would stay at a certain distance and pulverize the strongpoints; under cover of their battering, the foot soldiers would work their way up to the embrasures, spraying the insides with their goat's legs, hurling in quantities of grenades like coal flung from a shovel, crawling in themselves, bursts of automatic fire at close range in the choking interiors. The flame tanks too began to appear more and more. Shrieking fisheyes could be seen writhing through gaps blown in the walls, through the pitted embrasures. It was not yet called napalm, these jellied flaming come-jets.

But from time to time the tanks would withdraw to replenish their ammunition, which they expended with frenzied extravagance. Or if as much as a single German antitank gun remained in action, somewhere, then five or six T-34s might be knocked out in five minutes, leaving the foot soldiers bereft of their pulverizing support.

Rather than regroup their men to wait for more tanks to come up, the Russian commanders would often continue their attacks regardless, as they had their own schedules to adhere to, which did not always synchronize with the stupid bastards in the armor. Besides, it was all very well to attack judiciously and methodically when the tanks were there, but only a pervert coward saboteur would suspend further assaults when the tanks were not there. So the commissars would declare to benumbed, outraged (Russians in particular would know the fusion of numbness and outrage better than almost all other peoples) soldiers and regular officers, the more cowardly commissars then watching the attacks continue from some safe vantage point; the braver commissars leading the attacks in themselves.

"ONWARD! ONWARD, COMRADES!"

Into the same fields of machine-gun fire that had laid flat so many men at Cholm the year before, at Cholm and elsewhere.

The spirit of Comrade Josef rose up in the smoke and peered at the backs of these men—always at their backs, never at their fronts—through the smoke and the insane shouting and roaring.

The Lovat bridge went first after a terrible fight lasting many days. Apart from the wounded and a few antitank weapons Strongpoint Hamburg was nearly empty, with all available men sent up to the bridge. The bridge fell to the enemy. Sergeant Gipfel disappeared leading his platoon in a counterattack. The survivors gave contradicting accounts of where he had last been seen. Karstner from Freitag's team was dead; Razlitt, his place up in the office taken by a wounded man, was dead, or missing, presumed dead. The same for many others, some immolated in a machine-gun pit by a flamethrower, remains unidentifiable; some killed by their own shellfire from the city center, trying to drive the Russians away from the bridge. Men killed a week earlier, among them Lieutenant Gebhardt, lay among those killed during this last fight at the bridge perimeter. Hasenclever received orders from von Sass in Sing-Sing to blow the bridge. The charges failed. The remains of the company fell back to Hamburg. In front of Hamburg itself the Russian dead lay like a wrack washed in by the tide, then left there as the tide ebbed back, the bodies exposed, every which way, like anything that is tumbled into senseless clutter by the movements of the sea.

And then the cold dry wind brings in another blizzard and the gloomy pall resumes; throughout the siege the sun would

be visible on only a few days. Strange dry snow gusted horizontally through the streets, like a bitter white dust. Snow
blew off the dead before it could cover them. Their iron features were powdered this way and that way, the hair on their
scalps still rippling in the wind.

That was the only proper time to suspend an attack. When
everyone who had gone in, or almost everyone, lay dead. A
commander at this point would have done all he could do, and
a commissar might acknowledge this with terse graciousness.

It would take a while for more men to come up, and perhaps by then the tanks would have returned.

Meanwhile the artillery fire would continue, in order to
keep the German bastards preoccupied and to kill them.
There had been that desultory hiatus of five or six days, when
the fire had been infrequent and random, when Kordts had
taken Heissner to the field hospital, when the one rocket salvo
had taken the supply column by surprise. But after those few
days the fire would almost never cease. The heavy assaults
had resumed on 10 December, the barrage then almost unearthly; then the several hours of unearthly quiet while von
Sass rejected the terms of the Russian parliamentaires. When
the barrage resumed at a precise minute, it was of equal force.

Hamburg collapsed bit by bit under the weight of the shells.
It was a strong place. The luckier defenders were too stunned
by the endless blows to react much. But many were edging
nearer to hysteria. This took different forms.

A few had already been put under sedation. Because there
was nothing else to be done with them. If they simply stared
out of a lost world of horror they would be left alone. But
when they would not stop shouting or yammering something
had to be done with them. Slaps to the face came first, even
threats to throw them outside into the bombardment so the
others would not have to listen to them. These threats were
not carried out. Then perhaps the barrel of a rifle pointed between the eyes to make them shut up. If none of this worked
the last resort was to put them under sedation.

Only a few—and these few to be shunned for long after-
wards by any of their comrades to survive this ordeal. A man
might long to be sedated, but he prayed to hear the orders to

abandon this place and if he were sedated he might be left behind.

Those who had endured this far continued to endure. Parts of the building began to collapse and numbers were killed, more of them killed by this shelling than by the other ways. The luckier ones were too stunned to react much. They communicated by the briefest of grunts, too shattered to speak. The radio operator, simply to make his reports or to respond to queries from elsewhere, must make the greatest effort to open his mouth and let a few words come out. Only a few times would a blast so enervate his whole system that he would suddenly start shouting, hardly aware that he was.

They endured in their dead stoic enervation, really thinking they were dead already yet too tired to any longer apprehend frontiers between life and death. The dead lay all about—from concussion or mangling or from the collapse of things upon them, occasionally from suffocation if a concussion knocked the breath out of them and they choked to death on stinking fumes. Yet after a certain point they seemed little separated from a still-living comrade, who occasionally must quell the urge to speak out loud to a dead man sitting next to him. Either because he had become somewhat cracked or because he couldn't resist the urge and didn't care any longer. "Hey, you. Heh. Goddamn you."

But when the flame tanks came up again something further drained out of them and Hasenclever doubted he would be able to stem a panic. The men were like plants clinging to life in some stunted yet persistent form; then when the flame tanks came up they began to wilt all at once, not at first from the heat and the fiery fire but as if some element had poisoned the soil they were rooted in.

For a few minutes they reacted, firing from all guns with actual hatred, actual mechanical hatred and loathing. Firing their weapons was better than sitting in the barrage. A single antitank gun had been reassembled out of the wrecked pieces of itself and two others. It was the last heavy weapon still firing in Hamburg. A flame tank was knocked out a few yards from the flame tank that had been knocked out the week before. The others continued to come on.

The spurts began slowly to approach the embrasures, as if

the tanks were covering their approach behind the screen of
their own flames; they were. The flames and stinking oil
blocked the tank crews' vision but they knew where Hamburg was anyway. Each sheet of flame burned out quickly,
leaving guttering flames here and there, here and there, there
being little out there to burn except crushed stone and bodies
that were consumed so quickly they did not burn much either; each sheet of flame lifted away or simply vanished and
the tank approaching a few yards closer then flamed again.
The man who first began to shriek and recoil was as steadfast
as any of the rest could hope to be—Hasenclever knew the
man. He was nearly hypnotized by the weight of command
but he smelled the panic, saw it. No more time to slap sense
into people. It was time to get out.

To make any decision weighed upon him like the fear of
death. Theirs was a critical point and von Sass had spoken to
him directly that one time. He had to force himself.

"All right, we are getting out of here! Take your weapons
with you, is that understood? Do not abandon your weapons.
Head for the next row of buildings and stay there. Platoon
sergeants assemble by me at that point. Yes, that's it, we're
getting out of here! That's it, that's it!"

A few bolted toward the rear entrance. Others did not quite
hear what he was saying, thinking perhaps that he had gone
mad. Still it took only a few seconds. Schrader and the other
sergeants echoed Hasenclever's words and it did not take
much repeating. To restrain some of them long enough to see
to the wounded—to carry them out in this flight—was difficult but they tended to be pretty conscientious about these
things, even in a horror.

Most made it back to the next row of structures. The barrage had lifted so the flame tanks could work. The enemy did
not react quickly enough to the sudden flight. Most of their
foot soldiers nearby were staring at the forward embrasures
of Hamburg, hypnotized by the action of the flame jets.
Sharpshooters with automatic weapons were set up nearby to
mow down any fleeing German bastards and they did get
their share; though they too were somewhat entranced by the
whole burning business and most of their targets were visible for only a moment between gouts of flame and erratic

piles of rubble. If they had kept their sights trained on the
doors and windows of the next row of buildings behind
Hamburg they would have killed many more, but they had
not thought to do this.

A gaping hole in a wall, screened by a fanlike cluster of
collapsed ceiling beams. To one side a finely carved interior
door, with upper glass panels still curiously intact. This was
where Schrader met up with Hasenclever again after their
flight.

He grabbed Hasenclever by the tunic as if he were a recruit. "You fat old bastard! I'll get you some kind of medal,
you fat old bastard! Show me the officer with the guts to
clear out like that!"

Hasenclever opened and closed his mouth but otherwise
made no response. They watched a few laggards dragging
wounded men in or running back to fetch wounded men in
the rubble-field with great heroism. They simply watched.

Some minutes passed before Hasenclever was able to
speak again. By this time Schrader had already begun having
them set up new defensive positions, snapping them out of
paralysis before paralysis could grow any stronger, and then
Hasenclever began busily looking about and judging this
new wreck they were inside of and going about the same
tasks as Schrader.

For a while the fire did not follow them to this new place
too much. The Russians remained fascinated by Hamburg,
perhaps understandably as it had stood thus in front of them
for over a week. Even pulverized it was still too strong to entirely raze to the ground, crush into nonexistence. The flame
tanks continued burning it and burning it, not certain if the
entire garrison had fled. They exhausted their flame fuel one
by one and one by one withdrew into the smoke, as if being
retrieved by invisible tethers.

A group of Russians appeared in the rubble-field between
Hamburg and the new place. It was a reconnaissance team or
else only a sacrifice sent out to judge the German fire from
the new location; either of these things being more or less the
same thing, after the Russian fashion. The defenders machine-
gunned them.

Other Russians began crawling into Hamburg, occasionally visible moving about in there.

Hasenclever, and probably only Hasenclever, was relieved when a lieutenant and a group of about thirty strangers from one of the battalions of 277 appeared about an hour later. Even though he feared being told off or worse for what he had done. But he was too tired to care and was relieved that someone else would assume command. The lieutenant did tell him off and made it clear that repercussions might be very dire. And so at last Hasenclever felt anxious. But the lieutenant at least in this respect was no more than a messenger and he uttered this dryly to Hasenclever before assuming charge of more urgent business.

"All right, don't think about that, Spiess. Not right now anyway. I'll still be needing you."

The lieutenant said this matter-of-factly while not knowing if the old sergeant major might later be made to face a firing squad. Probably it would not come to that. It was not his concern.

Many of the others, though, realized immediately that the lieutenant would want to organize a counterattack and thought very hard about shooting him in his tracks. Kordts, after all, was not alone; anyone would know this. They thought very hard but all the same did nothing. Lethargy, habit, resignation, inertia—to do nothing at all or to do whatever they were told. Also fear. Such hard thinking at this time would in fact be beyond their capabilities but it all passed automatically through their brains while they did nothing. Taking up their new positions around door frames and windows and blast-holes.

He did organize his counterattack, but laid this burden upon the men arriving with him with whom he was familiar. The covering barrage from German guns inside the city was meager though precisely accurate; Hamburg being precisely calibrated on the gunners' range cards, as was every other strongpoint. Still it didn't do much nor really last long enough—two minutes—to sufficiently stun the new occupants over there and they shot down the lieutenant and half his men when the raid went out. The rest fled back to rejoin

Hasenclever's company. Wounded men remained crying out there. No one wanted to do anything for them except the strangers, and they did nothing either.

Hasenclever in command once again after only half an hour was too weary to feel disappointed or confused. Inertia took over. He did not have the inner wherewithal to belay any further counterattacks though; in his inertia he simply tried to organize something that would work better. He spoke to Schrader and Schrader was also too spent to argue; instead they somewhat robotically began discussing this and that and surveying their surroundings for a better approach.

"That house over there," said Schrader.

"Yes, that will have to do," said Hasenclever.

Common sense took hold of him at the last moment and he had a message radioed back to the battalion headquarters detailing what had just happened and requesting more reinforcements and weapons support before another counterattack was attempted. Nothing available. Request denied.

"The commanding officer is dead," said Hasenclever.

"Very well. Resume command. Hamburg is to be retaken. Upon your exact count there will be a barrage of thirty seconds."

"Never mind the barrage," said Schrader when this was done. "It will just alert them again. Without smoke shells it will be a massacre."

"I know that. Help me get them ready."

By this time Schrader had settled down enough to have second thoughts but he merely thought them while getting the others in order. He experienced a brief hallucination—it was not really even that but other words are still more inadequate substitutes—of all of them standing out there in the rubble-field, Buxa, Hoppe, Chill, Reymann, Hermann, Knieppe, Sudau, all the ones left behind at the *Iltis Stellung*, standing side by side out there, each slumped down or drawn up in his own individual stance, staring, staring back at him, men he had known only a little longer than the ones currently under his charge but that was before his senses had begun to shut down in different little ways. Those men. He saw them even while distinctly hearing Hasenclever saying something at his side; he grunted and acknowledged what Hasenclever had said, then looked back out there. Krabel too. There he was too.

He led Freitag and Kordts's sections out some windows in the rear of the building, having already pointed out to them where they were going. A moment later Hasenclever followed them. Schrader walked back.

"You should stay with the rest," he said.

"I will," said Hasenclever. "Don't worry about it. Go on. Go on."

They picked their way behind the rear of the building, the lee of this place strangely silent-seeming even though it was not. From the corner of the building they fanned out behind piles of debris, each man spaced a few yards from the next; from here they could see the house Hasenclever and Schrader had settled on a few minutes earlier.

It was a solid place that stood not quite by itself among other structures that had collapsed. From where they were it was about two hundred feet away. Hasenclever brought out a machine-gun team to set up where they were. Freitag's people would take another machine gun into the house. From that place and from the building two fields of fire at right angles could be brought upon Hamburg. The next attack would go out from the house or from where they were now or maybe from both places; the Russians wouldn't know which, as Hasenclever himself didn't know yet.

The geometric lines of this plan had their own logic but neither Schrader nor Hasenclever knew if it really made any sense. There was little that ever made sense without support from heavy weapons. The thirty seconds allowed by the gunners in the city center seemed useless but Hasenclever began to think of calling it in anyway. It would be enough to get the men over to that house. He went back inside the building, neglecting to tell Schrader.

Freitag stared at the house. He stared at Hamburg. In the far distance between these two places stood the skeleton of the Lovat bridge, twisted up in smoke; this last sight catching like a burr in his field of vision, of no consequence for now. He stared at his own people and the machine gun and tripod and ammunition boxes they carried. He stared at Kordts and his people moving cautiously past them now, who would go first, to take out any Russians that might be hiding inside the house. Kordts looked back at him and said something that Freitag could not make out in the din; the two men extended their hands, touching each other. Now Schrader moved slowly past, creeping up beside Kordts.

Freitag saw Hasenclever standing at the corner of the building, wondering what he was doing there, not going with them, surely. Hasenclever was speaking to the first machine-gun team already set up at the corner of the building. The force of what was coming filled Freitag up to the roof of his skull. Suddenly a memory was wedged like a tiny shim between the top of his skull and everything else pressing up from beneath. He remembered a raid from months ago, from the trenches outside the city, some other business after that *Iltis* business that he and Kordts and most of the men with them now had been fortunate enough to miss. Hoep-la, hoep-la, hoep-la, hoep-la. That was Hasenclever, counting them out of the trench that day, one after the other into no-man's-land. He could not place Schrader and he could not remember any officer, though both would have been there. If he turned his head to the left or to the right he might see either of them in this memory, but the picture of it was gripped in a vise that looked only straight ahead. He could not see Hasenclever either but only hear his count. Hoep-la, hoep-la. At Freitag's turn he had gone up and out. In his excitement he had dashed headlong and closed up the distance to the man gone out in front of him. The man had been struck and fallen back into Freitag's arms, Freitag dropping his weapon in the mud.

Even these decent fellows—tolerable fellows, his friend Kordts never knew how to put it—like Hasenclever and not like Belzmann or others, just counting them out to their deaths. Kordts had said this later, after it was finished. Sometimes his remarks were as obvious as the ocean or the sea and Freitag for once had had none of his own two cents to add to it. Yes. What of it then?

He could not possibly remember all this, not now, though the moments of waiting were very long. But these moments were always poured in with concrete. House. Hamburg. Lovat bridge. Rather a series of pictures had formed in his head, wedged in with that tiny shim, for only a few seconds, and then everything else associated with it had followed along in one spontaneous instant. Hoep-la. He looked at the corner of the building and saw Hasenclever stepping back inside the building.

Then suddenly it was starting.

Schrader was there.

"Wait till we clear the place. Then come. I'll give you a signal."

Schrader went back to Kordts and his people and they went out into the rubble-field. They were not carrying too much and made it fairly nimbly without staggering under the usual burdens. The last man in line lost balance and spastically tried to regain it over the last fifty feet, flinging his rifle in through a window and then falling to his knees in front of it. He got up and hoisted a leg to the sill. Other hands and arms from inside the window helped pull him through. They had made it.

Freitag felt a hand clap like iron on his shoulder and he felt his legs go weak. It was Hasenclever again.

Hasenclever looked beset by something and he blurted something that Freitag could not catch. He looked at his watch, holding Freitag maddeningly by the scruff of the neck, and he looked over at the house. The machine gun set up at the corner of the building was hammering at Hamburg and the razed areas beyond Hamburg.

The curtain of shells fell mostly on Hamburg. Actually it was the lone shriek of an individual shell followed a few seconds later by another and then another. Thirty seconds. Freitag and Hasenclever and the others at the corner of the building were too close to watch except in quick stubborn glimpses. Freitag saw part of the house go up and was knocked almost senseless. A great surge of force—inside of him—got him at least back up to his knees but he waited till the barrage was over before he looked again.

He saw Schrader and a few others stumbling about outside the house in wreaths of smoke. Another man came out of the place. As if they could not ascertain that they were still in one piece unless they crawled out into the open air. Then just as quickly as they had appeared they all ducked back inside again. The wreckage of everything all about was such that Freitag could not really see if the house looked any different than it had before, except that it was now shrouded in smoke.

"Thank God," said a disembodied voice, Hasenclever. "Thank God, thank God. I thought they'd all be gone. All right, that's him again. Go now."

Schrader stood in the one window like a doom-beckoning woman. He signaled with one hand.

Freitag and his people flopped like ducks, like fools, under the burdens of the machine gun and other equipment, twisting their feet in every crack and against every block of stone or protruding shattered plank. Falling several times, drawing fire. They seemed almost to roll like tumbleweeds the last short distance, handing the machine gun and boxes up to the men waiting behind the windows then flopping through themselves. Freitag immediately got up and collared Schrader and when he could not get a satisfactory answer he began crying out and looking everywhere through the beams and hanging dust.

Kordts lay buried in darkness beneath the parts of the house that had fallen in, choking on smoke, screaming. He had a horror more than anything else on earth of being buried alive. Not of suffocating, not at all of suffocating; but of being pinned in some awkward position in which he could not move his limbs. His head was tilted down and his feet were tilted up and one arm was twisted behind his back. He stopped screaming, threw a lid down on the panic; but the panic continued to push against it with terrible force. "Help me! Help me!" he shouted loudly a few times without actually screaming. He managed to just lie still for a few moments. Hearing voices out there, feeling the pain for the first time. It was very bad but the panic was worse and the pain vanished, like a radio tuner momentarily losing some brief signal. This awful fear, throbbing from his twisted legs and arms up to his brain; he grunted and twitched his face back and forth like a man on the verge of convulsing.

The innermost reservoir of his soul was a kind of stone-dead calm, which he now tried to call upon but it was useless. He succeeded only in part, stilling his frenzy by clenching his teeth; but it continued to push at him from the inside and he wept. Not crying, simply weeping, and the feel of this on his cheeks sparked another panic because his hands were pinned and he could not move them to wipe this irritation off his face.

He made a last effort to calm himself. It was only tears wetting the filth on his cheeks and temples; no more than sweat pouring down a filth-blackened face. Being unable to wipe away this small irritation was worse than being thrown alive into a furnace. No it wasn't, no it wasn't. Just lie still.

He managed to calm himself by listening disinterestedly to horrible screams deep inside his head, by watching disinterestedly as he blew his brains out with his rifle as a last resort. He could only move his fingers a few inches and he could not feel his rifle anywhere but simply ignored this, grimly resisting the urge to grope about for it, as this would only start another panic. In his mind the rifle was there, the muzzle resting against the side of his skull in the softer place between his ear and the corner of his eye, his fingers curled relaxedly around the trigger.

If they had been able to get him out sooner . . . that is, if he had been able to see and hear that they were moving enough things out of the way to get him out before long, then he might have been able to rest there quietly for a long enough time, guarded by this peculiar mental talisman against his terror. But they could not get him out, try though they might. They heard him from underneath, no longer screaming but grunting like someone who has swallowed his tongue, a man in a straitjacket struggling against this restraint and convulsing in his own worst fears.

At last the savior came. The pain returned and only for a few moments did this drive him into hysteria. The pain and the way the pain magnified the terror of being unable to adjust his arms and legs, feeling the terror in ever more uncontrollable impulses.

He saw a man twisting in a bear trap at the edge of a beach, only to hear something and glance over his shoulder at a great wave coming. Thank God. The wave roared in and swept him away. He groaned in agony but he was released and carried off.

He could forgive Erika for having betrayed him; he had somehow suspected this while on leave and it had hardly bothered him at all. She was still there; she was still there; it was not her fault. But in the final blackness she was not there; there was only the betrayal, and the horror of this accompanying him alone into the last black rush was too much to bear. And so he did not bear it. The betrayal was gone. He saw her as a child descending some old staircase into a cellar, lit by calm panes of daylight from small windows high on a wall. With the springy step of a child she darted into some small space beneath the stairwell, part of some childish game or only a place for her to daydream.

There was a great grey electric shaking inside his brain. He could see it and hear it. An ice cold gas shot up his windpipe and when it reached his head he was gone.

PART FOUR

The Breakout

Chapter Twenty-five

From one end of the Soviet Union to the other there was violence, though none greater than in Velikiye Luki. At the opposite pole, over a thousand miles away on the far southern shoulder of the country, lay Stalingrad. All that remained of that place.

They had been under siege there for a month now. The last relief attempt, von Manstein's relief attempt, had been beaten back far out in the snowy deserts. By Christmas the three hundred thousand men under siege had not begun to starve yet. But they could see it coming now, feel it tightening back toward their spines; in that sense it had begun.

Even after a month the siege perimeter was still enormous; it was a small nation, like the small nation at Demyansk. Out at the edge, in the snowy desert, there was fighting, vicious though erratic, and on many days the fighting died down. In the city center, in the ghost of Stalingrad itself, there was no longer any fighting at all.

The city had been nearly obliterated by the bombing and shelling and house-to-house fighting in September and October and November, but all that was over with now; the two sides were exhausted, and silence lay over the city like a dead god sprawled in the ugly sky above.

The bled-to-death divisions of 6th Army had blasted the unbelievably stubborn Russian defenders out of ninety percent of the city. In essence, 6th Army held the place now, this endless mangled sculpture of an industrial metropolis. But what did they hold? Only ruins, the like of which they had never seen before, and might never see again—unless a few of them survived to see Berlin or Dresden or Hamburg after the bomber fleets from the West had come.

But they knew nothing of that, nor ever would; very few would ever escape from Stalingrad to later witness those similar scenes of devastation.

They held on to what was theirs—this place—but now they were surrounded by the Russian siege ring far out in the desolate steppe, where there was no city, no anything. The perimeter was still so large that the men inside the city could hear nothing of the fighting out at the edge, out there in the emptiness.

The remains of the city stood up in the silent sky like the ribs of men soon to perish from hunger. Locked within the heart of the vast desert perimeter, the city itself was also vast. Small groups of men passed here and there in the ruins, in the silence of a great dead city. They might wander for miles along the wrecked boulevards and see no one, be disturbed by no one. A car might pass by, tires humming on wet pavement, driving by itself toward some destination miles away, still inside the city.

The Russians, on the outside, were mostly content to wait. The city waited, ruined, twenty miles long, five or six miles wide, along the banks of the Volga. Some attempt was made to distribute Christmas packets to the besieged men. Soon after this, starvation began in earnest.

In the homeland Stalingrad had been featured in the newsreels for months, since back in August, since the day Schrader's platoon had gone in at the *Iltis*.

Every week there would be features of German soldiers fighting all over the world; all over Russia, and then all over the rest of the world. But these features would always vary from one week to the next. Stalingrad was the only constant. In August of '42, in September, in October, in November of '42, the rubble of that city appeared week after week in the newsreels like a strange kind of clock.

And then, early in December, the last Stalingrad feature was shown in the theaters of the homeland. When the next newsreel came out the following week there was no mention of that place. And in the newsreel the week after that, there was no mention of that place.

The great silence settled in, heard everywhere throughout the German nation. There were furtive conversations in the living rooms of homes and on street corners. The 6th Army was only one out of nearly a dozen armies scattered across the Eastern Front. But it was the largest army, at that time. In the cities of the homeland were many hundred thousands of kinsfolk, perhaps even several million.

On Christmas Eve the newsreel featured radio messages sent in from German outposts all over the world. The soldiers sent Christmas greetings and received Christmas greetings from the homeland.

"Tunis *hier. Stille Nacht.*"

"*Hier* Narvik. *Stille Nacht.*"

"Leningrad Front *hier. Stille Nacht.*"

"*Finnischerfront hier. Stille Nacht.*"

"Athens *hier. Stille Nacht.*"

"*Hier* Paris."

"*Hier* Bordeaux."

"Libyan Front *hier. Stille Nacht.*"

"*Hier* Demyansk. *Stille Nacht.*"

From a U-boat crew far out in the Indian Ocean, stripped to their shorts, sweating like greased machinery in the windless tropical furnace: "Seychelles *hier. Stille Nacht.*"

From a weather station in the Arctic: "*Hier* Spitzbergen. *Stille Nacht.*"

Then there was a pause. Then there came a voice slightly louder than the others. Or perhaps those listening in the homeland only imagined it: "*Hier* Stalingrad."

From all the other places, brief filmed vignettes had accompanied the radio voices, ten or twenty seconds long, showing the men engaged in quiet Christmas festivities, from the Indian Ocean to the Arctic.

But from Stalingrad came no filmed footage, but only the voice. And that was the last. The very last, those two words. *Hier* Stalingrad.

It may even have been staged—that voice—to somehow hearten the listeners in the homeland. Though it was true . . . there was still radio contact with Stalingrad at that time.

There was no Christmas greeting from Velikiye Luki. No one noticed. There had been no news from Velikiye Luki throughout the war. It was a smaller place, two hundred miles from Moscow, two hundred miles from Leningrad, a thousand from Stalingrad, eight hundred from Berlin. The news from Velikiye Luki had either been entirely indifferent or else very bad, and as it was a smaller place, the two words of that place-name had never been said.

Sweeping generalities are often tiresome. Yet their pronouncement often satisfies some urge. One satisfies an urge to be rid of it. That Christmas the greatest violence in the Soviet Union was taking place around the citadel and around von Sass's last redoubt at the Barracks Complex; thus, in all likelihood, the greatest violence on the earth's surface.

Such grandiose pronouncements may fill one with a deep disgust. But at least the urge has been dispelled.

Freitag stood on the wall of the citadel in the early, metal-filled, glowing winter dusk. Almost all of them were too tired to speak, too tired and too hungry; a kind of speechlessness existed inside their minds as well, inside their own thoughts. The remains of the company had made it to the citadel after Hamburg had fallen and too many men had been lost trying to retake Hamburg. Hasenclever had been killed and worried about command no more. They had joined up with a Lieutenant Ritter and his men and in an endless night they had crawled through the ruins back to the citadel, losing more men, killed or left behind or lost in the darkness.

The Russians had made headway everywhere and commanded much of the ruins. T-34s scuttled about like roaches crawling through a tenement. They had passed many of these tanks in the darkness, tanks silhouetted by flames, backlit by the wall of a building in flames, iron hulks silhouetted against the glowing white sky of the dark, large shapes probing everywhere, grinding into every debris-filled corner, shooting at anything. In the dark they were easy to avoid but there were too many to avoid entirely in chance encounters; shrieks, surprise, the grinding of motors, a turret swinging around, gunfire from the tanks and from any of their foot soldiers nearby; they were everywhere.

Twenty-seven men made it into the citadel on Christmas Eve, where about four hundred men already were. The place was immensely strong, stronger than any of the annihilated strongpoints. Set on the highest point of the city, some sections of the walls rose as high as seventy-five feet. These were ancient earthen walls, not stone, but they were thick and strong, absorbing the blast of shells. There were the four walls and the bunkers built deep within the walls, nearly impregnable, all surrounding a large courtyard about five hundred feet long, two hundred wide. An easily defended place, yet doomed all the same.

The next day, Christmas day, the Russians launched a useless attack and over sixty bodies were counted later, piled up around the great stone arch set in the earth wall that was the main entrance, some even inside the arch, some even inside the courtyard. They wouldn't have made it that far except for the two T-34s that had broken in first, diverting everyone's attention, roaring around the inside of the courtyard like trapped roaches racing around and around the bottom of a kitchen sink.

The noise of their guns firing at point-blank range inside the enclosed space had left every man of the citadel garrison deaf or partially deaf for hours. Yet the walls and bunkers within the walls were so strong that little damage had been done.

Their infantry had tried to follow them inside and been slaughtered and driven off. The two tanks had remained alone in there rumbling about for what seemed an eternity, frightening things, altering the space of minutes and seconds.

At last one had gotten out of the trap, driving back out through the archway, rumbling over the bodies there, escaping. The other tank had driven into a frozen pond in the middle of the courtyard, crashing through the ice, stuck there. Freitag still had the urge to prove himself and over the days had become further emboldened by despair. With him it was hardly even that but an emptying out of everything and anything except for exhaustion, hunger, and abstract murderous impulses. He had skidded out onto the ice and then broken through it where the tank had broken through it. The pond was deep and he had gone in up to his armpits, tossing the hollow-charge explosive onto a pane of ice that still floated beside him. He ascertained that he wasn't going to sink any further, picked up the charge again and held it with one hand above his head—he was almost too weak to do this but he did

it—and with his other hand grasped a fender or chain or
track-link, something. He pulled himself up and found a
place to set his feet and got up onto the tank.

He set the charge under the turret and got off again, landing on a place where he thought the ice was firmer. It was,
and he injured his shins and knees. He got to his feet again
and staggered off, terrified that he would fall again on the
ice before he could get away. The blast probably would
have killed him but the charge must have gotten wet or been
defective.

Still it went off. Everyone in the vicinity expecting a concussion to pierce their eardrums heard only a loud pop instead; it was a violent bang but less than what they expected.
The tank appeared little damaged but the crew could bear it
no longer. They crawled out the hatches and were shot down,
shrieking from terror as much as from the metal striking
them. The defenders continued to riddle the bodies with bullets even as they lay on the ice, and a number of men surged
out from their hidey-holes and ran out onto the ice and continued firing into the bodies from two or three feet away.

Two of Freitag's people helped carry him back to a place
under one of the walls. He was in a frenzy and once off the ice
needed no more assistance and shook them away from him.

There was a row of smaller stone arches giving onto a long
gallery beneath the earth wall. Schrader was sitting against
one of these arches with a Russian tommy gun lying on his
knees. He caught Freitag's eye and gave Freitag a long look.
It was a more than adequate substitute for praise; such a look
would have passed for an entire conversation. It did.

Many of the men that had surged from their hidey-holes
were struck by shellfire that now came down in the courtyard. Most were wounded. They fled back into hiding or
were carried off. The surgeons in the vaults beneath the
citadel were covered in blood and no longer knew where they
were or who they were; they did a great deal of crude hacking because they were too tired to work more precisely. Like
automatons they could still wield scalpels but they were too
tired to think properly about delicate motions. They made
mistakes, proceeded to the next man. Healthy men who had

to go down there for one reason or another, carrying people mostly, were gripped by a grim awe that had long since been sucked out of them in every other environment, in the combat places aboveground. They left hurriedly.

At dusk Freitag was on top of the east wall. He had no concept of whether it was the east wall or the west wall. He could have oriented himself in a second, because the Lovat flowed immediately beneath the east wall, but he simply stared blankly out there without knowing what he was looking at. It was all around anyway, all of it, everywhere.

The commander of the garrison, Darnedde, had come up to him earlier, down below.

"What is your name?"

Freitag knew his name but felt he must see it within his mind before it came out.

"Freitag," he said.

"Well done, Freitag."

From the top of the wall he could look out into the distance. There was only fire and stony shapes and darkness. Night had fallen. There was darkness and stone, and where there was not darkness and stone there was fire.

They would starve here. Supply planes continued to drop supplies but only a few parachutes floated down into the narrow space of the courtyard. So they would starve here; otherwise it seemed they might hold on to this pile for a long time. It rose up like a large, whole thing above a broken-apart wasteland. The earthen pile was here, and the wasteland was there, down there. Occasionally he saw light shining off black water, where holes had been blown in the river ice, and he stared with dull curiosity.

They were isolated like inmates who had staged a successful revolt inside a prison, in control of every corner of the four massive walls, yet isolated from the outside world and sentenced to extinction by the forces inevitably massed by the outside world. Inmates were noncitizens and having staged a revolt could expect no mercy.

All well to say, here in the place they called Sing-Sing, but Freitag thought none of these things. For some weeks names had had a certain force—Hamburg and other names—but too many days had gone by and they were too tired and hungry now. Sing-Sing had vanished, the citadel had vanished, and been replaced only by this place, where they were.

He had called upon a certain inner toughness to deal with Kordts's death. He had called upon it before—many times at Cholm—but felt he must call on it again, to prove and reprove something. But it had not been this personal before. One must expect a friend to be killed, he thought. What good did it do to know this? He didn't know.

Apathy and exhaustion helped; it helped a lot of them. At odd moments exhaustion could push a man over a certain edge and he would feel everything going to pieces inside him all at once; yet exhaustion was so tremendous that even this collapsing sensation would be only intermittent, ephemeral, swallowed up by more exhaustion.

Kordts's influence over him had grown somewhat less over recent months. He had wanted to prove himself as an NCO; Kordts had had no interest in that. Still in Kordts's shadow, and perhaps even in the deeper shadow of his own instincts, he had known it was stupid, but could not help wanting to prove himself anyway. Only a corporal's stripes after all, but it was not really the actual rank.

Even so, Kordts's influence had remained strong; even after over a year he could not quite figure out what it was about Kordts, something the future would gradually reveal, somewhere beyond; but now he was dead. He remembered Kordts's girlfriend, whom he had met once, a beautiful woman; he had been astonished when Kordts had told him her real age.

All of these things existed inside him and so it was not necessary to think about them, even in little bits and pieces. Things came in little bits and pieces, precipitated out of a fog. So what. Human beings may communicate with one another but nonetheless as separate beings they are utterly sealed off from each other. Such an elemental fact of nature was obvious but nearly impossible to grasp, just as fish can never really grasp that they live in the sea.

Each human being lived in an impermeable suit of his own being, thus strove to go on living after others had died, or strove to feel any peace at all while others continued to live in such suffering all about. The obvious was too unspeakable; the unspeakable was too obvious. Strange perceptions were suspended like invisible meaningless particles in a great sea of exhaustion. He could feel odd channels bending in his brain but hardly cared.

Surrounded by so much death and hopelessness—not just Kordts's death but death, death, death—one developed strange leaks in that seemingly impermeable suit. It was not despair and hopelessness—to the very end they might hold onto the idea that relief would come, and Cholm-fighter Freitag should know that better than any of them. No, the leaks were more nameless than that.

He had felt something entirely sucked out of him, leaving a void; simultaneously he had felt a great dead weight filling him up entirely. These two contradictory sensations were like opposing lines of force diverging from a single point around a circle; each following the circle all the way around until they met again at some other point, and became one, were one.

He thought none of these things; it was Christmas and he thought of his family. An inquisitive, philosophical, uneducated young fellow, Freitag, his brain churning with mud and cold. Kordts was gone and he felt alone.

The night before—that endless, crawling night, when they had come all the way back from Hamburg, convinced at every moment that they would not make it, leaving the ones who did not make it behind them the entire length of the night—they had arrived at last beneath the great walls of the citadel.

What were they doing, singing at such an hour? They had no idea what time it was, sometime before dawn; or perhaps only about midnight, winter darkness falling so early in Velikiye Luki. They had followed the Lovat the last few hundred yards, coming up on a bed of debris beneath the citadel wall, so finely pulverized that it was like scree at the base of a mountain precipice. Hardly daring to move in the bad footing, to make any sounds. The black pile rose above them.

It was here that they had heard distant strains of singing from inside the walls. *Stille Nacht*. It was unbelievable but nothing was unbelievable anymore and so they simply listened. Some sat down in the debris and cradled their heads in their hands.

For an instant Freitag had experienced a hallucination so disturbing it had made him giddy. He had heard the normal words of the hymn being substituted with obscenities, yet still sung with the same quiet longing. It had passed quickly though.

The lieutenant—Ritter—had to guide them around to the archway, to the main entrance. He knew where it was but seemed unable to picture it in his mind for a few minutes, which side of the four walls it was in. The Lovat was here, beneath them, a few dozen yards away; which side was the entrance on?

When he remembered they got up and moved off again, crawling painstakingly around the outside of the fortress. A while later, after a nervy exchange with the men posted on guard, they passed beneath the great arch and into the courtyard.

Now, positioned up on the wall on the following evening, Freitag heard it again. *Stille Nacht*. The strains drifting up from the courtyard below. Who had the energy? Perhaps an officer or a chaplain was leading them. In a way it was still more unbelievable than the night before, for he had had these twenty-four hours to see what conditions were like inside the citadel. He listened. He remembered the clear, startling obscenities from the night before, was aware that he did not hear them now; he gave it no more thought. The sounds of men singing could not help but deeply move him or anyone.

Schrader was there. Come up from below. He uttered a single word that Freitag did not understand, then slumped down beside him against the parapet, waiting for the singing to end maybe. Another man, Timmerman, had come up with him. He too lay low behind the parapet, which was simply a higher ridge of earth bulked up in places with beams or stone. The men posted on guard up there would take shelter in holes dug into the top of the earthen wall, like ordinary foxholes or firing pits.

Freitag looked at them, saw they had nothing to say, not yet anyway. He remembered his stupid drunken mother and the different drunken fools who had taken up with her. He had remained very close to her though, always, traumatized though he had been by many different things, twisted through and through with loathing and care.

The compartments holding different things within his head, memories, ideas, fears, anguishes, became suddenly muddy and things began flowing together in a dismal sinking sludge. This muddiness caused him great discomfort for a few moments; the exhaustion and hunger only made it worse. He cried a little bit, managed to fight it off, or else it simply faded away somewhere.

"God in heaven," whispered the other man, Timmerman. Down below the voices had fallen silent.

"You're early," said Freitag, looking at Schrader.

Schrader said, "Darnedde says you deserve a few hours off. He forgot to say so before."

"Well," said Freitag. "Here is as good as anywhere."

"No, it isn't. Go down now. You can sleep below. It's too cold up here."

"No, it isn't," said Freitag, smiling faintly in spite of himself.

"Suit yourself," said Schrader. "Have you seen anything?"

"No," said Freitag.

Schrader reached out and grabbed him.

"For Christ's sake, you're still soaking wet. Snap out of it, Freitag. You don't want to get sick in this place. Go below. Go below right now. For God's sake, man, you're wet through and through."

The note of concern was so genuine that Freitag began to daydream.

"Did you hear me?"

"Yes. Yes."

"You must be sick already. Aren't you freezing to death?"

"It is cold," agreed Freitag.

He did feel it too, the east wind, as he began to stand up, above the level of the parapet. Particles and ash were borne by the wind, not much snow. He turned to face it, an odd smile caught on his lips. It broke as his teeth began to chatter uncontrollably.

Gunfire. Chunks flew off the parapet, sailing far below. Thick but almost inaudible sounds of bullets striking earth.

Schrader kicked him and then grabbed at him when he fell.

"Idiot. Idiot." He breathed this quietly, almost to himself. Freitag felt frozen through all at once and began to groan.

The parapet was wide. The stairs leading below were narrower. Schrader helped him and they went down below. Timmerman watched them go.

"Kordts kicked Moll one time," said Freitag, trembling agitatedly. "Hard as a bastard. You weren't there."

Helping him along Schrader could feel how cold he was, like ice, though he hadn't been hurt otherwise. They came out in the gallery beneath the wall, where the row of smaller arches gave out onto the courtyard. The T-34 sunk in the pond was silhouetted by a fire from the other side of the courtyard. The dead tank was angled into the ice at just such and such an angle, the gun barrel slewed around just so. There you are, there you are, thought Freitag.

Chapter Twenty-six

Two weeks later they were still there. It was now 9 January.
The dead were there and the survivors were there. By now
they had given up hope. As long as they still breathed there
was a chance a relief column might break through, but they
had given up hope.

Hope required a small amount of energy, liveliness, and
they no longer had it.

Automatically they passed through the hours, which consisted mostly of shelling and grenade battles and tiresome
lulls occupied by their own thoughts.

This must be what hell is like, thought Freitag, thinking
this but not quite able to believe it, never quite able to believe it.

After all, hell goes on and on, doesn't it? On and on and
on . . . into eternity. But that was too big a word. It just went
on and on.

The dead were scattered across the courtyard, their own
and the Russians who had broken in at different times and
been killed. He thought enviously of Kordts, of black peace.
The T-34 that he, Freitag, had personally destroyed in perhaps the most singular act of his life was still there, sunk
halfway through the pond ice in the middle of the courtyard.
The broken-up ice had refrozen quickly and seized the iron
wreck. The bodies of the crew still lay beside it, their faces
pulped beyond recognition by the close-range firing of the
crazed defenders, lying among numerous bodies that had
fallen since that time. Previously they had gotten fresh water
by punching holes in the pond ice, but fuel and oil from the
tank had polluted it. Now men were killed in forays during

the dead of night, outside the walls, fetching water from the Lovat or from a few other water holes, shell craters sheeted over with ice.

For a few days the singularity of his act had given Freitag a little extra energy, this action replaying in his mind like a coil revolving around a magnet, to provide him with a little extra energy. It served that purpose and there was no vanity to it. But now, two weeks later, that small extra ration was used up. In these circumstances two weeks was an endless time and the tank tilted into the frozen pond seemed to have been there for as long as anyone could remember.

It was the plight of the wounded that was most hellish. Their agonies gradually drained the wills of those who were still fit. The chief medical officer in the citadel had collapsed from exhaustion—that is to say he had had a kind of nervous breakdown—during one of the days around the new year, no one could remember just when. After a few days of nearly comatose shame, exhaustion, weeping, and silent held-in hysteria he had made only a partial recovery, returning to duty in the ghastly vaults, working with mad, robotic slowness. His assistants were in little better shape and often took over for him when his movements slowed down to the point of no movement at all, when he would become fixed in an overly long pause, staring at the endless flesh.

The vault belowground became too crowded. It was not a big place, storage for religious artifacts from the chapel at the south end of the courtyard, perhaps a catacomb at one time though they found no remains down there. It was warmer down there but very foul, and the air was difficult to breathe, like a mine shaft where bad gases have been tapped. There was no more room and many of the wounded lay aboveground in the long galleries around the courtyard, un-attended for days, alone in their last hours, surrounded by no-longer-interested men who took no notice of their final moments in the world.

This is what hell is like, thought Griswold, who had no choice but to believe it was so, whenever he woke up into hopeless pain from troubled, intermittent sleep. For days he had stared at the cold stone archway above his head, at the patch of grey sky above the courtyard, just outside the archway. He had been shot through the ribs. Many of them were broken and the bullet lay lodged inside him somewhere. A little further to one side and it would have been a belly shot, a relentless agony that would have tortured him for days, though at least by now he would have been dead. A little further to the other side and it would have been a heart shot, killing him instantly. With the painful metal inside him he was aware of his other organs—heart, lungs, stomach. His kidneys were torn but he did not know this, as no doctor had been to look at him. This is happening . . . how could this be happening? . . . this is happening, he thought sometimes.

His kidneys were slowly failing and his scrotum had ballooned to the size of a water bottle, though this in itself was not painful and he was hardly aware of it in his general pain. He could not move without his ribs stabbing him. So he never moved and if he had been fully conscious all this time he would have gone mad from lying for days in this one position. But semiconsciousness, which was his only relief, crept over him frequently; or else actual sleep. To awaken from sleep was a dismal bitterness that occurred over and over again. Sometimes a man woke him to raise his head and pour hot tea, some kind of hot liquid, between his lips. But to be awakened for any reason caused him despair and he managed to whisper pleadingly that he not be wakened out of sleep. But they always forgot, whoever was tending him and the other wounded lying all about him. You could not tell if a wounded man was sleeping or just lying still with his eyes closed, or was dead. So you always had to shake him gently, to know.

He and the other wounded were covered with straw, with blankets, with greatcoats; and there was a fire going in the stone gallery about fifteen feet away. Sometimes he was warm enough. At night he was always freezing and he wondered how he could fail to die. He shivered and his ribs stabbed at him and he groaned among others groaning. He and the others beside him groaned at night, groaned in endless seizures of pain and disbelief; during the day they mostly lay silent.

Freitag walked beside this silent mass beneath the gallery, passing next to Griswold and the others lying there. He was so hungry that it was hard to concentrate on anything. He welcomed it when the Russians attacked or when they rained shells down because these were the only things that could distract him from his hunger. But when they attacked he had to raise his weapon and to do that took a great effort. He was too hungry to notice the suffering of the wounded or any kind of shame at his own inattention. In fact he did notice them—no one could avoid it—but it was like some kind of horrible premise from which no conclusion could be drawn, because he could no longer think except disjointedly. They were just there, just as he was just there. He took his turn with all the others in helping them to drink hot or tepid liquids, and sometimes holding a wounded man's head in his hand and raising it to drink distracted him for a moment too.

Still, even when they were too tired or mind-fogged to absorb it, the suffering of the wounded, poor bastards of Christ, drained the wills of the others . . . the others who themselves would join the ranks of the wounded day by day.

But he walked by them now, Freitag did. He walked across the courtyard, stepping through the bodies on the pond ice. With dull interest he heard engines roaring and thought the Russians would be coming with tanks again. Other men hearing these same sounds passed from lethargy to a kind of half-lethargy; officers began to shout.

The relief attempt of 9 January, conducted with great élan, was a pointless exercise doomed from the beginning.

Kampfgruppe Wohler had pushed a salient to within six miles of Velikiye Luki. This salient was harassed by Russian fire at all hours and was barely tenable. The ground was frozen and could not be dug into; yet the snow cover was too sparse to allow for the making of snow walls or other means of protection. The frozen moors were devoid of natural cover and the scraggy woods that dotted the moors had been blown away by the fighting.

It was up to a man of courage to lead this relief attempt. One of the Gebirgsjaeger officers that Scherer had admired did so. This was Tribukait, only a major; he had volunteered.

The jaegers had no armored vehicles and so Wohler had brought up the only available tanks—the understrength battalion sent over from 11th Panzer Division—and placed them under Tribukait's command.

This was a haphazard assemblage of nine battle-worn Panzer IIIs and Panzer IVs, along with an equal number of armored half-tracks—one of them mounted with a 20 mm Flak, useful for close-in melees on the ground. The drivers revved the engines and they howled in the assembly position about a half-mile behind the forward outposts. Tribukait went from one crew to another, speaking to all, to the armored men and to his own jaegers riding in the half-tracks, shouting above the din of the motors. Emphatically he repeated instructions already laid out in the dead winter silence several hours before: "You will stop for nothing. Disabled vehicles will be left behind. Wounded will have to remain where they are. Surviving crews will board vehicles still operable. Keep moving at all costs. Do not engage targets unless absolutely necessary. Panzer ammunition is to be spared as much as possible. Smaller targets will be left to machine guns and the half-tracks. Remember only that there is no stopping until we reach the citadel."

They understood. How could they fail to understand such urgent and simple instructions?

The panzer crews mounted their tanks, climbing in through hatches or through the curious armored swing-doors in the sides of the turrets. A few jaegers rode on the decks of the tanks while the majority climbed into the open rear compartments of the half-tracks. Russian nuisance-fire bloomed continuously here and there across the dead landscape. The vehicles bore winter whitewash and weeks of accumulated dirt and mud, streaked and nondescript-looking like the landscape itself. A few had been newly whitewashed and they stood out like new things in the dead landscape. The sky was pallid grey with sunlight seeping down the color of dried straw, lighting up a few dead trees and any other small deviations in the emptiness, vehicles, men. They wore heavy white one-piece suits just newly issued for this second winter of the war. They wore steel helmets except for Tribukait and a few other jaegers, who insisted—for luck or whatever reason—upon wearing the tall mountaineer caps, outdated and out of place a thousand miles from any mountains.

They moved off at 1330 hours, an hour and a half past the low grey noon, an hour and a half before the colorless sunset.

There was no barrage, no warning other than the revving of their motors. The latter noise might have alerted the Russians if not for the Russians' own continuous firing upon the salient. The tracks of the armored vehicles bit into the hard ugly ground, throwing out only small clouds of snow from the sparse gale-blown snow cover. Though today, at this hour, it was nearly windless.

They raced through the forward outposts, which were poorly fortified with no barbed wire or timber at hand. The outpost line barely looked like anything, only a few people standing around or crowded behind whatever shelter there was, somewhat like a sparse crowd spread out for no particular reason on a large white plaza. They watched the tanks and half-tracks roaring through, the urgency of the spectacle stilled even so by the immensity of the land.

The terrain rose and fell in small undulations, perceptible only in that they foreshortened the horizon. Ragged patches of woodland—marsh scrub—were so nondescript that they could barely serve for orientation. But even before they could see the city the pall of smoke issuing from the city was quite clear.

Tribukait's armored wedge was not adequate to achieve its purpose. But in and of itself, at the point of impact, it was a terrifying sight. The Russians were used to more methodical operations by the German armor, advancing almost always with a protective screen of infantry.

At this moment almost twenty multiton vehicles were advancing in a tight wedge at full throttle. They churned out billowing wakes of dry dusty snow and as much resembled a flotilla of high-speed torpedo boats roaring across the snow-ocean to a single point. The Russians seeing them coming were too frightened to react. Soldiers in dun-colored overcoats threw their weapons aside and fled the impact point. The panzers hit without any great crash but with great violence nonetheless, mangling those who had fallen in their panic or who had remained frozen in their trenches, fouling the tank treads with these bodies. Sheaves of fire in wide-sweeping arcs came from the machine guns on the half-tracks and cut down fleeing men or men anywhere. The tank gunners though admonished to spare their ammunition could not restrain themselves from firing at targets everywhere, any more than they could restrain their own adrenaline. Destruction, wildness. They fired at close range into Russian gun positions, guns perhaps already abandoned by their terrified crews; they fired at milling herds of people, they delivered high explosives into Russian vehicle parks behind the lines.

They were through.

Several of the half-tracks had been hit. They were thinly armored vehicles, vulnerable to destruction. Russian gunners further away on either side of the point of impact had not panicked and had been able to lay down their fire. Antitank cannon. *Ratsch-boums*. Glancing blows did not disable the tanks but brought the half-tracks to a stop with smoking engines or run-out tracks. The crews swarmed over the sides and ran desperately to climb aboard another tank or half-track before they were left behind to be slaughtered. Some were unable to board another vehicle and they were left wandering among their enemy, vainly firing their weapons before being beaten to death or bayoneted in the face, decapitated by a submachine-gun burst fired from a few meters' distance. Those who were only wounded could await worse fates. A few men had remained inside one disabled half-track, trying to defend it like a small fort, which they did for a few minutes. The Russians tossed hand grenades into the open-topped compartments and the occupants were ripped against the interior walls. A few lived still and the Russians opened the rear doors and pulled them out like accused men being torn from a police van by a lynch mob, to be tossed out into the crowd, torn to pieces, dropped, stomped on. This would be their fate or something similar. Screams, frenzy. Such were the casualties of Tribukait's foray; the armored wedge, still intact for the most part, roared on toward the citadel.

How to find the place in this hideous field of ruins? For they had passed through the outskirts now and the nameless rubble of Velikiye Luki lay scattered senselessly around them. Two things only could be distinguished in the maze of blocks, beams, crushed things. The first was the Felt Factory, off to the right, a few smokestacks and multistory concrete facades still visible as markers. The second was the citadel

itself, that high earthen mound rising like a black tumor
above the town. Even this they might not have been able to
perceive from a far distance. If not for the fact that the
citadel lay in the western half of the city, Tribukait's group
might have wandered from one rubble-clogged channel to
another, circling and angling through the debris toward God
only knew where.

But they could see it and they traveled still at high speed in
that direction. Then they were obliged to slow down to negotiate any number of obstacles that lay spilled across their
path. The Russians could guess their objective only too well
and artillery fire closely followed the panzer column, almost
as if the tanks themselves were setting off explosions on either side by passing over invisible trip wires. The vehicles
picked up speed again over any reasonably clear stretch of
street or avenue.

The entrance to the citadel was a massive arch of stone and
beams set within the earthen rampart. The arch was unbarri-
caded. There was no gate, no portal, nothing except a few
tangles of barbed wire and sandbags to keep the Russians
from pouring into the place over these long weeks. The defenders had felt their own nakedness for all this time, even
while bodies continued to accumulate in and around the entrance. The panzer column made for that singular gap in the
high earth wall. One after the other they roared through into
the courtyard, circling around the frozen pond, around the
sunken T-34 in the frozen pond. Tribukait looked at his
watch. 1500 hours. Three o'clock. Scarcely more than an
hour since they had started off.

And so they were here.

The tank and half-track crews might have been in a poor
position to judge the suffering of the men here, for the men
who now closed around the armored vehicles were over-
wrought with elation, shouting, letting out wild shapeless
yells into the strange grey light of the day. Many stood
speechless, staring out of black faces with eyes like flares, as
if petrified by an unbelieving ecstasy.

For they could hardly believe it; yet even not quite able to
believe, they were still flooded with overwhelming sensa-

tions. They stood rooted to the ground, or perhaps took a step or two forward, and then stood rooted again.

Schrader and Freitag stood side by side in the courtyard among so many others, yet so rapt within the force of the moment that they were scarcely aware of each other. They stared as if struck dumb and indeed a look of almost blissful stupidity seemed to possess them, Freitag especially. He stood with his hands thrust almost nonchalantly into the pockets of his greatcoat, the wide collar upturned to muffle his scrawny neck. The boy scarcely twenty looked aged all of a sudden, not from suffering or privation but from some curious almost senile look on his face. He looked like an old man standing by the side of a road, who had just seen something to remind him of bygone pleasures in his life, lost in these memories while staring fixedly with a strange absentmindedness.

If anything Schrader's stare was even more fixed, though something of his canny hardness remained fixed there too. For weeks he had assumed with uncomplaining, businesslike calm that everything was lost, that they were all lost, and he stared at the circled armored vehicles as if he could not adapt to the thought of releasing this notion from his head. He just looked at them, the vehicles, the men, the relief column, the rescuers. His eyes were wide and rigid in blackened sockets; his teeth were not quite clenched and his lips were set slightly apart and he stood there breathing quietly. His arms hung somewhat tensely by his sides, still primed by months of violent anticipation, his hands clenching and unclenching spasmodically inside tattered woolen gloves.

Two gunnysacks connected by a long string hung down from his neck, hanging shapelessly on either side of his greatcoat. For carrying grenades, though they were empty at this moment. Apart from his hands closing and unclosing he was as still as a statue.

Beside Freitag and Schrader stood another man, an officer of the garrison whom they did not know except for his face. He was a slightly larger fellow, as yet not so wasted by hunger, a steel helmet barely fitting over his broad head. He wore a dirty white padded jacket and dirty padded trousers. One gloved hand was raised to his face to wipe tears from his cheeks, yet trying not to be too conspicuous about this weeping.

Others stood all around them, or walked slowly a few paces at a time. After the initial bursts of wild shouting they were for the most part speechless, having some difficulty in saying ordinary words to the newcomers, though when they did speak it was ordinary almost laconic words that came out, or sometimes outrageous obscenities, their faces easing from disbelieving rigidity into an almost unspeakable relaxation.

Perhaps if they had been allowed a few more minutes here, to absorb it all, they might have commenced talking with greater animation, spilling out pent-up words. But the moment, this one moment, was very short, not even lasting a few minutes.

Freitag was the only one who had been at Cholm and so he could not help but think of Cholm, of the day the siege had been lifted there, though thinking this somewhat confusedly amidst all kinds of things. Maybe that was why he looked like he was dazedly remembering something pleasant, the memory of that other day of rescue almost nine months ago now. A lifetime ago, it might seem in one compartment of the brain; while in some other compartment it might seem only yesterday.

So, here we are again, he thought blankly, even though he was the sole member of this "we." It seemed to have some meaning though he had no idea of anything it could mean.

"I can't go through this again." Quite clearly he remembered Kordts saying this, grasping some kind of girder or bent metal rod to pull himself up onto a broken stretch of wall where he, Freitag, was standing. Maybe he hadn't said it at that exact moment; he no longer knew. This too seemed to have some powerful meaning that was incomprehensible but whose shape was at least there, whatever it was. He felt a void on one side of his stomach, not hunger, more like a momentary chill in his belly, an icy gas passing through.

The moment, after all, the one moment of Tribukait and his column arriving in the citadel, was very short; perhaps it lasted a long time in the minds of some and passed very quickly in the minds of others.

Then the mousetrap, death trap, such as it was, closed shut again.

Few were aware of exactly how things happened. Shells began to fall; that was all they knew.

A few laggards from Tribukait's column were still approaching the citadel two or three minutes after the other vehicles had first entered there. They were a Panzer III and a half-track running the gauntlet of Russian fire as the others had done before.

The enemy artillery response was violent but the gunners had difficulty tracking these swiftly advancing targets. Shells landed indiscriminately around the approaches to the citadel, killing a number of Soviet soldiers in position out there. But during this time, even while menaced by their own fire, the Russians had maneuvered several antitank guns into position to cover the arched entranceway in the earthen wall. The majority of Tribukait's vehicles had already made it through before this could be done, but the trailing Panzer III drew well-aimed fire from these guns. The stone arch, massive as it was, was only just wide enough to accommodate a tank, and so the tank was obliged to slow down to negotiate this passage, and was struck four times in quick succession.

The commander standing in the commander's hatch was mangled by an armor-piercing round entering the turret. The other crew members escaped the vehicle and fled into the courtyard. The driver, then seeing that his vehicle had entirely blocked the entranceway, had the nerve and presence of mind to run back and reenter the driver's hatch even while the tank continued to be struck from the rear. The engine howled and the tank lurched forward a few more feet before being disabled for good. Smoke boiled out of the engine deck and the driver climbed out of his hatch a second time and fled again into the citadel, the backs of his overalls drenched in blood.

The other three escaping crewmen were also drenched in their commander's blood. They entered the arena of disbelieving elation among the surviving defenders in the courtyard, a mood that would change now within seconds.

The smoking tank still blocked the archway, trapping the

other vehicles inside the citadel, and trapping the remaining half-track at the tail end outside the citadel. The jaegers aboard the half-track had attempted to lay machine-gun fire on the Russian guns, though unable to locate them in the quickness of the moment. They saw one that the Russians had dragged into plain view down a side street. They fired a few bursts and felt the heartbeat span of time before the Russians switched fire from the tank to their own thinly armored vehicle and tore it to pieces. They dismounted and fled past the smoking Panzer III into the citadel.

This wide interior space was now curiously empty of human beings. For a few seconds the dozen or so armored vehicles remained there unmanned in odd stillness. Their crews and all other living souls had fled into the bunkers, galleries, or other shelters. Seconds passed and then the wide area of the courtyard was transformed into a single mass of fire and smoke, like a great edifice of flame and metal spontaneously erected there. Thus had the Russian howitzers and heavier guns pounded the citadel week after week without being able to obliterate the molelike defenders within the vaults; thus they pounded it again now.

But for Tribukait's tanks and half-tracks there was no shelter anywhere. The crews along with the original defenders watched from the bunkers and hidey-holes as the fire came down. A few of the thirty-ton vehicles were flipped over like turtles by blasts that no one could see in the face of such violent concussions. Rubble from collapsed parts of Sing-Sing poured down upon other vehicles. One after another they were wrecked or disabled and in the suddenness of these minutes they seemed no more than toys.

The spectacle was so astonishing that the defenders watched in awe even before the demoralizing force of all this could begin to drain their insides away.

Then they began to understand. There was no letup though, as the Soviet barrage continued for well over an hour.

The panzer crews and Tribukait's jaegers joined the defenders and so the siege continued for another week into January. Now there were a hundred or so more mouths to feed upon the soup-water with barely a bit of horse gristle floating in a fifty-gallon drum.

Tribukait's foray had plunged through the Russian defenses like a needle penetrating the rubber seal of a serum vial. To no good end. There were no follow-up forces from Kampfgruppe Wohler and nothing this small armored column could accomplish on its own. The seal of the vial was now shut impermeably behind them, as if it had never been pierced at all.

The defenders were little more demoralized than they had been already. It had all happened too quickly. They had walked into a world of elation, even dumb ecstasy, for a minute or two, and then walked right out of it again. That was all there was to it.

They might hope that if Tribukait's people had broken through then other people might break through after them. They might hope anything at all, think anything at all.

It was discovered that two tanks were still drivable, though nothing useful could be done with them with the one Panzer III still blocking the entrance. In any case these last two were eventually wrecked by shellfire that continued to come down. Another week went by.

On 16 January the survivors were told via radio that no further relief attempts would be coming. They were to break out on their own and attempt to reach the German main line west of Velikiye Luki.

Chapter Twenty-seven

Schrader, Freitag, Timmerman, Griswold, Lieutenant Ritter, and twenty-two others had made it from Hamburg back to the citadel on Christmas Eve. The place then had seemed like the end of the world, a featureless earthen rampart rising at the end of those featureless square miles they had crossed, a long and nightmarish night filled with the roar of tank motors, sudden shouts and screams, flare-bursts, gunfire, abandonment of wounded and dead, of others who lost their way.

It all seemed so long ago that it might never have happened. The eerie strains of *Stille Nacht* heard from the base of the ramparts . . . perhaps they had only imagined all that, some confusion from the unending blur of days and nights. Mostly nights, long winter nights in the ruins of Velikiye Luki, filled with violent flashes and noise.

By 16 January they had been inside the citadel for over three weeks. It seemed they had spent the entire siege in this place; Hamburg, anything else before then . . . it was all too long ago now.

Almost all of the original defenders were wounded or dead. If not for the arrival of Tribukait's jaegers and armored crews, there would have been no one left to man the walls.

At times other men filtered in from the eastern part of the city, from the Barracks Complex and railroad station where von Sass was still holding out. It was even worse over there, they said; they doubted any but stragglers like themselves would ever get out of there alive. The field hospital had been burned to the ground by the flame-tanks, the building and almost everyone inside it burned, burned, burned. Men wounded since that time were left lying about aboveground, in the streets, lying unattended in the middle of firefights, struck and struck again by Russian fire and by their own, lying unattended outside von Sass's command post, lying everywhere. Medical supplies were gone and medical care had broken down completely. A staff officer reported that von Sass was taking this very hard. His determination to fight on to the end had not wavered (. . . not determination but resignation and obedience to the orders radioed in from the outside, from on high . . .) but the sight of so many men lying about helplessly in the ruins, staring into space, calling out to him, to anyone, lying at his very doorstep . . . he looked like a ghost now, the staff officer said.

In any case it cannot go on much longer now, these stragglers said. Not anymore.

There might have been sharp questions about dereliction of duty, from Tribukait or Darnedde, or even from the disembodied radio voices still coming in from the outside. For there was no way to know if these men had deserted their posts to flee to the citadel, or if they had simply become separated by enemy breakthroughs from von Sass's pocket, trapped in other isolated pockets, burnt and pulverized strongpoints, all over the city. The staff officer in particular could not give a coherent account of how he had left von Sass's side.

But such grim and pointed inquiries did not arise, not now, perhaps not ever. The newcomers, hardly more than a dozen of them in any case, crawling in from the eastern part of the city at different hours, on different days and nights, were merely assigned to positions along the walls with the other citadel defenders.

Schrader wanted to know about Krabel, though thinking resignedly that no one would know anything. He was right. No one knew, though whenever he heard that another straggler had come in from the east side he compulsively sought him out and questioned him. These conversations were short enough. Krabel, Ernst? Burn wounds in the field hospital? Never heard of him. And most would add that they were all burned now, inside what was left of the field hospital. After hearing this enough times Schrader almost felt a little peace . . . thinking that at last maybe it was over for him now,

Krabel, black face, black burns, black peace, black night . . .
good enough, after all this. He felt depressed and empty but
maybe also a little peaceful . . . like so many others he could
not think clearly about anything anymore. Besides being
dispirited he was too tired and hungry.

Then he remembered Heissner and started asking about
Heissner, thinking that if someone remembered him then
maybe they would remember Krabel as well. He did this
compulsively, matter-of-factly, without being disappointed
by the answers he got, because he did not expect anything. A
few of the newcomers were killed on the walls or in the
courtyard before he had a chance to seek them out. So be it.

The breakout from the citadel was decided upon on 16
January, toward the end of the daylight. The surviving officers and NCOs were assembled in the stone chapel, what
was left of it, at the south end of the courtyard. Schrader was
there with them, listening to how it was going to unfold, the
break for freedom. Tribukait, who as senior officer had taken
over command from Captain Darnedde, informed them of
the final radio messages from Kampfgruppe Wohler. Wohler's
leading elements were now only two miles from the outskirts, but they had no strength left, were under continuous
attack by the Russians. There were no reserves left anywhere
between Vitebsk and Velikiye Luki that might come to their
assistance.

Tribukait said, "This being the case, General Wohler has
informed me that the High Command has granted us freedom of action. We will organize a breakout attempt for
tonight. It must be tonight, as he cannot guarantee how much
longer his forward elements will be able to hold their positions outside the city. There is nothing left to defend here in
any case. I must inform you that earlier today Oberst von
Sass surrendered in the eastern pocket. We are the only ones
left now."

In the lamplight of the chapel he looked around for reaction from the others standing there. There were Darnedde
and seven other officers and a like number of NCOs. The latter had shared the burden of command equally with the officers, over the remains of companies and platoons, over
handfuls of even three or four men, for these weeks now.

Yet there was almost no reaction, apart from small changes of expression, resetting of facial features. Only a few said anything. They waited still, to hear the details of exactly how they were going to go about doing this, waiting to hear the plan and to add their own thoughts to it, now that this moment had finally come.

They all knew that the fate of the wounded would be the most terrible burden in a situation like this. Tribukait was silent for a few moments, either formulating ideas or perhaps reluctant to speak. They waited. At length Captain Darnedde said, "What about the wounded, Herr Major?"

"We will have to leave them," said Tribukait. "There is no other choice."

These remarks also evoked little reaction. They were too tired to react to either treachery or need, or even to distinguish between the two. Captain Darnedde could only reflect wordlessly that if Tribukait had not arrived the week before then this decision would have been his to make.

Another officer, who had made it in from the eastern part of the city two days earlier, reflected on certain sights he had seen. Wounded men whom the Russians had come upon, skinned, beaten to death, or otherwise disposed of . . . raw faces still bearing articulate human shape, sinews articulated, muscles articulated around the skull structures . . .

At the moment he said nothing of this, though it was no secret he was keeping—he had already told others about this when he came in. It was no surprise to any of them anyway.

Now one of the NCOs began to speak, the sole survivor of another strongpoint on the eastern side, which had become cut off from von Sass's pocket. He had hidden himself in the rubble of Strongpoint Innsbruck, under the floorboards of a house, and had witnessed the survivors of his crew being taken prisoner. The Russians had marched them off and he had not seen any of them being mistreated. He had fled hours later, and come across the bodies of a few of his comrades lying in the streets. They must have fallen out during their march and been left to freeze, or maybe shot, he hadn't been able to tell in the dark. They hadn't been mutilated though.

This story made none of those listening feel better or

worse. There was no predicting what the Russians would do
to captives and all of them had known this for a long time.

Tribukait said, "All right. Now listen carefully. I must ask
all of you not to tell the wounded men that we intend to break
out. You will all determine which of your men are fit to
march and you must tell them this as well. Anyone found
spreading rumors among the wounded will be left behind.
This is a dirty business and none of us can wash our hands of
it. But any sign of panic must be forestalled at all cost; otherwise there will be no chance of survival for anyone. I have
already spoken privately with Captain Kaufmann and Captain Baer. They have agreed to stay behind."

These were the two surviving medical officers. Neither
was present in the chapel.

"All right. If anyone else wishes to speak then do so now."

No one spoke. Tribukait then began to lay out how the
breakout would take place. At this time it was early evening,
dark outside, with a moon halfway risen. He fixed the ap-
pointed time for 0200, when the moon would be down.

Schrader was on the east wall shortly before this time, during
the last hours. All was quieter than it had been. In fact the silence was overpowering, and he noticed this, though it still
made little impression on him. The moon was down and
darkness was absolute except for a few small fires that
burned like mutilated eyes to the east. A few shots rang out
over there, Russians firing at nothing most likely. Or shooting some poor devil they had smoked out from somewhere.
The intermittent shooting seemed no different from the silence, which was stronger than everything else, absorbing
everything.

The treacherous business with the wounded did not trouble him overly much. The chances of any of them making it
back to their own lines seemed not so good anyway. He was
too tired to understand anything anymore; thus it was like a
strange revelation suddenly cropping up in his mind, when
he saw that his callousness had much to do with how little
connected he had felt to the men in his platoon since the *Iltis*
assault. Though once this occurred to him it seemed obvious

enough, as if he had known it from the instant Tribukait had
disclosed this aspect of the plan, when he, Schrader, had had
nothing to say like most of the others there. They'd all
known it was coming anyway. To break out with the
wounded would have been a stark impossibility . . .

How he would have reacted with his old crew, before that
day in August, he did not know. Or perhaps he did know, but
it didn't matter now and it was too long ago. Suppose Krabel
had been here in the citadel instead of over there in the field
hospital with von Sass, where it was all dark now? Even with
Krabel . . . my God, those burn wounds . . . if he had been
unable to move he might have had to say goodbye. And what
would that have been like? The horror, the shame of it, filled
him with a kind of giddiness. Suddenly some of his dullness
(it was that more than callousness really) fell away and he
put his hands over his eyes, probing his forehead with his fingertips, mouthing silent words to himself. Goodbye. Goodbye. Or would he have volunteered like a fool to stay behind
with the doctors and the wounded?

The shape of the dilemma suddenly appeared in his mind
like a field of right angles, a chess problem, sharp yet also
murky; the thought disgusted him somehow. Only one thing
he knew—he would not have left Krabel behind without
speaking to him, abandoning him without a last talk, no matter how bitter and strange it might have been. Ernst would
have forgiven him, he knew; that went without saying, but
what kind of look would he have had in his eye?

Then he thought, My God, how can I be sure. Forgive me?
How would I know . . .

The useless and hypothetical nature of his brooding disgusted him as well but he accepted that he could not help but
think about it. Better to think about it than to actually live
through such a farewell. And he figured that many of the
other men getting ready in the courtyard below, about to
leave their wounded brethren behind, would be facing the
same dilemma. Whoever had friends lying down there, or lying in the vaults still further below . . . better not to have
friends, as always. But such truisms in principle only indicated the frequent violations inherent in the reality. No doubt

some of them had already disregarded Tribukait's order and
sought out friends and spoken to them for the last time, not
giving a damn for Tribukait's threats. Schrader doubted the
man would carry out such a threat anyway, but there was no
knowing.

But if Tribukait had feared an outbreak of panic then he
had been mistaken. The courtyard down below, and the stone
galleries all around the courtyard where so many men lay,
were as silent as all the ruined darkness beyond the walls.
The silence, the absence of vile cursing or complaint, spoke
louder than any noise of mutiny or panic, the deep silence
down in the courtyard hurled up against the stars. He could
not think about it. God knew how many of those wounded
men were cursing them all now, wordlessly.

He looked at his watch. The time was nearing. Good.
Good. Enough of this filthy place.

He took one last look. To the east, nothing but darkness
and a few fires. The Lovat passed beneath the wall but it was
too dark now to see anything of it. Bitter wind blew from the
east as it had done almost ceaselessly since early December.
He thought he heard motors rumbling, the sound beating erratically against him in the wind; gun-tractors and tanks already getting organized, no doubt, getting ready to move
over here after von Sass's last bits and pieces had been pol-
ished off. With a kind of uncaring perversity he turned his
back to the wind and lit a cigarette, one of the last he had left.
He remembered that Russian infiltrators had actually gotten
on top of different parts of the walls on many nights and he
cursed and extinguished the smoke, crumpling it in his
gloved hand. An entire smoke wasted like that . . . Better
than a hero's death, maybe. He brought it up close to his eyes
and unbent what he could of it.

He grasped that he would have to be more careful now if
he or any of them was going to get out of here. It was time,
and so he forced concentration into his mind and became all
at once alert and ready, no longer did he have to combat exhaustion to do this; he summoned it automatically somehow,
canniness, readiness, everything.

Cautiously he made his way along the top of the wall,
coming across a few other men who would remain there un-

til the last moment, whispering a few words to them and they to him.

"Are you mad?" whispered one of them.

"No," said Schrader, irked with himself but refusing to show it.

If they still reproached him it was done in silence now.

Schrader asked if they'd heard the motors and one or two said yes, damn right they'd heard them. Schrader said, "I doubt they'll be rushing over here just yet. It's twenty minutes now. When I come back it will be time."

He went below.

Freitag was standing next to one of the gallery arches at the bottom of the stairs. He had no watch and looked anxiously at Schrader. He had been determined to stay on his feet, just to show them all, but now he slumped down against the pier of the arch so he could rest a little bit, recover his strength. Schrader had told him about Tribukait's order a few hours earlier; if he thought he could make it, Schrader had also said, he would stay with him until they made it through to their own lines.

Among Schrader's people there was no one left except for Freitag and Timmerman, who was still unwounded. Among the rest Griswold had survived the longest, dying yesterday.

Freitag could walk but his left shoulder was crushed and he did not know if he could walk very far. He could ignore the pain and was utterly determined to do so, but his breathing was becoming more and more laborious. Part of his lungs must have been hurt too though he didn't know how. He could not tell if some bone was pressing against them or just what it was. A grenade burst had brought a wooden beam down on top of him two days before, outside the walls. He had been scouting around out there with two other men, dead of night, looking around for some route that might possibly lead through the Russian lines. Freitag had volunteered to do this and Darnedde had recommended him to Tribukait. At that time word from Wohler, from the High Command, had not yet come through but Tribukait had wanted to be ready with an escape avenue, if one even existed, approval or no approval.

Freitag had made it back to the citadel under his own

power, along with the other two. Tribukait had then sent out another patrol to find another route. Freitag, meanwhile, remained in much greater pain than he let on, to Schrader or to anyone.

Even now, at the last moment, he dared not tell Schrader anything except that he was ready to go and nothing would stop him.

"Don't worry," said Schrader. "Don't worry about anything now."

Freitag laid his head back against the stone arch and looked up in the darkness at the shape of the other man.

"Thank you. Thank you for not leaving me," he said.

"*Ja,*" said Schrader.

He reached out with his hand, not quite able to see Freitag in the dark, his fingers touching the top of the boy's head.

"How are you feeling?"

"Fine. Fine," said Freitag.

"Good. Just tell me if you need a hand."

Schrader did not know why he was doing this, saying these things. The tension during these last minutes filled him to the brim but even so he was calm enough.

Strangely the escapees were able to leave by the main gate, by the same way they had come in, a week ago or three weeks ago or months ago, however long it had been for different parties of men.

Strange enough that for all this time the stone archway had never been closed off to the Russians, who even so had never managed to break into the courtyard except on one or two occasions. As if the defenders aboard a spacecraft had withstood for all these weeks despite having a large unobstructed leak where the void might rush in. Machine guns across the courtyard had been kept sighted on the archway, which in fact had become more of a hideous bull's-eye for the German gunners than an access point for the Russians. The dead lay scattered and stiff there. Some lay crushed beneath the treads of the one tank disabled there the day of Tribukait's arrival.

Still it was unaccountable somehow. And strange also that they were leaving by this same gaping hole. They felt naked, departing in groups of ten or a dozen, filing past on either side of the disabled tank and then out into the ruined city. In fact in the profound darkness they were as invisible in the archway as they would have been if issuing from the very molecular structure of the earthen walls on either side. But they waited with extreme tension for flares to expose them. No noise, that above all. As best they could they had padded or else discarded every bit of loose metal on their persons, most of them leaving their steel helmets behind.

Outside the walls a dead zone lay between them and the nearest Russian posts. An enormous field of craters. Previously the enemy had been much closer, and escape through the main gate would have been nearly impossible. The last concerted assault had taken place two days before, nearly finishing them all; indeed it would have done so, for the Russians had gotten right on top of the walls in many places. That had been the worst day, the day when most of them had wondered what their last thoughts on earth would be. Tribukait had pleaded with Wohler to send Stukas in; it was either that or the end. At last they had heard the planes droning through the clouds, knowing that a misaimed bomb landing in the courtyard would finish them before the Russians did. It had been a close thing. The detonations had ringed the entire citadel right up to the walls, atomizing many of the enemy out in the open, rendering many of the defenders inside nearly senseless for long minutes afterward. Even before their senses had fully returned, still dazed and deaf, they had surged out of their hidey-holes to butcher any of the enemy still found staggering about, the defenders themselves lurching about like sleepwalkers in a nightmare, acting out this nightmare in merciless fashion upon any Russians they found still clinging to life, or horribly wounded, or even dead already, hacking at them indiscriminately, riddling them with bullets.

So the walls had been cleared. Beyond the walls lay a moonfield of craters. The Russians had pulled their perimeter back, as much as several hundred yards in some places.

Now in the black early hours of 17 January the first order of business would be to somehow traverse this crater-field undetected. Schrader led Timmerman and Freitag and seven other men. They were crouched in the deeper blackness next to the disabled tank; three other groups had issued out before them. A fourth group, led by Darnedde, then went, vanishing utterly after a few steps, out into the moonless dark.

Schrader whispered to Timmerman, "Freitag goes with me. I intend to stay with him no matter what. If we fall behind then you're in charge. Try to stay close to Darnedde if you get separated from me."

"All right," said Timmerman, his expression impossible to determine in the blackness.

Freitag was only a few feet away but Schrader could not see him. He whispered to another man and Freitag approached.

Schrader whispered, "Take this between your teeth. Somebody's bound to fall down out in that mess, especially you."

"I won't cry out," said Freitag.

"You can't know that. Just take it. At least until we get to a more level stretch of ground."

Freitag took the rag that Schrader placed in his good hand. He still had enough difficulty breathing normally as it was. He wasn't about to mention this now anymore than previously. He held the rag dubiously for a moment, then set it loosely at one corner of his jaw.

They stared out into the dark waiting for the first flare to come up from the Russian side. As if the intensity of their stares would cause this to happen, as if they wanted it to happen, just to get it over with. They'd all studied the crater-field during daylight hours, knew how very difficult it would be to cross that area without making any noise. They were blind not just from the dark but because the tension seemed to suck every sensory impression into their listening ears, and indeed they were almost certain they could hear faint noises now from the groups gone out before them. Every man wore felt boots stripped from the enemy.

Schrader led them out in single file. Immediately they turned to the left, along the base of the wall. They found a twisted metal rod protruding from a small rubble heap, which had been agreed upon as a marker from which they would break across into the crater-field.

Darnedde was waiting there; Schrader could barely recognize him. Neither spoke. Darnedde pointed to a place within the silhouette of the nearest still-standing buildings, about two hundred yards away. Schrader paused, kneeling, to study everything as carefully as he could. The city had been so thoroughly flattened, not just around the citadel but everywhere else as well, that the individual buildings or haphazard rows of buildings that still remained stood up in peculiar isolation from each other, as if they had been erected according to some strange haphazard plan, scattered about across the floor of a stony desert with wide spaces between them, spaces filled with every manner of low mounded debris. The starry night, like a cold desert night, creaking with incessant wind, hung down behind the buildings and made their deeper blackness easy enough to see. But the crater-field immediately in front of them lay in the deepest blackness and try as he might Schrader could make out almost no features in that landscape.

This is no good, he thought.

The first groups had been led across this initial obstacle by men from the scouting party—the second one to go out after Freitag's patrol had been turned back by the Russians—who had chosen this path. Even the few men who had crossed this area a few nights before would have had difficulty leading larger groups of men through it in pitch blackness. But now they were all out there somewhere. There was no one left to show Schrader the way.

Goddamn it, he thought.

About two hundred yards to the structure Darnedde had pointed to, maybe a little more . . . distances hard to perceive in the depthless gloom.

There was nothing to do but get started.

Still he paused to listen for a few seconds more. He could hear actual voices now and again, sounds drifting or winding between gusts of wind from God knew where in the night, from some distance away, Russian voices. Far away, in open spaces visible between black standing hulks, he could see what must be a few campfires, or else flames guttering in the aftermath of some destruction. He thought they would be campfires though. They were far off and not of immediate concern.

He turned around and touched the man just behind him and then they began.

As they went out they began to sense the voids of craters on either side of them, straining their eyes, feeling for these edges with their feet, crouching and feeling with hands and feet both. The Stuka craters were deep and wide, some of them thirty or forty feet wide. They began to have a better sense of these voids, able to avoid stumbling into them; Schrader felt a little better. Still it was difficult to stay upright without stumbling over something, and so they were all crawling, not on their knees but on the balls of their feet with their fingertips spread before them, the fingertips of one hand with the other hand gripping a weapon. They made little noises, it was impossible not to, noises maybe carried away by the wind or else indiscernible among the wider intermittent noises out in the city, though in their tension any slight skid of their boots among loose gravel or stones seemed magnified.

Schrader looked back for Freitag, could not make him out. He hunkered down behind a pile of blocks and as the others came up he saw Freitag's odder, injured shuffle; and he was the only one not carrying a weapon in one hand. When Freitag came by Schrader reached out and lightly took hold of his greatcoat.

In some apprehension they heard other faint noises behind them now. The next group must be coming out into the craters. They were all too alert for their own good; it was impossible to judge how audible sounds really were. Schrader was bathed in sweat; they all were, like a kind of liquid armor that conveyed the bitter cold to their skin in strange ways. At the moment they cared nothing for the cold.

Schrader was about to lead them on when they heard rubble sliding back there. The inevitable had happened. They all froze.

Perhaps it was the Russians who had made the noise, startled by coming face-to-face with their enemy in the dark. Shouts and gunfire erupted behind Schrader's group. Schrader felt his stomach turn over and piss dribble down his thigh. There was the flash and crump of grenades between where they were and the citadel wall. Russian shouts, German shouts, screams. The first flares went up.

Two of Schrader's people bolted now; the nearest build-

ings were not that far off. In the shock-light of the flare they
threw themselves down again, one yelling wildly, down into
a crater maybe.

Behind them, terrifyingly near, Schrader saw men etched
in the light, shooting at other men only yards away, flinging
things, grenades or blocks of stone, grappling with each
other, stabbing, crying out, falling. The ghastliness of it all
in the flare-light, the fizzling, sputtering, hanging light, like
house lights dimmed then brightened at crazy intervals, was
indescribable. The flare sank and another went up; several
went up. They had reckoned with the possibility of Russians
being in the craters, patrols or individual listeners. At the
next full shock of light Schrader saw three Russians running
in his direction, running and stumbling in the mess of everything everywhere; one turned to fire back in the other direction. Thinking in a way seemingly both instantaneous and in
slow motion he considered taking them out without shooting, stabbing them or crushing their heads with something;
but there were three of them and he had no sense of where
anyone was except for Freitag right next to him. They were
only yards away and he raised his goat's leg and fired. Simultaneously a grenade burst behind the Russians, flinging
them down or else Schrader's gunfire did it; he was momentarily blinded and felt grit hurled against his face. Freitag
yelled something, a man had risen and stumbled right between them. He fell to his knees, bleeding visibly and pro-
fusely in another shock of light; Schrader sent him fully to
the ground with a blow from the gun butt, straddling the
man's body between his knees and raining more blows on the
man's skull until he felt sick. He rolled off and lay as low as
he could, still trying to look everywhere at once. Three of his
men were huddled in terror only a few feet away, staring at
him or staring around wildly as he was doing. Freitag
groaned a few times, groans like choking; his face was paler
than white in the ghastly illumination, the strange rag clenched
between his teeth spilling down his chin. Schrader looked at
the skull of the Russian lying next to him and gagged a few
times. Violent noise rushed past them all from every direction.

He looked back for any sign of the other group behind

them, but they were lying low, either dead or else lying low. The melee had ceased. It seemed to have all happened at once but had probably lasted several minutes. It would take that long for one side or the other to kill everyone they could come to grips with. The noise and light had not ceased but it was coming from everywhere now, gunfire, one flare after another, networks of tracers from a dozen or more positions along the Russian perimeter. And also, Schrader saw, from the wall of the citadel; they were firing back from up there.

He began to consider this, though still scarcely able to breathe and thus scarcely able to think. He waited for his senses to clear, staring fixedly at the intense bursts of firing from the top of the walls. Not from the archway, from the rest of the men who must still be there, but from the upper part of the ramparts.

He considered. They were trapped like rats in these craters, but with luck, with luck, the Russians might not understand what was happening. Their hides might be saved by the men still firing from atop the walls. For it would seem that the defenders were still inside the citadel, that whoever had run into the Russian patrol out here might only have been another handful of scouts.

Would they think that? He didn't know.

The gunfire from atop the wall continued in a frenzy and the Russians answered it. Some fire was also laid down on the craters but not so much now.

Freitag moved and spoke painfully into his ear.

"They'll lay mortar fire down on us."

He wanted to make a run for it now, badly injured or not. The other three close by looked on the verge of it too, unless they were too frightened to move. Schrader fought with the same urge, but the flares were still going up.

"They won't risk hitting their own patrol," he said.

"You must be joking," said Freitag, a fierce and twisted utterance unlike anything Schrader had heard from him before. He was holding the rag in his uninjured hand, spots of blood on it.

"No," said Schrader. "They'll want their people to make it back to report what's going on. Just stay still."

Freitag made some kind of noise. Schrader's jaw began to

tremble and he opened and shut his mouth until it stopped. He thought he was right, convinced himself of it; but this guaranteed nothing. If only the goddamned flares would stop . . .

After a while the gunfire from atop the ramparts diminished, then ceased entirely. Just as well, thought Schrader. If they kept it up for much longer the Ivans might really start to suspect something. He found that he could no longer think clearly. He was a little calmer now, but he couldn't think. The other three had crawled up beside him and Freitag, asking what they should do now. Their eyes shone through twisted masks of fright, though their expressions were layered as well with the weary stolidity laid upon them by all the endless weeks of this madness.

"If they don't start shelling us they'll send out more patrols," said one.

Schrader said nothing though to himself he thought, yes, that was probably true.

"We ought to go," said another. "We can crawl. We can make it that far."

"Freitag can't crawl," said Schrader.

The others did not respond, thinking their own thoughts.

After a while Freitag said, "How are those poor bastards ever going to get out now?"

The men still back in the citadel.

"They'll have to think of something," Schrader said.

The flare bursts were less continuous now. There were intervals of blackness.

"Give it a few more minutes," Schrader said.

They could hardly stand it, none of them could.

There was still intermittent firing from the Russian side; a few answering bursts came back from the walls too. That would help, thought Schrader, the noise of it.

At the next interval of blackness they began to move forward again. They were not quite so deadly careful now, as if they couldn't stand it any longer, making quicker little movements during the black intervals, kicking stones and loose stuff down into craters. The black shapes of the buildings began to seem near enough to touch. They came across a body, one of the two men who had bolted when the firefight began. They left him in the dark, unable to see what had happened to him. They kept going, dropping like rags whenever another flare went up. Freitag gasped through clenched teeth; Schrader could see blood on his lips. He'd thrown the rag away. Schrader cursed him silently. They were almost there.

They heard noise. They lay still again, wanting to cry out just to ease the pressure of their hearts beating in their chests.

They heard it again, people moving quite close by. The Russians sending more men in to investigate the crater-field. Except they were moving in the wrong direction. Perhaps survivors then from the original patrol. Another flare went up and the shock of seeing men so close by was almost as great as the sight of the butchery during the firefight. Schrader and his people were already dead-still; the other group went down behind the edge of a crater.

They were German.

Schrader even thought he recognized Darnedde. But he did not dare say anything, fearing someone might fire without thinking. Christ, he thought. There was no telling what Freitag or the other three with him might do or say. But they did nothing, as transfixed as Schrader was by the fear of being fired on accidentally. When it grew dark again they heard the other group climbing out of the crater and moving off again.

They could not risk following them immediately; the same fear continued to prey on them while minutes passed by. Schrader felt physically ill from willing himself to stay where he was, from willing the other four to stay where they were without being able to speak to them. Finally he whispered this command toward the face of the nearest one simply to relieve himself of the impulse to say it. Not a sound came in response; but he judged that good enough. At length another flare went up and he saw all four staring at him like devils. The light sputtered, fizzled, sank. Went out. In the dark they got fully to their feet, too spent to sustain themselves in a crouch any longer. Then instinctively they hunched over again and in utter exhaustion made their way forward.

They made it into the first ruined buildings. They might have just made it all the way through to their own lines, so great was the relief they felt. Miraculously the other groups that had gone out before them were still waiting there, men cool as stones in the dark, looking about grimly like stones with eyes. Tribukait, who was there with them, had ordered them to wait for the people still trapped out in the crater-field, the ones with Darnedde, and now Schrader with his four men who had just made it across.

All in all they were in luck, or so it seemed. Every man judged for himself what had just happened, or whispered tensely with a comrade crouched beside him. But it seemed that the Russians had not grasped that a full-scale breakout was under way. Many of them understood what Schrader had understood, that the heavy return fire from the citadel wall had disguised what was really going on.

Inside one of these buildings, Tribukait, Darnedde, Lieutenant Ritter, Schrader, and another NCO huddled together.

Tribukait said to Darnedde, "Who was the last to start across?"

"Schrader," said Darnedde.

"The rest are still in the citadel?"

"As far as I know. Unless they've started out by now."

"No, it's too soon," said Tribukait. "We would have seen something in the flares. We could see everything from here."

"The flares have subsided," said Darnedde. "They might be coming now."

They fell silent. They looked out through windows or shattered gaps. They could see nothing except a few stars; even the wall of the citadel over there was almost impossible to distinguish. They waited for another flare to go up, but minutes passed by and none did.

"They'll be sending more patrols in there, most likely," said Tribukait. "They don't want to light up their own men."

He decided. It had already been hard enough to wait for Schrader and Darnedde's groups to get across. He suspected that some of the men in the building had already taken things into their own hands, taking it upon themselves to keep going, toward the German lines outside the city. Most of them had remained, however, upon his orders to remain.

"We can't wait any longer. It might be an hour before they decide to try again. If they even risk it at this point."

"They will. I know they will," said Darnedde. "It's tonight or never."

"We're moving on," said Tribukait. "If the rest are coming they'll have to find their own way."

Darnedde voiced no further disagreement. To succeed at all they had to keep going, come what may.

In the meantime Tribukait had sent two scouts out further into the ruins. These men had returned. They had come across several Russian outposts, been unable to find a way to get around.

They could expect no better. They would have to fight their way through. They moved off, sixty or so men assembled now. The scouts led them to the first outpost line and they were upon the enemy without hesitation, lobbing grenades that killed most instantly, machine-gunning the rest, taking their own casualties. Men too badly wounded to keep going were asked if they wanted the coup de grace, or just to be left there.

All this took scarcely a few minutes. The survivors kept going. The severely wounded remained behind to die of exposure, or to be captured, or to be shot, or to be mutilated. None had asked for the coup de grace. A few were in tears, a few just accepted it in terrible resigned silence. They had all been waiting for the end for so long now.

The element of surprise was lost and the survivors moved rapidly. The stone chaos of the city worked to their advantage. The deep blackness worked to their advantage too, though the enemy must know something was afoot now. Gunfire followed them without finding them. Russian voices shouted here and there, as frightened as their enemy, perhaps more so. Once through the outpost line they found the city ghostly and dead, empty again. Russian and German dead lay everywhere, outnumbering still-living occupants. They moved rapidly like dogs with the scent of prey, except it was freedom they were smelling. They passed by scattered rear-echelon camps, and came upon frightened sentries around a vehicle park and wiped it out with another grenade volley, their descent so swift that they took no casualties here; they kept going. A single well-sited machine gun could have cut half of them down, perhaps all of them. A flare at the right moment would have illuminated them like steers in a corral. But it didn't happen. The ruins out here seemed as endless and as lifeless as they had long been inside the German siege perimeter, these months past, the enemy presence scattered here and there, still in some confusion or even entirely ignorant in the deep inscrutable night. They moved that swiftly now, Tribukait's men; the enemy reacted and came to places they had already passed through, finding burning vehicles and bullet-riddled bodies. They shot a few Germans too severely wounded to speak; they pointed pistols at the skulls of a few who could speak, interrogating them, then shooting them.

And so they came to the edge of the city. It was a shock, for scarcely an hour had passed since leaving the citadel behind. The citadel had always been near to the western outskirts; they knew it, yet even so it was strange to see the dark barren snowfields suddenly spreading away before them. The city had been its own shattered universe, their own universe, for months now; none had seen the outside world during all this time, none except for Tribukait and those few who had come in from there.

Schrader and Freitag had become separated from the rest by now. Freitag had seen the men being left behind and he wanted to say something to Schrader. But he couldn't bring himself to do it. He wanted to reassure Schrader that he could make it, but as they went on he was beginning to think he could not keep going. He wished Schrader would reassure him but he could not bring himself to say that either. He didn't think Schrader would abandon him now but he wanted to hear it again. He was gasping and raling with every step. There was no hiding it and time and again Schrader looked at him with maddening silence.

As they came at last to the edge of the city they paused, looking about to see if they might have caught up with some of the others here. But it was too dark. They could see no one, hear no one. They were on their own.

"What's the matter?" said Schrader finally. "Are you hurt that badly?"

He had expected Freitag would be able to walk with the rest of them, more or less, so long as he could stand the pain from his shoulder. If the moment came when they had to flee for their lives he knew Freitag would not be able to keep up, and he had promised both Freitag and himself that he would stay with him if it came to that. But he had seen for a while now that the boy could hardly even walk.

Freitag sat down, harassed by glumness and fear. He started to say something but then he sat silently, breathing, trying to collect his breath.

Then he said, "There's something sticking in my lungs. I don't know what it is. I can't breathe very well."

"Broken rib," said Schrader.

"I don't know. I can't feel any broken ribs. My shoulder's broken. I don't know what the matter is."

"How is your shoulder then?"

"Like the devil. I suppose you were right about that rag. But that's not what it is. I need to catch my breath. Just a few minutes more."

To say these few words was more than he could manage and Schrader could barely hear the last of it as his voice hissed away like something being squeezed.

"Take your time," he said. "It's all right. You've made it this far. We need to think things over before we set off again."

Freitag feared he might catch his breath here for an hour, yet still be unable to go much further when the time came. He said nothing of it, tried to relax, tried to dispel his fear.

Schrader moved off a little ways, trying to see out into the dark. Without even the silhouette of buildings the landscape was as featureless as the ocean. Lonely winds blew, and he could barely make out disturbances that must be snow gusting out there, rolling up like small waves and then settling again in the intermittent wind. Much of the cloud cover had drifted away and the stars hung above in stubborn brightness, spread rim to rim over the perverse and utter blackness of the ground below. Patches of snow reflected dimly, but the snow cover was sparse and served only to give an illusory, shifting quality to distances and anything else.

He hoped to see traffic, or to hear it, moving along the main thoroughfare from the city out to the west, the Novo Sokolniki road, because he knew of no other landmark or way to orient them. He saw nothing, which did not surprise him, but neither did he hear anything. From the ruins at his back he could hear motors, he could hear intermittent gunfire. But out in the void to the west he heard nothing. At this point he was dismayed to know he was not entirely certain where west was; he had a general sense of it, but reckoning on that alone might lead them miles out of their way.

He should have had a compass; he should have figured that at some point they would become separated from Tribukait and the others. He cursed himself while continuing with his peculiar matter-of-factness to consider what they should do next.

Finally he did hear motors, off to the left somewhere. He felt better and continued listening. He listened intently, trying to ascertain if these were traffic sounds diminishing off into the distance—along the main road, in other words—or if it was merely some fool rumbling about at the edge of the city. The motor noise faded gradually, at a steady pace; that's the road then, he thought.

He began creeping back toward Freitag.

"How do you feel now?" he said.

Freitag gave no response.

"Freitag," whispered Schrader, reaching to touch his head, feeling his cold greasy hair. Freitag mumbled something. A surge of anxiety communicated itself invisibly from him to Schrader; Schrader thought he had only been gone a few minutes. But no doubt the time had seemed much longer to the boy.

"Please tell me if you do that again, Schrader."

"All right. I will," said Schrader.

He related what he had been able to see, to hear.

"For God's sake, I could have told you where we were," said Freitag.

"Where then? Why didn't you say something?"

Frietag breathed quietly, loudly enough but still quietly in the immense darkness.

He said, "I couldn't see it at first. You were already gone. There. You can see the factory over that way."

Schrader looked. He continued to look and gradually began to make out the distant structure. From their vantage point it seemed almost to be still connected to the city. Yet he realized that Freitag was right. The Felt Factory stood by itself beyond the southwestern outskirts. He forced a mental map to come clear in his mind, summoned from memories of actual maps of the city he had studied both recently and at countless times over these months. It jibed well enough, and the main road went out not far from the factory. Staring intently his eyes began to piece out the place, the taller walls and the decapitated smokestack that the starlight offered him, silhouetted for him.

"All right. Good eyes," he said.

He patted Freitag on the back and sat beside him, staring intently at the ground, at nothing, summoning another mental map of the city and of the country to the west beyond the city. For long minutes he was at this, gazing down at features and landmarks as they became pinpointed within his mind.

Finally he said, "Now listen to me. It's only two or three miles to the main line. Maybe closer if Wohler's people have managed to get any closer. You can make it that far. If you have to rest, well, rest. We might have to track around a bit in the dark out there. So just remember that there's not far to go."

Freitag felt the intake and escape of air within his lungs. What is the matter with the goddamned thing, he thought, referring thus to his own body. He nodded, but Schrader couldn't see him nod.

"All right? Have you got that?" Schrader said, trying to repress the apprehension he was beginning to feel about the man sitting next to him.

"Yes," said Freitag. "Two or three miles, two or three miles," he muttered, more to himself now. He remembered Cholm all of a sudden. He remembered that the German main line had been less than ten miles away, for all those months, for all those months. And yet no help had ever come. No, no, he thought. It had come. After all those months, at the end of all those months, it had finally come. It was here, where they were now, that help had never come. He discounted the arrival of Tribukait and the tanks, or maybe it no longer even occurred to him, so fleeting had been those few minutes of apparent salvation.

All of this seemed to take on some deep significance, a kind of moral force. Or some kind of force. But he could make no sense of it and didn't try to. He was too tired and confused.

"You're sure it's only that far? Two or three miles?" he said.

"You know it as well as I do," said Schrader. "They've been saying it for days now."

It was true; Freitag had heard this along with every other man inside the citadel. But somehow he had never been able to grasp it. Only a few miles . . . only a few miles . . . He had heard this so many times at Cholm that a few miles had begun to seem the equivalent of an infinite gulf of space. Suddenly he recalled how very acutely he had perceived this at Cholm, during certain bright winter nights, during certain winter nights and winter days, perceiving this hopeless gulf very acutely and yet also stoically, even imperturbably, as simply a raw fact of that endless trial; for an instant he felt a strange subtle electric shock as if he were actually back there again, at Cholm . . . as if all this at Velikiye Luki had only been some strange distorted dream of Cholm, of some other, dream-Cholm that would vanish utterly as soon as he awoke, awoke somewhere in the maze of those snow walls, with Kordts huddled next to him, or somewhere in the GPU building. . . .

Christ, he thought.

Yet the force of this strange sensation was dissipated by the way it passed so quickly through him; he felt it, felt it clearly enough to acknowledge what it was, but then it was gone.

In any case Schrader was speaking to him again.

"We have to get as far as we can before daylight. Are you ready, Freitag?"

Freitag said he was and they set off into the darkness, accompanied only by small winds. In spite of his anxieties Freitag was refreshed enough that he could walk at a normal pace for a while. The snow was not deep, hardly more than a skin laid across the ground; they had no trouble walking through it. The bitter wind, gusting violently then falling still, was at their backs; they didn't have to fight it. Needles of fine dry snow were driven into their backs but they hardly noticed that nor the cold either in their single-minded urge to keep going. In the darkness the land seemed flat but as they walked on they noticed how it rose and fell in endless small gradients, but it was not too bad, they were moving on all right. The sky was almost entirely clear now and Schrader wondered about being skylined atop one of these slight rises. He saw nothing they could do about it, except to stay alert; instinctively he felt they were alone, out here. The darkness and the emptiness and the dull noise of the wind gave them a certain feeling of invisibility; they felt as invisible as two souls lost out at sea somewhere, out on the nighttime sea. They walked fully upright, remaining wary and alert yet shed for the most part of the deep coiled tension that had forced them to crouch and hobble so fearfully through the ruins of the city behind them.

At this rate they would cover those two or three miles, thought Schrader, they would do it. And so it would not be long before they would have to crouch in that tension again, in order to get through the Russian lines and then their own lines. But he felt prepared for that and all in all felt his confidence growing now. If only Freitag was able to manage.

They paused every so often, if only for a few seconds at a time. Schrader would murmur something and Freitag would reply that he was doing well enough. Schrader didn't know if this was true or not; if the boy stopped then he would know.

They looked back sometimes, at Velikiye Luki. There was little to be seen of the place, even the silhouettes of buildings were low on the horizon now, insignificant-looking. There were different fires rising into the sky back there, columns of smoke blotting out the stars like squids' ink, clouding various local regions. And gunfire still, and shellfire. Intent on their own escape they would forget all about the poor bastards who had not been able to get across the crater-field, after the run-in with the Russian patrol; but then they would see and hear the shells bursting and remember the ones still inside the citadel, the wounded men and the other ones who had not been able to get out in time. Except perhaps they had gotten out by now; perhaps they had bided their time before making another attempt to get out. No way to know. No way to know, either, about Tribukait and the others with him; they were alone, Freitag and Schrader, they moved on. The city

receded behind them like a small planet, asteroid, barren lifeless stones, except for those few fires and smoke columns, a
small black matrix of rocks and human events drifting away
into space. For a while, as they moved further out into the
darkness, they were more clearly able to discern the Felt Factory off to the left, as their changing perspective detached
this ruin more clearly from the outskirts of the city. A
ghostly-looking heap off in the distance there, glimmering
with a few fires, campfires of the enemy. Again they heard
the rumble of motors, passing along the invisible road over
that way, audible for some time before fading into the wind
and silence.

They came across bodies strewn in the snow and stopped
dead. Freitag collapsed, though he made no sound. Schrader
squatted beside him, then laid himself flat in the snow. Freitag
was breathing heavily, gasping for air. He supported himself
with his good arm, half-lying and half-sitting, unable to lay
himself fully flat without bringing renewed agony to his
shoulder. After a moment he did manage to lie down entirely,
seeming to set his body down piece by piece, carefully into the
snow. He rolled on his back and stared up into the sky. His ex-
halations rose quietly up there like the faint milk of galaxies.
Schrader felt at the first body, stiff as iron wrapped in the
frayed cloth of a uniform, then crawled forward a little further.

Their entire path through the city had been marked by the
bodies of dead men, yet out here they had come across nothing and were understandably unnerved. His night vision had
improved to the point where he could make out jaegers' caps
or steel helmets on the heads of some, fur caps or nothing at
all on the heads of others. He saw the wrecked half-track in
the midst of these bodies, saw the shape of another one a little further away.

It did not occur to him that these were the remains of
Tribukait's men, killed a week ago during the attempt to
break through to the citadel. It did not occur to him to think
anything. All this might have been lying here for months for
all he knew.

To come across anything at all out in this emptiness would be
enough to set his nerves on edge. Nothingness and the dark

were the only comfort, the only security. Both consciously and subconsciously he absorbed his impressions of this scene, what he could see of it. He judged there was no one living here, nor anywhere close by. He gathered his nerve and trotted over to the nearest half-track, looking down the barrel of his weapon at the ripped-open rear doors. He saw what he expected to see, though still barely able to make it out. He accepted the hearty greetings of the mangled dead, poking at the nearest one half-hanging out the doors, stiff as mangled iron, like material no different from the vehicle in which they lay. He crept around to peer into the driver's cab, then went back to Freitag.

Freitag needed to rest longer. He had lost his momentum, feeling as if he had held his breath for half a mile or more, now gasping and gasping, fighting with the urge to groan as if that might help him to breathe better. Schrader told him there was no one about and he did groan then, faintly, just to let it out.

"Take your time," said Schrader, as he had said a dozen times already. "Things are looking up, boy. If you've made it this far you can make it the rest of the way."

Freitag was still lying on his back, staring up at the sky. The stars began to make him feel dizzy.

"Help me sit up," he said, reaching with his good arm. Schrader stood up and pulled Freitag to a sitting position, then sat down next to him again.

"I want a cigarette," said Freitag.

Schrader nodded.

After a moment he said, "That will help you breathe just fine."

"It wouldn't hurt," said Freitag.

"Would you trade a bullet for a smoke?"

"Yes," said Freitag.

"Don't be stupid."

"You know better than that," said Freitag.

They had both hoarded a few last cigarettes. Neither knew why they hadn't just smoked them all before leaving the citadel. The urge then had been overwhelming and they had chain-smoked them all except for one or two. They should have smoked those too. Now the temptation was just another aggravation; Schrader felt it too, having to imagine very clearly how one would taste right now, before being able to put it from his mind.

"How long before daybreak?" said Freitag.

"Long enough. Two or three hours."

Freitag was silent. Then he said, "That doesn't seem like very long."

"Maybe. Maybe not. Just tell me when you're ready."

Freitag felt irked somehow. He thought of saying something, but to say more than a few words at a time was too exhausting. He thought he might feel easier if Schrader just went on and left him. He knew he could make it, he would not think otherwise, even if he had to go on with such damnable slowness, even if he had to hide out somewhere when daylight came. At least then he wouldn't have to think about Schrader, and Schrader wouldn't have to think about him.

Still, he did not want Schrader to leave.

"Just a few more minutes," he said, his voice beginning to tighten with fear again. He really didn't know, he didn't know how much farther he could go.

Schrader meanwhile had fallen into his own fit of glumness. He had a watch. It was not quite four in the morning. But he did not know just when dawn would come. He should have asked about that long hours before but it had completely slipped his mind. He racked his brain in futile weariness, thinking he must know it anyway. Was it seven o'clock? Or eight? Or even later? The winter darkness. He pictured himself in the citadel again, waking from troubled sleep, peering up at an ugly, smoking dawn; or standing on the walls through the long night hours, watching for the first flare of daylight to the east, checking the time on his watch.

He knew that he knew but his mind was a dead blank. I won't last much longer at this rate, he thought, as if he could foresee his own weariness, his own carelessness, his own eventual death . . . not tonight, not even tomorrow or the next day, but somewhere in the weeks or months to come. For in the strange immediacy of the present instant—as opposed to the exhausting grey vagueness of the future—he still thought they would make it through tonight, that somehow they would find a way through. In fact, since that eternity back in the crater-field . . . everything since then had been less difficult than he had feared.

He blinked, as if snapping out of a trance. Somewhere between seven and eight o'clock, he was pretty sure. What difference did it make? When they saw the first dull ghost back in the eastern sky they would know.

A violent firefight distracted them from their own situation.

It was a long way away, though both highly visible and very loud in the blackness.

They both spoke at the same time, not loudly enough in the noise to hear one another. They glanced at each other, they kept looking.

Off to the southwest was where it was. More or less where the Novo Sokolniki road lay.

Freitag raised his voice.

"They've run into the Russians."

Schrader continued to watch. There was small arms fire and the more extreme concussive violence of heavy weapons, intense bursts of light. He could make out heavy guns firing from two different places.

"No," he said. "No, I think that's our own lines over there. Tribukait doesn't have any firepower. I think it's the Russians going at it with Wohler's people."

Freitag grew more animated now, staring at the place, trying to talk.

It did seem to be artillery fire and then answering artillery fire. They could both see it was that.

"Maybe Tribukait is trying to get through," said Freitag. "Maybe they're caught between the lines."

Schrader wondered. At first he thought they couldn't have made it that far, not yet. He thought again. He looked at his watch. Maybe they had then, if Tribukait's people had been able to move on at a fast enough pace.

They stared and saw freedom out there, in the intense violent light. They stared with hunger and apprehension. Schrader saw how close the bursting light appeared yet he also knew how far away it really was. Two or three miles was right. Or maybe more. And even if they headed in exactly that direction . . .

But they couldn't do that. They would walk right into it. They would have to steer to one side of all that.

"Goddamn it. We need to get going."

"I'm ready," said Freitag.

"No. Not yet. We might be seen. Goddamn it anyway."

"No one will see us. It's too far away."

"No," said Schrader.

Freitag was ready to move and he wanted to move before he dwelt any longer on how spent he was. He clenched his teeth and felt his breath pass icily between them. He felt tears welling in his eyes and he shut them. He opened them and clearly saw the half-track for the first time, strobed in the distant violent light. Bodies lay everywhere in the snow and Schrader looked at them too, more of them than he had imagined in the darkness. Flashes of light revealed hideous distortions, untrue twistings of limbs or trailings of scalps . . . more mutilations, or else only the aftermath of hand-to-hand stabbing and grenading; they couldn't see it clearly enough in the convulsive inconstant light.

Freitag looked at the half-track, gutted by explosions; gutted a second time, if he bothered to think of it, by the Russians making off with wheels, guns, gun shields, engine parts, anything not completely destroyed. The vehicle was a skeleton. He saw the heads of dead men still peering out above the side wall of the rear compartment; he knew what they were but he was startled all the same. In the lightning light they seemed still alive somehow, staring as he was staring; even one with a skull bloated like a melon above a twisted smashed-in grin seemed to be staring at the distant violence, just as they themselves were.

A creature, thought Freitag. An actual creature. Hardly knowing what he meant. Panic began to seep through him.

"They might go on all night like that," he shouted at Schrader.

"Keep your voice down. The damned bastards. Goddamn it, maybe they will."

He had hoped for the firefight to settle down, been waiting for that. But maybe it wouldn't

"All right, let's get out of here. Here. Give me your hand."

It was still dark when they came to the edge of the woods. Freitag was chewing on another bit of rag now, to keep himself from groaning. He would chew on it rhythmically, then he would take it out of his mouth for a few minutes so he could breathe better. Then he would start chewing on it again. It was a kind of distraction, something to occupy him while he set one foot in front of another.

From prolonged suffering he was lurching more and more into a state of complete agony.

What is the matter with this goddamned thing, he would think again, wanting to shout it aloud out of pure frustration. From the beginning he had been resigned to his difficulties, determined to overcome them, though he knew he might have trouble keeping up. But he had thought he was not really badly wounded after all; he couldn't understand the trouble he was having.

They came to the edge of the woods. It was something anyway. They had marched across the snowy void for a long time and at last felt they might be getting somewhere.

They went into the trees, stopping to rest again after only a few feet.

They had come across the first Russians only a short time before. Still out on the plain. The firefight off in the distance had diminished somewhat, though there were still bursts of light over there, muzzle flashes, explosions, sometimes flares soaring in silence, odd and feeble-looking in the distance. They had seen the gun barrels outlined against the sky, a Russian artillery battery.

For a long time they had waited, listening, barely raising their heads. Smelling too, smelling the odor of cordite, of gasoline or lubricating oil, of horses; odors of dirty majorka carrying through the clear air to hypersensitive nostrils. They listened and heard the small noises of horses in the night, tethered somewhere; and human voices, relaxed, weary, businesslike. Noises of people moving things about, carrying loads somewhere, dropping them in the snow.

They could sense the attitudes of men who did not perceive themselves in any immediate danger. Voices ordinary
and tired, quiet yet carrying clearly enough during windless
intervals. Even so there would be sentries about. And if
there were Russians here there would be other Russians
somewhere else not far off, another battery, foot soldiers; it
seemed they had come to the end of the long empty space.

They felt tension that was no worse than it had been in the
crater-field; no moments could be more acute than those had
been. But they lay there and felt their hearts beating and their
nerves tightening more and more, stretching out the last coils
of elasticity inside their bodies. They wanted to cry out, or
they thought about it anyway, imagined themselves crying
out just to dispel this stress, to finish everything. The Russians would come, take them prisoner, lead them off, and do
whatever they were going to do with them.

They dared not move for fear the battery might start firing,
expose them in the muzzle flashes. The artillery duel off in
the distance still rumbled intermittently and they expected
these guns they had stumbled into would also be in action.
But nothing happened and the guns nearby remained silent.
They waited, not knowing what to do. Schrader listened, listening for the peculiar noises of men readying their guns for
a firing assignment. He was not entirely sure what he heard;
then unexpectedly the salvo began.

They felt stripped naked in the blasts of light. They burrowed their heads in the snow, cupping their ears, their jaws
hanging open. Freitag wept when the shock waves thumped
against him. But he made no sound.

Schrader could hear them loading the shells now, after the
deafness cleared from his ears. Another salvo went out.

The guns fired for about ten minutes, or whatever the time
was; they had no real sense of it. Then they fell silent again.
Voices were louder now in the aftermath of this, Russians
deafened as well talking loudly to one another. The chink of
metal, of any small sounds, was louder.

They waited a while longer. When they had first noticed
the guns they knew they were close by, silhouetted by the
rumbling lights on the horizon. But it was an illusion of objects existing at a certain distance in space, in the dark; for in

the long minutes of firing, of intense haloes of light thrown out by the muzzle flashes, they saw they were much closer to the battery than they had realized, as if they had somehow been transported to within only a hundred feet of it. They stared at the guns in front of them and they looked from side to side and also to their rear, their nerves crawling with the feeling that instead of coming up to the edge of some group of the enemy they had somehow wandered right into the middle of them. Schrader kept glancing back over his shoulder, into the blackness. Freitag did this too, until his discomfort became so great that he simply laid his forehead down into the snow, aware only of Schrader's dim shape out of the corner of his eye.

When the darkness finally resumed they still felt utterly exposed, a feeling of helplessness leading almost to resignation, which perhaps made it a little more bearable; but not that much. At last they crept away. They did not try to circle around this place. They retreated directly back the way they had come. Schrader had studied the muzzle flashes of other batteries beyond the first one, off in a certain direction. For hundreds of yards they retreated directly back into the void they had crossed, until they dared to begin making a wide arc around the entire area. It was hard to move carefully now, they were so tired, without losing their momentum altogether; they feared more than ever they might stumble into a Russian patrol.

So when they came at last into the woods they counted it a blessing. They stayed for a long time just inside the edge of the trees, sitting like dead men in the deeper snow that had collected around the boles and fallen branches.

"We'll never make it," Freitag said sometime.

"Yes, we will," Schrader said stubbornly.

He was glad to be in these trees. He thought of nothing but this relief for a while. By now he had given up any hope of making it through before daylight. In the forest it was easier to accept that.

He said this to Freitag. Freitag began to feel less anxious, sinking into dead exhaustion; it was almost comfortable there. My God, my God, he thought. Now he felt unburdened of his most immediate source of anxiety, that his pace would slow them both down, that daylight would come and they would still be wandering, that it would be his fault.

But now he didn't have to worry about it anymore. Daylight would come and there was nothing they could do about it. Schrader had said so and he accepted it as Schrader did. In the woods they felt safe. Nothing else mattered.

The snow was deeper in the woods, hanging from the branches of firs and caught in windblown drifts among all kinds of other tangled branches, undergrowth. Freitag lay on his back in the snow with his head resting on a snow-covered log, feeling almost as if he were lying in a bed. He wanted to go to sleep. Schrader did too. This was the second winter they had endured in this country; by now they had enough sense of the cold and their own bodies to know they weren't going to fade away and freeze to death.

Or at least they thought they knew this. But some dim worry or uncertainty would prevent them from feeling secure enough to just nod off; they could never quite shake their anxieties about drifting into sleep and never awakening.

In fact this was the last thing to pass through Freitag's mind, this dull hook of fear in his belly, before he did nod off for a while.

Schrader spoke to him, gripped his cheekbones with one hand, and shook his head slightly. Freitag mumbled something. Schrader let him be, thinking it would be all right for the boy to sleep for a few minutes.

It was nothing, this cold, compared to what they had endured the year before. He thought so.

He sat with his knees drawn up, with his forearms resting on his knees, staring straight ahead at the impenetrable blackness of tangled firs, which made the memory of the open plain seem almost like a kind of daylight. He stared straight ahead or sometimes propped his forehead between his fingers and stared down at the equally dark ground between his boots. His boots, Russian felt boots, were thrust halfway into a snowdrift, giving him a feeling of support, steadiness. It was comfortable. He leaned back against a tree trunk and it was comfortable. He stared at nothing.

He felt the vacantness in his mind for a while, it seemed to do him good; he tried not to disturb it with any worries or planning ahead.

He looked overhead, where there were stars between the fir crowns, jagged treetops silhouetted in some profound design the way the ruins of the city had been. Vague patches sometimes blotted the stars, moving along, more clouds coming in above. Just as well.

At length, then, he began to think things over some more.

He broke off part of a branch, shook snow from it, then set it down flat in the snow between his feet. That was Wohler's group. He stared down at it, even though he couldn't see it in the dark, but he felt it nudged against his left boot. It helped him to concentrate. Left boot was west, right boot was east. North in front of him, south behind him.

The branch, Wohler's group, had been coming from the southwest. They would have advanced beyond the main line, forming a salient reaching almost to the city. So that was it, the branch, the salient, angled out from his left boot.

Two or three miles, he had been thinking; but that was just to reach the tip of the salient, to the southwest somewhere. From the activity they had heard and seen during the night, that whole area would be swarming with the enemy. Perhaps by now Wohler's group would even have been driven back a ways.

What remained of the rest of the main line he really didn't know. Tribukait had sketched it out for them in the citadel, but reports from units other than Wohler's group had been spotty. They would be off to the west somewhere, perhaps only a few miles, but his sense of this was vague.

His sense of these forests was also vague. He remembered a few marked with names on the maps, but many of these wooded areas were too patchy and irregular to have names. These woods where they were now, for example—he could not picture what or where they might be, in relation to anything else. He could not picture it and did not try to, remembering crossing these areas at different times during the year gone by, last winter, also sometimes in spring, in summer, autumn.

There was never one big forest but only a crazy patchwork

of wooded areas. He remembered marching for hours across empty plains and moors, like the stretch they had crossed tonight. Yet all of a sudden there would be a patch of forest on the horizon, or several patches; and they would march on and enter those woods, deep, tangled places, and after they had been in there for a while the forest would begin to seem as endless as the plain outside it.

At length they would emerge from the trees and come upon another plain, or boggy, mosquito-infested moorland, and across the distances in one direction or another they would see other woodlands scattered about, like small worlds, each seeming insignificant from a distance, yet each becoming larger and deeper whenever they tried to penetrate into them. Gloomy places, tangled, pathless.

He remembered all this. He remembered the operations from the year before along the Velizh road, to clear out the Kamenka Wald, the Kasten Wald. Woodlands named only because they had had to deal with them, named only because men had been lost trying to clear them out.

Otherwise it was nothing but a crazy quilt.

The operations outside Velizh . . . also other operations during the fall, after von Manstein's offensive had finally been called off, and they had been detached from the line to take care of business in the rear areas for a few weeks, before finally being posted inside Velikiye Luki . . .

So he knew these woodlands, he thought . . . but only well enough to understand that trying to use them as landmarks, to help find their way, would come to nothing.

Why was he wasting his time thinking all this through then? He didn't know, yet sensed a faint satisfaction all the same, establishing the landscape within his mind, however feeble his grasp of it might be.

But then he remembered the point of it all—that if these woodlands kept on then they could keep on as well, even during daylight, without being seen. If dawn had found them still out on the plain they would have had to lay low, to wait, to freeze, to suffer the crawl of the hours until night fell again. But in the forest they could keep going.

So they would just keep on going to the west. Sooner or later they would come to their own people. If they were lucky, the Russians would have only intermittent positions over that way. If their lines were more built up, they would just have to find a way through regardless.

He felt more animated suddenly and reached over and shook Freitag. Freitag rose slowly, covered in snow.

"How are you feeling?" said Schrader.

"I was dreaming."

"You feel any better?"

"*Ja*. Maybe so," said Freitag.

He tried to stand, he managed to get up without assistance. He hurt all over. But the pains in certain places weren't quite so sharp. Or at least he felt he could breathe a little better.

"Let's get going then," said Schrader.

"Through the woods?"

"No, not yet. We'd just get lost in the dark. And you'd wind up stumbling all over yourself. We'll follow along the edge until daybreak."

"All right," said Freitag.

They followed along the edge of the trees in what he judged to be a southwesterly direction. He looked for patterns of stars he had seen earlier, while crossing the plain, constellations whose names he didn't know but which he had studied carefully. But there was too much cloud cover now; he couldn't find any markers up in the sky. They kept on going regardless, inertia, momentum, pushing them along at the edge of the trees. It seemed it should be near dawn but they trudged on for a long time still in the blackness of night. On their left, or sometimes behind them, they could still see a dim glow across the void, from the city, from Velikiye Luki.

They heard vehicles again. The Novo Sokolniki road up there, or some road. They began to fear running into a Russian patrol flanking along the trees. Dawn would be coming now anyway. They broke off into the forest again, pausing to rest again in the dark trees, until daylight came.

They both slept a little, some kind of sleep. Nodding off, awakening, nodding off again. Dreaming fragments of dreams that seemed very real, even after they opened their eyes again. Dreams that seemed like memories of actual events rather than the distorted figments that they were. Schrader opened his eyes and was surprised to see the darkness still absolute, and he wondered when the night would ever end. He remembered Freitag screaming in agony, disappearing down into one of those craters, left behind there; he remembered the rest of them scrambling madly to escape, to get across that awful death-field, in the flare-light and the gunfire, leaving Freitag behind, his screams drowned out by the noise from everywhere.

His eyes were open and he considered all this, as if it had actually happened that way. The gradations of his consciousness were curious and vague and there was no distinct moment when he realized that Freitag was still with him, his body huddled against him in the deeper snow of the woods. He felt Freitag's body crouched against his own, yet still he reached out with his hand to touch him, to feel that he was there. The memory, the dream-memory, was still very real but nothing about it surprised him, as if two alternate courses of events, of life and death, might both exist. He mused over this without the slightest sense of mystery or confusion, because he knew it meant nothing, and he was too tired and there was no strangeness to anything anymore.

Freitag in his own deep inner darkness beside him remembered being buried alive in the same house as Kordts. That infuriating pain deep in his chest or lungs; it was from being crushed along with Kordts underneath all those beams and stones, that was how it had happened; it all came clear now. It was a horror but to understand it all now finally was a relief and it detached him from the horror, he floated slowly away.

In the dawn they got up and looked at each other. The small clouds of their breathing drifted up in the air. Schrader felt strong now, hungry, yearning for something to eat; but strong all the same. They had nothing with them to eat. Freitag felt stronger too, a little bit anyway. The cold actually made him feel better, revived him somehow. Dawn. Morning. Another day and both still alive, and at their strongest at the beginning of the day.

They felt safe enough to have a smoke. They smoked and appraised each other and looked at their surroundings; for a few minutes it all seemed possible, even more possible than during the night. That they would just keep going, that they would get through sooner or later.

Schrader expected clouds but again they had drifted off and again the sky was clear. The deep snow-blanketed woods had a kind of utterness all about, an unspeakable quality in the crystal air. The sky was blue and there was an agonizing beauty to this place where they were; they perceived it now, at the peak of their strength in early morning. They stared about, smoking, breathing quietly.

Then they moved on deeper into the woods, marking the sun to the east, following away from it toward the west. The sun would follow its winter arc along the southern horizon during the course of the day; Schrader understood this and studied the sun to keep it always somewhat to the left of them, to keep it in its right place. The sky was clear and it was easy enough to do this.

But the physical act of going through the woods became harder and harder, because the firs grew close to each other, and their heavily laden branches grew close to the ground. And the ground itself was littered with logs and fallen branches that seemed to have accumulated there for a thousand years. They followed their noses, that is to say they followed any thread of open space through the trees, regardless of direction, zigzagging, meandering about, Schrader constantly checking the left-hand sun; or if they were facing directly into it then that meant they were heading south, and they looked for the next thread of space through the thickets that would lead them west again, with the sun returning to its station up there.

Thus they kept on a true enough path toward the west, even though their progress kept shifting back and forth, back and forth like a meandering river. The air was very clean and they noticed this after the endless filth-clogged, death-clogged bitter air of the siege. The snow had mostly blown off the tops of the firs, and the treetops were a terrible green in the clear air; while closer to the ground, where more snow still hung accumulated on the branches, the light was reflected off a thousand little suns, dazzling them from time to time. All in all, though, there was a clear emptiness all about them that mostly sucked the glare away. Between objects, between trees and tangle and snowdrifts, they seemed to move within an almost palpable invisibility; as if the atmosphere were constructed from plates of invisibility that they might almost touch if they reached out with their hands in certain ways.

It was too laborious though. They both began to curse the denseness of the woods, silently at first and then cursing out loud to each other. They kept thinking that the trees would thin out somewhere, grow more parklike, easier to move through; but they didn't and they began to have the gnawing feeling that they weren't getting anywhere. For Schrader it was not so difficult; he could struggle through this all day if he had to, but even for him it was difficult because he was worried about Freitag keeping up.

It was impossible for Freitag to keep going without hurting himself, bumping into things, struggling with low-hanging branches, stumbling over things. They both did that, but with Freitag it kept bringing new surges to his pain, that he thought he might be able to deal with today, and the pain continually surged through him and surged out of him, sucking his strength out with it, filling him with exhaustion. He didn't want to stop anymore, to rest, but more and more often he had to.

Continually he would let out little noises, not quite groans or cries, the continual grunting mumble of his pain, trying to breathe in some steady fashion. His right arm, the one that dangled uselessly from his smashed shoulder, was supported in a makeshift sling tied around his neck. His right hand and forearm swayed back and forth in the sling from the movements of his body, bumping endlessly against his chest. He remembered chewing on the rag the night before but disdained that any longer. He only wanted to take in air, gulp it down easily, without hurting so much. For hours at a time he was crying, tears running down his cheeks; he was hardly aware of it except when the moisture became irritating and he wiped it away with his good hand. Schrader could easily see how the boy was struggling; but Freitag was sealed inside his own body and the pain was worse than Schrader knew. Freitag was young and determined, determined to keep going on until he dropped. For hours at a time he had almost nothing left but his own pigheadedness.

The sun followed its southerly arc. Noon came. The sun hung in a direct perpendicular upon their left-hand sides. Schrader checked his watch. He thought of resting because it was noon but he said nothing and they went on. They had already rested several times and would have to do so again.

Finally the woods did thin out a little. The firs gave way to more naked tangles of branches, scrub woods, swamp woods. The scrubby growth was not so tall as the firs, the bare branches frailer, flimsier, easier to push through. Schrader considered that in the summer all of this would be overgrown like a nightmare. But not now.

The scrubby thickets gave way to dead reeds standing in the sun. The old stalks had a singular presence standing in the clear air, just as everything did. Schrader stared at them, he stared on ahead. Some kind of small marsh bird darted among the reeds, coming to rest in a dead bush; he watched it with feelings difficult to ascertain, he was too tired to feel astonishment, though it was the first creature he had seen in many months.

"A bird," he muttered to Freitag.

Freitag noticed it too, the darting movement, though he was seeing nearly double for long moments now, or so absorbed in his difficulties that he no longer saw anything other than unfocused blurs. The crisp air that had made him feel a little better in the morning was now just another source of pain. It felt like lumps he was swallowing, cold heavy lumps in his throat and down in his chest. He hardly made any noises now, of pain or anything else, apart from his breathing. He stared at the little bird but his vision swam and he narrowed his eyes and looked at nothing. He had been plodding on and on in the company of strange thoughts, purposeful self-deceptions that might keep his exhaustion at bay. Over and over he reminded himself that his legs were fine and that they would carry him on, that they would be able to bear the entire miserable leaden sack of his upper body like the legs of a draft horse hauling a burden, plodding mindlessly on and on. At times he lapsed into a vague purplish state of semiconsciousness, no longer aware of anything except the dull shape of Schrader moving just ahead. He felt the things an injured man feels while trying to keep up with someone fit—jealousy, vague impulses of hysteria, gratitude and resentment, both as if they were the same thing, all of this swam through him in a blur which he more or less ignored, as unable to focus on these things as on his surroundings.

More and more he wanted to be left, thinking it would be better for him that way; but he was still afraid of that too.

They walked out into the reeds. They came to the edge of a pond, small lake, snow-covered. An open space, marked by a few more clumps of pale reeds out there, tilting slightly in a faint moaning breeze through the blue sky. Schrader saw a few tracks of small animals. Freitag saw hardly anything.

How to get around this open area? Perhaps a quarter of a mile across. Or should they just walk on out there, keep going that way?

Schrader's mind was becoming leaden as well, intent only on his own momentum; he didn't want to think about anything. He pushed thoughts of anything aside and almost began to walk out there, unable to imagine, stubbornly refusing to imagine, that there could be any living souls about for miles.

But his gut tightened and he stopped. He couldn't do it. Yes, all right, don't be stupid, he thought, whispering this to himself with himself barely listening; don't be stupid, not now, not at any time.

Freitag was even more a slave to his momentum—it was the only thing he had—and he dumbly followed Schrader and then bumped into him when Schrader stopped. His legs were wobbling, he bent over slightly and turned around in a small circle, afraid to sit down. He understood what the problem was, why Schrader had halted, but couldn't say anything, couldn't think anything. He would just do whatever Schrader did, until he collapsed. Schrader was studying the circumference of the lake. He backed up a few steps, then turned around, taking hold of Freitag's good hand.

They retreated back through the reeds to the scrubbier edge, until they were hidden again. They began to make their

way around the lake, moving more cautiously now, Freitag
coming up to Schrader and leaning against him several
times, resting his forehead against Schrader's back.

At length they saw that they couldn't go around. The lake
didn't end. It narrowed into a place like a neck or channel,
but this went on almost as far as they could see. In the distance the neck appeared to widen out again into another,
larger lake. There were more reeds out there, no backdrop of
trees; they sensed the presence of this other lake or clearing,
saw it in the blue emptiness of the sky hanging close above.

The passage in front of them was clumped with more
reeds, rushes, too sparse for concealment. A distance of a
few hundred feet lay between them and the other side.

Freitag looked at this fixedly, his eyes glazing over. He
was afraid Schrader would want to keep going around, following the circuitous path around the edge of that big indefinite space in the distance. The idea of this filled him with
dread.

"It's too far," he gasped, as if Schrader would understand
him. He was leaning against his back again. Schrader understood, and he also thought it was too far. He just didn't want
to go on in that direction. It was the wrong direction and he
didn't want to go any further that way.

"Let's just go," he said, not indicating which way he meant
but looking at the nearer edge of woods across the channel a
few hundred feet away. "I'll go across. You come when I get
over there."

"No, let me go first," said Freitag. "You've got the gun."

"All right," said Schrader, thinking it didn't matter who
went first.

Freitag went across, reaching out with one hand as if the
frail reeds might support him. Schrader waited, clenching his
teeth, momentarily maddened by his crazy sense of caution,
as if he could hear the loneliness and emptiness of everything mocking him, gnawing at his strength. He calmed himself. He looked at Freitag and studying him from a distance
saw more acutely how pitiful he looked; still he could not
help but admire the boy's determination. It was always like
this, he thought, thinking of the woods and the marshes. The
damned woods just seemed to go on forever, until you got to

the end of them, and you never knew when you would get to
the end of them. He had pretty much lost all sense of how far
they had come, could no longer imagine how far they had to
go, maddening as it was to still think it could not be that
much further, not that much further. The utter silence of
everything except for the dull wind, the dull faint moaning
of the firs, had been all right throughout the course of this
day. But now he wanted to hear something again, gunfire off
in the distance, anything to indicate they were getting somewhere. He stared at Freitag, plodding laboriously as if
through deep drifts, though the snow was not so deep. He
found himself staring at Freitag's shadow, a long dark pencil
in the snow, in the lowering daylight.

He vanished into the woods over there and Schrader followed him across. As he walked across the open space he
suddenly noticed the tracks Freitag had left in the snow, the
tracks both of them were leaving in the snow. A goddamned
highway. All day long and he had never thought of that, nor
last night either for that matter. He shook his head.

They went on. After a while the firs grew more densely
again, as they had done before, the snow-laden boughs and
the snow-draped tangle of deadfall everywhere underneath.
They couldn't stand it anymore, Schrader no less than Freitag. The daylight was short; evening was coming. For them
though, the daylight had not seemed so short; even on a short
winter's day, the time would stretch out into a kind of eternity for two men trying to find their way through an unknown wilderness. So it seemed to them that they had been
walking on and on for endless hours—dawn, morning, noon,
afternoon, evening, dusk—each interval of the day bearing
its peculiar kind of light and seeming as long as an entire day
by itself, all of these hours stretched out chaotically behind
them now, the time seeming to them much longer than it actually had been. It was real enough to them, but even so the
pace of the sun remained unchanged and the winter day remained short; and so it was evening now, dark blue light,
shadows. They had had enough of this infernal struggling.
Finally they stopped in a small space—you couldn't even
call it a clearing—only a few yards across.

Freitag was near to delirium and when he understood they

were going to be in these woods another night he stopped
trying to fight it, he let it wash over him in purple-spotted exhaustion and utter senselessness, weeping copiously. In fact
for hours now he had hardly tried to resist it, it didn't make
anything more difficult or less difficult, maybe it made it less,
he didn't know. But now at the end of another day he gave in
to it entirely, hearing a mad babble of voices inside his head,
much the same as the blood roaring inside his head. He
wanted to talk, to blurt things out in a senseless rush, but he
just sat where he was, too spent to say anything.

Schrader crouched beside him, saying a few things to him,
grasping the back of Freitag's head, patting him lightly
there, smoothing the dirty hair on the back of his head.

"It's all right, boy. You'll feel better after you've rested a
while. You've done very well, Freitag. Very well."

"*Ja,*" said Freitag, nodding his head back and forth, his
eyes still glazed over. Schrader could almost see the spots
dancing in front of the other one's eyes.

"I want to look at you," Schrader said.

Freitag nodded again.

Carefully Schrader drew back the empty sleeve of the
greatcoat, pulling the right half of the greatcoat off Freitag's
shoulder. Old blood was crusted on the shoulder of the tunic
underneath, hardly distinguishable from sweat, dirt, grease,
all encrusted there. Shapeless stains. Schrader unbuttoned
the tunic. He pulled the collar a little to one side so he could
see Freitag's shoulder. Freitag winced but he was still so
done in that he didn't notice the pain much, didn't complain,
continued to stare senselessly into the trees all around the
tiny space. He felt he could tolerate anything so long as he
didn't have to walk any further.

Beneath the tunic he wore an undershirt, several undershirts, sweaty, bloody, dirty. The stains there were moist and
reeking from perspiration. Schrader had some idea of the
damage now, knobs of bone thrusting at the thin cloth layers.
When he attempted to stretch the collars of these undershirts
a little to look better Freitag trembled, still uncomplaining
like an injured horse or dog, his eyes flared wide.

"I'm going to cut the collar open a little," said Schrader.

"No, don't do that," said Freitag. "It feels better with the undershirts. If you cut them away my tunic will rub me there. It will hurt worse."

He said this calmly, sensibly, as if his normal faculties had returned all of a sudden. Schrader paused, the bayonet half-withdrawn from the belt scabbard beneath the folds of his greatcoat. Freitag looked him in the eye.

"Go ahead and feel it if you want. It's not so bad."

Freitag reached over with his good arm, still encased in the other sleeve of his greatcoat, touching the ugly sunken knobs with his fingers to show Schrader it was all right to touch him there.

Schrader set the bayonet on his knee and reached out and carefully felt along the bones through the cloth undershirts. The clavicle . . . smashed down in a V-shape almost to the top of the ribs. Freitag winced, flaring his nostrils. Schrader winced too. He then reached around and felt along Freitag's back, felt the shoulder blade, several pieces of it like cracked tiles. Freitag made a noise deep in his throat.

"Damned right," said Schrader. "I'll bet that hurts."

Freitag exhaled quietly. He said, "It doesn't matter about that. Look at my chest, why don't you, if you have to look."

"Just take it easy," said Schrader.

"All right. All right. Just lift my shirt up. Don't try and cut anything."

Slowly Schrader pulled up the dirty layers. He looked at white skin that had not seen the light of day, nor felt the touch of air, in many weeks. The shadows of trees were long now and he could not see very well. It was still light out, the low sun sitting quietly up in the trees; but he had been staring into bright sky and bright snow for hours and it took a few moments before he could see very well, somewhat color-blind in the evening shadows. There was darkness along Frei-tag's ribs beneath his shoulder. He blinked and saw the discolorations a little better, deep bruises, purple, yellow. He felt the ribs to see if they were broken; Freitag kept saying they weren't. Schrader passed his hand over them lightly and could feel no breaks.

"Hurt?" he said.

"No," said Freitag. He was lying, but when he was sitting at rest the pain didn't seem to matter. "Go ahead, smack it a few times, ha, ha."

He winced again, but it was only from talking, from making this little laughing noise.

Schrader didn't know what to make of it. He leaned over, sniffing for gangrene. You don't get gangrene in your chest, he thought. This seemed like common sense, but in fact he wasn't so positive of it. He smelled nothing, nothing but the odor of sweat and the snowy cold. Tenderly he rolled the undershirts back down.

He wondered if there could be blood poisoning from the broken shoulder bones, or some kind of internal injury.

"Let me look at your shoulder again, Freitag. I'll have to cut it to see."

"It won't make any difference until we get to a doctor."

"Let me look. I'll give you a piece of cloth to put over it so your tunic won't rub."

"All right," said Freitag resignedly.

They spoke to each other with a strange patient mixture of tenderness and withheld hostility, weariness, stress, ongoing fear.

Schrader sliced away the undershirts at the collar, one layer at a time. The blade was sharp enough but it was difficult to get a good purchase while doing it delicately. The flat part of the blade bumped against bone and Freitag made a gagging noise. Impatiently Schrader grabbed the collar in one hand and ripped upward with a single jerk.

"All right, it's done. Just hold still."

Freitag was gasping violently. He squeezed his eyes shut. More tears ran down, through the dried paths of tears that had covered his cheeks all day.

"It's an ugly mess," said Schrader.

Freitag turned his head to see but he could not see his own shoulder very well. He lifted his head at some indefinite angle, tears still streaming down his face, staring dully into the black evening trees.

"Are you satisfied, Schrader?"

Schrader touched the swollen flesh, red and ugly, stretched

over the fractures like a collapsed tent. It was infected but he could not tell how badly. He felt for pus, swells of fluid underneath, squeezing a little harder, watching Freitag to see if he would cry out. Freitag shut his eyes harder, weeping and weeping, making no sound. He opened his eyes and stared again at the evening trees through a glistening film of tears, breathing with hoarse, steady patience.

"All right. You've got guts, boy. Remember I said that."

"Sure," said Freitag, in a distracted whisper, still staring vacantly out there.

Schrader stared at the shiny white chest, rising and falling, at the white belly beneath it, quietly rising and falling. He rolled the undershirts back down. He made to help Freitag with his sling again, with his tunic and greatcoat, but Freitag said to just let him be for a minute.

Schrader took the bayonet and pulled out part of his own undershirt, cutting out a patch of material and laying it on Freitag's leg. He said there was an infection and when they got through, a doctor would take care of it. Freitag nodded, still staring with a strange fixation.

Schrader imagined him looking at nothing, concentrating on staying calm while he had been hurting him and probing at him. Dully he ran his finger along the edge of the bayonet, staring at it, thinking things to himself, thinking nothing at all. He slid the blade back into the scabbard; he stood up, felt his muscles stretching, felt deep pangs of hunger.

What the devil is he looking at? he thought. He turned around in the small, claustrophobic, snow-covered space where they were.

It was only the sun. Schrader sat down again, studying it too, for no better reason than Freitag had.

The sun was setting but there was no real sunset. The sky was not red but only a deeper blue, a deeper blue. The sun was the same white disc it had been all day. It seemed very close to them somehow, as if it were not setting beyond the earth's rim but merely sinking into the woods no more than a few hundred yards away. It sat quietly in the tree limbs like a presence or a being.

Freitag stared as if in a trance, thinking it odd that he

could stare directly into the evening sun without hurting his
eyes. The dark clarity of the world had annihilated any glare
and there was only the light, though light stripped curiously
of its most forceful element. All was still. Cold air continued
to moan faintly in the tops of the firs, but the nearby sun
seemed to diminish everything within a profound stillness.
Freitag stared through the tears that still coated his eyes, as if
he were watching the sun from beneath the surface of shallow water. He blinked the tears away after a while and saw
better. Still he could look straight into it without any hurt to
his eyes. The sun hung in the tree limbs like a presence or a
being; it seemed to be speaking to him, though he knew it
was not, and he did not hear anything in his ears or within his
mind. Still, it was like that somehow.

Schrader saw some of these same things. The sun setting
in the winter woods. The firs were black jagged spears, but
there were also bare deciduous woods over there, tangled in
stranger patterns. There seemed more space between those
trees, and Schrader became fixated on an illusion of the sun
going down in the middle of another clearing or frozen lake
only a few hundred yards away. He did not believe this but
the strange appearance of the light was so convincing that he
decided he had to go see for himself. Perhaps the woods
came entirely to an end and there was another empty plain
over there. Which would mean . . . if Freitag could recuper-
ate for a while . . . that they might keep on going during the
night without getting lost. And they would have to cross it
during the night; they couldn't do it during daylight. He
didn't know, he had to go see.

He said this to Freitag.

Freitag was calmer now, not so unnerved at the prospect of
Schrader disappearing.

"There's nothing over there, Schrader," he said, though he
wasn't arguing. In fact even as he it said he began to acquire
the same illusion, which was only another form of anxiety
after all, the gnawing urge to see if there might be an end to
all this only a little ways away.

"I'll only be a few minutes," Schrader said. "Don't worry,
I'll find you. I'll just follow my tracks."

"*Ja.* Go ahead," said Freitag, more dully now. His head began to hurt suddenly and he blinked and turned his gaze away, staring into the shadowy snow where he sat. Schrader was standing now, the tommy gun cradled in one elbow. Freitag glanced at him as he moved off, the light playing strangely about him as if he were a figure moving offstage in a play.

Freitag felt a surge of some incomprehensible emotion and wilted a little where he sat. With dull methodical movements he picked the scrap of shirt off his leg and folded it and placed it on his shoulder, spreading his fingers and moving it an inch this way or that, patting it lightly. With the one hand he pulled the tunic carefully over this padding, pressing it again to settle it as comfortably as he could. Then he buttoned the tunic, using both hands to do this, though his fingers were so numb he was almost unable to. He had been not much aware of the cold for a long time, other than in his lungs; in fact he had been sweating for most of the day. But now he felt it very acutely all of a sudden, in the evening shadows; a layer of ice seemed to descend entirely through him. He cursed, fumbling at the brass buttons. He pulled his greatcoat over his shoulder again, drawing the flaps tight against his chest, hunching over fearfully in the snow.

He too felt hungry now. His belly twisted and his mind felt black with hunger.

Schrader kept going a way further than he had intended. He knew he was following a chimera but could not resist thinking that you never knew, you never knew. . . . He went out a few hundred yards into a tall bare deciduous copse where his progress was not so difficult, he could move in a straight line easily enough. He went out to where he had imagined the sun to be setting in the middle of a large open area; but there were only more woods. He looked out at the same quiet white sun that again appeared to be illuminating some open space yet a few hundred yards further on. He went on into fir thickets again. Finally he had to force himself to turn back. He was not satisfied, for the illusion, the chimera, still persisted. He felt the gnawing disgruntlement that a man always tends to feel when pushing on and on through the woods, never finding anything. But night was falling now. He looked back at the blue marks of his tracks in the snow.

He went back. The sun was down by the time he returned to the small enclosed space. A red bar of sunset as thin as a blood vessel lay among the black trees behind him. The blue-blackness of night descended slowly down to this.

He tossed his weapon irritably down in the snow.

"Reminds me of the damned partisan woods," he said.

Freitag looked up, muttered something inaudible.

Some last thread of light fell on him, striking a dark gleam off the shoulder of his greatcoat, a bronze heaviness, the Cholm shield there. Schrader glanced at this. Cholmkampfer, Cholmkampfer, he thought senselessly.

The night would be an ordeal, a different one from the previous night, worse in some ways.

They sat dully apart from each other as night fell, shrunken up with hunger, their heads aching. But it was too cold and they moved next to each other, huddled against each other. They ate a little snow, though they knew that snow was not so good for assuaging thirst. They ate some anyway. It was clean at least, not polluted with the endless filth of the siege.

"Damn it to hell," said Freitag, saying this or something similar every few minutes, trembling in the cold, wracked with dull pain from this trembling. "It wasn't this cold last night."

"Probably it was," said Schrader. "We were moving last night."

Such a matter-of-fact remark still sounded reproachful to Freitag, his mind was disordered and he was sensitive to anything now. Again he imagined sinking down for good, starving or freezing to death or dying of his wounds, leaving Schrader free to move on at his own pace. He felt so terribly cold.

He kept thinking of building a fire, not wanting to be the one to say it. Finally he had to, just to relieve himself of the urge to say it out loud.

"Why don't we build a fire, Schrader? It will do us good."

It came out like a whine, or in his ears it sounded that way. He felt disgust for himself and trembled again.

Schrader said nothing, thinking there was nothing to say. He had been mulling over the same temptation, unable to put

it from his mind—the desire for a fire gnawing at both of
them like their desire for tobacco. He could read Freitag's
thoughts; they were no different from his own. In this place
they could make a fire without being seen; the chances of
it seemed infinitely remote, were certainly infinitely remote; it would not be careless. He recalled the momentary
fit of craziness when they had crossed the passageway between the lakes, the silent woods cruelly mocking his stupid sense of caution. Self-preservation seeming infantile
and perverse . . . let fate have its way, the silent ranks of trees
seemed to be saying with terrible persuasion.

"Goddamn it to hell," said Schrader.

"I know. I know," said Freitag.

Freitag was not satisfied, he was just so cold, but now that
he had said it aloud he thought he might be satisfied to just
suffer mindlessly, to endure in his misery. Now his hunger
seemed worse than anything he had endured during the day,
and the cold worse than hunger, the prospect of the freezing
night hours stretching on and on.

He began to talk of one thing or another, his normal way
of filling in idle hours, he didn't know what else to do. He
tried to force himself to sound cheerful, usually this came
more easily to him than to most people. He tried to force
himself to keep hold of this.

"It was worse at Cholm," he said. "Even before we got to
Cholm it was worse than this."

"Yes," agreed Schrader. "Those were the worst days of my
life."

He said this without a trace of irony, after existing for
fifty-three days within a ring of horror in Velikiye Luki. For
it was true. Nothing was worse than the cold, and nothing
else could be like those winter months of a year ago.

"Where were you then?" said Freitag.

"In Velizh," said Schrader.

"Where . . . where was that?"

"Not all that far from here. You haven't heard that name?"

"No. No, I don't think so."

"Christ. Christ," muttered Schrader to himself, meaning
nothing at all. He went on, "It couldn't be more than thirty
miles from here. Something like that. We were in France,

boy. No Russia for us. No Ostfront for us. Then just like that, right at Christmas, they packed us into a train. Two weeks later we got off. Vitebsk, I think it was. Then we marched to Velizh. We just had the clothes on our backs, the same stuff we'd worn in France. The worst days of my goddamned life. Jesus Christ, Jesus Christ."

A wave of madness exploded through him; he shut his eyes but otherwise hardly stirred a muscle. He was remembering Velizh, but that was really only part of it; the madness was that and everything else, everything, right up until this very instant. And yet the dull miserable force of the present instant was strong enough that the madness just swirled away, as quickly as it had come.

And so he continued to reminisce with Freitag for a while, the different things they had endured. He talked about France a little bit, the pleasures and easiness there; that seemed a good thing to talk about. Of Velikiye Luki they said nothing; they talked of things from before then.

Schrader shared none of Freitag's talkativeness but he talked for a while and listened to the story of Cholm for a while, to somehow fill in these black freezing minutes and freezing hours like sands trickling into an hourglass. Over these months, at least before it all began in Velikiye Luki, he had heard them both talking about it from time to time, Kordts and Freitag. They would be talking to some of the other men; Schrader himself had never listened very carefully, he hadn't wanted to, he hadn't wanted to hear any of their stories. Kordts had never said very much; mostly it had been Freitag, Schrader overhearing fragments of conversation now and then, hearing of things as he was hearing of them now. He listened more attentively now, thinking of keeping the boy preoccupied for a while.

There was the night cold and their attempts to talk for a while, to distract themselves, to keep from thinking of building a fire—even though they both found themselves gazing fixedly into the blackness as if into an invisible fire at their feet, into warm and hypnotic flames. Schrader listened and answered quietly sometimes and on some other simultaneous level he also found himself pondering, wondering how he had come to be with Freitag in this place. He wondered if he would have done the same if it had been one of the other men. He felt no allegiance anymore, not much anyway; he might have just gone on with Tribukait, severing all ties with some other wounded man unable to keep up; they had all done it then, only twenty-four hours ago. Only last night? Could all of that have only been a single night ago?

Strange questions arose in his mind which he felt no impulse to answer. Over the course of months he had felt somewhat relieved to see Freitag not lying so much in Kordts's shadow. Because he liked Freitag better, that was simple enough. The bond between them was obvious for anyone to see, but it had grown less irksome. Kordts was a strange case and often enough he didn't know whether he liked or disliked the man; he didn't know because he wasn't going to trouble himself about that. If he had troubled himself about anything it had had to do with that fixed unforgiving look that Kordts so often walked about with. Instinctively he had thought it might lead to something, but somehow it never had. Maybe it would have come to a head sometime; but instead he was dead. A few times he had talked about it with Krabel, wondering if there might come a moment when Kordts would endanger them all with some crazy refusal. It would have been of greater concern to him, no doubt should have been, if he had not withdrawn himself so much from all of them after the *Iltis* attack.

But Kordts had been dead for weeks and whatever he thought of the man had been dispersed already into obscure corners of his memory, dead obscurity shared out haphazardly and indifferently with the other dead who also resided there, coming to his mind now and again like corpses floating to the surface, then sinking away again. Only with Krabel was it not like that . . . and even Krabel, even Krabel shared that exile now, along with all those others.

These things came to him disjointedly, even while he listened to Freitag and spoke of other things to Freitag. A single moment of awareness would have sufficed to compress all these things into a single instant, because he already knew them, even if little trains of words filled up space in his mind for a few minutes, redundant activity of the brain.

Freitag's trembling, his shivering, aggravated his hurts

again. Still it was not as bad as walking. He could just sit here
and suffer, just sit here and suffer. . . . He dreaded the ordeal
of another day just as he dreaded the eternity of the night
hours before then. Every time he trembled he felt a crushing
sensation in his ribs, or beneath his ribs. Weird figments of
light and radiation and blue sky from the day just past played
in his mind again. For hours he had played a kind of game, if
you could call it a game, wherein instead of ignoring his pain
he had concentrated on it with a sort of absolute concentration, wherein the pain would achieve a kind of absolute state
that would release it from itself, and from hurting him; it
would become simply a thing or sensation like any other
thing or sensation—a snow-branch, a little bird, a breeze on
his forehead. Many times he had done this at Cholm, so he
could endure the frostbite in his hands and feet without
moaning and moaning. This strange little mental trick had
worked sometimes, or he seemed to remember that it had, for
as long as he could keep it up anyway, which had not always
been very long. So he had done this again today and in the
freezing dark he remembered doing it again today. But it was
all too unspeakable and he didn't know if anything had
worked or not, helped him keep going or not. He had just
kept going . . . and he feared having to do it all again tomorrow. Somehow this strange game had included the idea of
Kordts's dying, crushed to death beneath those beams and
stones, in that house, this idea becoming part of that strange
terrible concentration on his own pain, every time he felt his
breath being cut short in that one place beneath his ribs . . .
and so he was there with Kordts again, or maybe there instead of Kordts, buried beneath the wreck of that house. . . .

This idea had played over and over in his mind through the
day, repetitions blurring into utter senselessness, till there
was only the sense of some abstract rhythm repeating endlessly, like a fragment of a tune that he could not, or would
not, get out of his head.

Maybe it had helped. He couldn't think about it now. He
was too cold and too weary. He trembled and felt that dull
crushing sensation again and so Kordts came to his mind
again but then left just as quickly; the day was over now, the
cold was worse than the pain, he could no longer think of

anything except in the most disordered fashion. For a moment the evening sun—that evening sun of several hours earlier—seemed to hang within the exact center of his brain, the calm white sun hanging in the tangled branches, speaking to him with an utterness beyond language. Then that disappeared as well.

For some minutes he had exhausted his ability to speak normally and reminisce about one thing or another. In fact they had been talking for quite some time, he and Schrader; but still it was early in the night, the winter nights were so long.

"A fire would be nice," he said, as he had said before, though feeling no shame now.

"*Ja*," said Schrader. "A nice fire. A cozy little bunker in Russia."

"Ha, ha," said Freitag, a dry little rattle. He lifted a little snow to his mouth, feeling it settle on his cracked lips, on his tongue.

"How far did we come today?"

Schrader sat silently. Freitag was huddled close against his bulk.

"I tried to figure it out. But how can you? Too much walking back and forth. Maybe three or four miles, as the crow flies. I'm only guessing."

This was not very reassuring but it had come out before he could think of a better way of putting it. What better way was there?

"We might have to go another ten or twenty miles," said Freitag. The idea came to him with an awesome horror which even so he observed with indifference.

"No. No, it couldn't be that far," Schrader said.

He firmly believed this, though knowing at this point he could no longer be certain of anything.

"It's just these woods," he said. "Everything seems slower. We'll get there. We'll get there."

"Why don't you try to sleep, Freitag? I'm here. I'll keep an eye on you."

"It's dark," said Freitag.

"Don't worry. I'm right here. Try to rest."

"You must wake me every so often."

"The damned cold will wake you. It will wake both of us.

Believe me. For Christ's sake, it will be all right, boy. It's cold but it's not that cold. Try not to think of that."

"All right," said Freitag.

Maybe it made sense. His hands and his feet were very cold but there was not that agony he remembered from the bitterest days and nights. But the core of his body was terribly cold, an icy void inside him that sometimes shrank and sometimes expanded. It was all too much. He tried to sleep but it was too cold to sleep. He listened to his teeth chattering. Then finally he slept.

He awoke feeling that he was dying of the cold, dreaming it first and then feeling it exactly the same when he awoke.

They had both settled into sleep, no longer huddled so tightly against each other, their limbs too weary to cling to each other.

He was too cold to know of anything else. He rolled over in the snow, so cold that he did not bother to move carefully on his injured side, huddling against Schrader's body again.

It occurred to him that he had awakened. Schrader had been right about that. He felt a small measure of relief, not much. His jaw trembled back to its hinges. Again he was too cold to sleep and he lay there until the fever broke over him. He was awash in liquid heat but was too disoriented to grasp what it was; he stared overhead at a thick agony of stars; he drifted into sleep again.

. . . Her. Heissner backed away, picking his weapon up out of the hay and firing from the hip, his trousers still down around his ankles. The stupidly screaming bastard outside the barn door collapsed. With maniacal enraged calm he shuffled a few feet to where he could see out the barn door and raised his rifle to his shoulder and fired at the other bastards, the ones they were all firing at now, the ones fleeing toward the ugly woods. A few went down. The machine gun Horstritt and Griswold had set up in the road, in the middle of everything, cut down several more before its field of fire was blocked by one of the burning isbas.

He couldn't see who . . . two or three went around the

smoking isba and continued firing with rifles and submachine guns at the ones fleeing toward the ugly woods.

Heissner looked around to see if anything else might interrupt him, catching his eye, nodding with a calm lust-
maddened toothy grin, then shuffled back into the grainy
shadows of the barn, throwing his rifle back down in the hay
and throwing himself down again, in the hay.

He could use a little himself, he felt the rage burning in his
own crotch; he let out a wild croak of laughter when he saw
someone had set the other end of the barn on fire; he strode
up to the door and shouted at Heissner in there; Heissner
looked up, saw the flames licking the miserable beams, a red
flash in his glasses, smiled twistedly and continued what he
was doing.

The idiot . . . but he felt it too, the urge nearly overwhelming him, to go in there before the damned place burned
down, or drag her outside and finish her in the dust.

Half the village was burning now. They'd found no
weapons but set about burning the village anyway. The fool
Rebec had been shot in the throat and whoever had the
weapon had fled to the woods with it or else ditched it somewhere where they'd been unable to find it. The ones who
hadn't fled, most had not fled, cowered in different clumps
of terror on the dusty road . . . screams, wails . . . with half a
dozen other men, Kordts, Krabel, somebody, ringing them
around with rifles raised, a split second from shooting or not
shooting. Others were running about shooting at anything, or
racing past the last isba to fire into the ugly woods. The
damned fools would be shooting at each other if they didn't
watch what they were doing. A few simply stood about in
wilted shock, or wandered about in wilted shock almost
dragging their weapons in the dust, nearly walking into
somebody else's fire. He could see it coming and ran out to
the machine gun and told them to stop firing.

He heard a crashing noise behind him, glared back that
way. The barn, or part of the barn. Part of the roof had fallen
in and the other part burned wildly above the walls that
would take longer to burn. Heissner walked out the barn
door, rearranging himself, savagely appraising everything.

Another man had been in there too, darting out behind Heissner and running around behind the flames, making himself scarce.

He thought of the woman . . . get her out of there, enough was enough. But he did nothing or was distracted by some other thing. He found himself by the last burning isba, staring with exhausted disgust at the ugly woods, the same ugly woods they had marched through for hours before coming to this place. He yelled out to the men scattered in the ugly stubble-field between the burning isba and the woods, waving them back, intent on finding out how many of the bastards had escaped. It was always the guilty ones who got away. But what difference did it make.

It was no dream. Or maybe part of it was, but what difference did it make. The freezing night just dragged on and on and he had nothing at all except his memories, which bored him to death in the bitter cold, hour after hour. The ugliness of certain things was dispersed amongst the ugliness of everything else, all of it, all of it, and even while he pondered savagely over certain things the night just dragged on and on and he would find himself thinking about something else entirely, a thousand different things, while wishing only that he could be shut of every last bit of it and sleep a little longer in the cold. He remembered so many endless nights from the winter before this one, long nights like this one, when it had been so cold that it had been impossible to sleep in more than brief snatches, and a man wound up keeping himself company hour after hour in the freezing dark, keeping himself company until he could stand himself no longer.

It was all so familiar that he hardly even cared, except he was still so cold and depressed. It seemed possible now in these long and useless hours that they might not make it through; he still refused to really consider this but he could not prevent the idea from popping into his head, absorbing it with grim acceptance. He had rested enough by now and if he had been alone he would have just gone on, gone on through these black woods, fighting through his hunger and the sick headache of his hunger, reckoning the stars as best he could—anything better than sitting still like this, wasting

hour after hour, strength and resolve rattling uselessly away
in the cold.

He did not want to abandon Freitag, but he could not struggle through the woods with the boy, not in the middle of the
night like this. It had been bad enough during the day.

The urge to move on distressed him, but his cold and
hunger distressed him too; it was all only one thing or another, one thing or another. Sometimes his mind lapsed into
a black empty dullness that was a little bit better, but still the
night went on. He rose and walked about a few times, stamping his feet in the ugly little clearing, this little hole in the
trees. Freitag awoke a few times, spoke lucidly once, inco-
herently a few other times; he was sleeping again, when
Schrader knelt over him and touched his face and felt the
fever burning there. That does it, he thought. Yet somehow
he was relieved to see Freitag sleeping, to be getting any kind
of sleep at all. Schrader lay down beside him, sheltering him
somehow, gingerly putting his arm around Freitag's body,
drifting into sleep himself again, awakening yet again. The
night passed. They had not gone very far the next day, the
next morning; the Russians on skis caught up with them.

The dawn always brought a little hope, dreary and sunken-
looking as it was. And then the true morning light came and
brought a little more hope. At least, just like that, they were
no longer so cold. The day came and they were ready to
move and they were no longer so cold. They moved on
through the woods, where they had seen the sun settle down
into quiet open space the evening before. But now in the
morning they saw only more woods. Their hunger sometimes made them walk in a hunched-over fashion, though
they tried to fight it off and walk normally. Their hunger induced as well a kind of sick headache that came near to inca-
pacitating them, draining them of the will to stay upright.
They both suffered and they both thought over and over that
they would suffer less if they could just lie down in the snow
and stay there.

Freitag was invigorated for only a few minutes in the
morning light. The fever ebbed a little bit upon his first arising and he scarcely recalled being awash with it during the
night. But he had not gone very far before the fever intensi-

fied again and made him feel so weak and ill, weaker than anything the pain had done to him yesterday or was still doing to him now. He was nearly delirious again but the misery of his sickness forced a kind of perverse consciousness upon him, because he was staggering more than walking, leaning against tree trunks; he could no longer achieve that dumb momentum, inertia, grimly setting one foot in front of another. He tried to keep doing it but he just couldn't. He tried, but it was getting harder and harder.

Schrader wondered what would happen if it came to that, if he had to just leave the boy somewhere. Would he ever be able to find him again, if he got through and then tried to bring help back to him? He doubted it. He didn't know what to think anymore.

They heard artillery fire, a rolling sound carrying through the deep woods. The pressure wave dispersed over a long distance and they felt it thump faintly against their breastbones.

"Ah, Jesus Christ," gasped Freitag, sinking to his knees. They heard the sound of other human beings roaring in quiet dissipation over their heads.

It was a long way away. They were not entirely sure which direction it came from, the sound so dispersed in the cold air; they had to concentrate, or Schrader did. They had felt the first shock of elation—though that was hardly the word for it, not in their state—but they felt something anyway, something other than despair tugging on their spirits. But he ascertained that it was coming from the south, a long way off to the south. It was just too much to turn in that direction now, and whatever that gunfire had been was still miles away. They continued on to the west as if fixed with an obsession, obsessed with the idea that they would have to come upon something pretty soon. They heard the artillery fire again a few times, far off to the left, to the south.

They had not really come very far since the dawn. They came out upon the edge of an open area that must be another snow-covered lake. Freitag observed Schrader with dread, wondering if he would insist on going all the way around it again. The band of forest on the other side was not so dense anymore. They saw only a few isolated fir trees among a tangled grey scrub. The weedy naked scrub, hardly more than tall bushes, was penetrated with a strange radiance that seemed to stretch across the snowy ground into the distance. Perhaps only another lake lay beyond all that, or marshland, or perhaps they might at last be coming to the end of something. Schrader led them directly across, and when they reached the other side Freitag collapsed beneath the low branches there.

He no longer looked exhausted or in pain but merely sick to death, which he was. His eyes were sunken deep, shadowed in the sockets. Schrader studied the frozen surface they had just crossed, distressed by the tracks they had left but trying to tell himself there was nothing they could do about it now. He wondered if Freitag might recover after a time if he simply left him here. He studied the edge of the lake so that he could remember it, marking the precise spot along the edge where they were so he might be able to come back for him somehow. He thought this automatically, with dull yet growing desperation, thinking he would not leave him behind until there was no other way, no other hope, knowing there would be almost no hope of returning to find him again anyway. He knew this very well and so even now he did not know how to think about leaving him behind; the various useless-seeming possibilities merely passed mechanically through his mind. He had lapsed into a kind of senseless state, still staring back at the frozen lake, when he noticed the Russians on skis off to one side, already several hundred feet out from the edge of the woods.

He stepped back to where Freitag was. Freitag had no weapon except a knife. He drew it out, staring at nothing, unable to see the lake through the tangled branches. Schrader moved to where he could see, only a few feet away. The lake was not large and the Russians came across their tracks in a few minutes. He heard their voices in the blue distance, in the blue middle distance, only a few hundred yards away. So this is how it ends, he thought. Still, there were only three of them. A terrible alertness had come over him like a flash of lightning, yet still he could not think very clearly. There was no time, they moved very quickly on their skis. He thought it would be better to get over to one side, give them a flanking burst just before they got to the bushes. But the bare branches

were too sparse and he was afraid of being seen. There was
no time. He stayed where he was. With luck he could get all
three. He felt a stab of dread, certain the tommy gun would
jam or misfire—he ignored it.

He waited these final seconds for them to come close
enough. With a dull stoic horror he saw them stop, talk
quickly to one another, within range but he could not be sure
of getting all three. Two shucked their skis and lay prone in
the snow with weapons trained on the woods, upon almost
the exact spot where he was. The third shucked his skis and
trotted off at a quick angle from the tracks leading to the
woods, clad all in white, clean-looking. What bastards, he
thought in helpless rage. The third man was almost to the
woods, off to one side, glancing back this way. Schrader
fired and the man went down. Schrader lay flat in the snow.

The return fire from out on the lake was instantaneous.
Branches broke everywhere and snow slid down or burst in
little puffs. Long bursts of automatic fire. He lay flat in the
snow and waited to be hit. He heard the air tearing next to his
head. Perhaps thirty seconds went by. The noise changed. He
raised his head a fraction. One was firing still and the other
was coming forward at a run. He had a grenade in one hand
and Schrader shot him from fifty feet away. He pressed his
face into the snow. Seconds passed. The grenade did not go
off. So this is how it ends, he thought again. He exploded
from the branches and saw the last one still lying out in the
snow, just beginning to raise his head again when Schrader
ran out and began firing. He stopped and braced himself and
fired again and then ran on madly until he was only a few feet
away and then fired again into the body which he could already see was spotted with bright blood. Without pausing he
ran back, staggered back through the snow, to the other one,
jerking to a halt only when he saw the grenade still lying in
the snow beside the man. He stared at the grenade, bright
black in the snow. He clenched his teeth and walked up ap-
prehensively and stood over the man and fired two more
shots. He stared at the grenade in the snow, thinking he might
have need of it, but he couldn't bring himself to pick it up
and he backed away.

He looked about with sharply distilled hysteria. Adrenaline thumped against his forehead and behind his eyes and he felt a flush of panic when he couldn't see the first one right away, the first one he had shot. Then he saw him, lying near the edge of the bushes where he had shot him. He collected himself for a second, glanced at the magazine of his weapon. He began to run again and then slowed to a walk and gazed fixedly at the white-clad body until he was standing over it, thinking for an instant that the man was still alive and firing several shots into the back of his head without knowing what he had seen.

By the time he returned to Freitag there was other gunfire all about. He was alarmed but it was with a canny resignation now; it was better that way. Freitag's eyes were glazed over but still a beseeching look in his eyes penetrated through that glaze. Schrader had an extra tommy gun, ammunition, and a few grenades taken from the one at the edge of the bushes. He set the weapon down on Freitag's thighs, that and two grenades.

"There were only three," he thought to say. "I got them all."

"Who's shooting now?" said Freitag.

"I don't know," said Schrader.

He stepped back to the edge again, trying to get some sense of this other gunfire. He ran back out to the farthest body, retrieving ammunition and a few more grenades. He looked at the other body with the grenade still lying black and shiny beside it in the snow. He still couldn't bring himself to go pick it up; he told himself he was being foolish but he didn't care. It didn't seem to matter anymore. He ran back into the woods before some witless anxiety caused him to change his mind. They were surely cooked now; they had enough firepower anyway, to put up some kind of fight before the end came.

Freitag was holding the tommy gun now, staring listlessly at it. He was sitting in the snow with his back cradled flimsily by one of the bushes. Perhaps he shared some of that canny resignation; he almost looked a little better, his despair fading away all of a sudden . . . because it would all be over with now. He waited for Schrader to say something but Schrader looked preoccupied.

"Are they coming?" Freitag said finally.

"I don't know. Not just yet anyway."

He was considering moving deeper into the woods. But what would be the point . . . they couldn't hide their tracks. He was afflicted with a ridiculous image of sweeping their tracks clean with a broom, an old woman sweeping out a gutter. No, it would just be a mess, making more tracks trying to erase the first ones. He was tired, wildly pumped up now but still tired. He hunkered down beside Freitag, staring around through the woods.

His first thought had been that there must be more of them over there, firing after the noise of the first firefight. Firing wildly maybe, laying down gunfire ahead of themselves as they came to this place. He still thought this was what it must be and he craned his neck so he could see out onto the lake. The gunfire continued and after a few minutes it came to him that it must be something else. He hardly dared think this, but he listened and it became obvious. They were shooting at something else, somebody else, and somebody else was returning fire.

"Get up," he said to Freitag. "This is it. This must be it. Can you do it? There must be some of our own people over there."

Already Freitag seemed to have understood. He looked jolted somehow, unnerved with hope, with the necessity of having to make a last effort after he had settled into the dignified peace of waiting for the end. Still he stood up, rising quickly before Schrader could assist him. Dried saliva shone at the corners of his mouth.

Schrader tried to think of some plan of action but he had no ideas except to move on and get through. It could wait until they got close enough to see how things lay. He considered angling away from the gunfire, to avoid walking right into the middle of something, but as he became convinced it must be their own people over there the sound drew him like a magnet and he gave up trying to resist it. He went through the woods with Freitag, through the bare scrubby woods, bushes or small trees only a little more than head high. He could not move quickly without leaving Freitag behind and in this measured pace he began to calm down a little, con-

sider things more clearly. He sensed that the Russians had no
established positions or main line over here or they would
have seen some sign of it by now. So what was it then? Ski
troops . . . a scouting party running into some German
group. He didn't know. The idea of seeing his own people
again brought a kind of fever over him that drove him on
faster than he could think. Freitag lagged behind and several
times he walked back to Freitag, encouraging him, looking
about warily all the while for snipers, for anything, for any
sign of anything. Freitag had discarded the tommy gun, too
weak to carry it.

"I'm sorry," he said.

"It's all right," said Schrader. "Come. Come."

Freitag looked like a ghost weaving through the woods,
like a ghost that might weave aimlessly because it could pass
through trees or any obstacles; but Freitag could not pass, he
stumbled drunkenly into the frail branches, clawing his way
through, staggering, collapsing.

"Ah, God. Ah, God," he said.

"Get up," said Schrader.

Freitag got to his knees and began to gag, collapsing again,
shrieking a quiet little shriek as he fell on his shoulder.

"Schrader. Schrader," he said.

He held out one hand.

Schrader reached for his hand and with arms locked
around each other they stumbled a little further. Freitag
moaned and cursed, driving himself a little further with this
anger. He went down and Schrader could not drag him.

He told Freitag he would come back for him, he would
bring people back for him.

"Yes, that's it," said Freitag.

He closed his eyes. He lay in the snow. He opened his eyes,
staring half-liddedly at nothing.

Schrader stood over him, nearly paralyzed. He opened his
mouth to berate the boy, he raised his hand to cuff him in the
back of the head. He couldn't do it, knowing Freitag would
keep on if he had any strength left at all. Then he did it anyway, slapping him in the back of the head, shouting at him.

"Don't. Don't," said Freitag. "Just do as you said. Do as
you said."

Schrader closed his eyes. He mouthed something silently to himself, pressing his lips together. He had to force himself to go on. He left without looking back.

In spite of himself a wary calm began to settle into him again after he had gone a little further. He was very tired but this did not bother him because he was not exhausted; he felt no more exhaustion. The gunfire had diminished somewhat, ragged bursts of fire and answering fire, individual rifle shots. It seemed not far off but still he had to go on for ten or fifteen minutes and in these crazy bushes this time seemed very much longer than it was. He cursed to himself but remained calm and determined, ready. When the gunfire ceased entirely he quickened his pace, as if beset by something. He outran his own strength and had to pause gasping a few times but then he pushed on. The deep silence had returned and it began to sink deep into him. He had a terrible picture in his mind; if it was not yet the main line but only some patrol or mobile group then perhaps they would have moved on before he could get to them, retreated or moved on God only knew where. He moved less cautiously, forging through the scrub like a blunt instrument, thrusting branches aside. There came another crackle of gunfire. He stopped dead, collected himself, moved on more carefully again. He bolted across a narrow thread of open space, only a few yards wide, like the border of something. The ground sloped up gradually and he looked back and understood they had been coming through a frozen swamp, overgrown with all those things. He walked up the rising ground into a band of taller trees. Very quickly he saw open space through the boles.

He saw them out there on a wide undulant snowy terrain. He leaned against a tree to look carefully and make sure of what he saw. He set the Russian gun down behind the tree. Many had been using these weapons for months now but he did not want to offer anyone the least provocation. Still, he could not avoid the dread of being fired on and so he simply set his teeth and walked on out there, waving his arms, unable at first to even bring himself to shout German words. Then he did that too, hearing the strangeness of his own voice, the first mantle of disbelief beginning to descend over him.

There was a miserable-looking group huddled together, then an outlying ring of other men kneeling or lying in the snow with weapons trained out in all-around defense. Some of these men started to get up but then there was shouting and they resumed their positions and waited for him to come to them.

When he had approached to within a few yards of the nearest ones they carefully stood up again and walked out to him. Schrader saw the black faces, black with beard stubble and exhaustion. He was out of breath and put his hands down on his thighs and then found himself kneeling in the snow.

"Velikiye Luki," he said.

Several men helped him up and the touch of their hands broke him down and he embraced one of them, gripping him tightly, screwing his eyes shut, gasping little noises.

He understood all at once. He recognized the man; already he had recognized several others.

He stepped back, swaying from one foot to the other, breathing.

"It's Sergeant Schrader," he heard someone say.

He pointed, explaining about Freitag. They looked over that way, gaunt faces of men he recognized, recognized from the citadel, from all of it. They looked back along the foot-prints in the snow, back into the forest. Their faces were ravaged by wind and cold and fear, their expressions grave, calculating the sense of plunging into the forest, into another ambush. Schrader sensed their hesitation but not refusal. They were not about to leave someone out there who had made it this far.

"All right, Schrader," said one, another NCO. "Can you show us?"

He said yes and turned around but could go only a few steps. He did not sink down; he stood there, fighting for breath.

The other man came up, gripped him on the shoulder.

"We're almost there, Schrader. We've almost made it. Darnedde's gone on ahead. He should be back soon."

Schrader could not really grasp it all, though he could not fail to understand. He said nothing. He put his hand out on the other man's shoulder; he seemed to need to feel him there.

"Just give me a moment," he said. "I'll show you."

"We can follow your tracks. Is it far?"

"No. No. Not far. But let me show you."

An officer was with them now. It was Ritter. He had led them on that terrible journey through the ruins on Christmas Eve. There had been nothing but darkness and fires then and Schrader might not have remembered his face. But he remembered it from the citadel, from all the weeks since then.

"You were at Hamburg," said Ritter. "You were with us that night."

"Yes," said Schrader. All of that was too long ago now. He explained about Freitag again. "You know him, Ritter. He got that T-34 in the pond. In the courtyard."

"All right. Don't worry. We'll get him. I'll go get him myself. Stay here, Schrader. Help is on the way."

They all looked terrible, thought Schrader, wondering how he must look. It didn't matter. He was out of breath from driving headlong throughout the overgrown swamp but he was not exhausted; he felt no more exhaustion. If they could just give him a minute.

But an urgency seemed to possess them. Then there were ragged shouts, different voices, from the larger group huddled tightly together behind them. Schrader turned, they all turned. In the distance a flare curved up in the blue milky morning sky. A faint reddish burst, carried away in a small breeze. Schrader looked to see them in the distance, it must be Darnedde bringing help back, but he could not make anything out and he turned and looked anxiously into the forest where he had come from.

Ritter said to the NCO, "All right, I'll wait for Darnedde. Go ahead. It's Freitag. You know him. Be quick. The Ivans might show up again."

Schrader ignored Ritter's telling him to stay there and went with the other men, the NCO and four men. But they moved urgently into the forest, into the band of tall trees, down into the thick scrub of the swamp, and he couldn't keep up with them. They could see his tracks plainly and they followed them quickly and he lagged behind a way.

Doggedly he followed them, not satisfied to wait. Time passed. He saw them coming back, struggling with Freitag whom they bore in a white snow-cape. Their breath rose in translucent clouds through the infinite branches and the sunlight. They labored, exhausted, having no proper stretcher; they had already been exhausted before this. All five struggled to carry him and then Schrader helped too, carrying him back, back through the swamp. Freitag groaned from being manhandled and Schrader felt better to hear it.

"It's me. It's all right now," he said.

Freitag looked at him, his head lolling to one side. Greasy sweat covered his face.

"Good, good," said Schrader, putting his palm on Freitag's forehead, clutching at his scalp for a moment.

They had to set him down and then they tried to drag him across the snow on the snow-cape. It was difficult; the undergrowth was too thick. An infinite latticework of thin tangled shadows fell upon them, upon their efforts. Freitag's face was grey, or red, it was hard to see what it was; he looked very bad. The other NCO sent one man back to get more people. The rest stopped, nearly falling down, sitting down or supporting themselves among strange branches.

"Can you talk?" said Schrader. "Are you all right?"

"*Ja,*" said Freitag.

Schrader was too exhausted to say more and Freitag said nothing more. They began to drag him on again, slowly, through the thickets. Freitag groaned when they dragged him across roots or tugged him through dense growth. He was awash in his sweat. The sunlight dazzled him through the brown thickets. He imagined himself being pulled through the thorns on Christ's forehead. When he lost consciousness it was for the last time. Other dreams, inner life, remained locked inside him for a while; he had not ceased breathing yet.

They reached the strange thread, alleyway, of open ground that ringed the swamp, separating it from the rising ground beyond, other people meeting them here and dragging Freitag more quickly the rest of the way. They dragged him through the bigger trees and out across the open undulant ground and up among the other men who had all escaped from Velikiye Luki, laying him to rest among other huddled men who had been wounded or who could go no farther, waiting for help to come, waiting for Darnedde, who was coming now, they could all see him and a larger formation of men coming in the distance now. Horses, wagons, men.

Schrader was mad with thirst and he asked if anyone had water. He wanted real water. Someone gave him a canteen and he drank. The water was cold and it coursed through what felt like raw skin inside of him. He tried to get Freitag to drink but he wouldn't; Freitag rolled his head vaguely, his eyes shut. Schrader poured a little on his lips, tried to get a little into his mouth. He saw his face and wet his cheeks and forehead a little bit.

Ritter was there again, kneeling down next to Freitag.

"They're almost here. They're almost here," he said to Freitag, to Schrader, himself.

He stood up.

"I'm going out to meet Darnedde," he said.

"Ritter," said Schrader. "How far is it to the main line?"

"Not far. Not far at all. That's them. He's coming from there."

"What happened to the major?" said Schrader. The man's name escaped him.

"Tribukait's dead," said Ritter.

Ritter was dead too. The lieutenant was rough and resourceful, often aloof, sometimes unpleasant, a man with the somewhat vain, self-reliant remoteness of the lonely people in the mountain country where he came from. His face was large and bony, a tall face, from which his eyes tended to peer down narrowly, almost with a certain loftiness, but he was not too bad really. He had few endearing qualities but did not really need them, especially among some of the other men who came from the same place he did. He spoke with a rough and quiet voice and had a good share of whatever it was that constituted leadership. Calm and common sense above all. Schrader did not like him particularly but thought he was one of the better officers; so did some of the others.

Ritter was pretty much as they all were now, features carved by weariness and exposure. His steel helmet was covered with white cloth and a scarf or muffler or some kind of rag was wrapped entirely around his head. He looked at Freitag again and then stood up and collected a few men.

They went out to meet Darnedde, who had been visible for some time now, approaching with painful slowness in the clear air.

About noon, it must have been, as the others huddled on the snowy undulant plain—dotted in the distance here and there with some of those same patches of woodland— waited to make this contact with the outside world.

Ritter and the men with him had gone out a way, about halfway to Darnedde and the approaching wagons, when the shells fell. Only two of them, the incoming roar louder than the muffled thunder of impact in the snowy ground.

The men still huddled near the swamp-forest had crouched with fright, but the shells had landed out there a ways. They waited for more of them to come down, still showing little more than utter weariness. About a minute passed; when the ringing left their ears they heard screams faintly from out there. With resigned horror they waited a few moments longer. There was no more fire; there was hardly any sound at all. Then a few men went out to where Ritter was.

In the distance some of the men with the wagons, panje carts, also began to run forward now. Still the horses and the wagons themselves labored so slowly. But it was only five or ten minutes longer now, anxious as this time was. One of the wagons halted to pick up Ritter and the others killed with him, others who were badly wounded, agonized cries carrying a certain distance across the noon stillness. There were two other wagons that Darnedde led up to the larger group, even as some men from here rushed out to meet him now. Men shouted hoarsely and embraced one another, some of them did, unable to contain themselves regardless of this violence and death that had descended at the last moment, regardless of what chance it might fall again at any second.

There was only so much jubilation. They could not linger. The wagons carried those who could not walk, and Ritter's body and the other dead. The rest walked on, led by Darnedde and two other officers who had come out with him. It took less than an hour. They passed through, still less than forty-eight hours from the moment they had left

the main gate and entered into the crater-field. There was
only a little barbed wire, resembling jumbled scrap snowed
over at the perimeter of some abandoned farm. There was
none of the heavily fortified network of trenches that some
recalled from back in the summer, from outside Velikiye
Luki, outside the city. There were a few weapons-positions
behind piles of deadfall or in shallow holes mounded up
with snow. Small numbers of men were there, or coming
out to greet them. They passed through all of this, which
was not much.

Schrader walked alongside the cart that bore Freitag along.
So did Timmerman, whom Schrader had last seen in the
crater-field. They greeted each other quietly. He looked over
at Freitag every so often but was too weary to watch him
continuously or even to speak to him. Freitag was unconscious. Schrader could have ridden with him in the cart but
somehow he did not think to do so, as he was not wounded.
The cart was for the wounded or the badly frostbitten and
anyone else who could no longer walk. All the rest, with
Schrader or in front of him or behind him, walked on between the scant disruptions in the landscape that formed the
new main line. They had made it through and the mantle of
disbelief settled in its peculiar way upon each one of them,
incomprehensible as it was, and thus still not disrupting too
much the ordinary presence of all things that they walked
through, walked slowly past.

Freitag might have died just before they got there, or moments afterward maybe; that was when Schrader checked on
him again. He couldn't be certain at first; he had looked like
this since the first light of day. He climbed onto the cart,
among other men crowded in discomfort and pain. Still he
could not be sure or could not quite believe it. Then he did
believe it and he got down again. So there you are, stupid
bastard, he thought. Once or twice he might have overheard
Kordts speak to Freitag in this peculiar fashion, but he had no
thought of that whatsoever, and possibly might never remember it.

He was possessed by some unspeakable thing, whatever it
was; he could expect nothing else and even so walked on
silently for a while before he had to sit down by the side of

the road. There was no road, only the passage of men and things through the snow. He sat there holding his head in his hands, he had to, not quite sobbing, or if he did it would be all the same, all the same.

Chapter Twenty-eight

Kordts had much of his attitude beaten out of him during training. He was disciplined on a few occasions, humiliated on many others. Humiliation and infantile exercises formed an essential part of training and this had caught him off guard more than physical punishment; of course it was designed to do that. He was a hard man to embarrass or humiliate but eventually they wore him down, especially when such punishments included working him like a dog, beyond the limits of his endurance, at any number of degrading tasks. This was only standard procedure for dealing with people like him.

So he learned to keep his mouth shut. This was not too hard on him, as he was generally a close-mouthed person except among people he trusted. There was always that look in his eye though. NCOs and officers noticed him as someone who would bear watching. While some merely resented authority, or even accepted it willingly, he despised it the way some despise snakes or spiders.

In fact he feared running afoul of some officer or NCO who would see him for exactly what he was, and make life hell for him whether he kept his mouth shut or not, simply because they didn't like his looks, goading him until he revolted.

Indeed there were many who did not like his looks, but he was fortunate to never run afoul of any particular antagonist who would single him out.

After training life was somewhat easier, and his attitude gradually began to resurface, his self somewhat rehabilitated. But only somewhat—fear of reprisal still kept him in his place. He was not alone in his thinking; the penal battalions and stockades were full of various miscreants. Sometimes he wondered if he was a coward to keep it all inside himself, to never lash out with some outburst or tirade or flinty-eyed refusal that would get him sent to a penal unit. How bad could that be? Plenty bad, he knew. Still he tormented himself; for a long time he did anyway.

He had a sense of humor and he laughed good-naturedly at a lot of things; it was not always soaked with cynicism. He was also blessed with a certain stoicism, so that he rarely felt sorry for himself, thus avoiding the attention a whiner attracts. These traits often served to distract superiors from the deeper contempt he bore; they might wonder about him, but not too much, with so many other men under their command to wonder about, to lead, to enforce obedience upon, to punish when necessary.

He was twice under siege and a siege changes everything, changes everyone, drawing them closer together whether they like it or not. Then there was that strange extended period of contentment, or whatever it was; it seemed that he had almost been content, after Cholm, after his long furlough, though he really could not understand it and indeed refused to try. He might have grasped that he was in the grip of prolonged shock, but grasping this only barely, if at all.

They were all resigned to death, especially by the time of their second year out in Russia. All of them were. Not so much because of the relentless violence—there were, after all, long periods in the trenches that were fairly quiet—but because by the second year it had become clear that there was no end in sight. A man still hoped to live, and thus still feared for his life; but for some, even for many, the force of their resignation eased their stress in some ways, the stress that would eat men away and which was worse than any hardship. Kordts was not immune to this. To be released of this stress—engendered by fear, engendered by hatred—was to experience, never enduringly, but intermittently, intermittently, the ability to look quietly about oneself and see the world on a few days, to see the clouds drifting calmly across the world among the deep shafts of sunlight, even out there in Russia.

As the weeks and months went by, during that summer and autumn, his understanding of himself began to diminish, if only because he already understood, or as much as he was ever going to. Perhaps he never quite reached the necessary state of apathy and exhaustion, but he came close to it; and so had that much in common with the rest of them.

There was a low hill beneath a gentle blue sky, the sky reaching up and up as far as he could see. It was all in the distance, and the crowds of people atop the low hill were further obscured by the strange gentleness of the sky, a softness that blurred things. There were a few small structures there, he thought, or maybe just a single structure at the top of the hill, with the people around it. He could almost see a road leading up to the hill, coming from the distance maybe, from the distance where he was. All of it was vague and far away, but even so the picture lingered in his mind with a certain forcefulness. Perhaps he would have remembered it from time to time, for no particular reason.

Hours later the flame tanks were crawling forward again, and all of them shrank behind the blast-holes and embrasures, crouching back near the limits of their endurance, like a wall they could feel behind them. Several men had already been burned and how the rest tolerated the horror of this none could know. The stinking jets swelled forward again like ocean swells coming to break upon a shore. A man began to scream. Hasenclever gave the order to abandon the place.

An hour later he was crouched behind a pile of rubble, beside the row of ruined buildings they had fled to. Several other men crouched next to him. Their faces were black with smoke and grime and white with terror. Schrader was speaking to him; Kordts listened and understood, though feeling almost deaf within his fear.

There was Hasenclever standing at the corner of the building and speaking to a machine-gun crew set up there, then speaking to Schrader, then walking back next to the rear of the building. There was Freitag and the three men with him carrying another machine gun and ammunition boxes out among the rubble piles.

Freitag crept past him, he reached out and cuffed Freitag on the shoulder. Freitag looked at him. Kordts returned the look somehow but had nothing to say, he only nodded very slightly. Freitag thought Kordts wanted something but understood from the look on Kordts's face that he had only meant to touch him that way. He crawled on with his men a little further, crouching behind another pile of the stones and dust, barely covered with snow, that lay everywhere.

The noise seemed unending, ever-present, like the roar of a highway that one becomes used to and no longer hears. Sometimes there were gaps in the noise, a few seconds of quiet. Then he could hear the cries of men from the other company that had come up, lying out there, after the first try to retake Hamburg. But he hardly heard them either, so many cries he'd been hearing for days and days. He did hear them but he hardly knew it.

Schrader was coming up again, putting his hand on his shoulder, then crawling out a little further to say something to Freitag. Kordts looked at the house over there, the one still standing among a few others collapsed beside it. He looked at Hamburg, a few hundred feet to the right; he had been inside that place for so long that he hardly recognized it from the outside. He did recognize it but it was all unfamiliar; they were moving about in there, the Russians were. The machine gun at the corner of the building opened fire; a row of dust plumes erupted along the rear face of Hamburg. Between the house on the left and Hamburg on the right there was space, distance, though almost unseeable in the tension that squeezed his vision down and fixed it on a few things only. House. Hamburg. Lovat bridge, the skeleton, out there in the distance. He caught a glimpse of the flame-tanks pulling back in the distance, scuttling like roaches, little toys pulled away by a child on an invisible tether. Ha, ha, he thought witlessly. "Thank God for that," said one of them beside him. "Thank God for nothing," muttered another. Kordts thought this too, though he could hardly think. He glanced up at the cold suffocating overcast; part of it came apart, like a belly coming apart, showing a thread of blue sky like something to be revealed to him alone, he didn't know what.

Schrader was beside them again, hoarsely repeating a few things he had said a few minutes before. The machine gun hammered from the corner of the building. He gave the signal and they rose and went out. Their ankles and knees turned every which way in the chaotic mess that they crossed; fear was like a physical barrier that might slow their progress, block their access to that house only a few hundred feet away, but it didn't do so, it slowed them not at all, they moved as fast as they ever could. They spilled through a doorway or tumbled in through windows, a man cut on broken glass, crying out. Schrader looked at them all; they were all inside the house.

Schrader went to one wall, a crack there offering some view of Hamburg. Kordts and another man went through an interior doorway, firing into another room as they entered. A Russian was dead. A second one came at Kordts with a bayonet. He turned to fire but the man was already on him. He fired anyway. The other man with Kordts had the Russian around the neck, grabbing at the knife-hand, pulling him away. Kordts was cut. He beat the Russian in the face with his rifle butt, gagging at the sound of it even while he was doing it. The other man picked up the bayonet and turned his face away.

The other man asked Kordts if he was hurt. Schrader was in the room now, asking the same thing. Kordts shook his head. He was cut somewhere, it didn't feel like much. He couldn't say anything, he just shook his head. He wanted to vomit. The sick urge passed through him as quickly as it had come; it left his mind. He leaned against the frame of the interior door. The other man offered him a cigarette, his hand visibly shaking; Kordts couldn't take it. He pulled out his water bottle, his own hand visibly shaking. The dead shall rise again; and then be dead forever. The other man walked dazedly into the outer room where the rest were. Kordts had trouble drinking, he didn't have much water left; he rested the canteen against his neck, against his collar bone, until he felt he could swallow. Someone was on the upper floor, shouting; he dropped down to the first floor and said something to Schrader. Kordts saw a low hill with a soft blue sky rising far, far above it. The picture startled him and he jerked his head back, knocking the back of his head against the door frame. It left his mind as quickly as it had come. He tried to drink again, slowly pressing the canteen to his lips. He saw Schrader standing in one of the windows they had come in through, signaling, beckoning to the others waiting over there, out there. He closed his eyes for a moment, opened them again.

Epilogue

Velizh was unchanged. A ruin. The fighting had died down and the place took on a quiet familiarity. The wind blew clouds and snow across the sky.

Scherer was here. The remains of his division were here. While 277 was being wiped out in Velikiye Luki, 251 and 257 had been ground down outside the city, until they could continue no more. At the beginning of January they had exchanged sectors with another division and moved into these quieter positions around Velizh. Many of them remembered Velizh from the year before. It still looked the same.

The division's two surviving regiments still existed on paper, but in reality they were almost finished. At Tchernosem, the cornerstone that had protected Wohler's flank, Scherer's men had gradually been driven back from the railroad embankment and into the open country, the desolate country. After the long filthy mud of late fall and early winter the terrible cold had come at last. The ground was too frozen to dig into and the snow cover was too sparse, so they could not dig into that either. One of the last Russian armored assaults had brought horror, too much horror. The men had fought from positions that offered almost no protection on the open, frozen ground. The wind, that strange, dry, particle-gnashing wind, had blown into their faces as the tanks came. They had no antitank weapons left. The tanks overran them and one company was annihilated and Scherer discovered that many of the dead, the commanding officer and many, many others, had been crushed into the hard earth beneath the treads of the tanks. In this one place a waste of pulp and shredded clothing adhered to the earth.

The incident had a bad effect on him. The last straw, almost, except there was never a last straw. The days went on. And even at this time von Sass and 277 were still holding on inside Velikiye Luki.

The incident had a bad effect on the men and this feeling was conveyed to him directly, the agony not precipitated out, filtered out, by the normal stratus of high command, because he was too worn out and had no more perspective on things. For weeks he had been filled with an intractable sense of mission, not the carelessly arrogant and goal-obsessed sense of mission of commanders spilling blood to get somewhere, to achieve something; no, it was only the pitiless urge to do whatever he could to help the men dying under siege in that city a few miles to the north. If he could not participate in Wohler's relief attack, then he was determined nonetheless to hold and hold at Tchernosem to guard Wohler's flank. And so Scherer's other two regiments had bled and bled there, leaving scraps of their flesh clinging to the track-links of the Soviet armor, leaving parts of their limbs embedded in the hard ground like mangled flesh-trees and flesh-bushes.

The dead soil was fertilized. The survivors were reeling and Scherer became frightened for them, for himself. In his exhaustion he felt very clearly his mental resources bending and stretching, very clearly like a kind of elastic bending in his brain and down his spine, stretched into tenuous, exhausted, ghostlike shapes by these two divergent agonies: the visible horror at Tchernosem and the invisible one borne along the radio waves from von Sass in Velikiye Luki.

For even now von Sass and the rest were still holding out there; the weeks went on and on.

Otherwise he would have requested relief for the men at Tchernosem much sooner. He knew this. But he could not bring himself to do this, not with von Sass's voice coming over the transmitter day after day. Finally von der Chevallerie arranged for the survivors at Tchernosem to be relieved by another division. This was in the first week of January.

Scherer led them down to Velizh, only twenty miles away. But the ring of agony swelling out from Velikiye Luki did not reach this far; it was quiet here. From the old command post at Novo Sokolniki Scherer had said goodbye to von Sass. Goodbye. Goodbye.

But it was not so. For even at Velizh he could not help himself; through the first weeks of January he remained almost
around the clock beside a powerful transmitter and continued to speak daily with von Sass. There was nothing left for
Scherer to say, but he could not help himself. He kept von
Sass informed of Wohler's progress, of Wohler's wormlike
progress across the land; but von Sass already knew of this
because he himself was in contact with Wohler. So for
Scherer there was nothing to say; he repeated things he had
said before, he listened to von Sass's replies, he repeated
what he had said before about Cholm, about how they had
held on at Cholm, on and on. Perhaps von Sass wearied of
this; Scherer suspected it, but he could not bring himself to
break off contact entirely.

And then, finally, it was over.

He felt relieved when it was all over. He could not help that
either, a burden lifting away from him and leaving him hol-
lowed out and inwardly no longer sure of himself, ashamed
somehow, but still it was a kind of relief. And it was hardly
shame either, he knew it was not his fault, but even so it was
something like that. What else could it be? For about a day he
could hardly speak. Metzelaar spoke to him a few times, but
then stepped away when he understood that Scherer did not
wish to be spoken to, did not wish to unburden himself, did
not wish any companionship. Later . . . maybe.

He still had Cholm, he thought to himself, like a miser
hoarding a pile of gold that could not be melted down or ever
dissipated or changed into something else. He tried not to
think that way, for without a doubt it was a shameful way to
think, but he was too tired to prevent thoughts of Cholm
from coming to his mind, supporting him a little bit. At least
on the conscious level, though, it did not make him feel much
better; he would not have wanted it to.

Even at the end, after von Sass had signed off for the last
time, he had remained by the transmitter to hear the fate of
the group that had broken out from the western pocket, from
the citadel. The hours went by. He could bear it no longer. He
desperately needed sleep; he needed it so badly that he
thought he might drop at any moment; but he had been needing sleep for days—weeks—and mostly had found himself

unable to sleep, lying awake for long hours, listening at nothing. So instead he had left the building, the communications center, and walked out into the night air for a while.

Much as he had done the month before, at Novo Sokolniki . . .

He did not walk far. He was too tired, and he did not know his way around Velizh too well. Novo had been a ruin, but it seemed it must always have looked that way, miserable hamlet, only a few buildings there. Velizh was larger, a town of sorts, gaunt faces of blasted stone buildings along rutted streets, piles of timber everywhere from the razed isbas, burnt, razed.

The division that had occupied Velizh before them had left curious structures all over the town. The demolished isbas had been a good source of lumber and the windows and doorways of almost every occupied building in the town were screened by long wooden planks, set endwise on the ground and propped against the stone buildings like wooden awnings. They functioned as screens that would absorb shrapnel bursts and Scherer thought them sensible enough devices, though the town had not been under bombardment since their arrival and he wondered how effective they would really be. In any case they gave a peculiar look to the town, which in the dark he perceived somewhat—a look of dark smooth angles sloping down evenly from the faces of the buildings, among the shattered aspect of every other thing. He did not wander far and by and by found himself pulled back there, drawn back there, to the building housing the divisional signals unit. He stood smoking for a while in the cold dark across the street. Soldiers walked by from time to time, only a few recognizing him and saluting. Others walked past a foot away but did not recognize him.

To the few who stopped he said quietly, "How goes it, *junge*?" in the noncommittal tone of a weary sergeant major. He had been a staff officer for most of his career, rather than a leader of men. Perhaps he had thought for many years that he must lead men someday, if he was to feel right with himself, with his life as a soldier. He must have gained some deeper cognizance of this at Cholm, but he did not think of it now.

"Well enough, Herr General."

"Watch your step in these streets," said Scherer.

The men acknowledged this, laughing quietly. The mud streets were deeply rutted, frozen in abstract iron corrugations. Other men had walked by unaware, distracted by having to step carefully in the dark, cursing as their feet twisted one way or another.

"*Hals und Beinbruch*, Herr General," said one.

Scherer laughed quietly, closing his eyes tight for a moment. He opened them and they were walking off, alongside a few others whom he saw glancing over at him in the dark.

"Herr General," one of them said from the dark. They walked on.

There was light in the building across the street, showing in threads through the shrapnel screens. Metzelaar came out. He looked about, seemed to perceive Scherer across the way, called out to see if it was him.

Scherer walked back over there, his boots twisting.

"Survivors from the citadel have made contact with Group Wohler."

"How many?" said Scherer.

"The report says about one hundred. Major Tribukait was killed."

"What about the eastern pocket?"

"No more reports from there, Herr General."

"Will there be more from the citadel?"

"Hopefully so. There are others unaccounted for. Only small groups though."

Scherer was silent. The night was frigid. Overcast revealed stars and then shrouded them. Tribukait had been with one of the jaeger units but Scherer knew the man from Tchernosem, when the jaegers had fought there for a few weeks. His deep weariness and hollowness was no greater or less than it had been. His deep hollowness was weighed down paradoxically with lead, no heavier or lighter than it had been.

"All right. Thank you," said Scherer.

It was another two days before the last reports came in; until the reports ceased, of any more survivors of that siege. One man broke out alone and struggled for nearly fifty miles in a great semicircle to the north, at last reaching safety many miles north of Novo Sokolniki. He was the very last. Before then another small group of eighteen men had made it through, a group of wounded men who had discovered their abandonment by Tribukait in the citadel and refused to stay behind there. These men might have been haunted by thoughts of betrayal, eighteen wounded men fighting to survive, somehow encouraging each other to go on in the wake of those who had left them behind for the Russians, yet when they reached their own lines they seemed only desperate and utterly spent, no more nor less than survivors from other groups. The lieutenant leading them was killed in the same fashion as Lieutenant Ritter of Darnedde's group, by shellfire immediately before crossing through the German lines.

And so it was all over.

They continued to hear reports from Stalingrad, one thousand miles away. They pretended a sullen lack of interest, in light of their own ordeals. In fact it was not really a pretense, though they could not entirely contain some mechanical curiosity about the fate of Stalin's city, word of which had been carried by rumor, communiqué, and newspaper ever since the previous summer. Sixth Army had been ground down throughout the late summer and the autumn, capturing almost all but never all of that city. Then in November they were all surrounded there by the great Russian counteroffensive, exactly a week before Velikiye Luki was also surrounded.

Velikiye Luki was entirely in Russian hands on 17 January 1943. The men at Stalingrad were left, for the most part, to starve to death. The immense pocket held by those three hundred thousand men, the size of a small European nation, was reduced by 3 February to an area of a few square miles around von Paulus's command post. Von Paulus surrendered on that day. Scherer heard about this in Velizh. Every other man in the German army heard about this in their own positions along the three thousand miles of front in Russia.

Velikiye Luki, so much smaller than Stalingrad, a pinpoint, a nothing, had been garrisoned by about seven thousand men—total casualties there running in the neighborhood of ninety-nine percent. Cholm remained in German hands until 1944.

Scherer, long retired from the German army, boarded a

plane from Germany to London in 1977. Some hours later he arrived at his destination, a row house in Kensington. He had noticed the street number in the letter and now noticed it again on the front door. Four twenty-three, the same street number as his own house. Many strange coincidences had begun to accrue in his life over recent months. He did not believe in their import but could not fail to notice them. He did not believe in the presence of an unknown guiding hand, but lately as small coincidences—some of them quite striking, if one cared to think that way—had begun to appear more and more frequently, he had begun to ponder the presence of an unknown guiding hand, sometimes ruefully, sometimes in other frames of mind. It was the kind of thing he noticed at the moment and then forgot about entirely until the next instance of it.

He mentioned this to the owner of the house after he was invited in, who declared that he had noticed it too, the street number. The two men had never met each other and it was a pleasant way to begin talking. A house in Kensington and a house in Halle. They took refreshments in an upstairs room, comfortable, overfurnished, lit by lamps, with other light from the street passing through gauze curtains. His host was a stout man, ruddy with food and alcohol, or earlier years of it; he suffered from diabetes now. He was writing a book about Cholm, but he had also fought in the war, so the two men took to each other quite easily. Lucas was no dilettante. They spoke gregariously after a while, and were comfortable enough in the silences in between.

"They fought like lions," Scherer said.

He said this with quiet stubborn pride, not caring how it sounded, remembering the truth irrespective of the forms in which it was spoken. Lucas had learned much of the obscure, almost mythic lore of the Russian war and had long been struck by the inexplicable survival of Scherer's battlegroup for one hundred and five days at Cholm. He wanted to learn the smallest details and Scherer obliged, speaking genially and also in a kind of dream-state, hour after hour. In thirty years he had never recounted those events in such minute fashion, had never been asked to do so, had never expected to do so, expecting only to take it all with him to his grave the way the dead had done back in 1942, the way the survivors had done in the dying years of their lives since then.

He was a wizened, smallish man, his glasses very thick, the beard still on his cheeks, white beard; he looked like an old Jew, resignedly tragic, enduring, calm. He said they fought like lions and he seemed to be staring narrowly at something as he said this, not drifting back within himself into grey memories but staring outwardly as if at some enduringly mysterious thing. Yet also after thirty years it had settled back into the mere familiarity of something that had happened. It had happened.

They talked of Cholm and might have talked of nothing else, like a small universe that contained everything, with seemingly an endless number of deep recesses opening up into the events of those months. But then they did talk of other things now and then. Scherer spoke of meeting Hitler in 1942, after it was over, on his celebrated leave in the homeland. Lucas said, "Tell me your impressions of Hitler," and Scherer obliged him. Scherer said his next home leave, in 1943, was much different. He was drained in ways he could not describe after Velikiye Luki; even after those months at Cholm it had not been like that. He had not been due for leave again; von der Chevallerie, along with Wohler and Kluge, commander of Army Group Center, had arranged it for him.

"The privileges of rank," Scherer said quietly. He stared again, somewhere. The light caught on his glasses, from the outside, or from other reflections elsewhere in the room.

"Poor von Sass," he said. "I knew him only briefly. He was a Prussian, but not so typical of that kind. He had a pleasant manner, the way Guderian did. I thought him too inexperienced at the time. But he did everything that anyone could have done."

He handed Lucas a slip of paper. It was a page torn from a book, with a list of men who had been hanged by the Russians in 1946, in the ruined town square of Velikiye Luki. Lucas had heard of this before, in the course of his investigations and reading, and his many interviews with other German veterans. He stared at the list, at the names there. Von Sass and four other officers had been hanged. Then there were the names of a number of other officers and one enlisted man, sentenced to twenty-five years hard labor; they were paroled in 1955 and allowed to return home.

Lucas was curious. It did not seem like the typical Russian war crimes trial, in which legitimate grievances and trumped-up charges would often be cobbled together helterskelter. There was still much that was a mystery; Lucas knew this, but as far as he knew von Sass had been guilty of nothing other than twice rejecting the surrender terms of the Russian parliamentaires, of dragging the violence out to the bitter end in one of the most violent episodes of all that war. That the Russians would exact this kind of vengeance, just or unjust, did not surprise Lucas. What struck him as curious was that the hangings in the Lenin Square in Velikiye Luki were unique. Many had been executed in Siberia, or in prison cellars in Moscow, he knew this—but he could not recall any other incidents of hangings in the ruined town squares of Stalingrad, of Demyansk, of Kharkov, of Kiev, of Minsk, of Smolensk, or Sebastopol, of Rzhev, of Vitebsk, of Orel.

He imagined von Sass in a Russian prison for three years, before being transported back to the ruins of that city, of Velikiye Luki, to meet a fate of such cruel distinction. He asked Scherer his thoughts about this, but Scherer seemed not to grasp the distinction he was making, merely referring to the Russians in so many words . . . as being the way the Russians were.

There was still much to say about Cholm, their conversations probing this subject at great length, raking over stones and then raking over them again. Several days passed, with Scherer as Lucas's guest.

He returned on an evening flight, after seeing some of London. The vacuousness of the present day, the flickering and noise of television sets, made no greater impression on him now than at any other time over these decades, even in a foreign city where many things might have seemed new or unusual. His opinions about the present era had in fact been stronger a decade or so before. Anymore he had fewer opinions, their absence being filled in by a certain mysteriousness, the nearness of death maybe, the nearness of memories almost forty years old. He was cognizant that there was no more war, and sometimes wondered what this might mean. He knew that small wars and concerted murders were still taking place in many parts of the planet; but there was no great war, no war of annihilation, and anymore he understood that he lived in a culture where there was neither war nor expectation of war, and he wondered what this might mean. Would people live for generations, on and on, without war, and so achieve some kind of other life? For years he had expected it all to come crashing down, as it had always done in the past, but more recently he had begun to wonder if it might maintain in this way for generations, with people living however they were going to live.

Such curiosities did not astonish him, nor had they ever astonished him; some things worked their way in a slow and translucent manner that could not provoke astonishment. He remained skeptical, of course; only a fool would not remain skeptical. But he had been waiting for the next war for too long and in these later years he had given up waiting for it, given up wondering when it might happen, wondering instead about the things that were and how long they might last.

And even such reflections as these had become more or less subliminal by now, passing through his mind now and again; or fermenting on subconscious levels that in many ways were no longer of any concern to him, even were he to become aware of them. He was old; death was near, or nearing; old memories were near.

He flew back over the continent, looking down at the waters of the channel and then at the continental land mass in the eastern gloom. He ate and drank with the other passengers in the filtered air, in the faint ever-present rushing sounds of a pressurized compartment. Another plane crossed the evening sky in the distance, lights blinking, moving through the air with silent force; he heard nothing but the small noises of the cabin where he was.

He saw towering clouds backlit by the sunset to the west, and space, the sky, between these clouds. A man from Cholm had told him once, at a small reunion after the war, that from time to time he would look up at the clouds in the sky and see his dead comrades standing up there, gazing down at him. He had been one of those disturbed men, Scherer remembered this, gesticulating and making other strange statements. Scherer had resented nothing, felt only the same sympathy he felt for them all. The man had been raving, making some people, even Scherer, uncomfortable; but all the same the man could have approached him and called him a butcher and sunk his teeth into his neck and his sympathy would have been no more and no less than for all the others.

It was not the first time he had remembered this, these dead men standing in the clouds. One could not forget such a thing, and so he had been reminded of it different times, over many years. He stared out the window at the towering clouds, solid masses in the evening air. Thoughts come and thoughts go away, with ninety-nine percent of them vanishing forever into nothingness; and memories do the same, though perhaps with some greater fraction of them surviving to return again.

He closed his eyes and the plane flew on. But he did not sleep and he opened his eyes now and then, drinking from a glass on the tray before him. He saw the GPU building, with one whole face of it caved in after that last great barrage, the May Day barrage when Bikers had been killed. After the barrage the interior of the GPU was laid visible as in a cross section, with a few men in white snow-capes standing in the exposed upper floors, and a few men in white snow-capes standing on the exposed lower floors, the lower men partially hidden behind all the stone that had collapsed. White snow-capes . . . even though the snow had all melted by then, by the time of those first days in May. The snowless, strangely dusty appearance of all the ground inside and outside the city had made a strong impression on him, associated with Bikers's death perhaps, and because, also, it had looked that way when the siege was finally lifted, only a few days later. That strange dustiness, calling to mind an alien world more strongly than the cold glittering snowfields had ever done. The thaw had come in April, the deep mud and standing water spreading everywhere; but all this had dried up by the beginning of May, yet still before the slightest trace of green sprouts had appeared anywhere in that land. And so for those final weeks, until the day of liberation, there had been nothing but brown dirt visible for miles beyond the city, and brown dirt on the banks of the Lovat, and brown dirt on the open spaces within the city, that the wind would pick up and carry as dust through the ruins, through the empty sunlight that was neither winter nor spring. That was how it had looked on the last days, when the relief column broke through. It reminded him of northern China, where he had been posted briefly as an attaché before the war, in Peking, the endless brown dust of that land. China, of all places.

Night fell. The plane descended, landing at Frankfurt at seven o'clock in the evening.